"Ingenious! Beautiful writing! Captivating! A fascinating account of America's most controversial First Lady."
— *Dr. Eugene Griessman, author of "The Words Lincoln Lived By"*

"Everyone loves Abraham Lincoln and everyone wants to know the real power behind the greatest Presidential leader of all time. Kay duPont has written Mary Todd Lincoln's story in a captivating, page-turning style that will wow your soul."
— *Mark Victor Hansen, co-creator of the #1 New York Times best-selling series "Chicken Soup for the Soul"® and co-author of "The One Minute Millionaire"*

"An engaging idea. Sensitive appreciation of Mary Todd Lincoln and good descriptions of Mr. Lincoln. The mechanism of a diary for modern readers is unique, and the chapters are lively. The book reflects both the person and the age. Measured against the odds she faced, Mary Todd Lincoln deserves to be remembered as an important part of Mr. Lincoln's life, and I'm pleased that Kay duPont has reminded us of this."

— *Jean H. Baker, Goucher College, author of "Mary Todd Lincoln" and three other books on the Civil War period*

"Kay has obviously done a lot of research, and certainly has an imaginative idea of what to do with it. She ably captures what many would take to be Mary Lincoln's personality and character, warts and all."
— *William C. Davis, Center for Civil War Studies, Virginia Tech, author of "Lincoln's Men" and more than 25 other books on the Civil War era*

"If Mary Todd Lincoln had kept a diary, it might have read very much like Kay duPont's fictional representation. Offering new insights on both Mary and Abraham Lincoln, *Loving Mr. Lincoln* is a poignant and gripping story of their life together facing personal tribulations and national crises."
— *Dr. James M. McPherson, Princeton University, author of the Pulitzer Prize-winning bestseller "Crossroads of Freedom" and more than a dozen other Civil War era books*

"Kay duPont has done a great job. She has clearly defined Mary Todd in a way that has never been done. She made both the Lincolns warm, loving and real people, with human feelings, faults and sensitivities, rather than the stiff, stilted figures we see in the history books in black and white. The book moves rapidly and is an excellent read."
— *Richard Freeman, Lincoln and Civil War Presentations*

"Mary Lincoln has often been described as somewhat cranky and, while Kay duPont doesn't shy away from this issue, she offers insights into the reasons. duPont beautifully reveals this intriguing woman's fragile side: her capacity for love, drive for a better life, dreams of prominence, and deep sorrows. This reality-based novel shows Mary Lincoln in a new, surprising, and more compassionate light."
— *C. Leslie Charles, author of "Why is Everyone So Cranky?" and "All is Not Lost"*

"duPont has done a marvelous job of capturing all the historically accurate details of the Civil War era, and gives us insights into an extraordinary woman who had the vision and influence of Eleanor Roosevelt, the social impact of Jacqueline Kennedy, the political acumen and ambition of Hillary Clinton, and the pioneering spirit of Anne Morrow Lindbergh. You'll lose yourself in this fascinating saga of a woman who was ahead of her time…a woman who was every bit as capable as the man she married and propelled into becoming one of our most respected American presidents. Read it and reap."
— *Sam Horn, author of "Tongue Fu!" and "Take the Bully by the Horns"*

"Whether fact or fiction, *Loving Mr. Lincoln* gives us powerful and at times 'delicious' insights into a misunderstood era of American history. But this is primarily an easy-to-read story of a woman—a complex, strong, driven woman. One who became a power, if not *the* power, behind a president. Mary Lincoln comes alive in this book as a visionary and a romantic. The author has such insightful compassion for Mrs. Lincoln's struggles and personal losses that you will want to comfort her in your arms…while scolding her at the same time. Most of all, you may come to realize that had Mary Todd been a woman of the 21st Century, perhaps Mr. Lincoln would be known as the man behind *her*."
— *Ron and Paula Eichner, retired but still reading*
  Review posted on amazon.com

To The Readers

Thank you for reading this labor of love. Although this book is fiction, all the people were real and all the events actually happened on or about the dates recorded here. The newspaper clippings are authentic, although I may have shortened or clarified them. I wove history and imagination together into a story of love and ambition to show two of America's most famous legends as people just like you and me.

Most of Abraham's and Mary's words are documented, although they may not have said those words to each other. Some of Mr. Lincoln's fans have contended about certain phrases, "But Mary didn't say that, Abraham said it." How does anyone know? Perhaps Mary said it first and he later repeated the words or wrote them to someone else. We can't be certain where most good ideas originate, and I believe Mary and Abraham were partners in his political efforts during their early years, so they would have bandied around many thoughts and concepts.

I know you've probably heard that Mary was a very controversial woman, and I've not tried to sugarcoat that. She wasn't a saint by any means, but neither was her husband. As William C. Davis so eloquently said, I've tried to show Mary Todd Lincoln as she really was, "warts and all." I hope I've fairly explained her erratic behavior and Abraham's role in it; shown how much she loved her family; documented her maturation and her decline; and given her credit for what I believe was the germinal strength behind her honored husband.

Acknowledgments

To all the Lincoln fans, Civil War buffs, and editorial assistants who helped me with the facts and flow, especially Jeff Disend, Richard Freeman, Morene Marcus, Dr. Jean Baker, and William C. Davis. To all the people who encouraged me for the three years it took to write this book. And to my friend, Helen Kahn, for her wonderful cover rendition of Mary Todd Lincoln.

Loving Mr. Lincoln: The Personal Diaries of Mary Todd Lincoln

M. Kay duPont

Published in the United States by Jedco Press, Atlanta, GA

ISBN 0-9614927-5-9
SAN 693-4005
Library of Congress Control Number 2003091592

Manufactured in the United States of America

Cover art by Helen Kahn

DIARIES OF MARY TODD LINCOLN FOUND AT FLEA MARKET

On a cold, gray afternoon last week, Chicago resident Trisha Morgan wandered through a large indoor flea market looking for something unusual she could use as a bedside table. After about an hour, she found just the right piece: an old trunk with a flat top.

Morgan, a graduate student at the University of Illinois, describes her find: "It was late in the day and the dealer was eager to bargain, so I bought it for only $40.

"As I struggled to pull the trunk up the stairs to my apartment, the worn leather handle gave way, sending the old case tumbling to the bottom of the entryway.

"When I turned the trunk upright, a false bottom fell forward and out spilled 26 hand-written books, each about five inches wide, seven inches high, and one inch thick. I carefully touched the gold-bordered pages, ran my hands over the maroon leather bindings, and

traced with my finger what remained of the embossed "L" on the covers to determine if the books were authentic."

To Morgan's surprise and the amazement of the US government, the "books" were actually diaries written by the 16th First Lady of the US, Mary Todd Lincoln, wife of Abraham Lincoln, the Great Emancipator.

Morgan continued, "After opening the first volume, I was bowled over to see that I had uncovered Mrs. Lincoln's personal diaries.

"Over the next few days, I saw Abraham and Mary Lincoln in a way I had never

imagined—up close and personal. I soon felt like part of their family. I laughed at their idiosyncrasies; cried when their loved ones died, especially their little sons; rooted for them during their personal and political struggles; shared their anguish as the issues of the day—from slavery to the Civil War—dramatically unfolded; and marveled at the deep love between them.

"I also discovered great strength and determination in Mary Lincoln that I had never heard about. She was a determined, goal-driven woman, and very much the driving power behind Lincoln, especially in the early years. Everyone should read her story."

And now you can....

<u>Dec. 13, 1839, my 21st birthday:</u> My dream last night was the same one I've had off and on since childhood:

I'm sitting next to my husband, the President of the United States, in a meeting upstairs in the Executive Mansion (though we used its more current name, White House). I'm counseling him, and he is nodding in affirmation. His features are not clear, but he's obviously taller than the others at the table. The large room is magnificently appointed in shades of royal blue and deep gold, with navy carpeting and fresh yellow roses in tall crystal vases on mahogany tables. The fragrance from the roses permeates my senses.

There is conversation, but it's not significant. At some point, my husband reaches out and places his hand over mine and we smile knowingly at each other. I feel happy, needed, and totally complete.

After reluctantly casting off the cobwebs of sleep, I jumped from my bed with a flutter in my chest, a rush of hope, and fresh determination to make my vision a reality. I'm going to live in the White House!

I sit now at the small desk in my room, where Elizabeth has just wished me a happy birthday. This birthday is especially exciting because it's my first since leaving Lexington to live with my sister and her husband, Ninian Edwards, in this exciting new Illinois capital.

Their home sits atop the highest point in Springfield, which the townsfolk call Aristocracy Hill. Because Ninian is a prominent legislator, I'm meeting many important people. I have new friends, new places to shop, new marriage prospects.

My family and friends think it's shameful to be unbetrothed at my age, and Elizabeth and Ninian are determined to find a proper match for me. But there's still time. I would like to marry, of course, as I'm nearing the age of spinsterhood, but I won't marry just anyone. My future is predestined. I will wed a man of importance—a governor or senator. My precious mother told me I could even marry someone capable of becoming President if I waited long enough and chose prudently. Mother...my heart bleeds at the sound of her name. How desperately I miss her. She's been gone 14 years now. She would be 45 now. I still see her in my dreams, calling to me, holding me as she did when I was a child. How sadly my life changed when I walked into her bedroom. It was only four nights after the birth of my brother George, her 6th baby. I still wonder why someone didn't tell me. I was only seven, but I can still feel the floor dissolving beneath me.

And very soon there was Betsy, who always called my ambitions ridiculous, no matter how often I stamped my foot and insisted she was wrong. She never supported me. She said women are meant to marry young, have children, and give up fun, excitement, and romance.

"Grow up, Mary," my stepmother taunted on my birthday last year. "It's impossible to live as grandly as you dream of. Forget politics. What good will all that learning do you? You'll never be anything but a rich man's wife. And there's certainly nothing wrong with that! It was good enough for your own mother and it's good enough for me. I know you don't like me very much, but trust me when I tell you that storybook love and ambition have no place in a woman's life. You're a foolish, willful child, always woolgathering instead of making yourself useful. Go live with Elizabeth in Springfield until you find a husband, like your sister Fanny did, and get out of this house. We have enough little children to watch without also being responsible for a grown woman."

Father encouraged me when Mother was still alive, but his responsibilities deepened when Betsy brought her three youngsters into our home, where there were already six, and then gave birth to seven more in quick succession. He never told me to give up my dreams, or to leave home, but my needs became less important to him after he remarried.

But I know he understood my desire to live in the White House, because he once dreamed of it himself. He often said when I was a little girl, "Since you can't run for office yourself, you'll marry into it. But to attract a man capable of attaining a high position, you have to understand the political world. Successful politicians need astute women beside them. So you have to listen carefully to people you trust and to your own inner voice, and choose the men you back wisely, both in politics and in life."

Then he usually added a caveat: "Dream big and shoot high, Mary, but always be careful what you aim for." I promised to do so.

What will my future husband say when he learns that I have planned and envisioned his presence?

Dec. 14, 1839: Elizabeth and Ninian are hosting a ball tonight to honor my birthday, so I must begin my preparations soon. To attract the best prospects, a lady must look fetching and aristocratic. I'll wear my black velvet. The neckline is scooped, but not terribly low cut, which will satisfy Elizabeth and Ninian. "You reveal too much, you're too daring!" are their continual comments about my gowns. I want their approval, of course, but I'll wear what I please tonight. My senses tell me the evening will be special, and my senses are never wrong.

Dec. 15, 1839: A wonderful night, with dancing from candlelight till cock crowing. Waltzed with Edwin Webb, quadrilled with Lyman Trumbull, and polkaed with Andrew Keyes. Even shared a glass of port with Edward Beckwith! We toasted with champagne at supper, and I slipped away with Stephen Douglass[1] for a second portion.

I like Stephen, though he's a funny-looking man, with his hair pulled back over his huge forehead and styled like a woman's! A dwarfish fellow, only slightly taller than I, with a thick trunk and spindly legs—almost looks misshapen. But very cultured, political, and a splendid dancer.

Everyone of importance attended the bash, even Cousin John Stuart's law partner, Abraham Lincoln, whom they say seldom attends events not associated with politics or law. I saw him speak several weeks ago when I went with Ninian to the courthouse, and he's quite amusing. Lincoln says he moved here from New Salem and joined up with John only a few years ago. He's part of the Long Nine, the group of Whig legislators who were instrumental in getting the capital moved from Vandalia to Springfield.

Cousin John says people call his partner "Humble Abraham Lincoln" or "Honest Abe," because he's shy, trustworthy, and a fighter when he believes he's right. John said, "When Lincoln gets a case, he seems bewildered at first, but he goes after it, and before long he masters it. He has a tenacious grasp of a thing once he gets hold of it. Rather like you, Mary." Lincoln serves as Whig floor leader in the Illinois House, but he lost the election for House Speaker. He campaigned last year on John's behalf for Congress against Stephen, but that didn't turn out well either.

Lincoln is ugly as a grizzly bear, and he seldom smiles. Very tall and thin, with swarthy skin and black hair, resembling a dark-feathered crane. His head is small, but he has a large nose and protruding ears. His arms are long, with huge hands that hang way out of his sleeves. He walks on enormous feet and puts his entire foot flat on the ground at once, which causes him to lean slightly forward and appear off balance. His frock coat was too short, collar too limp, gloves soiled, shoes unshined and much too

---

[1] Stephen Arnold Douglas spelled his name with two *s'* until 1846.

informal. His lack of schooling is evident in his substandard contractions, particularly "y'all," and "t'wont," and "ain't," which he uses frequently. He must be at least 30 years old. Oddest of all, he carried a twig in his mouth all evening, which Cousin John said was sarsaparilla. Perhaps he can't afford tooth powder. I find him very puzzling.

Dec. 21, 1839: Saw Abraham Lincoln in town. He tipped his stovepipe hat and said, "Why, Miss Todd, how lovely to see you. You're sure shining brightly in the dreariness of winter." His hat appeared to be filled with paper, and a small piece fell to the ground. He quickly retrieved the scrap and stuffed it back inside the lining.

He's pleased about the Whig nomination of William Henry Harrison for President, though he shares my disappointment that Henry Clay's bid was unsuccessful again. He says Harrison will make an "all-fired good President" and most likely won't "back and fill" — waffle between principles. He also believes President Van Buren is a strong candidate for re-election.

He is preparing for the upcoming rallies with Stephen Douglass. They will speak in Springfield on eight consecutive evenings about Whig and Democrat policies, explaining the party differences and trying to sway votes. Hope I can attend some of the speeches!

Dec. 23, 1839: By lighting the candle in the west parlor window, Elizabeth has made it clear that gentlemen are welcome to call. She is even "interviewing" marriage prospects for me. I'm embarrassed by this, but that's her role as my oldest sister. She sets great store by James Shields, a 23-year-old Irish soldier with a bushy moustache that bounces when he talks. He's our state auditor, after serving a year or so in the Illinois House. A generous nature, and intelligent, but somewhat pretentious and high-faluting. I want a man with feet closer to the ground.

"You're too particular," Elizabeth said when I showed little enthusiasm for her favorite.

I felt the irritability course through me, but was helpless to stop it. "Perhaps," I said. "But a man has to be capable of attaining political prominence before I'll even consider falling in love with him. I wouldn't be happy any other way. I dream of...."

Elizabeth shook her head. "Yes, yes, I know, you've told us a dozen times about being the President's wife. You need to stop acting like a child and marry a flesh and blood man, not a dream. Father shouldn't have encouraged your silly ambitions and fairy tales. He colored your thinking." Betsy's wagging finger flashed before my eyes. I stood up and braced myself, hands on hips.

"No," I shouted, "my thinking is just splendid. I want a husband, but he must be my choice. I won't be told whom to marry! And I won't squash my dreams just because you don't believe in them!"

I regret raising my voice, but Elizabeth just doesn't understand my pain or my passion. I need a mate who cares about our country and its political workings. An ambitious man, a fighter, someone not easily scared by an owl. A decisive man who is always honest with himself and those around him. A husband who accepts me as an equal partner, who has enough confidence to put me by his side instead of under his thumb. A man who will honestly confide his deepest fears and hopes, and listen to mine. One with spirit, courage, and the drive to be President. Will I find this man in Springfield? Perhaps. Where there's a will, there's a way.

Dec. 25, 1839, Christmas: Much of our family is here to celebrate. What a joy to see them again — Father, Ann, Levi, George, Sam, David. Betsy is in the family way again and stayed in Lexington with the younger ones. I can't say I miss her.

The children are awed by the candles on the tree. Boxes and papers are strewn from room to room. Father brought silk-velvet from France, merino and other luscious fabrics from New Orleans, jewelry from Spain. He also confided that Mother left me some farmland in Indiana, to be deeded over when I marry, so I'm now a landowner. Of course, it's still in Father's name, but....

Christmas always reminds me of Mother, and our conversation brought her vividly into my mind. I feel so alone without her, especially when everyone is telling me what I "should" be doing with my life. When I mention her to Father, he grunts and hurries from the room with his head down.

Dec. 26, 1839: Went to the final debate tonight to hear Abraham Lincoln's closing with my friends Eliza and Simeon Francis, owners of the *Sangamo Journal.* They have known Lincoln for years, and they love him like a son. To my surprise, he joined us in the carriage after the event, and we all went to the Francis home for refreshments. He sat with his eyes sunken and non-seeing, one eye practically at the top of its socket. His knees were wedged under his chin, hands clasped tightly around his ankles. When I asked what troubled him, he replied, "I've got the hypo."

Simeon explained that Abraham suffers from hypochondria or depression. Tonight he was doleful over the low turnout at the debate and the poor press review of his previous speech. I tried to uplift him with mimicry and riddles, but he would not be cheered.

Jan. 1, 1840: New Year's Day is very festive in Springfield, with much visiting, hand shaking, eating, toasting. Practically every prominent Illinois Whig came to call on Ninian — county officials, senators, governors past and present, congressmen. Even Henry Clay stopped by! I always enjoy seeing him. When he served as Secretary of State a few years back and had been nominated for President, I asked about visiting him in the White House. He said, "Not just visit, Mary. You'll live there with us and help Mrs. Clay entertain the dignitaries. She's not much for socializing, and you would be a great asset to her. You can serve as hostess, like Dolley Madison did for Thomas Jefferson and Emily Donelson did for Andrew Jackson." How I wish that prediction would come true, but his chances now seem dim.

I talked at length with the men about the upcoming elections. One discussion was whether Ninian or Cousin John Stuart should stand for Congress next year. Either way, I'll be pleased, because it puts me in a position to meet eligible congressmen. I've learned a great deal about the judicial system since arriving here. My male cousins respect my knowledge and ability to discuss politics, but my sisters and female friends call the topic "unladylike." It's disappointing that women don't see the need to understand these matters. Having no interest in how our country operates is pure naiveté.

Mr. Lincoln did not visit today. Or perhaps he came when we were out and just had no calling card to leave. At any rate, all that rushing around in the cold gave me a sick headache, so I took a dose of laudanum[2] and I'm off to bed. Hope I can sleep; I've been very restless lately.

Jan. 17, 1840: Saw Lincoln in the *Journal* office this morning. He serves as one of the assistant editors, in addition to his law practice, and asked me to contribute an article or poem. Of course the piece would have to be anonymous. The only times a lady's name can be publicized are at her birth, marriage, and death. How unfair! Women can do many things as well as men! I didn't commit to an article, but I'll probably try, especially considering by whom I was asked.

He interests me. I've never met a man quite like this one. Very quiet till he opens up, and then he's filled with laughter. He will occasionally chuckle right out loud for no apparent reason, as though he just understood a joke from yesterday. His manners are horrible; it's easy to see he has no breeding. Still, I'm intrigued, and yes, attracted. He's very different from the other men I know. They are always posturing to be the center of attention, but he allows others to have the limelight. He has a subtle power that's hard to resist.

---

[2] A painkiller consisting mainly of opium used through much of the 19th Century, especially for severe headaches. Paregoric, mentioned later, was a liquid mix of opium and 10% alcohol.

Feb. 1, 1840: Horrid, wet weather today, though certainly better than thunder and lightning. The icy streets have turned to filthy slush, and even horses have difficulty getting through the quagmire. I've read every available book of interest, and today searched for humor and romance stories. Not likely in Ninian's library! The room's dark paneling and massive chairs would blush and shrink under the weight of frivolous love stories! I would like to go to town and buy one of those dime novels from the pharmacy. A little intrigue in my life would be wonderful, even if only through a book.

Feb. 10, 1840: It stormed again late in the afternoon, causing me to retreat to my room and hide under the covers. I know I seem brave to others, but no matter how hard I try, I can't overcome my terror of thunder! Mother understood this even when I was a baby; she would rock me until the crashing noises stopped. How I wish someone would hold me now. Now that I'm "grown," no one wants to dry my tears.

Though I would never admit this to anyone, I feel desperately alone, even with so many constant visitors. I feel worthless, useless, uninterested in anything around me. I wish someone would come into my life and liberate my heart and soul. I long for a sense of belonging and togetherness, someone to share my dreams and physical yearnings. When will he come?

Elizabeth says, "Mary, you're too melancholic. You go back and forth from despondent to euphoric. You sleep and eat too much or not at all. You're either crying or laughing. We certainly prefer your happy mood, but sometimes you're excessive. You talk too much and too fast, and you annoy people with your mimicry. You need to find an even keel, settle down somewhere, and stay there."

I know my moods vary; I've always been temperamental. Mother said it wasn't unusual in the Parker family. Said she and Grandmother Parker both went up and down, and I shouldn't concern myself. But how can a person be "overly happy" as Elizabeth claims? Why is happiness a bad thing? Bah!

Feb. 14, 1840, Valentine's: Abraham came round this afternoon with a small box of crème-filled bonbons, and we sat in the parlor talking for an hour. I'm beginning to truly enjoy his company. Stephen Douglass sent roses—red, the color of passion. Edwin Webb brought his usual peppermint cakes because he thinks they are my favorite sweet. No matter. My dear best friend, Mercy Levering, loves mints. I'm so glad she's staying next door with her brother for a few more months. I'll miss her when she returns to Baltimore.

Feb. 17, 1840: A fearful headache and nausea yesterday. My pains seem to come with activity, and I've truly been racing around lately. Sometimes my stomach seems full of gnawing worms and I wonder if my last meal will stay down. And the spots of light that often appear before my eyes make me question my sanity. The cramps and visions ease only with paregoric and rest, but it's hard to close my eyes. Am I dying?

Feb. 24, 1840: I shivered with horror as I read in the *New Orleans Bee* about a man who chained his slaves in the attic. While they were there, the house burned down. The account says the city's people wrote vile inscriptions on the remaining walls. Surely there is some way to stop such horrid, sinful treatment.

I remember the slaves being dragged down Main Street in Lexington — hundreds of men, women, and children manacled together. They were taken on to Louisville, shackled to riverboats, and shipped to the New Orleans markets. I still have vivid dreams of it, and hear their cries in my sleep. If I were a slave, I would defy the traders and kill myself instead of being sold like cattle! Abraham says the American Colonization Society is collecting money to send free negroes to Africa or Haiti. He said Thomas Jefferson first proposed it, and he thinks it's still the best idea. Seems to me that the free ones are not the people who need help, it's the ones in chains.

Mar. 2, 1840: I went with Elizabeth and Ninian to hear the debates at the courthouse. Benches lined the room from wall to wall, and yet no sitting space was available. Even with the pounding rain, there must have been 250 people! Stephen Douglass spoke on the state of the country, Abraham Lincoln on the need to establish slave-free states. Edward (Ned) Baker, a Whig, also spoke briefly on politics in general.

Stephen and Ned are fine speakers. Abraham delivers quite well too — in a folksy, homespun way. When he speaks, however, his gray eyes light up and he's not so plain. In fact, he's almost attractive. He talked for two hours about Whig beliefs, state banks, and what he believes were the intentions of the founding fathers to induce eventual emancipation.

Stephen claimed the Whigs are only interested in money, the federal bank is "a tool for elitist financiers," and the Whigs in office are "aristocrats and reactionaries." He said the Democrats are "poor, simple folks interested in the welfare of the people." But seeing Stephen in his fine store-bought clothes and hearing his well-educated speech, then looking at Abraham in his tattered, ill-fitting coat, using rural words like "tweren't" and "reckon," debunked the whole concept. I wonder if Abraham presents that image as part of his campaign strategy? Surely he knows it's not becoming.

I greatly admire speakers who can move a group to accept their concepts, and believe Abraham could be as good as Stephen with practice.

He holds the audience, but prefers yarns to hard politics. His tales often focus on his poverty, rural upbringing, and poor education, which I believe hurts him in the press. I heard a reporter behind me say, "The story that yokel told wasn't totally impure, but it's certainly not suitable for publication."

Worse, Abraham is frequently the first to laugh at his own accounts! Sometimes he can hardly get to the end because he's gasping for breath between guffaws. I would like to caution him on this but, of course, that's not my place. If he polished his skills, he might have real political potential.

Mar. 4, 1840: What a day Mercy and I had! I was desperately bored and beside myself with restlessness and the need for fresh air. So I convinced my dear friend to walk to the courthouse with me. I thought it would be fun—it's only three blocks—and perhaps I might see Abraham. But there was so much mud from the unrelenting rain that a dozen carriages had been abandoned in the square.

So I collected some old wooden shingles from the coach house and convinced Mercy that we could jump from one spot to another by throwing the shingles in front of us as we went. She resisted until I threatened to take off my shoes and stockings, pull my skirt up to my knees, and walk through the sludge alone.

We made it to the courthouse without falling, but were out of shingles, and Mercy wanted to go home. She has no sense of spontaneity or adventure. We headed back by trying to hop from one dry area to another, but it was just too difficult. So when I saw Mr. Hart in his hay wagon, I called him over and asked for a ride. Mercy wouldn't get in the cart, so that silly goose walked home and ended up soaked to the bone, mudded to the bloomers, sneezing horrendously, and being disciplined. I told her she should have done it my way!

Mar. 6, 1840: Abraham intrigues me, but he's truly a strange character. I don't understand why he doesn't try harder to make friends and learn the ways of society. He seems so ill at ease and lethargic when off the platform. Sits with his hands folded in his lap and hardly ever looks at anyone. Sometimes when standing, he puts his arms behind him so his elbows extend sideways and then quickly drops his arms as if trying to hide them. My sister Fanny claims he's the plainest man in Springfield and always appears to need a good oiling.

Have I said he's six feet four inches tall? Fourteen inches taller than I! When he crouches over to talk with me, he looks like old Father Jupiter bending down from the clouds. His height is mostly in his legs, like a man on stilts. And what must I look like when craning my neck toward him? Possibly a calf reaching for its mother's teat. Or a daughter reaching for her father's hand. Does he remind me of Father? Perhaps, although they seem to have nothing in common. I had dreams of marrying Father when I was little — until Betsy came.

I do hope Abraham will call on me again. It would be kind and proper for Elizabeth and Ninian to invite him, but they refuse. Ninian says he's ill mannered and uncouth, and Elizabeth continually harps that he doesn't fit into our social group. So I myself have asked him to visit. They have too much breeding to reject a man from the parlor after he has been greeted. I will not be told whom to see!

Mar. 7, 1840: Abraham called tonight. I love the way he can sit still and listen for such long periods, his head slightly bent to the left, hands on his knees or in his lap. Even though he looks out of place among Elizabeth's dainty furnishings, he perches on the old horsehair sofa and watches when I talk as though he's never seen anyone quite like me. His attention encourages my conversation. Once he blurted out, "Mary, you speak just like a book, only faster." How poetic!

Odd, however, he has asked to call me Molly. When I asked him why, his answer was characteristically evasive: "I knew a girl named Mary once before and it didn't turn out too well."

Mar. 9, 1840: Mercy and I chatted for a long while this afternoon as we worked at our embroidery. She also says Abraham has no future, and her judgments are usually sound. But I wonder in this instance. He has a quiet energy, a determination, a natural brilliance, that others lack. I sense in him past hurt, sadness, insecurity, and even fear. Other men are often hypocritical, egotistical, and uninteresting. Even those who promise a secure future seem frivolous with their affection and wavering in their devotion. I need someone who will share my feelings, be devoted, and understand my longings and loneliness. Only one who suffers can understand suffering.

Mar. 17, 1840: Abraham stopped by at noon today. I fixed a small lunch from leftovers and we ate in the kitchen — roast turkey, brown bread, potato salad, red cake for dessert, and the strong coffee he prefers. He hesitated to join me, but then gobbled as if it were his first meal in a week. He said it was "plumb toothsome."

He told me about defending Springfield's first-ever murder trial, as co-counsel with Stephen Douglass. They must have appeared quite odd to the jurors — one so tall, the other so small. Their client was acquitted.

Mar. 20, 1840: All my friends are marrying. I've been a bridesmaid four times in less than a year! Perhaps the adage, "Always a bridesmaid, never a bride" is true? Now Mary Jane Parker is married, Mercy will soon marry James Conkling, and I still have no serious interest. Not that I haven't been considered. But all my beaus are hard bargains for the eye or heart, and I still wait for the perfect mate to fill this emptiness in my soul.

Mercy laughs when I tell her about my feelings. "Oh Mary, you're just too hard to please. Lots of men would come rushing if you would only wink an eye or toss your curls in their direction. You could marry tomorrow if you would just give up your grandiose dreams and calm down a little."

Perhaps. I know my face is pretty (some have even called me beautiful), though to be chosen for my looks alone would not please me. I'm well versed in literature, French, composition, piano, drama, dance, and history. Although I can't yet cook, I am a fine seamstress.

And, because practically every man in my family has been in the legislature, I understand government and the affairs of the country. Not that anyone sees such as an asset. Most of my family ridicules my passion for politics, but I don't listen. Politics is not a pastime to be taken lightly. If we don't care how we are governed, we will be governed <u>without</u> care. Oh there I go again, getting fired up over the nation's future!

Mercy and Elizabeth also say my wit offends people, but I mean no harm. It's just hard for me to restrain comments or mockery when the occasion presents itself. I have such clever ideas! Mercy reminded me of the day Ninian's friend, Thomas O'Dooley, hinted that he might consider me for a wife. I replied, "Well, you can consider it all you please, but it would take more intellectual consideration on my part and more financial consideration on your part to ever make it happen." I was fluffing, playing with words, but he felt wounded.

Why are people so touchy about humor? Is enjoyment of life a wicked frivolity? I think not. Abraham and I often laugh together; he understands my personality. I find it boring to be boring, absurd to be unheard, bad to be sad.

But if Mercy is right and I should marry, whom would I choose? All I want is a good man with a love of family, a devotion to liberty and justice, a drive for political position and commendation, a strong moral mind, and bright prospects. And a sense of humor, of course. Is that too much to ask? Betsy always said it was.

Could I choose the wishful merchant Thomas O'Dooley? I don't think so. Marshall Prescott still calls, but I have no serious thoughts in his direction. Edwin Webb is 15 or 20 years older than I and was left with two "little objections" when his wife died. Red-haired Patrick Henry speaks eloquently but no real thoughts come out, though Uncle John Todd thinks Pat surpasses his noble ancestor in talents and pushes him toward me. It's true that he's the handsomest man I've ever met, but I can't envision myself in his arms...or his bed.

Stephen Douglass is my favorite dance partner and Springfield's upcoming political star. He served in the Illinois House for three years, and is now one of our youngest senators. He makes sufficient income as a land speculator even if he forsakes politics. I likely could live with him, and sense he would ask for my hand if I gave the signal, which would certainly please Elizabeth and Ninian. But it would not make me happy.

They call him the little giant, but I don't think he's such a big man. Besides, he's a Yankee, a Democrat, and a partisan who favors slavery. He said recently, "I'm opposed to negro citizenship in any form. White men created this government for the benefit of white men and their posterity." I don't believe clear-headed voters will stand for such an attitude very long. Stephen will be revealed as a slavist and vanish from political sight. I would rather tie myself to a man who is coming rather than going.

I told him once that we could never marry because he would never be Chief Executive. I said, "I will become Mrs. President or I am the victim of false prophets, but it won't be as Mrs. Douglass."

He laughed and said, "How sure you are of yourself, Mary!"

I admit my goals are high-minded, but believe I can accomplish more by reaching for the stars than the shelf. My precious mother used to say the stars <u>are</u> possible. I want to be the nation's *grande dame,* and I see no reason that can't happen.

And now Abraham Lincoln comes to mind. We enjoy talking about literature, poetry, politics, states rights, theatre, elections, and many other topics. More importantly, he listens to me. He respects me as a person, not just a woman, and he appreciates my mind. He too has fears and, much to my amazement, says rain depresses him. What a sight we'll be in a storm!

<u>Mar. 22, 1840:</u> As Abraham left tonight, he kissed my cheek. Then blushed and quickly backed out the door, his ebony hair falling in his down-turned face. I wish he had kissed my mouth instead. I often wonder how his lips would feel on mine, and think I may be falling in love with this scrawny man. But it must remain a secret for now. I sense he would run all the way back to New Salem if told, and Ninian would surely offer my bedroom to the first taker.

My senses tell me that something unique lies underneath his roughness; he may even have the makings to someday be President. No one else sees his greatness, but I think Mother would have recognized that beneath his awkward exterior breathes a truly decent soul.

<u>Mar. 29, 1840:</u> To my amazement, Abraham accepted my invitation to attend church with us this morning. He looked quite handsome in his black

suit and overcoat. Had even oiled his hair! After lunch, we went for a drive, and I asked, "Are you a God-fearing man, Abraham?"

He hesitated before replying. "No, Molly, I don't fear God, but I'm on speaking terms with Him and I've read the Bible. Some of my kinfolk were Baptist and some were Quaker, but I don't go in much for organized religion. I wouldn't know how to behave in a regular church."

I was elated. "Quaker? My distant relative and the woman I most admire in the world was a Quaker!"

He slowed the buggy and turned to look at me. "Who might that be?"

"Why, Dolley Madison, of course, James Madison's wife, the most popular First Lady ever. She served as hostess for Thomas Jefferson for eight years and then served again during her husband's terms. In fact, she lived there longer than any other person! She saved George Washington's portrait and the Declaration of Independence when Washington was burned in 1812! You must know that, everyone knows it! I want to be just like her when I get to the White House."

His lips twitched upward and his eyebrows rose. "Get to the White House?"

"Oh yes! I fully intend to live there someday. I've had regular dreams of being the President's wife since I was a child. My heart is set on living there, and I believe a person can achieve whatever she wants badly enough, don't you?"

He looked straight out at the horses and stroked his chin. Then he asked, "And how would you be kin to Mrs. Madison?"

"Well, I read that her first husband was named John Todd and they had two sons. Only one lived, but Dolley and I are so much alike that I know I'm descended from that son!"

He smiled and squeezed my hand. "Yep, I reckon you might be."

Apr. 1, 1840: At the Whig rally last night, I asked Abraham to dance. He hesitated and looked down at his long feet, and then at the dancers on the floor, with a most chagrined expression. He wrung his hands in that annoying way, rubbing his knuckles as though they were tarred.

He replied, "Molly, I want to dance with you in the worst possible way, but...." I waved away his words and led him inside the pavilion.

After the first round, I could take no more. When he led me off the floor, I said, "Abraham, you said you wanted to dance with me in the worst possible way, and you're a man of your word. That is the worst possible way I've ever been danced with."

We both chuckled and I felt honored to have such a droll man find amusement in my quips. Honestly, when he laughs, he's quite handsome. His eyes crinkle up at the corners and he enlivens. His pouty lips open to reveal broad teeth and the aroma of sarsaparilla, and he appears powerfully different from the stone-faced man people often see in court.

Apr. 6, 1840: I'm alone again. Mercy has returned to Baltimore, and most of the fellows have left to canvass the state for the elections. What a wonderful time they must have, traveling from town to town, being admired by the crowds, hearing applause for their words.

Although he didn't come by the day he left, I know Abraham is campaigning for William Harrison throughout Illinois and Kentucky. Stephen always calls before he leaves, and when he returns, and he brings me gifts from his travels. Of course he does the same for several others. I suppose he thinks we ladies never speak about such things.

I while away my loneliness by shopping. I truly don't need anything, but it's such a luxury to go from store to store, being recognized as Ninian's sister-in-law. I seldom pay—my purchases are simply added to Ninian's account and money is never mentioned. I worry that some of the items will never be used, but I can always have one of the servants return them.

May 21, 1840: Sister Fanny's first anniversary. I remember their wedding so clearly. Most of Illinois stood in Elizabeth's parlor, which was smashingly decorated in white and gold.

Abraham refused my invitation to the anniversary celebration. With his eyes down and chin on his chest, he said, "I'm sorry, Molly. I just can't go. I have no energy for such shindigs. Please just ask somebody else to escort you." The poor man dances so badly and feels out of place at soirees. But he'll learn to enjoy them in time; I'll teach him.

Because the affair occurred in our home, I felt no shame in attending alone. We had an exciting discussion about suffrage and I asked, "Why aren't women allowed to do the same things as men? I believe we should have the right to vote and the same chance to be educated. Why do we need to remain 'intellectually inferior,' as the *Kentucky Gazette* asserted? I get tired of sewing and visiting and being 'ladylike.' I'm as tough and as smart as most of the men I know. Sometimes I think women are perceived as no better than negroes." Most everyone nodded in agreement.

Cousin John Hardin asked if I was "interested" in anyone, and hinted he might be a willing suitor. Of course, we're cousins, but what of it? So were Mother and Father. And Grandmother Parker married her first cousin too. They say marrying a close relative causes mental instability in children, but that's poppycock. I turned out all right!

Although John is highly respected, easy on the eye, slated for higher politics, and even being groomed as a possible Presidential candidate, he is not the one for me.

May 27, 1840: Saw Abraham in town, hurrying to the courthouse for a case, but we chatted for a moment. I chided him for declining my invitation to the celebration last week and he said again he's not much of a frolicker. "I'm defective in those little links that make up the chain of socializing. I'm also not sufficiently educated in the female line to talk much to women. And you, Molly Todd, are very much a woman." I stood with mouth ajar as he smiled, tipped his tall black hat, and scurried off.

June 10, 1840: Abraham came to call before heading out again on the campaign trail. As he was leaving, he took me in his arms and said he "thinks very fondly" of me. I returned the compliment, and he murmured into my hair, "You always smell like roses." Then he kissed me fully on the lips for the first time and my entire body trembled. I've never experienced such an intense pounding of my heart and thought for a moment I might swoon. Is this love? Whatever it is, I want more of it!

June 20, 1840: Abraham came to see me so early this morning that the curling papers were still in my hair! I covered them with a lace bandeau, slipped on my blue flannel robe, and went downstairs to greet him. He didn't appear to notice my attire. He stared at his feet, then jerked a small bouquet of orange wildflowers out from behind his back and shoved it toward me. When he dropped the bouquet, we both bent to pick it up and our heads touched. I grabbed the flowers to save him the embarrassment of giving them to me again. Then I made chicory coffee and we talked for an hour before he had to leave for his office. He's very excited about the Presidential campaign!

June 28, 1840: I've seen Abraham every evening since he returned — talking in the parlor, visiting friends, a long walk or horseback ride, a soda in town, a carriage into the countryside. We even went to the new Samuels and Mackintosh troupe show! I find his mind extraordinary and his humor endearing, but I must admit, for your eyes only, that being seen with him in public is embarrassing at times. His swallowtail coats are usually wrinkled, trousers are too short, tie is a clump of black knots, socks rarely match. He looks like a scarecrow put in a field to protect the corn. No! I sound denigrating, like the others. Financial wealth does not define a person's character. I've been rich all my life and what has it gotten me? I certainly don't feel "rich," and I'm certainly not fulfilled.

July 1, 1840: Abraham and I went on a most delightful picnic. We spent the entire day just talking, reading poetry, and nestling. We both try our hand at writing poems to share with each other. His words are nice to hear, but he has little rhythm. He is surprisingly knowledgeable in the classic poets, especially Burns and Shakespeare, though he still reads out loud like a child. "When I read aloud," he explained, "two senses catch the idea. First I see what I read, then I hear it. I can remember things better when they hit me twice." His memory is practically flawless.

He told the funniest story about the answer he gave recently to a lawyer who called him rich. It went something like this: "No, Sir, I've always been poor. When I was a boy, I got hired on a flatboat at $8 a month. I only had one pair of breeches to my back and they were buckskin. Now, when buckskin gets wet and then dried by the sun, it shrinks. My breeches kept shrinking till they left several inches of my legs bare between the tops of my socks and the lower part of my breeches. And while I grew taller, the pants became shorter and so much tighter that they left a blue streak around my legs that can be seen to this day. If you call that rich, I plead guilty to the charge."

I made him show me his legs and was amused to see that "Honest Abe" does occasionally tell a white lie! Lots of dark hair, but no blue streak!

July 2, 1840: After supper, I asked Abraham how he came to be a lawyer. He told me, "We moved around a lot when I was a boy. From Hodgenville, Kentucky, where I was born; to southern Indiana, where Maw died; to Decatur, Illinois, where we finally settled. When I was 22, I got hired to take a raft-load of goods to New Orleans. The boat's owner promised to take me on as a grocery clerk in New Salem, so I headed there after the trip. Eventually I bought into a store myself with a chap named Berry, but I wasn't cut out for clerking. A couple of years later, I got the postmaster's job and began to study surveying. I was working all sorts of jobs to keep soul and body together.

"I ran for the Illinois House in '32, but lost to your friend Steve Douglass. Then all those folks I'd been surveying for got me elected in '34. That's how I met up with your cousin John Stuart again after the Blackhawk War—he was elected that year too. We were stumping together and he invited me to share his room in Vandalia. We got to be friends and I was always asking him questions about the law.

"One day John said he'd lend me some law books to study, and if I learned well, he'd give me a job. Then when I got elected again in '36 and his partner moved on, he asked me if I wanted to go in with him. I reckoned I could make a better fist at lawyering than storekeeping, so you can blame it on him." Thank you, Cousin John.

July 4, 1840, Independence Day: The grandest holiday in the nation! We had a glorious time at the town picnic. Abraham looked all slicked up in his boiled white shirt and blue pantaloons! They offered games of all kinds for the children and even a few attractions for us, including a three-legged race. How exciting to be so close to him in public!

Elizabeth won first prize for her apple pie again and Abraham won the log-splitting contest. With his experience, no one can best him. He looks so strong when he rolls up his sleeves and reveals the muscles under his thin white under-sleeves. He has coarse, dark hair down his arms! That shouldn't shock me, I suppose, with the unruly mop on his head and my glimpse of his legs. I long to discover whether he also has hair on his chest.

July 7, 1840: I'm sitting on a train roaring to Columbia, Missouri, to visit Uncle David and Cousin Ann Todd. The train is said to run at over 20 miles an hour! Though I hate to leave Abraham, Ann writes so heartily about her home that I couldn't refuse. The car is comfortable and I have a smart number of magazines to read, so time will go quickly.

July 14, 1840: We drove into town today and visited a phrenologist—a woman who said she could read one's intellect and personality through the skull's bumps and shape. She charged very little, so we invested. She said Cousin Ann has a nurturer's bumps and will make an efficient and loving mother. I, however, have an "adventurer's skull," and will never be satisfied in a purely domestic life. She prophesied Ann will be married this year, but not I. She foresaw much happiness for my cousin, but sadness for me. Bah! I'm just glad we didn't waste much money on such silliness. Tomorrow we leave for a little town on the river called Boonville, so I won't write for a week or so.

Aug. 2, 1840: What a surprise to receive a letter from Abraham—entirely unexpected. He is well and staying out of mischief. I wonder if he's beginning to miss me as I do him? Will my continued absence make his heart grow fonder? He sounds worried about his re-election, but that's a silly fear. He's a fine representative.

Aug. 5, 1840: Another almighty short letter from Abraham: "Not much news to tell you, except I've been elected for a 4th term in the General Assembly and indigestion is again in command of my body. Otherwise I'm doing well and look forward to seeing you soon." He will visit here soon.

Aug. 8, 1840: Abraham arrived in Columbia last night from Rocheport, where he delivered a speech, so the Missouri end of the family has had an opportunity to meet him. I sense that no one here is overly impressed. He was quite irritable and withdrawn—probably because of the rain.

Aug. 9, 1840: After a serious discussion today, we have decided to marry!! Can you believe it? I'm betrothed!!

Abraham wrote to Father for permission, and addressed him as "Mr. Tod." When I informed him that "Todd" has two "d's," his eyebrows puckered in wonder. I told him how Betsy always ragged Father that one "d" is good enough for God but not for the Todds! He laughed deeply, filling my heart with joy. In the end, we decided to postpone the letter. My family won't be happy with the arrangement, and deferring unpleasant news is usually wise. It's certainly not unpleasant news to me! I am overjoyed!

Aug. 10, 1840: Another long conversation with Abraham about my hopes for the Presidency. He doesn't want the position as strongly as I, but I countered each argument well:

"Oh Abraham, you'll make such a fine President. You have everything it takes—more so than anyone in recent past. You're kind, intelligent, caring, tactful, honest, temperate. Unlike Gen. Harrison, you truly are an abstainer. You're spiritual at heart and believe in equality. What more could the people want?"

"I don't know, Molly, I ain't sure I even want to be President. And I don't think I've got the other things the country needs."

I brushed at the lint on his coat. He never notices things like that. "Whatever do you mean?"

He watched his hands clasp and unclasp. "Well, for one thing, I ain't very handsome. I remember once on the circuit I looked into the mirror and resolved that if I ever saw a more unattractive man, I'd shoot him dead. The next morning, I saw a new lawyer in the tavern, pulled my pistol, and said to him, 'Halt, Sir. I promised myself that if I ever saw an uglier bloke, I'd kill him on the spot. Well, I've found him. Make ready to die.'

"'Please, Mr. Lincoln,' the man said, 'if I'm any uglier than you, fire away.'"

I smiled indulgently but didn't allow the conversation to be diverted. "And which of our former Presidents was so attractive that you would be ashamed for your portrait to hang beside his? Rotund John Adams? Smileless Madison? Drunken Jackson? Or perhaps Van Buren the Dandy has a more pleasant face? And if you believe yourself to be less attractive than Gen. Harrison, you are badly mistaken."

He sat up a little and his face brightened. "Well, they certainly had more learning. You know I hardly went to school. I've got maybe a year's education in total. Everything I know came from borrowed books."

I shook my head. "You've always said experience is a better way. We can learn together what we need to know."

He continued. "And what about money? I don't have the funds to invest in electioneering or paying for the expenses of the office if I should win."

I loathe it when he brings up his financial straits. The issue exasperates me and he is so unreasonable. I said, "I have money, Abraham, and what's mine is...."

"No," he interrupted, holding his hands in front of his chest and waving them about. "I'll never spend Todd...."

"I know. You'll never spend Todd money on your own needs. But this would be for me and for the nation. Surely you can make an exception for your country and your wife. If not, I guess we'll raise funds some other way."

He sat quietly for a full minute as he looked out over the lawn. Then we came to the matter's heart. He said, "I've got no experience in politics to speak of. A man can't become President without any background. I'm not prepared."

I smiled. "That's exactly why we'll start gaining experience immediately. I have a plan all set out for us. You, my handsome candidate, will run for the House next term, and then for Senate, and then for the Presidency in '52, or '56 at the latest."

"You're a wonder, Molly Todd. You line up things so perfectly and never worry that your plans will go off course. There's just one thing you ain't thought of. What if the people don't want a ripe old scarecrow like me in Congress?"

I took his hands and fell into his eyes. "We'll make them want you. I am committed to the task."

His eyes flickered and he said, "You remind me about the man who got nominated for town supervisor. When he left home on election morning, he said to his wife, 'Tonight you'll sleep with this town's supervisor.' When the man came home defeated, his wife immediately put on her best trappings. 'Where are you going?' he asked. 'Well,' said the missus, 'you told me I'd get to sleep with the supervisor tonight, so I'm going over to his house.'" He took me in his arms and I could feel him chuckling above my head.

Aug. 11, 1840: Abraham left Columbia today, back to Old Tip's campaign trail. My heart ached to see him go. Each time he departs, my soul goes with him a little more. Though he thinks himself incapable, he will make a magnificent President. I only hope we can really pull it off.

Aug. 28, 1840: Today begins the long journey home. While I'm sad to leave such kind company and beautiful surroundings, I'm eager to see

Mercy, who has returned for only a few months before marrying James Conkling and moving to Baltimore forever.

Sept. 12, 1840: Last evening Elizabeth and Ninian gave a delightful party for Mercy and James. Almost 100 graced the festive scene, but I had eyes for only one. Abraham wore a new blue suit that fit his frame well. He seemed free from the depression that often controls his soul, and confirmed that he hasn't had a bout of hypo in several weeks. We sat on the veranda after the others left and talked about the future of our country and our relationship. I continue to discover how many things we agree on; he is a most learned man. He still has no interest in becoming President, but there's time to change his mind!

Sept. 15, 1840: We discussed our marriage intentions again, and agreed to save ourselves physically until the knot is tied. I don't know if I can keep my word. It's hard not to kiss him more passionately. My heart pines for his body, and yes, even more. I'm eager to enjoy the physicalness of the marriage bed.

I blush to admit it, but I'm crazy to feel his lips more deeply embedded into mine. My heart tells me that our bodies will blend into one and I'm heated just to imagine it. According to *Godey's Lady's Book*, there is much to learn about pleasing a husband. Which parts of his body will he like to have caressed? Will he be shy? Will we couple with the lamp lit? I taste his skin in my dreams and frequently wake up longing for him in a way I have never known, tingling with anticipation. When we're together, I can hardly restrain myself from touching him. We're careful not to spark too much, because his desire is as great as mine. But, most wonderfully, we are also happy to simply sit and hold hands. There is peace in that.

He has presented no gift of commitment and we've told no one, but I know I'm finally and completely in love. I can do so much for him, and he will fill this void in my life. He's the only person who has ever fully respected my intelligence and wit. He can listen to me for hours and hardly open his mouth! Just smiles and nods, though sometimes he does seem to drift away. He teases me when I talk too fast, and prods me when I don't feel like talking at all. I've chosen the best of the lot and can teach him whatever culture he lacks. He will be a good husband and father, honor my opinion, and ask my judgment in all things.

And he will be faithful; no other woman will turn his head. At least he will most likely not turn hers, unless it's with conversation and humor. He told me that, in his first three months in Springfield, only one woman spoke to him and that wouldn't have happened if she could have avoided it. There is wisdom in choosing a homely mate. We will always be partners in life and in task, and nothing will ever take him away from me. I am no longer alone, no longer frightened. I will be somebody after all!

He said, "Molly, if you decide to throw in with me, I'll do everything in my power to live up to your needs, and I can't imagine anything that would make me unhappier than to fail in the effort."

How deeply I love him! I feel it every time he smiles at me—that joy which begins down deep in his heart and slowly works its way up to his mouth. Had I missed the moment and not seen the spark that drives him, I would never have known how beautiful love is through his touch.

Sept. 18, 1840: Abraham mentioned tonight that he hopes to have a large family. I agree children are a fine idea, though raising as many as he would like may not be wise on our political journey. He wants to leave a legacy, but I'm sure we can find ways to be remembered without having a dozen offspring, though I didn't say as much! "Proper" couples probably don't talk about such things at all!

Still, we listed names we like: Eliza, Dolley, Elizabeth, Nancy, Sarah, Joshua, Bob, Henry, James, Abraham. I asked why he has no middle name, and he said they had no need for such in the woods of Kentucky where he was born. I think children should have at least three names.

Unfortunately, our conversation threw him into sadness and he withdrew from me again. He later told me that I suddenly reminded him of his mother—the dearest person in his life. Mrs. Lincoln also had brown hair and blue eyes. She was also an excellent seamstress, and was often hired to sew for others. She was neat, cheerful, and intelligent, as I am. She taught Abraham to understand goodliness, truth, and moral principles, as I'll teach him social graces and political maneuvering. She nurtured and encouraged him, as I'll do all his life.

He said, "I confess the corn, Molly. I still want Maw to be proud of me, because all I am or ever hope to be, I owe to her. I just hope, for her sake, that I can leave the world a little better place than it was when I arrived." You will, Darling; I know that in my deepest heart.

Sept. 20, 1840: Today, as we strolled hand in hand, I asked Abraham how he would vote if the slavery issue were put to the people. He said, "That's a hard question. Overall, I reckon I'm more free-soiler than abolitionist. I'm against the spread of slavery, and think new states should come in free. I'm afraid people ain't ready for sudden abolition. Some things have to be taken slowly. Like Ben Franklin said, haste makes waste."

So our views differ somewhat. I've always disliked the system. I begged Father to release our slaves right up until I left Lexington, though they were treated tenderly and lovingly. Abraham says emancipation would cause a riot and the country would be torn apart by war and upheaval; that the slaves wouldn't know how to care for themselves and would turn to stealing and begging, which would increase poverty and disease; that slavists would hire the negroes for pennies a day and in effect keep them in bondage. I hear some logic in what he says, as always, but can't believe the situation could get any worse.

Oct. 15, 1840: Love is glorious! I'm so happy, happy, happy! I never knew I could feel like this. I've given my heart fully to this gangly, somber man. He says little, but his touch is deep. Sometimes we read together—almost motionless, arm to shoulder, knee to chin, heart to soul. His presence soothes the turmoil of my mind; his hands generate warmth around my waist. I see passion in his eyes, crimson feelings reflected in steel gray.

But I admit that I sometimes wonder if what I see is really fervor for me. I ask if he loves me and he says, "Course I do, Molly. We're getting married, ain't we?" Not overly emotional, but always truthful.

Certainly he has known women in his travels, but all men need physical gratification. He says he has never loved another in his heart and I believe him. He told me about his only close female friend, Ann Rutledge, whom he treasured as a sister. She died when they were both hardly more than teens. Perhaps the friendship would have blossomed into romance if she hadn't been betrothed to another man, but Abraham would never betray a trust. And that other Mary—Mary Owens? He quickly saw the folly of that relationship and ended it.

Oct. 22, 1840: I asked my beloved to set a wedding date and he agreed to New Year's Day, though he still hesitates and asks me not to tell. Doubts intrude on my heart, and I worry he may be changing his mind. Have I offended him in some way? Has he decided I'm too plump, too plain, too outspoken? Do my varying moods or jealous questions annoy him? Has he found another? I have not been able to sleep or eat for worrying. If I lose him, life will not be worth living.

He says the issue is money. "I've only got minor prospects for the future and nothing saved up. What little money I do have could disappear as fast as the funds of the debtors I represent. In a blink, I could lose the means to give you the ease you ought to have."

"But I have money," I told him yet again. "Father will give us a handsome dowry and I already have funds from Grandmother's will, and the land Mother left me."

"No," he said, folding his arms across his chest, "I never use any man's money but my own." Stubborn old goat! When people are married, yours and mine don't exist. It's all ours. But he won't give on the issue of financial independence, and our future may be lost for it. The world would be an infinitely better place if someone could figure out how to run it without money!

Oct. 25, 1840: When Abraham read in the *Family Monitor* that love won't pay your board bill, he muttered, "I reckon I'm a bored Abe." He meant for me to hear it.

I tried to calm the dry quiver in my voice when I asked why he felt bored. He said he might be happier just roaming around as a traveling lawyer or judge instead of being tied in one place.

I said, "Well, now is a fine time to be deciding that! What about those dozens of children you claim to want? How do you expect to raise them if you're always on a horse? And you're not getting any younger, you know."

I stared at his wall of silence. "Do you not love me? You certainly never say the words. Have I shunned all the others in vain? Is there another woman? Answer me!"

No, he said, there's no other woman. It's a worry about money and his natural restlessness, so I finally consented to his riding the circuit as long as he feels the need. Then he told me he will be "courting" most of next April, May, and October, and a week in June, July, November, and December! He promised to write every day or two. Surely I can manage such a schedule without losing my sanity. He again committed to January 1st for our nuptials, and I agreed to remain silent a while longer. That will be difficult, especially with the trepidation I now feel.

Oct. 30, 1840: My sweetheart has written to me more about his life, and I understand now why he's so concerned about funds. I know, of course, that he doesn't come from a moneyed family and his father had no ambition. Now he has revealed his father's many financial losses, and his own as well.

Apparently Abraham himself failed at several businesses, and once even had his horse, surveyor's instruments, and law books levied against. When Mr. Berry died, Abraham became responsible for all their liabilities left over from the general store and he borrowed money to cover it. He's still repaying this "national debt," as he calls it.

His letter was filled with sadness and he complained of leg pains. I continue to sense how lonely he is, and yet he's frightened of intimacy. He has never loved before, as I have not, and can't decide what to say or do about it. He tries mightily hard to avoid rejection and failure, and is afraid of saying the wrong thing. If he says nothing and does less, nothing wrong can come from it. I've always taken a different approach to life: If I say everything and do more, something right will come from it. We're opposites in background and temperament, yes, but our hearts understand each other.

Nov. 4, 1840: Abraham is still unwilling to make a public commitment of our betrothal. We have less than two months to make the wedding arrangements, but I won't hang up the fiddle just yet. I am determined now; he won't deny his destiny. With me beside him, he will have a brilliant future. He must understand that our hereafters are bound together and we are bonded forever. He has lived too long in Joshua Speed's loft and associated with unmarried men who spend their evenings exchanging crude jokes and smoking cigars. He needs a woman's culture, a woman with taste and breeding, a Todd woman.

Nov. 21, 1840: Elizabeth and Ninian are hosting a Thanksgiving supper Wednesday night. What a wonderful chance to re-acquaint with old friends. It will be lovely to dance again too, and Abraham has agreed to step out more often. I'll finish the gown I've been sewing—in Dolley Madison's favorite bright yellow—and buy new shoes from Gardams. I'll talk with Abraham tonight about announcing our engagement there. What better time? How could he deny me that privilege?

Nov. 22, 1840: Talked with Abraham for two hours about our wedding announcement, and he finally agreed we can declare our intentions at the festivities next Wednesday. If he had not consented, I don't know how I would have managed. If kept a secret until the last moment, I would have to do everything myself, and there would be few in attendance. Even our close friends must have some notice! Of course it's proper that the wedding be held here in Ninian's home since he's my guardian, though Abraham wants to be married at Rev. Dresser's home. If he had his way, we would elope and tell no one. Men understand so little about how important a wedding is to a bride.

Nov. 23, 1840: Everyone has now accepted Elizabeth's invitation for Wednesday. The menu includes stewed oysters, turkey with chestnut dressing, cranberry sauce, Spanish pickles, meringues, soft-shell almonds, and an amazing cream-filled pyramid cake with buttered icing. Almost as though she knows how special the night will be.

My nerves have worked themselves into nausea and headache. Not severe, but bad enough to require a sip of paregoric. Even though my hands are shaky, I've been sewing myself blind on my gown, even overlaying the sleeves with needlepoint. Abraham must be proud of me and his decision!

We'll be mobbed when we tell the news, but Elizabeth and Ninian won't be pleased. They tolerate Abraham's presence when they must, but not the idea of his permanence in their lives. They chant that he's not "Todd quality," I'm settling for too little, he's a rube, he'll never amount to anything, I should see others again. Stephen Douglass still comes around, and so does Marshall Prescott, but I'm only socially polite to them. After Wednesday, the world will know I belong to Abraham and no more acting will be required.

Nov. 24, 1840, Thanksgiving: I gazed in the mirror tonight and thought about upcoming events. Strange how a woman can look at her face for almost 22 years and really not see it. I studied myself and tried to see me as Abraham does. I know he finds me physically desirable; that has been evident from the beginning. And now, as we feel cozier in our caresses, his masculine desires become more quickly and obviously noticeable.

I believe I've gotten prettier since we met. I've become more womanly than girlish, more sensual, more ready to be loved. Abraham says he likes the wayward curl I've always tried to keep away from my forehead, so lately I have just let it be. He prefers my hair in coils, though he never has anything but praise no matter how I style myself. He says he can read my entire day in my eyes within minutes after he arrives. "Your eyes are the key to your soul," he frequently says as he touches my cheek with the back of his hand.

On Wednesday evening, we'll be under scrutiny by many eyes. People will look at us carefully to ascertain what we see in each other, how we'll blend our lives, whether we have enough love to sustain us. They will smile at our opposite sizes and Abraham will joke that we're "the long and the short of it."

When I came down the stairs to display my dress for Elizabeth, Ninian said, "Why, Mary, you're so lovely you could make a bishop forget his prayers." From Ninian, that's high praise indeed. Of course my costume is not the big event for tomorrow, but they don't yet know it.

Nov. 25, 1840: What a miserable night! After the meal, Abraham asked to see Ninian in the drawing room. Ninian poured a sherry and led Abraham through the halls. They came back in about 20 minutes and Ninian said, "Ladies and Gentlemen, I have an announcement to make."

I held my breath. The group gave their full attention, and Ninian stood stiffly with his arms by his side and legs spread as though for balance. He looked at the floor and twice cleared his throat. He did not glance my way. "I've just been informed that the Honorable Abraham Lincoln has requested the hand of my sister-in-law, Mary Ann Todd, in marriage. The ceremony will be held in this parlor on the evening of January 1, 1841."

A loud gasp came from across the table. I turned toward Elizabeth and saw her hand over her mouth and a mixture of emotions in her eyes. I knew she wouldn't be pleased, but I didn't expect to see terror and wrath. She slumped back into her chair and held on to the seat. I glanced at Ninian; he resembled a statue frozen in time. I turned toward Abraham; his skin was the color of day-old egg whites. The room remained totally quiet for a moment and then the congratulations began. I led the well-wishers over to where Abraham stood with his arms frozen behind his back, his elbows stuck out to the sides like prongs. He finally managed to twitch the corners of his mouth slightly upward and accepted the handshakes, but his left hand hung unused by his side. His jovial double-handed greeting was forgotten. He left shortly afterward, saying he had a case early tomorrow morning.

Elizabeth and Ninian are devastated. I hoped the anger and shock would pass by evening's end, but it didn't. After the guests left, Elizabeth asked me to sit on the settee in my room and talk. She said, "Some people aren't meant to be together no matter how strong their feelings. This man is not suitable for you. He's rustic, socially primitive, unattractive, uneducated. He lives in a room above a store, for Heavens sake, and he has no money. You're opposite in nature, culture, and raising. You're a Christian and he doesn't even belong to a church. You're so different that you will never live happily as man and wife. He'll disappear the first time you collapse in tears for no reason or go racing in circles around the house. And your dream of the White House? You can certainly forget that!"

I dammed back my tears. "Why can't you just be happy for me, Elizabeth?"

"Because Lincoln has no chance of success. Why, he can hardly afford essentials for himself, much less a family. And where will you live? Not here, you can depend on that. You've done some nonsensical things in your life, Mary Todd, but this is the worst of them. Father will be beside himself. You know he won't attend the ceremony. He'll disown you. You'll have nothing, do you understand? Nothing!"

"Isn't love important?" I asked.

"Dash it all, Mary, not in this case, not in this case." She stormed from my room, slamming the door behind her.

Nov. 26, 1840: Abraham came by tonight and told me he's worried. About our future, about public opinion, about his wanderlust, about money. He says he really can't afford to marry right now: "Molly, I can't whitewash it. I'm poor as Job's turkey and you're used to finery. I earn maybe $1500 a year lawyering, $200 as a legislator for however long that lasts, and a few coins at the *Journal*, but my income's not consistent. I never know how much I'll bring to the kitty. If I lose an election or a few clients, I won't be able to support a family. And don't bring up your money."

Ornery old critter! What in the blazes does he think marriage is all about? Besides, I believe this sudden change has more to do with Elizabeth and Ninian's reaction than with money. Perhaps they even discouraged him. Damn them all! Why won't people let me get on with my life?

Dec. 1, 1840: Abraham's moods fluctuate back and forth. Today he is not in favor of our marriage again. He said, wringing his hands and staring above my head, "This matter is harassing my feelings a good deal. I'm afraid you won't be satisfied with your life if you get stuck with me. There's a lot of flourishing about in carriages and the lot here in Springfield, which it would be your doom to see without sharing. You'd be poor without the means to hide your poverty. Your sisters and their husbands will never forgive you for hitching up with an uneducated country boy and depriving you of all you were born to have. And you'll certainly never have the President's House if you hook up with me. You're getting the little end of the horn."

I touched his arm. "Do you not love me?"

"You know I do. I just don't have the business sense to give you all you need and want. You could be powerfully rich with a man like Douglass or Webb. I reckon it'd be hard for you to give up the things you're used to and struggle on your own with the likes of me. You're young and beautiful; you can do a lot better."

He finally succumbed to reason and allowed his pendulum to swing back to favor. After January 1st, everything will be the way God meant it to be. Abraham will be happy with a nice home, a loving helpmate, precious children, and a strong political goal. His fear and depression will subside and the money will come.

<u>Dec. 13, 1840, my 22nd birthday:</u> I will be married by this time next month! Mr. and Mrs. Abraham Lincoln—tall and petite, thin and buxom, dark and light. He conceded to being married in this house, of course. How could he do otherwise? But he hasn't spoken to the minister, and he would prefer to keep the event quiet and small.

Elizabeth and Fanny are still quetching over the engagement. I don't care what they say, or anyone else either! Abraham loves me and will always tend to my needs. Marriage should be based on friendship, love, and physical attraction, not pocketbooks or pedigrees. Many of our Presidents have started their careers with less money than their wives!

<u>Dec. 14, 1840:</u> Abraham again insisted that we not announce our plans to anyone. Must we wait until the pear is ripe? Is he ashamed of me?

When I ask about his feelings, he hesitates. When I ask if he loves me, he nods that he does. I can't read his thoughts. He hasn't been this silent since the last debate with Stephen Douglass when so few people turned out.

He even came late for my birthday supper last evening, and brought only an arrangement of red and white poinsettias. He said he had been working at the courthouse and lost track of time. I waited patiently for an hour, refusing all requests to dance, but finally waltzed with Edwin Webb. I even allowed him to kiss me on the cheek as he said goodnight. Abraham's eyebrows rose slightly at the occurrence, but he said nothing.

Is our behavior normal? Isn't this supposed to be a happy time in our lives? If so, why do my eyes sting and my belly roil? Why must I struggle to stay calm? Why do I feel such jealousy when I see beautiful women near the courthouse or Speed's store? Why does he seem so indifferent, so unemotional?

Dec. 16, 1840: Abraham has been resurrected! He arrived for supper tonight looking powerfully dashing and smiling from ear to toe. He had a small package hidden behind his back, which he held out to me as though it were still my birthday: a perfectly marvelous hatpin, gold, with a mother-of-pearl tip, just the kind I love.

I said, "You're looking fine and fit tonight. Has something good happened?"

He answered, "No, My Dear, only that we're to be hitched up in a fortnight and I reckon it'll be a day of wonder. I just hope you don't soon wonder why you did it."

He chuckled and reached out for me. As his arms encircled me, I laid my head on his chest, listening to the slightly irregular beat of his heart and wishing time would stand still. He continued, "I stopped at the Globe today and asked about rooms. I didn't mention my reason for asking, so our secret's safe. I hope you'll be pleased to learn that the same room Fanny and Willie lived in after they got married is available. Does that make you happy?"

"Yes, for a while. I would like to get our own home as quickly as possible."

He released me. "Now, Molly, this arrangement will give you a break before we set up housekeeping, and it'll help us put back some money. Some folks board for a coon's age before getting tied to a home."

"Yes, but they are not the Lincolns. We have great things in store for us. We can't manage properly in a hotel for long."

He didn't answer.

Dec. 17, 1840: Abraham was here for supper but, as usual, Elizabeth and Ninian created a reason to leave soon after the meal. If not for their political association, Ninian would probably not speak to him at all. I prefer to eat with them alone and visit with Abraham afterward. He says it makes "no nevermind" to him where — or whether — he eats.

After Abraham left, I asked Ninian why Abraham is good enough to be Whig Party leader but not good enough to marry a Todd. Ninian puffed deeply on his cigar and said, "Politics and family are two different things, Sister Mary. I want you to have the best, the kind of life I've provided for Elizabeth. While his political sense is strong and he speaks like a preacher, Lincoln is a plebian.

"He has no business ability and will never be able to charge enough as a lawyer to keep you in gowns and shawls. You know he only owns one hat, which he uses as a briefcase. You own dozens of bonnets and hundreds of gloves. You'll have to give up everything—carriages, servants, fine clothing, jewelry, all the things you love. Do you understand that?

"Maybe your sister won't tell you, but I will. When you marry a Todd, your life changes, and in a way, you become a Todd. Lincoln is not capable of being a Todd."

My words spewed out from some hidden place in my soul: "You don't understand, Ninian. I don't want him to become a Todd! I want to become a Lincoln! He has more wisdom and potential than any of those other men you keep throwing at me. So what if he's not 'old' money? He'll someday have both fame and prosperity, you can count on that, and already he's serving a 4th term in the legislature—is that a 'plebian' accomplishment? Most importantly, we love each other. This won't be a marriage of convenience and 'family.' We have a future together and we'll make it a grand one, with or without your blessings!"

Then I went to bed, after stopping by the library for a small glass of sherry.

Dec. 20, 1840: I am so angry I may never speak to Abraham again. We are invited to a continual round of events during the holidays, but he refuses to take much part in the festivities. As usual, he says he's not a social man. What to do now? What would Dolley do?

"Abraham," I said this afternoon over peach dumplings, "it would be embarrassing for me to attend these soirees alone. Do you want me to refuse all social invitations until after we're married?"

He sighed and lowered his spoon. His eyes focused on something deep inside himself, not on me, as he said, "I've got to work in the courts right now. I'm handling nine cases before the Supreme Court this month alone. I'm tuckered out and my mind's in the law, not in frolicking and silliness. I'm called to help people, not to make a damn fool of myself."

I watched mutely as he resumed eating. When he wiped his mouth for the last time, I rose and he followed me to the door. He left me with only a dry peck on my cheek. Bah! Let him work all the nights he wants. I won't be held back from my own social obligations because he refuses to attend. We have a reputation to build.

Dec. 24, 1840: Abraham promised to escort me to the Bunns' party tonight, and I promised to suppress my temper and concerns. I'll wear my soft blue silk with the flame-colored roses across my bosom, with only a few petticoats so we can dance closer, and coif myself in ringlets. Some rose-pedal dust will add youth to my cheeks, and powder under my eyes will hide the sleeplessness. Yes, I'll dazzle the Honorable Mr. Lincoln tonight!

Dec. 25, 1840, Christmas: God Rest Ye Merry, Gentlemen. Seven days from marriage, yet I don't rest merry. Father and the children couldn't come from Lexington for Christmas, and I miss seeing them. Perhaps they fear being obligated to stay through the nuptials, which they have already "sadly" declined. I feel like a stranger in my own home and tread lightly around Elizabeth and Ninian to avoid their drawn faces. I remember Christmases past ringing with laughter and joyousness. Tonight my heart is shredding like bark on a dead tree. The only true joy is Elizabeth's Baby Albert and his youthful innocence. He has yet to learn that the world can be a confusing, cruel place.

Last night Abraham sent word that he would be very late. Feeling it more socially correct to go without him than to be tardy, I rode with Elizabeth and Ninian to the Bunns'. When he finally arrived, I was dancing with Edwin and didn't immediately notice his presence. He stood silently near the dance area, looking like he had been on the receiving end of a moving fist. His eyes showed streaks of red pain, his voice was hoarse and whispery. When we were alone, he accused me of wanting to end our relationship and continue my life as a "belle." Why has he any right to be jealous in light of the way he has been acting? Bah!

Dec. 26, 1840: Abraham has vanished. He didn't appear for supper, and sent no word. Thoughts race through my mind. What to do now? Prepare for my wedding or give up the idea completely? I said nothing to Elizabeth about our spat, so she continues to plan for the event next Saturday—less than one week. Oh Abraham, I love you so much. Where are you tonight?

Jan. 1, 1841: *C'est la vie.* It's over; we have parted. Abraham came this morning while the moon still shined on the snow. He said he had not slept in two nights, and it certainly looked to be so. He was phantom-like—face peaked and pale, eyes sunk deep into his skull, lips dry and parched, cheeks hollow. His wrinkled clothing testified that he hadn't changed in several days, nor had he bathed or combed his hair. I've never seen such a pitiful specimen. I wanted to hold him in my arms and comfort him, wash his face like a child's, feed him ox-tail soup and apple brandy, then tuck him into bed and let him sleep till his nightmare ended.

"What on earth has happened?" I asked. He bowed his head and remained silent. I led him to the red velvet love seat in the sitting room.

He put his elbows on his knees and laid his head on his upturned palms, breathing in labored bursts. He spoke to the floor: "I've come to ask you to free me from my promise, Mary." The loving "Molly" was gone.

I hurdled through dark tunnels of fear and confusion before finding my voice to ask why. He took an eternity to clear his throat, lift his eyes, and tell me. I have never heard him so tenuous. "I'm not fit to be a husband. I've got no social culture. I lose track of the clock and forget those little obligations you care so much about. No, let me finish.

"I ride the circuit for months at a time, and my income is sparse and scattered. Me and John Stuart are nearing the end of our partnership because there just ain't enough fees coming in. Our caseload is down by half this year and it predicts to be even less next year. I owe heavily and I'm currently taking free food and board from friends. You need a life in society and I ain't the man to give it to you. Hell, I don't even like society very much! Go marry Webb or Douglass or Henry. You've got a slew of other choices that would be better for you."

He looked toward the east windows, focusing on the dark wooden frames, and sighed—a deep sound that started at his heels and tried to break free of the walls around us. "I'm sorry, but you'll find in time that this is best. I want in all cases to do right, and I believe it's right to let you go."

My knees were buckling, so I eased into the wide leather chair where he used to hold me on his lap while reading. I took a shaky breath and asked, "Do you love me?" Quiet filled the house like a mantle of obscurity. His breaths shuddered from his lungs. My heart was racing, and I prayed for it to stop altogether. The silence screamed.

I stood and moved in front of him, wanting to lift his chin in my hands and force him to look at me. I persisted, quietly but adamantly, "Abraham Lincoln, do you love me?" Perhaps it was the unusualness of being called by his full name, or perhaps it was my tone, but I reached the ears in his heart. He lifted his head without assistance, met my gaze, and nodded.

"Yes, I've always loved you. Since the moment I looked into those clear blue eyes. Since the night you bedeviled me about my poor dancing. Since I first put my arms around you and smelled roses. You're a vision, Mary Todd, and you have a real knack for love and joy. You deserve a man who can give you all that in return. I'm full of moods and not good at saying how I feel. I even question my judgment at wanting to marry a woman who would be blockhead enough to have me."

He forced a tiny smile, but I could not reciprocate. I asked, "Then why can't we work this out and marry tonight as planned?"

He slowly shook his lowered head, as though watching a mouse scurry continuously from left to right. He squeezed his lips together and rubbed his nose. Then he whispered, "No, Mary, I can't afford to marry you. Your family has made that obvious. Odd, too, because I thought Ninian was my friend. But he's right, of course. You deserve more."

I turned toward the foyer, my tears fighting to remain invisible. "Then go," I said. "I release you from your promise. You win, Counselor. You have plead your case magnificently. I won't ask again."

He stood and walked to the door, hat in hand. He turned back, fingers still on the knob, but I refused to look up, and he left without another word. Now I have to tell Elizabeth and Ninian.

Jan. 20, 1841: I have accepted that I won't be entering into marriage with Abraham Lincoln. In fact, I've given up the idea of marrying at all. I'll be a white-haired spinster living alone with boodles of cats and baking cookies for the children who come to see me wilting into death.

Elizabeth and Ninian have already begun to invite gentlemen to the house in hopes I will like one enough to dress up and go out. I'm still an attractive woman, and since Abraham forced me to keep silent, my availability has not been questioned. I'll simply like all the men and give myself to none, remain independent and fun-loving, ride horses, dance in the streets, go to Paris and buy all the latest styles. I will not give in to matronly ways, and will find my own glory rather than submerge myself into a husband.

Feb. 12, 1841, Abraham's 32nd birthday: I considered sending a card, a note, a small remembrance. Would he be happy or angry? No, I won't make the first move. It would embarrass him if he doesn't want to see me, which is certainly the way it seems. Happy birthday, My Love. I think oft and long of thee, pining to dwell where we used to be.

Feb. 14, 1841, Valentine's: The post contains many lacy cards, but none from my heart's desire. I continue to work with Simeon and Eliza Francis at the *Journal*, proofreading and filing, but Abraham never appears.

His cases are still reported in the papers, so I know he's working. He recently tried a divorce suit (how appropriate), and Simeon says Abraham is now "lobbying" — meeting with other legislators in the State House lobby for informal debates. They set up mock committees, and Abraham heads the committee on Etiquette and Ceremony (how ironic).

I also heard that Joshua Speed plans to return to Kentucky, so Abraham will soon be ousted from his loft in the store. Simeon says he has arranged to board with the Butlers. I pray they take better care of him than Speed did.

Feb. 15, 1841: My social life has increased dramatically since the legislature resumed. The Shakespeare troupe is in town, there are parties almost every night, and the city is alive with excitement. I have expected to see Abraham on the street, crossing the square, buying a paper, attending a play, but it hasn't happened. He is a specter. But he appears in my dreams almost every night.

Last night I dreamed of being locked in a damp, smelly cellar.

There are small windows above my head. I can see feet walking past the windows and I cry out. I run up the stairs to the door, but it remains locked. The feet pass again and I notice how large they are, then I recognize Abraham's boots. I search for something with which to reach the windows, if only to make noise, and I see a brown rattlesnake with black markings. I scream, but the snake doesn't move. I run to the stairs again – up and down, up and down – but the door remains locked. I begin to cry and call out Abraham's name, but he walks on by. This happens again and again.

Feb. 16, 1841: Cousin Steve Logan invited me for supper tonight and told me he plans to ask Abraham to be his new law partner after the legislature adjourns in March. Abraham and John Stuart have agreed to split up, and my cousin's partner, Ned Baker, is moving back to Chicago. Steve's red curls bounced happily as he talked about his many upcoming cases. They should do well together, the crane and the gnome. I hope the arrangement will give Abraham the financial success he needs to feel secure in life.

Feb. 17, 1841: Stephen Douglass called at the house tonight for the first time in many weeks. Elizabeth and Ninian were overly happy to see him. He smiled to hear that Abraham no longer visits, and announced his own good news: He has been appointed Illinois Supreme Court Justice! Of course, he himself wrote the bill setting up the five new judgeships and handled the political maneuvering necessary to ensure that Democrats would fill them. Stephen is a crafty politician and a dear friend but, to Elizabeth's consternation, he is not in my heart.

Feb. 19, 1841: Elizabeth and Ninian invited approximately 50 couples for a handsome supper tonight to celebrate their wedding anniversary. After nine years, they have a wonderful home, a beautiful baby boy, social and political friends, a prosperous career with a strong future, and a jilted sister! Will I ever see my 9th anniversary? Will they ever let me forget what happened?

Feb. 20, 1841: Despite my mood, I attended the event last evening and found myself in delightful company. It's hard to remain sad in so much gaiety, and mourning is not my style. The townsfolk seem to believe I asked Abraham to stop calling, and I said nothing to change their impression. If he knows the rumor, it's kind of him to keep silent. A lady's future can be badly hurt by a rejection. Of course, I did release him and ask him not to return, so there is truth in the story.

Mar. 1, 1841: Eliza Francis told me Abraham has applied for a position in Bogotá, Columbia. In Central America! As far as he can possibly get from me, I suppose. What a dilemma that could be! Any hope of reconciliation would be gone forever. I miss him so dearly — the way he held me for long moments as we parted or greeted, how we laughed at our poetry attempts, how his eyes closed in reverence when I read to him from Ninian's history books, the way he hardened against me when we kissed. No, I won't give up my faith that this pain will be over soon.

I also hear rumors that he is ill and confined to his bed at the Butlers'. People say that he, like myself, sleeps poorly, suffers indigestion, and eats little. He has asked that Dr. Anson Henry be appointed as Springfield postmaster to keep his much-valued doctor from moving away.

Mar. 3, 1841: A letter from Cousin Steve says Abraham has returned to the legislature after an absence of almost a week, but his cheeks are sunken through to his bones, and he is "reduced and emaciated, with scarcely strength enough to speak above a whisper." Abraham told Steve, "Since the 'fatal first,' I've been the most miserable man living. If what I feel got equally distributed to the whole human family, there wouldn't be one cheerful face on the earth. Whether I'll ever be better, I can't tell. I figure I won't, but to remain like this is impossible. I've got to die or get well."

Does this condition have to do with me? The "fatal first" must be January 1st, the day we parted. If he feels this way, why doesn't he call on me, or write? He must know I still love him. Will he allow himself to die rather than risk marriage? My poor darling. What can I do?

Mar. 4, 1841: President Harrison was inaugurated today. What a festive day across the country! This nation is ripening and yet seems to be splintering at the same time. Too many political groups, too many territories, too many disparate ways of seeing life. I hope Harrison is strong enough to bring the people back together.

Mar. 6, 1841: The newspapers say Harrison gave the longest inauguration speech in history — almost an hour! In his shirtsleeves! Perhaps he's not as intelligent as we think?

Mrs. Harrison was too ill to travel from Ohio in this frigid weather. She is 65, almost as old as the President himself. Their widowed daughter-in-law, Jane Irwin Harrison, will serve as hostess till his wife arrives in the spring. The papers say Jane is outgoing and like Dolley Madison in temperament. Perhaps I should write to her and express my willingness and capability to serve in the position of hostess on the chance she would care to engage a substitute at times. I could easily preside over those lavish state dinners with great style in beauteous new clothing and elegant gloves, being admired by everyone. All I need is the opportunity. Yes, I will write to her!

Apr. 4, 1841: President Harrison has died of pneumonia! No presiding Chief Executive has ever passed away, and the nation is in shock and mourning. Black wreaths and banners adorn Springfield's every door, and people clamored to the *Journal* office to read the report. According to the Constitution, John Tyler will be sworn in tomorrow, but no VP has been named to replace him. Abraham should make himself available. It's a better choice than Bogotá!

Apr. 11, 1841, Easter: I could find little to be happy for today. I could hardly hear the minister's sermon for the sounds of my own loneliness. Wonder if they celebrate Easter in Bogotá? Though he has rarely been seen in church, Abraham now apparently deems all society unworthy of his presence.

I journal little these days, because little appeals to me. My writing would be flat, stale, and unprofitable. Like my life. I think mostly of love and tears; these alone will fill my years. I live in a world of just me. Sometimes I feel like I'm the last person alive on earth.

Apr. 26, 1841: Ninian relates that Abraham's hopes for Central America have proved fruitless and he is off again on the circuit. Even knowing he's away, I often hear his footsteps in the foyer, or his high laugh in a crowd. He still comes to me in dreams, and I feel his lips on mine before waking to desolation.

Last night's storm brought me terror. The grumbling thunder and bursting lightning caused me to shriek and squeam till Elizabeth came to comfort me. I slept wrapped in blankets until daybreak allowed a light sleep, but I needed several laudanum tablets to rouse myself this morning.

As Elizabeth wiped my brow last night, she reminded me that Mother died during a thunderstorm. I don't remember the weather, just the overwhelming fear and loneliness of that day. And this one.

May 1, 1841: I visited Eliza Francis today. She was so concerned about my health that I finally told her about my torment. She made strong horehound tea and forced me to talk until it all lay out in the open. I love him! There, I've admitted it, I still love him! I will never want another man. But what can I do? I can't—won't—go to him. What would he think of me if I did so? No, he must come back to me.

May 25, 1841: Elizabeth and Ninian threw the season's final soiree last evening. Everyone waltzed and sang, gay and merry as a marriage bell. I played the piano for hours and managed to enjoy myself. But my days are marred by sick headaches, agitation even at little things, and my family constantly reminding me of Abraham's defection. They invite suitors and wag on about high qualifications and eligibility. They continue to kick against the only man I'll ever love.

Elizabeth wants me to forget Abraham ever existed, but that would be impossible. She has never lost love, or loved as deeply. Life has always come to her as she wanted, so she knows nothing of emotional pain. How can she profess that I ruin my life by hoping for his return? Perhaps she secretly envies the love we felt for each other.

June 5, 1841: Cousin Steve told me Abraham will be back this week. He says Logan and Lincoln has many cases to try in Circuit Court and also in Supreme when it begins later in the month. Apparently the months of travel have been good for Abraham. Steve assures me that he is fully recovered and practices law more astutely than ever. Bully!

Father has invited me to spend the season at our summer home in Alton, and Uncle David Todd has sent an invitation to visit Missouri again, but I have no energy for either. It looks to be an unbearably hot summer, and I can't fathom the idea of riding in coaches and rail cars for any distance. I would rather be left to the solitude of my thoughts.

July 2, 1841: Six months. How time has wrought its changes upon us. The passing days have not lessened the love I feel, though everyone assured me they would. Time and absence only serve to deepen the intensity with which I remember my beloved. I have been with many people lately, yet remain still very much alone, and my thoughts are often with him.

This invisible band around my skull keeps pushing inward, inward, trying to crush my brain. My stomach lies in corded knots. I have cried so long that my tears are no longer salty. My hands are cold, but my body burns from intense fever. I would welcome death. How could a person arrange such?

Sept. 1, 1841: Today my heart-sister, Mercy Levering, married James Conkling. I am so, so happy for her, and know they will be harmonious in their new life. Tonight they will experience marital love in all its splendors and I am ever so envious.

How I wish my darling were near. I'm afraid he may never be mine again. His reply to Mercy's invitation arrived from Kentucky, where he visits Joshua Speed. That will be a good excursion for him, because they were as close as Mercy and I. Speed told me on his recent visit here that he still encourages Abraham to marry someday. I hope he heeds the advice.

Oct. 10, 1841: Winter has fallen early this year and looks to storm as cold as summer raged hot. No wonder I suffer; weather variations surely add to my physical discomfort. I have been abed for almost a week, taking calomel, jalap, and bitters. I have also been quarrelling with Elizabeth. She says I'm malingering; I say she's too harsh. I hear myself lashing out, being caustic and disrespectful, but I'm powerless to avoid it. I feel like I'm watching from a distance.

Even visitors who come to offer health wishes annoy me. Stephen Douglass still pays overmuch attention, and Marshall Prescott, bless his heart, is like a sickbed nurse. I am soured on them all. I hear that Abraham has returned from Kentucky, but have neither seen nor heard from him.

Nov. 24, 1841, Thanksgiving: The baking turkeys and mincemeat pies coat the air with spices. Dried orange wreathes adorn the doors, beans and corn decorate the walls. On the tables are crook-necked squashes, cinnamon and corn breads, juicy hams, and dried beef. Everything is festive except my soul. I picture it differently in my mind. It's the Lincolns' first Thanksgiving in our new home. Abraham and I sit side by side before the hearth, watching the kettle simmer, drinking cider, and toasting our love. I can scarcely realize that almost a year has passed since the "fatal first." Please, God, don't let another year go by in separation. Only shopping seems to ease my loneliness. Odd, I often can't even remember what I purchased, nor do I truly care. The act itself whiles away the hours and lessens the emptiness.

Eliza Francis shared my agony with her husband, even though I asked her to keep silent, and they asked to speak to Abraham on my behalf. Of course the answer is no. He must be the one to make the first move. I instructed them to say, if anything, that though I have released him, the matter will be held open. I understand that his reluctance came from love for me and shall forgive if asked. Time alone will tell the outcome of this saga. What will be will be.

<u>Dec. 13, 1841, my 23rd birthday:</u> My dream was different last night.

I sat as always in a regal, aristocratic office, facing my husband, the President. I held a small, delicate glass of red wine in my hands. I was smiling and nodding at a Chinese emperor. Suddenly an Indian man burst in. He slightly resembled Stephen Douglass but his hair was straight and black. He was naked except for a loincloth, and he carried a tomahawk. The savage grabbed the glass from my hands and threw it into the fireplace. As I reached out to try and save the glass, my bright yellow hat fell to the floor. Then the man sat gently down on the President's lap, leaned back, and melted into him. Their features combined into a new President, who smiled at me and said, "Thank you for coming, Miss Todd. I know how long you've waited, and I'm sorry we can't accommodate you. That will be all."

The room dissolved around me and I woke in my own perspiration-soaked bed.

<u>Dec. 14, 1841:</u> How can months crawl so slowly and sprint so quickly at the same time? The world, like my recent dream, has changed since this time last year. Not just my life, but elements around me as well. The State House is now sufficiently husked out for the legislature to meet within its walls, and Springfield is vibrating with the nominations of governor and legislature. A familiar name is being mentioned as a candidate for House re-election.

The Second Church has added another bell to its steeple. It clangs so long and loud that no one could mistake the hour. I'm sometimes forced to cover my ears with pillows to shut out its incessant ring. Uncle John Todd must send laudanum more frequently to ease the headaches caused by the noise. I'm blessed to be the niece of Springfield's foremost doctor.

Cousin Steve says Abraham has argued 14 cases in Supreme Court this month and won 10 of them. Such posturing will get him elected for certain. Keep up the momentum, Dear One. You will see Washington despite yourself. I pray to be by your side.

Jan. 1, 1842: What a fine winter day to begin a year! We rose early to be ready for the guests who would begin arriving around 8am. Many of the afternoon callers had been to the horse races and shared stories of money lost and won. The house dazzled like a bazaar. Reception tables staggered with cakes, preserves, wines, hot oysters, taffy, chocolate and whipped cream, lemonade, and eggnog. May this year be peaceful and loving. And may my gray-eyed ghost reappear as surely as the spirit of Hamlet.

Feb. 1, 1842: There is little to record. My time is filled pleasantly enough, with sleigh rides, ice skating, evening singings, church events, chess games by the fire, and the endless winter mending. But the air is too frigid to get about much, so everyone stays close to home. I did call on Eliza and Simeon Francis a week ago and had a pleasant evening. They tell me Abraham is safe and well.

President Tyler, now being called "His Accidency" because of the unfortunate way he gained office, is suddenly against the tariff and internal improvements such as construction of roads, harbors, and rivers. He now resists the distribution of receipts from public lands, believes in slavery, and considers Andrew Jackson's nullification proclamation unconstitutional. How he can claim to be a Whig is hard to fathom!

Feb. 14, 1842, Valentine's: Returned last night from a weekend rail trip to Jacksonville with Lyman Trumbull, Julia Jayne, Anna Rodney, Stephen Douglass, Lizzie Todd, Marshall Prescott, and Martha Rathbone. Stephen spent the time trying to taunt me into admitting feelings for him. When I would not, he finally said, "I won't ask you again, Mary. A man can only take so much rejection. You've thrown away your best opportunity to live in the Executive Mansion."

Perhaps I should consider him more seriously. He is carving a fine future for himself as a Supreme Court judge, and his orations continue to improve. Rumors abound that he plans to run for Senate next year and he doesn't deny them. He has a path planned for himself that Elizabeth says is "fitting for a Todd union." But no, now that I've known love, political success alone can't take my heart.

Mar. 15, 1842: A letter from Joshua Speed with the most incredible news: He married Fanny Henning on February 15th! Imagine Speed a married man, finally faithful enough to make it to the altar. He says he is far happier than expected. He mentioned Abraham only to say that he writes regularly, is in good health, and doesn't plan to run for the legislature this term. How disappointing.

My health might be good too if the dratted snow would let up. My bones are chilled and my hands and feet are never warm enough. I'm sleeping better, but feel doleless—no energy or interest in social events, piano, or even sewing. I have surrounded myself with books, and I write sad poetry and play with Albert. How I wish for my own child! I would name her Dolley. Or if a boy, Bob, James, Levi, or...Abraham.

Apr. 2, 1842: Sunshine today for the first time in many weeks. Perhaps now I can finally warm up. We haven't seen the ground since December, and I'm soured on the white drabness. Spring brings beauty and love to life. I long to see hyacinths bloom, feel spring breezes brush my cheeks, ride horseback, and walk along the river with shoes in hand. I'm eager to return to the *Journal* office to help Eliza and Simeon, and perhaps write a paragraph or two myself. They are so good to encourage my creativity.

Elizabeth says we will have a large dinner party next month to start the season, and she'll invite all the eligible men who have arrived in Springfield since last year. Some few actually seem to be interesting and, in her estimation at least, are gifts for the belles.

May 6, 1842: Sadness has returned with the spring sunshine I so ardently desired, because I remember days like this when Abraham and I strolled hand in hand along the riverbank. Alas, the icy, destroying hand of time writes on us all, even as it passes into warmth. The stars shine down as before, yet not with the same mellow light. But hope will remain my guide as I dream of a reunion. May the day not be far away.

May 13, 1842: The papers and the coterie talk of secession and war! Surely it can't be allowed to happen. The abolitionist *Liberator* encourages readers to take up the separation cause even here in the north. The article mentioned the withdrawal attempts in 1806, when Louisiana's admission so outraged New England leaders that Sen. Plumer of New Hampshire encouraged the eastern states to form a separate government. Sen. Pickering of Massachusetts even proposed a northern confederacy. How absurd, and how dangerous the talk. Surely it is only talk. If the parts were gone, what would become of the whole?

Dear God, save us from ourselves! I fear the rancid smell from the streets comes not just from the manure and dead waste in the gutters, but from our homes and newspaper offices as well. Ninian says disunion will never happen because the south needs the north too badly. I pray he's correct.

July 4, 1842, Independence Day: A celebration day in Springfield, but a fearful headache kept me abed until evening. The heat, the smells, the intensity, the talk of secession are sometimes too much for me. At those times, I can eat nothing, and the draperies must be drawn because the window light hurts my eyes. I don't understand my temperament lately and the confusion is harrowing. I feel fuzzy. I sway from contented and optimistic to bewildered, alienated, and helpless. At night, I dream of being unable to pull myself from a railroad track going only downhill.

I miss my mother so terribly. I want to feel her cool hand on my cheek and accept small ice pieces from her to soothe my fevered throat. Sometimes I see her in my room and cry out, "Mother, help me. Tell me what to do." But she cannot, or does not, answer. Oh to be an angel with golden wings and fly beyond this earthly existence.

July 20, 1842: I have seen him. My greatest hope (or was it trepidation?) came to pass. Eliza and I worked at the *Journal* during the morning, setting type and editing articles, and she suggested we go out for sandwiches and tea. As we crossed Fourth Street, I saw his tall figure coming toward us. Other than a white shirt, he was dressed all in black, even on such a humid day.

Several children walked with him, looking up at Father Jupiter and begging to be swung from his long arms. Eliza and I stopped, speechless, as we watched him approach. He also paused and our eyes met. Then the youngsters began to drag him again. He tipped his beaver stovepipe and said, "Afternoon, Ladies," as he passed on by.

That was part and parcel of an event for which I have waited 18 months! But I sensed recognition in those dreamy gray eyes. I saw in his face all I felt in mine: sorrow, pain, apology, love, hope, memories. Or did I? Am I still so enamored that I only pretended to see the emotions I want to see? Was it nothing more than a simple passing—an event for which I alone have prayed?

Now that the meeting has occurred, I wish I could do it over. I would exclaim, "Why, Mr. Lincoln, what a fine group of children you have acquired since last we met." I would enthuse, "Why, Mr. Lincoln, how fine you look today." I would say, "Why, Mr. Lincoln, I adore you and want you in my arms."

Eliza knows my feelings, so I asked if she noticed anything in his glance. She confirmed that something did indeed pass between us. Now we will wait and see. The king and queen have both moved; who will advance and who will remain to defend the board?

Aug. 5, 1842: The chess match is over and neither king nor queen lost face! This was the most amazing night of my life, one I will never forget or be able to repay.

The Francises invited Abraham and me to supper without telling the other. When the carriage deposited me at their front door around 6pm, I had no idea my life would soon change so completely. Walter opened the door as always, but he wore a low smile as he said, "Welcome, Miss Mary. You're expected in the library." Eliza sprinted out from the parlor, smiling and adjusting her skirts, and gave me a fierce embrace. Still I had no hint of what was to come. She opened the library doors.

I'll never forget the scene. Simeon and Abraham stood beside the fireplace. My beloved had a sarsaparilla twig at the corner of his mouth and one elbow on the memento-congested mantle. He was dressed in dark blue striped trousers, brocade waistcoat, white shirt with upright collar, and a pale yellow cravat secured with a pearl pin. A watch hung from his pocket. His ankle boots were shined. His hair touched his ears and hung loosely on his forehead—longer than I had ever seen it.

When the doors opened, both men turned and saw me standing there with Eliza at my back. Simeon began to grin—I know no other word for it. Eliza whispered, "Please be friends again."

Abraham looked at me as he had in town, but this time no children were near to drag him off. We stared at each other in silence for what felt like hours. Then he held out both his arms and I took my first wobbling step toward him, feeling like a toddler who has finally turned loose of his mother. Somehow I reached him and he took both of my hands into his. I felt the strength of his long, thin fingers; saw the soft black hair on his knuckles. I vividly recalled the touch of those hands on my neck and against the back of my head when we last kissed. He led me to the large gold settee and we sat, still holding hands and looking into each other's eyes. Eliza and Simeon quietly closed the doors behind them and left us alone.

Finally Abraham spoke, his voice uneven. "You look fit, Mol...Mary."

"So do you, Abraham. And, please, I like hearing 'Molly' from your lips. I see Mr. Hypo is on sabbatical."

He smiled at my personal teasing and we were strangers no more. Suddenly no time had come between us, no distance crossed, no feelings hurt, no promises broken. We were the long and short of it again. We were one. Music and laughter returned to the world.

In less time than it takes to say, "I love you," he wrapped me in his strong arms and we kissed with a passion I have never felt—or even imagined in my own bed as I pretended his presence. We had so much time to make up for! A kiss for every month, a caress for every day.

When we could separate ourselves, which we both knew we must do if we were to retain our deportment there in the Francises' library, he said, "I'm so sorry. I was such a pig-headed fool. I've suffered hell since our parting. There was a lot of trouble in my mind, but I never meant to hurt you. I was poor and making so little headway in the world that I dropped back in a month of idleness as much as I gained in a year's rowing, and I thought I might miss the long hours at my office and talking with the men down at the store half the night. My health was also a worry, but nervous debility is always a conductor of other ailments.

"Mostly, I guess, I was scared of a lifetime commitment, and I couldn't reason myself out of it. You go so fast and dream so high. You know I'm not a demonstrative man. When I feel most deeply, I express the least. I didn't know how to tell you all this. My excuses all seem pretty lame now."

We didn't remember the Francises again until they brought in boiled ham sandwiches, Saratoga chips, and iced tea. Eliza said it was picnic food we could eat with our hands—fare that didn't require much work. We had concentration for only each other.

Abraham told me, "I never felt my own sorrows any more keenly than yours. Knowing that you were still unhappy, and I had helped make it so, killed my soul. I could only reproach myself for even hoping to be cheerful while you weren't. My desire for you never lessened and I was mighty lonesome without you. I've been seeing Dr. Henry frequently for hypo. Did you ever notice how often he inquired after you and your health when he called at your house or met you in public? He would tell me about your doings and well-being.

"How miserably things are arranged in this world! If we don't have love, we don't have pleasure, and if we do have it, we arrange in our own stupidity to lose it, and then the loss doubly pains us. I wanted to see you real bad, but decided to wait for a sign. My text was, 'Stand still, Lincoln, and wait for the Lord's direction.' And now He's spoken and you're here."

When he reached for a glass of tea, I replied, "No, My Darling, hush. It was my fault. I knew you loved me, and sensed you were suffering. I wanted to see you, and thought about you every day, but I was too stubborn to contact you. I wrote letters never sent, birthday and valentine greetings you never saw. I lived in agony all those months without you. I've been practically bed-ridden with guilt, fear, and longing. My nerves have become more defective every month. I should have been stronger for you, shouldn't have rushed you. Can you ever forgive me?"

He pulled me into his chest and inhaled deeply. "Ah, roses," he whispered. Then, "I don't need an apology, Molly. You're my darling child and I gladly take the blame, if blame has to be given, just to have you here with me again."

After a while, I looked toward the windows. Daylight had faded and the lamplighter had already passed by the house. We had been there more than three hours! In what seemed to be one quick beat of our rejoined hearts, we needed to part. If I had stayed longer, Elizabeth and Ninian would have questioned my doings.

Abraham, in the playful manner I remember so well, said, "Since tomorrow's not a court day, how about I come by in a carriage around 11 o'clock and we'll go rowing on the river?"

I panicked. "No, My Darling, I think it's best for us to meet here for the time being. My senses tell me we should spend some time in approving company while we accustom our feet to walking together again. Elizabeth and Ninian will only spoil the joy we feel tonight. Let's ask our devious hosts if we can meet here again. I'll manage somehow."

Eliza and Simeon brought me home and no questions were asked. I excused myself almost at once to be alone with my thoughts. Sleep won't easily dissolve this mantle of joy. I can still taste his lips on mine, feel his body press into me as we held each other. I am loved!

Aug. 6, 1842: I slept more soundly last night than in almost two years. After breakfast, I ran down the hill to Julia Jayne's, knowing she has complete discretion and believing she would enjoy an intrigue. She thought it very romantic and Victorian, like a romance novel, and agreed to be my "alibi" whenever needed.

At 10am, we told our families we were going shopping and then to the *Journal* office to read the news reports. But, of course, we headed directly for the Francis home. Julia giggled as Abraham walked into the room, but Eliza quickly escorted her out, and we were left alone.

Abraham pleased me by saying, "Being with you like we were yesterday filled up my heart. I've hardly calmed down yet! My silly fears were all the worst nonsense. We belong together." I wholeheartedly agreed.

Aug. 20, 1842: I see Abraham almost every day now as Julia and I "shop" or "walk" or "horseback ride." We meet still at the Francis home, and they have become like parents to us—the family we haven't had to approve our relationship.

Our most confidential friends carry messages back and forth: Dr. Anson Henry, Eliza and Simeon, Julia Jayne, James Matheny, Lizzie Todd, Anna Rodney. It's astounding that Elizabeth and Ninian don't yet know about our trysts.

We also spend time at the *Journal*, as we both love to read and write the special interest articles. Julia has also taken a liking to them and we have helped Abraham compose several pieces. We especially like creating satires about politicians, mostly Democrats.

A favorite victim is James Shields, one of the beaus Elizabeth favored for me. Even then he created mirth with his drolleries. He serves in the legislature, and is pretentious and pompous, so he's an apt target for irony. Simeon wrote an especially amusing article about Shields recently. He crafted it as a "Letter to the Editor" and signed it "Rebecca," a backwoods woman from "Lost Townships." She poked fun at Shields' views on taxation, habitude, manners, even his clothing.

Abraham has also created a Rebecca letter. I love to watch him write. He sits at the editing table and approaches the long sheets of blank tally paper with determination. He bites his bottom lip when he thinks, and scribbles rapidly once he begins. He passes his pages to me for approval or laughter, and our eyes meet when we share the joke. If Julia is there, I hand the pages to her and we judge his humor. If the piece is especially amusing, I have no shame in kissing his cheek. He feigns embarrassment, but smiles.

Aug. 25, 1842: We spoke again about marriage. Abraham has made it clear that I'm the only woman he has ever cared for and he won't take "no" for an answer. I have made it clear I won't release him a second time. We renewed our vow of celibacy until marriage, but it becomes harder and harder to uphold.

Abraham mentioned Speed's recent marriage and seems emboldened by it. He said, "Speed's been hitched for nearly eight months. I know from the spirit in his letters that he's happier now than on the day he married Miss Fanny. That pleases me and gives me courage."

Eliza is determined to see us wed soon. Abraham says we shouldn't disappoint her, but I'm in no hurry. Just to be back in his arms is joy enough. I have such a wonderful arrangement now — the luxury of Aristocracy Hill and the excitement of love and intrigue.

We have crafted another Rebecca letter. I say "we," but I wrote the lion's share. This time, Rebecca ridicules Shields' views on banking, especially his decision that Illinois will no longer accept paper currency for tax payments — not even our own state bank notes! Abraham says that demanding only gold and silver is not legal.

Sept. 3, 1842: Shields is aflame, and has made his anger well known by publicly repudiating yesterday's Rebecca letter on the square. As he spoke, his eyes bulged, he jumbled and transposed his words, and little saliva streams spewed out at the few listeners who had assembled. Julia and I laughed uncontrollably.

Sept. 14, 1842: The *Washington Post* reports that the Council of DC has created an auxiliary night police to enforce the "colored curfew." At 10pm, all negroes outside without a pass are liable for arrest, fine, and flogging. Each officer carries an iron spearhead to club human beings who have committed no crime other than being outdoors. What is this country becoming when people can't walk the streets without being harmed? Damn them all!

Abraham is also angry. When he visited Speed in Kentucky, he saw slaves chained together on the riverboat like "fish on a trot line." It hurt his senses so deeply that he can't speak much about the scene. But we discussed the horror of slavery itself, and he vows to help make sure it doesn't spread. I would prefer to eradicate it.

He said, "I ain't totally anti-slavery, you know that. But I'm most definitely opposed to its extension and universality. Slavery's founded in man's selfishness, opposition to it in his love of justice. These principles set up an eternal antagonism. Half our country believes slavery's wrong and half believes it's right. I believe if slavery ain't wrong, nothing in the world is wrong, so we have to fight it. This is a country of compensation; a man who wouldn't be a slave shouldn't consent to have a slave. I don't believe this country can survive as half slave and half free, but I'll be damned if I know what to do about it."

I replied, "Run for Congress, Darling. The best way to win is from the inside."

Slyness twitched across his lips when he said, "You're quite the campaigner, Miss Todd."

Sept. 17, 1842: Shields has again publicly protested the Rebecca letters, so I assume they will be discontinued. He claimed the articles question his honesty and mock his physical courage, and demanded that Simeon reveal the author. We all participated, but Simeon, not knowing what to do, called on Abraham, and my darling claimed accountability.

"Tell Gen. Shields that I'm responsible," he said confidently. "Nothing will come of it, except maybe he'll thumb his nose at me in the street."

Sept. 19, 1842: Abraham returned home unexpectedly this afternoon with some frightful news. Shields tracked his whereabouts and found him earlier this week at court in Peoria. He demanded satisfaction for the Rebecca letters by challenging Abraham to a duel, even though duels are illegal. This is unthinkable!

I tried to talk Abraham into his own good senses again. But he said, "If I back down, that angry Irish will shoot me in the back and I'll have no defense. At least this way I might talk him out of it. I don't want to kill Shields, you know that's so. I've never intentionally harmed anything in my life. I don't want the damned fellow to kill me either, which I rather think he'll do if we use pistols. But I've got an idea. I've been practicing with a broadsword recently and believe I can defend myself. I also don't think Shields will be able to reach me if I'm holding out a sword. He's about your height and only comes up to my armpits. A broadsword is about four feet long, so I should be safe, even if I have to swing."

I stared at him. "Why not choose cow dung thrown over your shoulder at five paces? You're both good at slinging that!"

This is all my fault. I carried the rag on longer and ridiculed more in my Rebecca letter than the others. I even set Shields' shortcomings to rhyme. Abraham says he could have stopped my words from being published, claiming responsibility by omission. None of us realized how deeply my little verses would provoke him. Oh what have I done? I have truly trespassed on Abraham's tenderness and amiability this time.

Sept. 22, 1842: The duel is over and we are all victorious. No one was hurt, though I believe some egos were damaged.

Yesterday morning, Abraham and his seconds, James Matheny and Cousin Steve Logan, rode the 80 miles to Alton to prepare and practice. Julia, Eliza, Simeon, and I took a buggy last night, spending the night with Miss Thompson, Julia's friend.

Early this morning, we hired a horse-ferry to transport us across the Mississippi River to an area facing "Bloody Island," a sand bar in the river on the Missouri side. Since the event was so highly publicized, hundreds of onlookers were stationed on all sides of the island.

The duel was to begin at 8am. As defender, Abraham requested that the men draw an eight-foot circle and allow neither man to pass over the center line. The duelists each took a sword and began to test its value. Shields danced around, parrying with this tree and another. Abraham sat on a log, chewing on sarsaparilla and practicing swings and swishes. His calm demeanor surprised me. The seconds from both sides talked in the distance for more than an hour. Then there were several conferences with Abraham and Shields individually.

Finally, to my full relief, James Matheny made a loud declaration, "Though Mr. Lincoln wrote the September 2nd article, he had no intent to injure Mr. Shields' personal or private character. Mr. Lincoln did not think said piece would produce such an effect. Had he anticipated such, he would not have written it. He wrote the article solely for political reasons and not to gratify any personal irritation against Gen. Shields, for he has none and knows of no cause for any."

As usual, my sweetheart's planning proved sound. Shields must have looked at Abraham's long arms and decided he would be sliced into ribbons before ever reaching his opponent. He relented quickly.

To my surprise, Abraham is mortified over the event. He told Simeon he would never write another anonymous letter for any newspaper, and made me promise never to refer to the matter again.

Sept. 25, 1842: Abraham is still upset about that foolish duel. No harm was done, but he acts as though President Tyler himself witnessed it. He says it was illegal, immoral, embarrassing, and foolhardy. Why is he so reluctant to speak of it? He did it for me; he stood as my champion. He should be proud of his romantic behavior! Men are so unpredictable.

Sept. 26, 1842: Cousin Steve Logan was elected to the Illinois legislature and carries hopes of Congress next year. The Todds and their offspring continue to reign! I hope Abraham won't let another term pass without being a candidate for Congress himself. If both Abraham and Steve should win, the Whigs would be back in the federal light!

Oct. 1, 1842: This evening at supper, Abraham blurted out, "Molly, I've got to start on the circuit Monday and I'll be gone the whole month. I want to ask you a question, and now seems as fit a time as any. I want very much to marry up when I get back. Will you consent? My life's out of sorts without you."

I smiled and put my arms around his waist. "Then we must repair your life...and mine. Of course my answer is yes."

He gave my hand three quick pats and continued. "Still I'm worried, Molly. About what you'll be forced to part with, the changes you'll have to make. For a year or two, we'll live at the Globe, so you won't have to keep house, but someday you'll have to learn to cook and clean. Your beautiful little hands will get dirty and you won't have expensive gloves to cover them. Can you truly give up all the Todds and men like Douglass have to offer you?"

I nodded, too full of love to speak out loud.

"Then I've got a gift for you as a promise," he said as he reached into his long coat pocked. He handed me an envelope containing election returns for the last three legislative races. I looked at him with my silent questions.

"You're the only little woman I know who'd enjoy getting those." He laughed in his high, sensuous way and squeezed my hand again. "I thought we'd study them together and plan a strategy to set the Whigs apart from the Democrats in my run for Congress."

I jumped into his lap and flung my arms around his neck. "Congress! Oh Darling, I'm so thrilled."

He stood and set me on the floor so he could pull another small packet from his pocket. "I'd also like you to see the inscription I've chosen for this." He showed me a thin gold wedding ring. "Look inside the band and see if you approve."

I focused my trembling eyes and peered into the dark circle. Imprinted there, reflecting my own thoughts, was the vow, "Love is eternal." My tears flowed over layers of mental boulders, washing away years of doubt and insecurity. I will never be alone again. We are so greatly attached to each other that it's hard to imagine anyone being in love but us.

We discussed our plans. I would like a large, festive wedding, but it's not to be. We'll probably be married at the minister's home without any parade. "Can we take a trip afterward?" I asked, still fancying Paris.

"No, not right away. There ain't money for it. But soon. We'll go to Niagara Falls. Would you like that?"

I nodded. "Yes, that will be fine. Can we at least stay at the American House on our first night as man and wife? The hotel is so luxurious. I'm told it has a large nuptial suite with a private water closet. And food can be served in your room."

"I'm afraid not," he answered. "It's just not financially mindful right now." So we'll go straight to the Globe.

Some in Springfield will shun me for the secrecy, and rumors will spread because of the suddenness, but I don't care what anyone else thinks. Ritual is not important now. If people don't like the situation, they can just not come around. It will be their loss. We will have each other and we won't need outsiders.

I'll be content as long as I have Abraham Lincoln by my side and in my bed. I've waited a lifetime for this moment and endured much. Our glory will soon come as well. Abraham is like a shooting star—no one else can see him yet, but he's on his way to greatness. He swore me to tell our news only to Julia and Eliza. He doesn't want Elizabeth and Ninian to know until our plans are complete.

Oct. 29, 1842: Abraham has returned! He tried cases in Decatur, Clinton, Urbana, and Danville, where he talked to many people about being a congressional candidate. He believes the nomination is secure. He also met a law student named William Herndon, whom he has recommended as a clerk for Logan and Lincoln.

It was after supper when he sent for Julia and me to meet him at the Francises. When I asked why he waited, he explained, "Well, Molly, I wanted to rush right over, but thought you'd appreciate some cleaning up on my part after a month's riding. So I went to the tavern and took a long bath. I also got my hair trimmed and greased, paid a nickel for a shave, and put on this shiny new collar I bought in Clinton. Don't I look purty?" He did look "purty" indeed.

Oct. 30, 1842: We are to be married next Friday!! Elizabeth and Ninian, and probably Father too, will be furious. They have long disliked my darling Abraham, for his looks and station only. But I will not be told whom to marry and will prove them wrong very soon!

Nov. 1, 1842: Abraham is calm and leisured, but I have much to do, matters to decide, things to which I must bid *adieu*. Goodbye to youth, girlhood, family, home, name, luxury, independence. Hello to the Globe Tavern, sharing a bed, eating with strangers, and being an extension of my husband. And I share his future gladly. Being a helpmate is a loving way to be successful in all areas. I will shine because I help him be a star. After all, the power behind the throne is mighty in itself. I'm sure many Presidential wives have understood this.

Nov. 3, 1842: Tomorrow is our wedding night. Who knows what changes you will hear when I next write? I'm excited, yet nervous; terrified, yet more excited and eager than ever before. Mrs. Abraham Lincoln. The name has a strange and wonderful ring to it. Mrs. Senator Lincoln. Mrs. President Lincoln.

I'm full of questions. Will the 9 years difference in our ages matter? Will he become doddery while I remain youthful and sophisticated? It made no tilt to Dolley Madison. She was 17 years younger than President Madison! What will we experience in physical union? I have imagined it for so long, and my nerves spark to think about it even now. Will my fantasies be realized? Can I truly be a good wife and mother? My God, how will I learn?

Nov. 5, 1842: How strange to journal again. I feel as though my girlish musings should be put aside, but I want to record the memories of our nuptials. Our children may someday want to read them.

Abraham went out early yesterday, first to Rev. Dresser's to secure him for the service, then to James Matheny's to engage him as groomsman, then to the hotel for fixing up.

Meanwhile, I was to reveal the news to Elizabeth and Ninian. But Ninian was out, and before I could say a word, he stomped into the house and demanded an explanation. Apparently, he met Abraham on the street and my beloved revealed the plan himself. After I explained about the months of courting, Ninian said, "Mary, you're my ward, and as such, if you insist on this folly, you must be married at my house, not at the minister's."

Elizabeth began to cry, saying more than once, "Mary, he is a plebian. You're a Todd."

I finally squared my shoulders and said, "Yes, Todd for a few hours more. We're going to be married. If not here, then at Rev. Dresser's, but we will be married tonight."

She calmed slightly and then asked me again to wait. "Just one week, so we can follow proper etiquette and send out the appropriate invitations. And so I can plan a formal wedding like Fanny had in our home, a service worthy of a Todd."

I shook my head. "No, we've waited almost two years, and I don't intend to delay any longer."

Abraham arrived a few moments later and Ninian told him the ultimatum. He was not pleased to be married in this house. Why should he be? He has been ridiculed and ousted from here. We all talked it over, and though he would have rather gone to the minister's, he agreed. He also consented to a guest list, a formal supper, and extra attendants to stand with us! For a nuptial gift, he gave me white gloves trimmed with black satin quillings. Must have cost him a week's wages!

After Abraham left, Elizabeth began to prepare the house and worry herself about food and attire. She came to my room, where I was folding my belongings into a Saratoga trunk, and said, "You've not given me much time to prepare for our guests. I'll barely have time to send to Dickey's for gingerbread and beer. Perhaps we can still arrange for a macaroon pyramid from Watson's, but you'll not have anything splendid."

I couldn't resist saying what lumbered across my mind: "I'm sure it will be good enough for plebeians."

Elizabeth hung her head. "That's cruel, Mary, but I suppose it's deserved. I'm sorry we've been so rude to Abraham. We had only your best interests at heart." A moment later, she asked, "Who will be your matron of honor? I'm certain you don't want me."

My heart gave way. She is, after all, my sister. The woman who cared for me after Mother passed away and tried to protect me from Betsy's harshness. The person who took me in and brought society to my feet. She has been my friend and guardian; I couldn't shut her out at such an important moment. I said, "Will you stand up with me, Elizabeth?"

We fell crying into each other's arms. "Oh Mary, I just want you to be happy. If Abraham can make you happy, then I will accept him as a brother. Are you truly sure you love him enough to forego everything you could have with someone else?"

I pulled away. "That's what you and Ninian fail to understand. I'm not giving up anything. I'm gaining a gladiator, a protector, a confidant, and a future. If anyone can fulfill my dreams, it's Abraham."

Elizabeth and the servants quickly cleaned and decorated the house, polished the silver, began cooking food from the storehouse, and sent Raymond to town for the gingerbread and wedding cakes from Dickey's Bakery. One of the servants began writing invitations and another began delivering them. Everyone moved at thunderbolt speed. Except me—I could hardly plod through my mind's haze.

At 5pm, the service began. I wore a long white dress, white satin gloves, and the pearls Elizabeth gave me for last my birthday. Abraham was, as he said, "all slicked up."

I was honored to have Julia Jayne, Lucy Todd, and Anna Rodney as bridesmaids. James Matheny served as Abraham's groomsman, and Justice Brown of the Illinois Supreme Court stood with them. There were approximately 40 guests. Neither Abraham's parents nor mine were invited in time, but we'll travel soon to see them all.

One humorous event occurred during the ceremony, and this writing won't do it justice. Judge Brown, a rough old-timer who often says just what he thinks without regard to surroundings, stood beside Abraham. The room was silent except for the vows we were exchanging. When the time came for Abraham to put the ring on my finger, he repeated after the minister, "With this ring I thee endow all my goods and chattels, lands, and tenements." Apparently Judge Brown had never heard the line and the significance suddenly struck him. He screeched, "Lord God Almighty, Lincoln, the statute fixes all that!"

We stood in shock for a moment. Then everyone had a hearty laugh and the ceremony proceeded. My favorite words of the entire event were, "Till death do you part, I now pronounce you man and wife." May death be long in procrastination.

The ceremony took less than five minutes. We toasted our future with a glass of cider and Abraham whispered, "Now we really are the long and short of it, Mrs. Lincoln. You're beautiful tonight. I like the pink paint on your cheeks; it suits you. I'm glad we're married, in feeling as well as judgment. My obligations to you are 10,000 times more sacred than any I could owe to others."

We dined on Cornish hen, roasted potatoes, and Boston brown bread. And, of course, pastries from Dickey's. The guests laughed that the wedding cakes were still warm! Elizabeth played the piano and we danced until we could no longer stand. Ninian somehow secured a photographer, but I allowed only one picture. I'm not sure the variances in our heights, weights, and colorings will show off to advantage in an ambrotype.

We begged our leave around midnight, and after much hugging and well wishing, we gathered up the two carpetbags of possessions I would carry into my new life. I became a shade concerned as we rode through the downpour to the Globe. Knowing how rain depresses Abraham, I prayed it wouldn't thunder. What a wedding night it would have been with both of us crouched under the bedclothes!

The sign on the outside door greeted us, as it has hailed travelers for years: "Eight pleasant and comfortable rooms, as well as convenient resting places for the weary. $2 a week per person, meals and some washing included." I shuddered.

Breathing became easier when Mrs. Beck showed us the cheerfully decorated parlor and the long dining table covered in a yellow linen cloth. Inside our room, I was glad to see the almost new egg-blue woolen spread on the four-poster bed and a round tin bathing tub in the corner. We also have a French wardrobe, a small green sofa, and two comfortable easy chairs. The window fronts east and overlooks the square.

A fire already blazed in the hearth, and a bowl of fruit sat on the table beside a bottle of champagne from Elizabeth and Ninian. Their note read, "We know Abraham doesn't take to drinking, but if ever he wants to give it a try, tonight would be a good time. Congratulations to you both." We didn't open it.

We kissed until we could wait no longer. Abraham, my husband, my all, went down to the men's bathing room just off the kitchen, carrying his Windsor soap, towel, tooth powder, white nightshirt, dark blue wrapper, and buckskin slippers. His hand trembled, and his words came out falsetto: "I won't be long...Mrs. Lincoln."

I rang for hot water and soaked luxuriously in the tub, into which the maid had poured lilac water and a soap that made bubbles. Afterward, I put on my new white nightdress, and tried to relax in the horsehair chair near the door. Soon my husband peeked in from the hall, wearing a smile bigger than the bed he was trying to ignore. He took me in his arms, like a doll being folded into a blanket, and carried me there. He smelled of Old West India bay water.

When he pulled off his nightshirt, I couldn't resist commenting, "I've never seen a naked man."

He reached for me hungrily and replied, "Ain't I purty?" Once again I had to agree.

I can't describe the pain and pleasure we experienced that night. Our actions cause me to blush and smile even now. He is all man, my Abraham, and his body parts match his long lean fingers. I never knew I could utter such sounds, and undemonstrative Abraham found ways of demonstration I hope he will never lose.

From outside my cocoon of ecstasy, I heard rain crashing into the windowpane, creating a rhythm we seemed to match. The old bedsprings creaked as we moved and rolled, trying different positions as our imaginations took flight. We slept a short while and woke to find each other again in the dark. The night was worth the wait.

Nov. 7, 1842: Abraham has returned to the circuit for at least a week, and I'm alone with no chores, no responsibilities, and no one with whom to converse. The showers have stopped, so perhaps someone will come to pay their respects. While not the Turkish splendor of the American House, the Globe's parlor is pleasant enough to host callers. Meanwhile, I have decorated our room, as best I can, in a style befitting our new status. I put Abraham's many books into the shelves against the south wall with the figurines Elizabeth gave us and his bust of Thomas Jefferson. I will make new crimson curtains to replace these dirty brown ones as quickly as possible. The round table from my own room on the hill sits in the center of the room with a fine white turtledove cloth over it. It holds newspapers for Abraham to read: *Lexington Observer, Baltimore Register, New York Tribune, Sangamo Journal*.

I arranged my personal things—combs, brushes, jewelry box, perfume jars, Portugal water, magazines—on the bureau next to the bed. My things, his things, now our things.

Nov. 15, 1842: Because the wedding preparations and ceremony were so soon before her own birthday, Elizabeth decided she and little Albert would share a small celebration today, so I took wishes and gifts for both: a music box for Albert, a peacock fan for Elizabeth. Though I missed Abraham, who arrives tomorrow, I enjoyed eating again in their resplendent dining room with the elegant chandeliers. Mrs. Beck is not a gourmet cook and the Globe is not Aristocracy Hill!

I look forward to having our own children in year or so. We hope to begin with a daughter—a little girl to cuddle and dress in the latest styles, teach sewing and dancing, play with dolls. We'll enroll her in Mount Holyoke or Oberlin so she will receive a proper education. I'll teach her to speak fluent French. She'll grow up and marry a governor, a President, a baron, a king! Perhaps she'll be an author like Jane Austen. Or an actress. How proud we'll be!

Though I don't want to stay very long in this tiny abode, I'll always happily remember it as the first home of our lives together. Abraham is already putting on weight from eating regular meals, regardless of their quality. He looks forward to the family atmosphere in the dining area and hearing travelers' tales. He shows no sign of regret or hypo, and his need for the blue mass liver pills, which make him cross, is diminishing. My ailments are also reduced, though I carefully guard my medicine. Why do the books on marriage make the prospect sound so terrifying? It's the finest institution man or woman could have invented. Continual togetherness is a perfect life!

The oddest change is still being called "Mrs. Lincoln." It's a lullaby to my ears and honoring, but I don't yet answer to it easily. Abraham speaks the name almost every morning when he awakes: "Good Morning, Mrs. Lincoln." I reply, "Good Morning, Mr. Lincoln." Then we kiss deeply, and we're often late for breakfast because we find it so difficult to abstain from our marital delights. Abraham is the gentlest man I have ever known, and he takes great care to ensure I am as satisfied as he—sometimes even more.

Nov. 24, 1842, Thanksgiving: Thanks in great part to the efforts of Sarah Hale, editor of *Godey's Lady's Book*, Illinois has proclaimed the 4th Thursday of November (today) as an annual day of thanksgiving. Although the courts weren't in session, Abraham was busy with legal work, so we had our meal here at the Globe: roasted gobblers stuffed with walnuts; potatoes, corn, and other vegetables; mincemeat and pumpkin pies; oranges, cranberries, and winter sweeting apples. The food was good, but the ambiance is not what I prefer. I'm eager to find our own home.

Dec. 5, 1842: Quite a show in the federal courtroom! A habeas corpus proceeding for the Mormon prophet Joseph Smith, whom Gov. Ford arrested a time back.

Because of the massive audience, several other ladies and I were allowed to sit on chairs to Judge Pope's sides, so that we were facing the gathering as he faced it. Mr. Smith's 12 "apostles" sat on the front row. Mr. Butterfield, Smith's attorney, rose in silence, looked the judge and then at the group of women, and said:

"May it please the court, I appear before you today under circumstances most novel and humbling. I am asked to address the Pope (he bowed to the judge), surrounded by angels (he bowed to the ladies), in the presence of the 12 Holy Apostles, on behalf of the prophet of the Lord. How shall I proceed?"

I'll never get enough of the intricacies and workings of the Bench, and I visit the courthouse several times a week just to sit in. Of course my favorite attorney, and the wisest in Illinois, is a tall man from Kentucky with an adorable little wife. He shares most of his case stories with me and I pretend to be on the jury. My senses seldom fail.

Dec. 12, 1842: Goodbye again, Diary. With God's guidance, my blessed husband and I will soon move to a fine home, be elected to Congress, and begin a family that will fill our hearts with even more gladness—if such is indeed possible. I'll be a good wife and Abraham will never have cause to regret his decision to marry. When we're in the White House, he will be as proud of me as ever a President was of his lady. I will make the world proud of us!

<u>Dec. 13, 1842, my 24th birthday:</u> My darling husband, the completion of my life, is a kind man. We are physically compatible and gloriously happy in our marriage bed, as I knew we would be. His magnificent body looks hugely different out of those baggy outfits he insists on wearing. I delight almost every night in the firmness of his arms and legs—and other things. I only hope I can harden his political ambitions as easily as his romantic ambitions!

I once worried about our disparate heights interfering with our lovemaking, but we have no problems. He is compassionate, soothing, and tender—almost too gentle at times. He believes a woman should also enjoy the marriage act and ensures it. It's frequently hard to remain quiet enough that the other boarders don't nod knowingly in the morning. Often they do, but I just stare as though I haven't a guess.

He also asserts that women are intellectually equal and should never be under a man's thumb. I'll never be under <u>his</u> thumb, because he never leaves it in one place long enough to fall under it! He continues to be moody and erratic, but not so often or deeply as before, and he hasn't suffered from hypo since our marriage. Perhaps that, like my frightful headaches, disappeared along with our chastity!

<u>Dec. 18, 1842:</u> I'm tired of the Globe. It's boring, lonely, and extremely loud, with visitors constantly coming and going, slamming doors, barking orders. There's little to do and Abraham is always at his work. He has nine or ten cases in Christian County alone, and has been gone almost a week. I've read all we have of interest and my head aches when I sew too long. I'm stitching our new curtains and a linen shirt for him, but they progress slowly. Few people come to call. Will I find a way to kill time or will time find a way to kill me?

Dec. 23, 1842: Almost Christmas and no plans for festivities, though Elizabeth and Ninian invited us. Surely Abraham will agree to go. He can't work every hour, can he? I feel queasy and take calomel several times a day. Abraham said, "You're peaked and pale as bleached cotton. I reckon you're annoying yourself into bellyaches, complaining about the accommodations. Why can't you ever be satisfied?" Perhaps he's right, but if he was here more often, my complaints wouldn't all come out at the same time.

Dec. 25, 1842, Christmas: We spent the day with Elizabeth and Ninian, Fanny and Willie, and all their children. Father included a package for me in the family gifts: a black cotton shawl with just enough warmth to use near the fireplace. Abraham gave me James F Cooper's new book, *The Deerslayer.* How much we think alike; I purchased a volume of Byron for him! He always says his best friend is someone who gives him books, and being his best friend is my fondest desire.

Abraham and I had some time to talk alone, and we held hands on the black sofa like when we courted. I do truly love this man, and each time we're apart, I realize how lost I would be without him. But such is the life of a successful lawyer's wife. I must sacrifice now to gain what I want later. We'll live like my sisters someday, I vow it!

Jan. 1, 1843: Our first New Year's Day as man and wife. Abraham has settled into wedlock quite comfortably, already acting like a long-married man. After supper, he relaxes in his armchair, talks to me about his law cases, and then goes to sleep early.

What will this twelvemonth bring for us? We still talk about purchasing a house, but he said we have to stay here for a full year, maybe two. "Why Molly, Fanny and Willie lived almost three years in this very same room. Are we better than them?" he says in defense.

"Yes," I say emphatically. But he only shakes his head as though communicating with a capricious child. "My little child-wife," he calls me.

I'm not at all sure I can stay here another year. Perhaps Fanny had more patience, or more to keep her occupied. Maybe Willie remained at home more to entertain her. I abhor the blacksmith's constant clank and hammer next door. I despise the roof bell that signals the stablemen and porters when travelers come. Of course the ringing is also notice for me to go downstairs. Despite the noise, I love to see who has arrived and whether they came from the far-away places I long to see. The women from New York, Philadelphia, and Baltimore are so fancy in their city finery. The show of shawls, bonnets, feathers, furs, and pinched waists is grand entertainment. Abraham enjoys the lobbyists and officials who dine here. I like their stories too, but now the cigar smoke and racket affect my digestion. I continue to be nauseated, surely because of the food. Mrs. Beck is no New York chef, and yet I seem to be gaining weight. Could I be...?

Jan. 8, 1843: Have been shopping again. Going out relieves my loneliness and need for activity. With the small amount of money we received as wedding gifts, I purchased two small Currier landscapes, only 20¢ each from the peddler. Arranging them with the etchings I've received over the years from *Godey's* subscriptions gave us a nice art grouping. I also got a long blue wool carpet for Abraham to lie on and a small walnut desk for papers and correspondence, now placed at the window. His table is still heaped with books and the shelves can't hold the remainder. Still, the room is homier now. I try to involve Abraham in the decoration, but he doesn't care beans.

"Whatever you do is fine," he said. "As long as I have a place to stretch out my bony legs and read, this old codger will be happy." Then he added, "I wish you would settle in and be content." Bah!

Jan. 15, 1843: God has blessed us! I am in a delicate condition— expectant! I have suspected as much for a month, but didn't want to say anything until I was sure. After two months without flow, I asked Uncle John to stop by and examine me. Though Abraham said we couldn't afford a baby yet, it has happened just the same. I won't need to hide my increasing girth any longer, and soon will have a child of my own, my very own! I will never be lonely again!

When I told Abraham the news after supper, he said, "So soon, is it?" Then he left our room for quite some time. Worry was creeping into my mind, but he came back before I summoned help. He displayed his fine, deep smile as he handed me a small bouquet of ivy. "It's all I could find in the snow...Mother." Then he took me in his arms, drew me onto his lap, and covered my face with quick, tiny kisses until I pushed him away.

We talked into the night about our future, and he promised again to run for the House. I am so, so pleased! I'll work with him side by side till we can live in grand style. Our child must be raised in a fine, cultured place. This rooming house is not fitting for a daughter. She must have opportunities far superior to her father's, and even her mother's. She will live in a different time and place, in a country her father serves even as George Washington served.

Jan. 20, 1843: I saw the Hardimans in town today and they hardly spoke. The people with whom we socialized on Aristocracy Hill now think us unworthy because of our financial situation, and we're seldom invited out. It's painful to be rebuffed by those I considered my friends, but we'll show them! We're poor now, but someday we will have it all, and the Hardimans will not be invited to our White House!

Jan. 28, 1843: I imagine the baby is moving inside me, but I know it can't be true yet. Still, I talk to her and she eases my restlessness. I hope to name her Elizabeth, after my sister and Abraham's stepmother. Or maybe Dolley.

"But what if the tyke's a boy?" Abraham always asks.

"I suppose we'll just wait and see," I answer, but my heart wants a girl. A daughter to hold, to dress in the latest styles, to teach, to protect. But a boy with Abraham's mind and heart—that would also be a gift.

I haven't told anyone about my condition except Elizabeth and Fanny, and my dearest friends Julia Jayne, Eliza Frances, and Mercy Levering. My sisters both hesitated before showing any happiness. They think we're not in a proper position to raise a child, and perhaps they're right. But my beloved husband will take care of us.

I feel bad for criticizing my sisters' early offspring. Had I known the joys of the behavior that plants these seeds, I would never have wondered why they were at it so quickly!

I'm staying busy sewing for myself and the baby, fighting nausea, and writing letters to congressmen to gain their support for Abraham's campaign. I speak to anyone in the Globe who might have connections and tell them what a wonderful representative my husband will make. Like Dolley Madison, I will be a strong political wife—an asset, a secretary, a confidante.

Feb. 2, 1843: I discovered last night that Abraham is apprehensive about indulging in sexual congress now. Uncle John says it's perfectly acceptable for several more months, unless I should become ill, but Abraham is so gentle with me that we have lost the passion of our wedding night. I trust it will return after the birth.

I'm so sorry I lost my temper about the discarded newspaper. He didn't intend to throw it out. Luckily, I was able to calm myself before he went for a walk. Those strolls of his sometimes last for hours!

Feb. 10, 1843: My dear husband has been away for the last two nights with Herndon. I have discovered that Herndon is one of the wild no-count Sangamon boys who drink and run with loose women, though he claims to be married. I will talk with Abraham about firing him.

I try to be strong in my husband's absence, but fright sometimes overtakes me. Midway of last night's storm, I had to dress and go downstairs where the lamps are always lit. I could not abide being alone in our room—so many shadows and creaks. Each time it thundered, the child shuddered inside me and I fought her hysteria. "Don't worry, Dolley," I cooed as I patted her, "Mama won't desert you for others to raise. You will never be unloved, I vow it."

I visit Elizabeth or Eliza when possible, but it's not as fitting now to be going about unescorted. I have gained at least ten pounds, can no longer wear a corset, and must constantly keep a shawl over my bodice to hide its increasing size. Even though I eat mostly broth, milk, rice, vegetables, and fruit, the cramps and vomiting are unyielding.

Feb. 12, 1843, Abraham's 34th birthday: Abraham is fully committed to Congress now. But so is Cousin Steve Logan, who is already in the legislature. We may have a battle on our hands; Steve is crafty. We will need to write dozens of letters and shake many hands to best him. Ned Baker is also running, but Abraham's stronger nature can easily defeat him.

When he left yesterday, Abraham said, "Molly, if anyone downstairs or at your sisters' should say Lincoln don't want to go to Congress, please tell him directly that he's mistaken. And I'll be doing it too. I've also asked a few others to spread the word. August will be a grand month for the Lincolns—a baby and a nomination."

We're working on a campaign circular for the Whigs. It analyzes national issues, advocates a tariff for revenue rather than direct taxation, speaks out for the federal bank system, and urges the party to use the convention system for nominations like the Democrats are doing. We chose a phrase from the Gospels to encourage party unity: "A house divided against itself can't stand." My senses tell me the line will be a success. Abraham said he couldn't have written the tract without my help. Though he can craft a memorable phrase, I'm working on his grammar; he can't quite grasp verb tenses.

Feb. 22, 1843: My excessive free time allows me to think overmuch about the pleasures and dangers of giving birth. My mother, Abraham's sister, and many others have died from the process. Betsy was always sick and threatening to perish in her last months. How will I manage?

Abraham says I'm being silly. "You're a strong, vital, healthy woman, Molly, and the doctor will be standing ready. How can anything go wrong? Be brave. You're a Todd, remember? With two d's. Like Thomas Jefferson said, 'Courage is as essential in your case as a soldier's.'"

Thomas Jefferson indeed. I don't believe he ever gave birth. And he didn't have to live with these demons that threaten me: dying, a malformed child, being an incompetent mother.

Apr. 12, 1843: A letter from Mercy. She still teases me about wanting to be Madam President, but I have to share my dreams with someone, and one who rags is preferable to one who bites. I miss her; when a woman marries, she is so lost to her friends.

I am sewing tiny clothes, and Mrs. DuBois has given me some of her baby's outfits. I had hoped to receive one or two of Albert's beautiful dresses, but Elizabeth herself will soon have another child to wear them.

Apr. 16, 1843, Easter: I attended church this morning with Elizabeth and Ninian, and later watched the children search for eggs. I envision my own daughter giggling over colored treats and decorated cookies. I wonder if Abraham will go to church regularly after the birth? He knows the Bible so well he could rouse us to goodness even better than the minister himself. Still, he says he doesn't "take" to organized worship, and he still questions the truth of the scriptures, so I won't nag.

Apr. 24, 1843: I have been alone for almost a month now — too long for a new wife. I yearn for my husband's arms; his body; the dark growth on his back, shoulders, and chest; his wholesome laugh; even his improper style. I long to see that old black hat and all the notes tumbling from it. I miss our nightly conversations and his wisdom and humor. I feel as empty as his rocking chair by the fire. Visions of death haunt me.

Apr. 28, 1843: Many callers this week: Cousin Ann (who is now married and living in Boonville but visiting Elizabeth), Harriet, Helen, Lizzie, Julia, Hannah. It's good to see friends, but it's not visitors I wish to see. I want my husband, and I need him with me more frequently. I grow fat without benefit of indulgence.

Apr. 30, 1843: Abraham is home! How good to see him, hold him, feel him in bed next to me. How lovely to watch him writing at his desk, his mouth puckered in thought, his eyebrows pulled together in a bushy "V." I love the scratch-scratch of his pen.

He still travels the entire 8th Circuit, 120 miles long and 160 miles wide, from Springfield to Indiana. Cousin Steve is wiser — he stays here and handles local cases. When I ask Abraham why he must be gone so long, when other lawyers come home more frequently, he says he "cottons to" visiting all the counties, attending all the courts, hearing all the cases. He enjoys the travel, the blazing summer sun, the unrelenting sleet and snow.

"I've always been a wanderer," he said. "I like talking with other lawyers, finding out what they think about life and politics, learning what's happening over the rest of the state. It's enjoyable playing handball on the patched red barns and checkers on a pickle barrel as the sun goes down.

Some of the men I share rooms with are prominent and can help us in our goals. You do still have political ambitions, don't you?" Oh the lawyer pleads a good case. He can only stay home a few days; I must make the most of it.

May 10, 1843: Abraham again proposed to the Sangamon Whigs that they use the convention system to elect their congressional candidates. They adopted his plan, but not him. When he saw that Ned Baker had more support, Abraham bowed out. I'm disappointed that our own people didn't support us more adamantly.

"You're a better politician than Baker and would make a better representative," I argued. "And we've dreamed so long about going to Washington. Why give up your chance now? This is our stepping-stone, part of our goal. A year in the House, then the Senate, then the White House. Why did you concede?"

Abraham's lower lip protruded, his eyebrows furrowed, his head wagged. "For unity, Molly. Remember what we said? A house divided can't stand."

I shook my head. "You sweet, silly man. You have such high principles and I love you for it, but if the Whig Party can't stand behind you, why should you stand behind it? Don't do it, Darling, please don't give up this chance. Run against him anyway. I'll help you. We'll write your speeches together." But he won't oppose Baker.

To pile on the agony, the party named Abraham a delegate to support Baker. "Like the fellow who was made groomsman to the man marrying his own dear gal," he said. I find it ludicrous and insulting. Abraham is the man for Congress, not Ned Baker!

June 3, 1843: Fanny and Speed have invited us to visit them in Kentucky after the baby is born, but Abraham said we can't afford to go. I hope he'll change his mind. It would be good for us to get away from this tiny room and stagnant air.

He is still paying off the "national debt," so I suppose we'll do little until that is defrayed. We could have more money, of course, if he would be more diligent. He frequently forgets, or neglects, to charge his clients an adequate fee. Sometimes he charges no fee at all. He says money is not important, since he has no personal needs other than his horse and his inn bills. That we live in a second-class establishment, while my sisters live in luxury, is no matter to him. He never notices my needs. He has no idea how much fabric costs or how much a baby will require. Or how expensive a real congressional race will be in four years. Harrison's "log cabin and cider" campaign only worked because he had money behind the scam!

June 18, 1843: My dresses no longer fit, though I have let them out as much as possible. Abraham said I could purchase two outfits, but I can buy remnants and sew them together just as well for less money. I could follow Mrs. DuBois' lead and wear skirts so gored that no one would suspect till the child is born. No, I'm past that possibility.

I plan to visit Julia Jayne today. Abraham won't return for several days, and I don't believe I can stand another hour with only myself and my fears of motherhood. I can't be ready; I know nothing about babies. If only I had asked Mammy Sally to show me how to reach the spirits, then I could call on my angel mother and maybe I wouldn't be so scared. I'm so sure something is going to go wrong that often I can't stop myself from crying. Fanny and Elizabeth say this feeling is natural, but I wonder. Other mothers seem to smile all the time. Is something wrong with me?

June 23, 1843: Abraham has been melancholy for several days, perhaps because of the ongoing drizzle. He prefers silence in depression, so I try to be quiet and not startle him. Or I create witty stories, share all the gossip, and do my best mimics to make him smile, but they seldom help. It scares me that he sits motionlessly and stares at invisible scenes for such long periods. He can't hear me from his internal hiding place, so I often must touch him to rouse his attention and bring him back to this world. Occasionally I also have to remind him where he is. When asked where his mind went, he shrugs and says, "I don't really know, Molly, I don't really know." I wish I could go there with him.

He's happy about the child, but knows less than I what to do. I grow more concerned every day. Who will assist me? We have no servants, of course, and Springfield has no midwives. Uncle John, I suppose, or Willie Wallace, or perhaps I'll just give birth alone. If so, who will cut the cord? Abraham? How scandalous that would be!

What if the baby dies at birth, what if the thunder demon steals her away? Could we handle it? What if she's breech? Then I would be required to call in Uncle John. And I might die myself; I've seen it in my dreams. How would Abraham parent a child? He can hardly take care of himself, and as President, he couldn't raise a child alone.

So I'll have to grit my teeth and live on—for the good of our country and my beloved husband. But perhaps we'll conceive only one child rather than the dozens we discussed. *Godey's* reports that the average couple has seven children! Too, too many for me. I've read about ways to control conception; perhaps I'll investigate.

July 7, 1843: Two blessings today: a long quiet rain and a niece! Elizabeth named the girl Julia. Abraham says the child is the image of her mother. Better than looking like her father! I would like to ask her how the birthing felt, what she experienced, how much pain she endured, but I'm too large and ungainly to go. Fanny told me the wonder of birth masks the hurt, but that becomes more unbelievable as the months go on. I am half-minded to get out of bed and run down the stairs to see if I can speed the event!

July 14, 1843: Abraham had the most horrid nightmare last night! He woke us both by groaning loudly, tossing from left to right, and gripping the bed sheets with his hands, as though trying to strangle an intruder. I touched his forehead with cold water and called his name until he woke. He had no memory of his vision. I hope it doesn't concern our child or me. He saw his sister die in childbirth, so he must at least consider the possibility. He dreams wildly several times a month.

Aug. 4, 1843: Our precious son was born on Tuesday, August 1, 1843. We named him after my father: Robert Todd Lincoln. The birthing itself was hard suffering, but I managed with only Mrs. Beck in attendance. No physician had to be called, so we saved that $5 for our boy's future.

When Robert had hardly crawled from the womb, I opened my eyes and saw a most wonderful sight. My darling husband was bent over me, perspiration glistening on his face, sarsaparilla just visible inside his cheek to make sure I inhaled only sweetness, tears on his cheeks. He said, "Molly, you're a profound wonder and so is the baby. You showed real grit having this boy by yourself. I knew you could do it and I knew our son would be perfect. He has skimpy arms like yours, but I'm sorry to say he already has my nose."

I replied, "Let's pray he gets your weight too."

He answered, "Yep. I only hope he don't end up with one long leg and one short one!"

I smiled as best I could and held little Robert until I drowsed off. When I awoke, Abraham was sitting in the rocker beside the bed, humming tunes to a chubby bundle of flailing arms and legs. Our son, God's perfect miracle, a combination of Todd breeding and Lincoln goodness, was mewing like a new kitten. He will go far.

Aug. 7, 1843: What a strange turn of events at the election in Pekin. Cousin John Hardin showed up with more support than Ned Baker. A boggle to most, including Abraham, who then asked the delegates to make the nomination unanimous rather than splitting it between Hardin and Baker "in order to show Whig unity and keep us strong enough to whip our common enemy." Then he worked out a deal: Elect Hardin now, Baker in '44, and Lincoln in '46. The three men shook hands and called it a verbal agreement.

Bah! What good will a verbal agreement do four years from now? Abraham is too gullible. I know even now the agreement won't be kept. But no, he believes in his fellow man. I begin to think he has no head for politics after all. We must take what we can when we can, not four years later! Will he ever start thinking more like a candidate and less like a statesman? Being a politician is a skillful art and I seem to be the only one in this family who has it!

On the other side, as expected, Stephen Douglass was also elected to the House. His seat on the Supreme Court was taken by none other than James Shields.

Aug. 10, 1843: Abraham told me that while negotiating unity with the Whigs, he heard some of Baker's supporters talking about his rise to aristocracy: "Why, they called me the candidate of wealth, pride, and aristocratic family distinction. Can you figure it?" Wealth and aristocracy? Good Heaven! We can hardly afford $16 a month for a room in this tavern!

He works long hours at his office now, losing himself in cases to forget his defeat, and perhaps aiming toward truly being wealthy someday. Perhaps we'll be like that Frenchman who just died, Pierre Lorillard. The papers called him a "millionaire," a man worth more than a million dollars! The article said the US boasts several millionaires as well, including John Jacob Astor in NY. He married a Todd, so we're probably related. Perhaps I should write to him. Someday the Lincolns will be among the rich too, I vow it! The wheel of fortune is always revolving.

Sept. 10, 1843: I've been powerfully busy since Robert's birth, although he's an independent baby and doesn't want much attention from anyone. His little body is solid like his father's, though I sense he will be more rounded and low like me. His hair is brown like mine, his eyes gray like Abraham's, only lighter, and he has a dimple in the same place on his chin as his father.

He also seems to have a slightly turned-in left eye like Abraham, and he cries loud enough to wake bears in the winter. Uncle John says he will outgrow both; I certainly hope so.

Abraham is kind to get out of bed and walk him at night; I'm still too tired. Mrs. Beck, Mrs. Hardison, and Mrs. Bledsoe check in several times a day. They wash and dress Robert and bring my food up from the dining room. Eliza calls every afternoon about teatime, bringing news from the *Journal* and the town, and dear Hannah Shearer is always nearby. I couldn't manage without these friends to care for my needs, and will be very happy when my seclusion is ended.

Abraham has dubbed our son Bob or Bobby, and now calls me Mother. In keeping, I now refer to him as Father, but it doesn't yet seem real. I keep dreaming that Elizabeth or Fanny — or sometimes Mother — tries to take him away. Thank Heaven I awaken before he is pulled from my arms.

Sept. 12, 1843: I went to town with Julia Jayne and purchased two inexpensive books from the new store on Fifth Avenue: *American Frugal Housewife* for myself and *Manners for Social Entertaining* for Abraham. Etiquette is extremely important if we are to impress Washington. *Savoir-faire* is critical, because a rude man is labeled a bad man. Abraham doesn't care beans about protocol and etiquette. Why, he still eats with a spoon most times, uses his own knife in the butter, and refers to white meat as chicken "breasts" like a bumpkin! I finally taught him to use a napkin, but he still tucks it in his shirt collar. And I have finally assured that his socks match by buying them all in one color! "Why, ain't that clever?" he said a month later.

Sept. 15, 1843: Abraham has rented a house!! A three-room yellow cottage on South Fourth, just a few blocks from downtown. He doesn't really want to leave the Globe, but the other boarders are losing patience with Bob's incessant crying.

And, since no one has yet come to call (though we have received several congratulatory cards), we will make it known after our move that the caudle punch is ready for toasting, and mother and child are available for viewing. Elizabeth will help me make the caudle — we'll need oatmeal gruel, raisins, spices, and Madeira. Surely Abraham won't oppose a touch of Madeira for the ladies. He needn't know if there is a drop or two left over for later.

Oct. 1, 1843: Finally we have taken up housekeeping on our own! I have always believed a nice home, a loving husband, and a precious child would be the happiest elements of life. Now I know it's true. Everything will continue to improve from this point, and people will see that I was correct in my marital choice. Abraham will want to stay home more because it will be so cozy, and Bob will become more affectionate with his father close by. I'll try very hard to curtail my temper so they will both have a more pleasant environment.

I assembled what little furniture and fixings we have. The lithographs look nice on the large wall. I put Abraham's table on the far wall from the bed, leaving enough room for him to stretch out on the floor rug. My small desk, the three chairs, and the new maple bookcases are neatly arranged. New curtains and linens are next.

When Abraham came home tonight and saw the house, he picked me up, whirled me around like the old days, and said, "Why, Mother, ain't these bodacious diggings?" We will soon be making love again; I felt it in his caress. Surely a more devoted husband has never existed. Tomorrow he leaves again for the month, but there is much to occupy my time.

Oct. 20, 1843: Little time to write recently. Bob has been more cross than usual, and I'm learning from the book how to be a "frugal housewife." I have never really cooked before, and can now burn many dishes very nicely. Abraham will likely not notice. He'll eat anything put before him except turnips. He just doesn't care for turnips.

He is still traveling, but usually comes home in midweek for a night or two. He shuffles around this small house in his old slippers like a giant holding a kitten, often making Bob soar high and swing low. How funny to hear the great orator coo and sing little ditties. But the baby will stand it only for a short time, then he wants to be put down. He is not an endearing child.

Nov. 4, 1843, our 1st anniversary: After supper tonight, Abraham asked me to take a stroll with him. I bundled up the baby and we walked down to Rev. Dresser's home.

"Are we reminiscing about our wedding?" I asked, my hand tightly in his.

He stared at the residence. "Do you like this house, Mother?"

"It's a fine house. Why?"

"Do you realize it's only two blocks from my office? And look, it's got a story and a half. I reckon it's plenty big for the three of us, or even four. It's well built, sturdy, made out of oak. It's got a privy and cistern in the back, a well, a barn, and a carriage house. More room than we'll need for years to come."

"What are you saying, Father?"

He moved behind me so we both faced the house and put his arms around my waist, his chin on my hair—right there in the street! He leaned down and whispered, "It's for sale and Rev. Dresser wants us to buy it. In the end, it'll be cheaper than the rental house. Wouldn't this make a dandy anniversary present?"

"Do tell! Are you teasing me, Abraham? Our own home? With a yard and a room for Bob all to himself so we can be alone? What a wonderful gift! Can we really afford it?"

He took my hand and began to whistle as we started back. "We'll see," he said, "we'll see."

Dec. 1, 1843: Another nightmare for Abraham. Just before dawn, I woke to his loud, rapid, incoherent babbling to someone unseen. I listened for a name or a familiar word, but heard none. Bob began to cry and my teardrops lurked at the ready. We thought his hypo had ended, but perhaps he merely transferred it to the back of his mind. These somnolent outbursts are disquieting, and I sleep poorly for several nights afterward. Abraham can remember nothing, but he wakes unhappy, his heart galloping. These terrors are often followed with hours of melancholia in which he can hardly function as a lawyer, husband, or father. I can abide his inattention, deaf ears, shortness, and depression, but Bob senses the mood and responds with surliness. He has resumed his blue liver pills in hopes they will improve the situation. We must both try harder to show our love and joy.

Dec. 10, 1843: My father is visiting Springfield. He's staying with Elizabeth, of course, but has spent a smart amount of time here with us. He looks well. Betsy didn't come, because Kitty is just two and colicky. Father's children now total 16. Surely there will be no more at his age.

Father seems pleased that Bob bears his name; his other children haven't honored him in that way. He gave us a $25 gold piece to help secure his grandson's future, but I must not tell the others. As far as I know, he hasn't done the same for them. He also gave us a deed for 80 acres outside Springfield and $120 annually to keep it up.

So he's coming around and beginning to trust his son-in-law to safeguard his favorite daughter. He shook Abraham's hand and said, "I only hope Mary will make as good a wife as she has a husband." I will, Father, I will!

Dec. 12, 1843: What an eventful year! Time has borne many changes on its wing. We ran for and lost a seat in the House of Representatives, had a son, left a boarding establishment, rented a small house, and are buying a larger home! We are, thankfully, moving up and looking better. Abraham still walks around in his stocking feet and undershirt, with only one gallus holding up his trousers, but he's learning that he must behave differently in public.

Bob now crawls like a streak of greased lightning, and I'm thankful Abraham likes to chase the boy so I can rest. His eye still focuses slowly, but Uncle John continues to say he will outgrow it.

The Whigs are still in power, though President Tyler acts more like a Democrat every day. He needs a VP, but it doesn't look likely. Though impeachment is already being whispered, I can't see that he's done much harm and find no area of illegality, so I assume he will reign for another year. Life is good!

Dec. 25, 1843, Christmas: Bob's first Christmas! He's too young to understand the event, but was fascinated by the other children at Elizabeth's. He sat on my lap and watched as they squealed with abandon. It pleased me, as he so seldom sits quietly, and even more rarely on my lap.

Abraham is moody and scatty. He said little, though I believe he appreciated the umbrella I gave him. He certainly did not relish dressing up. We must show our best when we visit Aristocracy Hill, so I purchased a quality black suit for him and an embroidered linen dress for Bob. Abraham still doesn't understand why the items were so expensive, and almost refused to pay the bill. We may not live like kings, but we must never resemble beggars.

Now that Abraham is home for the winter break, he has thrown himself into his law practice and spends more time there than with his family. He said he wants to learn all he can from Cousin Steve so someday he can be his own man rather than a junior partner. He reads statutes and law books to Bob, who pretends to listen for a short time before nodding off. I, more than anyone else, want my husband to excel, but his managing a practice concerns me. He has little business acumen and is by no means a systematist. Will he be able to keep up with the daily activities such as billing and collecting? At least by working for Cousin Steve, he is paid regularly!

Jan. 1, 1844: With the new year comes hope of success. We'll see a richer future this year, I know it! Presidential election years always bring changes. Abraham is working hard, sometimes handling as many as 7 court cases a day! He's still talking with Rev. Dresser about our new house, and it shouldn't take much longer. Then a few years entertaining the Springfield *beau monde*, and on to Washington!

Feb. 5, 1844: I took Bob to see Willie Wallace and was told his eyes are crossed. I asked the doctor, "Will he also inherit his father's headaches and melancholy? You've seen Abraham's eye when it turns inward toward his brain. The condition precedes his partial blackouts and days of incurable depression. He's not an easy man to abide at those times."

"No, I don't think Bob will get them," Willie replied. "I've seen this in many children. He'll learn to use his other eye and vision shouldn't be a problem. If he hasn't experienced headaches by now, he will no doubt avoid them altogether." I am still worried.

Feb. 12, 1844, Abraham's 35th birthday: I served him a snug breakfast of flapjacks, eggs, ham-doings, biscuits, and gravy. Although he dislikes receiving presents, I gave him two pairs of heavy drawers. He still wears the long johns he had on the barge when he went to New Salem! The man has no sense of fashion, style, or propriety!

Apr. 2, 1844: Once again my beloved husband rides away on Old Buck to protect democracy, and once again I have no one to talk to. At least at the Globe there were people about when I chose to chat. Thank Heaven Julia and Ann aren't far away, and I'm always welcome at the *Journal* office. I can only baby talk for so long. Abraham is good about writing to me, but it's not the same. He does often put my own passions into words though, and I read those letters again and again. I urge him in every message to say how much he loves me, and when he forgets, I prod him again. He can't understand what those words mean to me as I wait alone and plan our future. I try not to be distrustful, but sometimes my imagination convinces me that he has no time to write because he's charming other women as he travels. I keep these fears to myself most of the time.

Apr. 12, 1844: Abraham is still working closely with the Sangamon Whigs, trying to elect Henry Clay again, even though the party turned its back on him last year. The Democrats will surely nominate Martin "Van Ruin" for a second term, because he's well supported in the southern states. And I'm sure he will accept, since he rejected President Tyler's offer of a Supreme Court position.

Apr. 27, 1844: Henry Clay has come out publicly in the *National Intelligencer* against the annexation treaty with the Republic of Texas. He fears war with Mexico, and possibly with the southern US states that oppose the addition. Van Buren agrees. Abraham believes these men are correct, but he would like to see Texas added, if it can be done without war, because of the land and cotton production.

May 1, 1844: Abraham is home for a week. How wonderful to be back in his arms! Henry Clay was nominated unanimously for President again and the Whigs have rallied behind him as never before. The platform is the usual plug — a regulated currency, tariffs to increase revenue, distribution of public land sales revenue, and a new idea: a single term for the Presidency. Clay surely will not back that position after all these years of waiting! I certainly would not.

May 2, 1844: We finally have our own home! Abraham paid only $1200 plus the lot across town he bought several years ago, worth about $300. The house needs redecoration and paint inside, but the pale brown color and deep green shutters on the exterior are pretty. The kitchen occupies almost a quarter of the first floor and a window from which I can see the yard and stable. It has five rooms, including a separate dining room, a parlor, a sitting room, and a loft where a nursemaid could stay. The 1/8-acre lot includes some outbuildings, a barn, a garden, a well, and a laundry shed.

We're still on the wrong side of Springfield, but it's a beginning. Abraham has no desire to live on Aristocracy Hill, though a rising politician needs a fine house. I sense he's still stung by the remarks about his being wealthy. This house is an improvement for us and will still allow Abraham to maintain his "humble beginnings" reputation. I haven't complained; he's so proud of himself! We purchased a nameplate for the front door engraved "A. Lincoln."

In time, people will see what Abraham Lincoln is capable of. We'll ask no odds from anyone. We'll make it on our own, the three of us, and in due time my darling husband will be one of the most powerful men in the states!

He is still campaigning for Henry Clay and we're all hopeful again, though his recent acceptance of the Texas annexation may have hurt his chances. Of course, he only yielded because the south threatened to secede. Bloody riots have occurred in Philadelphia, and the Democrats are accusing the Whigs of condoning — indeed encouraging — slavery, secession, and violence against foreigners and Catholics. Bah! Damn them all!

May 5, 1844: As planned, Ned Baker has won the Whig nomination for the House. Two more years and we'll have our turn! Abraham hasn't had a political position since our marriage and it's hard on us both to be away from the scene. He attended the festivities in Chicago and was named a Presidential elector. Ninian and Cousin Steve Logan have been nominated for the Senate. This will be a wonderful year for the Whigs and our Todd relations!

June 1, 1844: Charming spring-like weather today and my blessed husband's health has improved. He lay feverish in bed for several days after returning from Chicago. Though the city is plagued with diseases, Willie Wallace says Abraham is simply exhausted. Because he felt better on Saturday evening, we went to the theatre and then ate a late supper of mutton and vegetables with Elizabeth and Ninian. How lovely to be out with adults and have Abraham home for such a long time.

Harriet Hanks came back with him to live with us again and attend Springfield Female Seminary. She stayed with Bob last night and said he was as good as a bunny. She will help with our lad and the chores in return for room, board, and school supplies. She is slight, with dark stringy hair and deep-set eyes like Abraham's. She also uses the same poor grammar patterns, pronouncing "can't" to rhyme with "paint" and mistreating verbs! But she's good with the baby, and having her here will allow me to rest and perhaps see people more frequently. She sleeps in the loft and has made it quite homey.

The rest of our home is also progressing nicely. We have a large papered sitting room with a fireplace and several sizable windows, which I have covered with forest green draperies. Most of our furniture is in this room: desks, chairs, étagère, large round table, bookcases, and new red sofa. The parlor is carpeted, with crimson draperies, and there I have placed our lithographs and other valuables, a black settee, and a few chairs. The bright dining area is between the kitchen and the sitting room, and there is a porch off the kitchen for airing clothes in the spring and storing staples in the fall and winter. Our bedchamber is downstairs and, for now, Bob will sleep in our room.

It's a nice house after all. I'll furnish it more when we have the money, a little at a time. If not for the yearly cash allowance from Father, we wouldn't be able to decorate so nicely.

June 5, 1844: What an upset among the Democrats! Van Buren's opposition to annexing Texas made him unacceptable to the southern Democrats, and many resigned rather than support him. The remaining delegates couldn't agree on a candidate so, as a last-ditch measure, they offered up an unimpressive Tennessee governor and former congressman named James Polk. Van Buren withdrew and Polk won by a landslide.

But that's not all! The party nominated a senator named Silas Wright for VP and he declined! Can you imagine refusing an opportunity to serve in the White House? They finally settled on George Dallas from Pennsylvania.

June 24, 1844: The weather is so warm and dusty that there is no comfort in being outside. I presume we won't be free from dust till mud takes its place. But we have to keep the windows open to breathe inside, which brings endless swarms of flies. I constantly worry that Bob will pull away the boards holding up the frames and crush his tiny fingers. We'll all greet cool weather with exuberance.

June 30, 1844: What romantic news headlines the papers: President Tyler has married in New York! Her name is Julia Gardiner; she comes from a prominent NY family; and she's beautiful, charming, and accomplished. They met two years ago when the Gardiner family spent the social season in Washington. Then her father died in a gun explosion on a Presidential frigate excursion on the Potomac. Tyler and Julia were also aboard, and it's reported that they weren't in danger because they were "below deck" together. He is 30 years older than she! Had I known elopement could be so romantic, I might have allowed Abraham to convince me. The press calls her Lovely Lady Presidentress.

July 4, 1844, Independence Day: This country is undergoing the vilest and most raucous political campaigns ever seen. Where is our love for truth and justice? Honesty and equality? The Democrats are exerting open fraud against the citizens. Abraham says they are like the fence that's so crooked that whenever a dog goes through a break in the slats, it comes out on the same side.

Thousands have been naturalized only so they can vote for the Democrats, but many of these people are illegal. NY recently imported more than 20,000 new citizens to vote for Polk. Where is the freedom of honest choice for which we fought so hard?

Aug. 1, 1844, Bob's 1st birthday: Bob is deranging Harriet and me! He pulls at everything he sees, so I had to put all the breakables into cupboards. Abraham enjoys playing with him — when he will allow it. One of their games is "peek-a-boo" and Bob reacts well to his father's teasing. But he is still more aloof and distant than any child I have ever known, and doesn't care much for his mother.

Aug. 4, 1844: I have not been in a mood to write lately. My nerves are erratic and my movements often wearisome. The days have become one after another of housekeeping, sewing Abraham's tucked shirts and Bob's little dresses, caring for the baby and exercising his eyes, teaching Harriett, and looking after Abraham. He is so absent-minded!

I will admit to being tempersome this morning after putting away Bob's toys and Abraham's dirty clothes. "Father," I screamed, "can't you put anything away? You're bad as the baby."

Then I noticed his bare feet. "And why must I constantly remind you to take care of yourself? I have to chase after you with an umbrella on rainy days and a shawl on chilly days. I have to look you over every time you leave to be sure you haven't neglected some important detail—like the fact that your right pants leg is currently rolled up and your left is rolled down. Do I now have to find your socks and shoes?

"You forget to bill your clients, you forget to pay the ice man, you even forget to come home. The rest of us had to wait until 8 o'clock last night to eat supper because you disregarded the time. You're not demonstrating Presidential potential, Father. You're not even showing parlor potential. How will we ever get to the White House?"

I turned my back and stirred the soup. He put his arms around my upper body, squeezing until I could no longer move the spoon, and laid his bony chin on my head. He hummed one of the ditties he had created for Bob's pleasure, and rocked me left and right till I leaned back against his chest.

Then he said, "Now, Mother, I don't intentionally upset you. You know I've never had a head for little niceties. I do chop the wood when I'm home, don't I? And tend the fire, and light the boiler, and help with the canning? Maybe you could put proper clothes in a sack and teach Fido to run after me with the sack tied around his neck. You could put a chicken leg in his teeth for me too. Then you wouldn't have to worry so much."

I began to laugh in spite of myself, and turned to meet his smiling eyes. "You're a buffoon, Father, a pure tomfool. I only pray you never forget where you live and take up with another family. You probably wouldn't notice for days. I'll be sure to remind you when it's time to run for Congress again."

He let me go and began to twirl Bob round and round by his little arms. He said, "I'm mighty proud to have you as my campaign manager, Mrs. Lincoln." I forgave the sarcasm, as he had pardoned my outburst. We love as much as we argue.

Aug. 6, 1844: It's almost time to put Bob to bed, and Abraham has yet to appear for supper. I would worry about the street ladies near his office, except I know he's still hard at work. Cousin Steve plans to bring his son into the partnership, and Abraham wants to open his own office. Unfortunately, that may be another of those plans he never carries out. Steve has been good for him, and has taught him much, especially about organization and accuracy. But Abraham always allowed Steve to do the study and preparation for cases while he himself relied on internal inspiration to sway the judge and jury. How he would manage an office I can't imagine. His habitude is not one of constancy—he's regularly irregular in all habits. Except in caring for his family. Though I often accuse him of neglect, I know he loves us.

Aug. 10, 1844: We had the most smashing supper last evening. So many people we haven't seen in a coon's age: Julia and Lyman Trumbull, Isaac and Isabelle Arnold from Chicago, Mary Jane and Cassius Clay, Mason and Mary Brayman, Fanny and Willie, Cousin Lizzie Todd. Our newest congressman, Ned Baker, and our newest senators, Ninian (and Elizabeth of course) and Cousin Steve Logan. Harriet and I cooked all day for the event and received high praise.

The election is on everyone's mind and we spent most of the evening discussing the possibilities. Though they refer to him as a "dark horse," James Polk is gaining followers. I would hate to see Henry Clay lose again, and Polk is a "hard money" candidate—against both banks and paper currency. He also favors the annexation of Texas and Oregon at all costs.

It was so good to be with adults and talk about topics other than crying and colic. I felt like a true hostess when Mr. Arnold called me "witty and intelligent."

Sept. 1, 1844: Bob has finally weaned! He's happy now with a sugar tit and cow's milk, which eases my burden tremendously. What adds to my millstone is Abraham's talk about a partnership with William Herndon. Not an office with the heathen as clerk, but a partnership! I believe he relishes the idea of having a junior partner, after serving as such himself for the last eight years, and Herndon is easily accessible. But he once called me a serpent, and I believe he lies in other ways as well! I don't trust him much and like him even less. His reputation is tainted. It will do our congressional chances no good to be so closely associated with the likes of him. I wish Abraham had never brought him into Logan & Lincoln.

Sept. 8, 1844: I prayed very hard in church today that Abraham will change his mind about Herndon. The minister continues to ask if Abraham will come with me someday, and I continue to say, "My husband is a God-fearing man, Reverend. His soul is not in danger." At least going to services gives me a morning each week to put on a nice outfit, leave the chores to Harriet, and visit with Eliza and Simeon.

While I was out, Abraham was pulling Bob in the wagon and reading a book at the same time, and he didn't notice for several blocks that the baby had fallen out! I sometimes wonder if his mind is as extraordinary as I believed it to be.

Nov. 4, 1844, our 2nd anniversary: Sorry to say I've been rather irritable lately, and have argued with Abraham quite too much, even today on our anniversary. I purchased a bottle of Dr. Spolen's Elixir and am taking it regularly, but the medicine doesn't help. Some days I simply have to stay in bed and leave Bob's care to Harriet. Perhaps my motherly instincts are changing since my son weaned.

Nov. 15, 1844: Exceedingly tired this morning. Because we have taken up our impassioned marital relations again, I frequently need to sleep a bit later. Abraham is such a wonderful, caring lover. If someone should ever see this diary, he would think me wanton, but I see no harm in writing about relations with my own husband. I worry that I enjoy being a wife more than being a mother, and perhaps such adds to my frailty.

Dec. 1, 1844: The world goes on, but dear Henry Clay was defeated again. Our 11th President will be Democrat James K Polk. The race was neither close nor fair. The Louisiana papers report that the Democrats took a boatload of passengers up the Mississippi River and allowed them to vote in at least three different cities along the way. But the true defeat came because James Birney, the Abolitionist (Liberty) candidate, won in NY, and took those votes away from Clay. If he hadn't split the vote, we would have been victorious. Abraham is despondent and heading home.

Dec. 13, 1844, my 26ᵗʰ birthday: My favorite time of year. Abraham has returned until spring. No more long trips until the courts resume in April!

Dec. 20, 1844: Our future is tainted, our reputation is ruined, our livelihood will soon disappear. Cousin Steve hired his son and moved his office, so the firm above Seth Tinsley's store has become Lincoln-Herndon. No good will come from this partnership, but Abraham would not hear me. I'll watch closely to make sure my husband is not swayed into bad behavior.

He tried to explain. "Mother, you're the one who said I can't manage alone. You said I've got no money sense and will forget to invoice the clients. Billy likes paperwork and he's a smart boy. He'll mind the office and I'll win cases. You know how I loathe doing office work and drafting legal papers. It's a fine arrangement. Billy and I trust each other, and that's all that matters in a partnership. Besides, I'll have other partners — good lawyers in every county capital in the district."

"You mean you plan to keep riding the circuit?"

"Well, yes, of course. But I'll try to cut back to only a week or two in the summer months. How's that?"

What choice do I have? I'm just his wife. Worst of all, Abraham always troubled that his senior partners paid him only a third of the fees, so he promised Herndon half. Half! He could have partnered with anyone. Why must he always fight for the underdog?

Dec. 26, 1844: A lovely day today, snowing but not too cold. We spent yesterday with Elizabeth and Ninian. Even though Ninian is now a bullocky Democrat like his father, and their political views are contrary, he and Abraham tolerate each other for their wives' sakes.

We played Elizabeth's grand piano all Christmas day: *Oft in the Stilly Night, Land of the West, Auld Lang Sine, Silent Night.* I must admit to being envious of my sisters. Patience, Mary! You're poor now, but someday you won't have to pinch pennies.

Jan. 2, 1845: The country has gone wild for what's being called our "Manifest Destiny," and every newspaper story says God has ordained that we spread the democratic ideal to the world by annexing any and every thing around us. A Philadelphia paper actually proclaimed the US to be "a nation rightfully bound on the east by sunrise, on the west by sunset, on the north by the Arctic Expedition, and on the south as far as we darn please." I'm not sure that's truly what God intended.

Feb. 5, 1845: I gave up sweets for Lent. I must watch my size and regain a lover's shape rather than a matron's so Abraham will never have reason to stray. I find myself becoming somewhat green-eyed now when he speaks about his lady clients and surely that's wrong. Perhaps with less poundage, I'll feel more secure. He says I'm being silly, that he has always preferred plums to string beans. A humorous man, my husband.

Feb. 16, 1845: The annexation of Texas was approved! The newspapers say Canada is bound to join the Union soon, and possibly territories in the Caribbean also. After all, owning the world is our manifest destiny, and the American eagle is flying high and far! As President-Elect Polk says, "Our beloved country presents a sublime moral spectacle to the world."

Mar. 5, 1845: President James Polk, the youngest ever at 49 (Abraham is 36, so he has time), was inaugurated yesterday before a large gathering of dripping umbrellas. Polk made it clear that he won't give Texas back to Mexico. He also announced Florida's acceptance into the Union as our 27th state. He is a true expansionist.

Apr. 3, 1845: Abraham leaves tomorrow for the month. I pray he brings home a purseful. I'm tired of buying only remnants. Harriet will be leaving soon, so I will also need money to hire help for the chores. I dislike bringing strangers into our home, but suppose it's best. I'm not as strong as I once was.

Apr. 15, 1845: Fearful headaches again this week. How I despise them! Without perfect self-control, I'm apt to do something amiss, and I know how Abraham worries when my mood is dark. Why must women always be smiling and cheerful? Men may groan and bellow with a toothache, but women must bear all pain, including childbirth, in silence and decorum.

No, I shouldn't complain. God gave me a kind husband and a healthy child. What are my annoyances and occasional megrims compared to Abraham's daily legal battles? I know he works diligently for us. I only wish he were more politically active. He hasn't held office since our marriage and a man can't attain the highest office in the nation without positions beneath. God helps those who help themselves. I talk to him about this (he calls it nagging), but he's the eternal procrastinator.

Apr. 25, 1845: Abraham is "courting" this month and I busy myself being his "confidential secretary," as they call Mrs. Polk. I scan newspapers for rumors of war and expansion, read books and write reviews for him, keep him informed about the talk in town, and make sure he knows about any political developments published. We write nearly every day, though he writes less often and fewer words.

May 5, 1845: A moment to record while Abraham is playing with Bob. How wonderful to have him back home to help with the chores, the baby, and my personal needs and desires. But he leaves again tomorrow for three weeks. I long to go with him; I would love to go anywhere exciting. I feel so tied down here with cooking, cleaning, and mothering—like a nobody. The Bible says, "Riches come to those who wait," so we should be powerfully wealthy soon. I only hope I can wait.

June 1, 1845: Mexico has cut all diplomatic relations with the US and war is rumorous. Must we always be facing conflict? First we fought Great Britain for our independence, then England in 1812, now Mexico for Texas, possibly England again for more expansion. Will the thrill of battle never end?

July 5, 1845: I am with child again. I had suspected, but would not believe it. Uncle John says my time will come in late winter. Abraham is delighted, and says he will work harder at the law office so he can stay home more. I would rather he work harder at politics so we can move to Washington!

Sept. 1, 1845: No freedom to write lately; I've been too busy with the fall cleaning. I'm gaining weight and starting to look fleshy again. Sick almost every day, but at least this time the process isn't so frightening. I may be even bigger with this pregnancy, but won't mind the inconvenience if this baby is the girl I want so badly. Dolley Madison Lincoln, with her father's dark, thick mane, and my blue eyes and light skin.

Nov. 4, 1845, our 3rd anniversary: We had a small but most elegant anniversary supper, though we could hardly be romantic for Bob's playing with his father's legs all evening. Oh to be young enough to entertain yourself with only two scrawny legs!

"I'm sorry I don't have a gift for you," I said as the candles began to die.

My dear husband replied, "Oh but you've given me the greatest gift of my life."

"And what is that, Darling?"

He leaned over and patted my belly. "First you gave me a child-wife I adore. Then you gave me a fine son, and soon you'll give me another. What will we name him?"

"Her. This baby will be a girl, I know it. And we'll name her Dolley. Perhaps Dolley Elizabeth or Dolley Madison Lincoln. Do you like that?"

He smiled without showing his teeth and said, "Yes, Dear, but perhaps you should consider a boy's name just in case."

Dec. 12, 1845: This was a swift twelvemonth, and I'm surprised to see it end so soon. Next year will bring us another baby and election to the House of Representatives. I feel this in my heart. I don't know how I'll manage, as a 27-year-old woman with two children, to devote enough time to campaigning and pushing Abraham to move upward, but I won't give up! It's our manifest destiny.

Dec. 13, 1845, my 27th birthday: How will I ever handle the added responsibility this year? My husband is a noble man, but I frequently wish he would concentrate a bit less on humanity's troubles and a bit more on his family. I'm aging quickly, living alone so much of the time, tending an unaffectionate child, carrying another heavy load in my womb, and facing the upheaval of food almost each time I try to eat. I have few adults to talk with, especially now that I'm "confined" again. I chafe when reading, because the newspapers are filled with such tripe. So many rumors, so little truth.

The planks I laid around the house to keep people from tracking in mud are gone again. The pigs and wild dogs have uprooted and dragged them off. So I'm constantly dizzy from bending over to wipe slush off the floor. All that stooping can't be good for the baby, and I know it's not good for my back.

The weather is horrifically cold. Snow, sleet, rain, and ice fall endlessly. I dress Bob in woolen shirts and heavy trousers, but he won't stay in them. Like his father, he also prefers to go without shoes, and would die from the iciness if I allowed him to run as bare as he wants. We must keep the fires lit at all times to avoid rekindling. At a penny per match, I can't afford a box every week!

Dec. 15, 1845: Mine is a come-and-go world. Maids, money, visitors, health, happiness, husband—they all come and go. When Abraham is here, we have long chats, like in our courting days. Tonight we ate poached ham, potatoes, cornbread, and my own roasted coffee, which pleased him very much. He still prefers dark, thick coffee to the elegance of tea. I'm learning to cook rather well as time passes, though making a meal often takes the better part of a day. I don't even attempt to serve turnips—no one in the house will eat them.

After supper, we talked about the war and its implications. Then we cozed beneath the down comforter, and I fell asleep in the safety of his arms. We have no sexual union because of my condition, and I seem to miss the act more this time than he does. I have become quite wanton in my desires!

In to the weekly cleaning girl, when we can keep one, we have employed a nice colored lady who helps with Bob, sets the table, washes dishes and linens, keeps the fires lit, and frequently reads to me as I sew. She offered to help with the stitching, but I prefer to make my family's garments myself. I can't allow another woman to touch my husband's shirts or sit-down-upons!

I also sew for the Episcopal Sewing Society, a group of ladies who gather here once a week and make clothing for the poor. It's the least I can do. Being pinched ourselves, we have no money to donate, but I have capable hands. I get along with most of these women well, but some act like mice in a cat's bed and I can't abide their timidity. Two have stopped coming, allegedly because they didn't like my outspokenness. I certainly don't care, not as much as a snap of my fingers. Damn them all!

Dec. 22, 1845: We have lost another maid, right here at Christmas when there's so much to do. These girls can't seem to learn the simplest tasks, not even bed-making! I believe they are lazy; Abraham says they are frightened of me.

"You're too rough with them, Mother. You speak your mind right out when something displeases you. And not just with the help; you do so with our neighbors too. I'm used to it and know you don't mean harm when you snipe, but these girls ain't worldly like you and they don't realize that in just a moment the deed will be forgotten." Snipe! He called me a snipe! He can be a sap at times.

I admit my rancor now, but I responded calmly at the time, "Yes, and they can't just up and leave like you do when bad air comes between us. If they turned their back and left the room—or the house—the way you do, they wouldn't even receive a day's wage. And if I didn't love you so dearly, your sloppiness and slowness would cause you to go unpaid as well."

He dropped his eyes. "Try to be more understanding, and gentler if you can. Can't you remember that a drop of honey catches more flies than a gallon of gall? They don't mean any harm. They're only girls."

"Yes," I spit out, "and slothful ones as well. Laziness is the devil's helpmate."

As always, the tension subsided on its own, and we slept entwined like newborn puppies. Abraham doesn't like to argue, but I believe it keeps a couple activated. He simply stops responding or walks away, leaving me to solitary seething. That's the end of it, of course, except perhaps for some banging of pans or tins in the kitchen or a slammed door. This has been our way since before we were married.

Dec. 25, 1845, Christmas: Love is all around. We dined on Aristocracy Hill with many others. My sisters' children grow taller and more mature each year. They have a strong sense of confidence, and are allowed to express their own opinions on matters. Our children will have the same rights. We won't be overly strict. We'll never beat them, or keep them from youthful joys and frivolities. They will be educated in the finest schools and cared for by trained physicians. They will conduct themselves like young adults at all times. Of course, Bob is often moody, and my perfect sisters, with their perfect children, roll their eyes when he acts up for attention or refuses to be touched. He'll outgrow it in time.

Jan. 1, 1846: Guests arrived every hour today and Abraham wasn't here to greet them. He left this morning before sunrise with only an apple for breakfast, and didn't reappear until I sent Mr. Gourley to fetch him for lunch. I told the early visitors he was calling on friends, but he wasn't, of course. He was at his office working or reading or telling jokes with Herndon. Why didn't I marry a bank clerk?

Jan. 2, 1846: President Polk gave a reception yesterday and again Dolley Madison starred. 78 years old now, but the papers say she's still beautiful and the belle of Washington. Amid all the festivities, they announced that Gen. Taylor has been ordered to move closer to the Rio Grande and protect Texas from Mexico's retaliation.

Newspapers also report that Mrs. Polk replaced most of the White House servants with slaves and housed them in the basement! Surely Congress won't allow it to continue! Though slavery is still legal in DC, this hasn't happened since Andrew Jackson's term. What a horrible image it paints of the US!

Jan. 7, 1846: Cousin John Hardin, once an honest man, has shown his true colors. Even though Abraham worked so diligently to establish the Whig rotation process, and John agreed, when it became Abraham's turn, John said he had decided to run for the House again himself. It's mortifying to discover that someone we love is intentionally trying to ruin our future. If neither man had been to Congress, or if they both had, I know Abraham would back down and allow John to have the office, just to keep peace among friends. But turnabout is fair play.

Abraham says he will speak with John. If my cousin reneges on this agreement, I'll cut myself off from the Hardins forever. I may not forgive him for this intended slight as it is. Now, to make things worse, we hear that Cousin Steve Logan is also seeking the nomination.

How will we achieve our goals if people keep shoving us out of the way? If we lose this election, Abraham will be dissuaded from politics. No! We can't fail unless we allow our minds to be improperly directed, and I will not. Damn them all!

Jan. 25, 1846: As I write, Bob is balanced on Abraham's head, screaming, "Papa more, Papa again." He can say "Mama" too, but seldom does. He is hugely independent and often says, "Me do it" when we try to dress or undress him. His favorite word for the past few months has been "No," especially at bedtime.

"Now, Bobby," Abraham will say, "big boys have to sleep a full night so they can grow strong. You don't want to sprout up skinny like your old Paw, do you?" Then he throws the boy onto his broad shoulders and off to bed they go, both giggling like two-year-olds.

Bob is fearless—except for spiders. He will scream like death at the sight of a spider, but he'll hug a filthy pig in the wink of an eye. Though he has my tendency toward plumpness, he's now dark and dusky like his father, and he has Abraham's moods.

Feb. 7, 1846: Abraham rode to Jacksonville to speak with John Hardin, and my illustrious cousin proposed that, rather than nominating by convention, the Whigs should open a poll in every precinct and no candidate should be allowed to electioneer outside his own county. Abraham distinctly told him no.

He told John, "I've always tried to accept almost any proposal a friend makes and I'm truly sorry I can't in this. I don't believe you mean to be unjust or ungenerous, and I'm slow to believe you won't yet think better of this matter. I'm entirely satisfied with the system you and Ned Baker were nominated and elected under. It's fair to all three of us candidates, and the local Whigs are well acquainted and well satisfied with the system." John rightly backed down and withdrew his name. The Whig House seat will be ours!

Feb. 12, 1846, Abraham's 37th birthday: Jane, our new girl, made the traditional flapjacks and jam for Abraham this morning because I was too nauseated and tired to be sociable. I abhor the illness, confinement, and embarrassment of the entire childbirth process. After our girl is born, I won't go through it again!

After doing the marketing, Abraham read the papers to me. As I dozed, he snored in the rocking chair beside me. When the sun began to fade, we dined on eggs, cheese, and biscuits from a tray. As he lit the lamps for the evening, I marveled again at his fine chiseled features. When he returned to my bedside, I asked, "What do you want from life, Abraham?"

"Want?" He sat up straight and leaned forward, elbows on knees, lower lip slightly protruded. "Well, yes, I suppose every man has a peculiar ambition. I want nothing more than to be well thought of, to be worthy of my fellow man's esteem, and to be a good husband and father. Why do you ask?"

I paused, then spoke my mind. "I want so much from life that you often seem oblivious to."

"I know. You want things like...."

"Like the White House. You know better than anyone that my ambition has always been the Presidency. I want us back in politics. I want my children's father to be famous and respected, and I want us to live in Washington."

I sat up and curled my feet under me. "I want you to pursue the House with all your strength and not let anyone or anything stand in your way. You know we're at the first step now, and we need this office to move upward. You said it yourself: 'If you're resolutely determined to make a thing of yourself, the thing is more than half done already.' I've waited patiently for our turn and now we must have it."

"Patiently?" he said with a roguish smile. "You've never waited patiently for anything in your life, especially when it had to do with politics."

"You're wrong, Father. I patiently waited two years for you to return, remember?"

If I hadn't been on the verge of childbirth, I believe we would have achieved new marital heights after that conversation!

Feb. 14, 1846, Valentine's: I can hardly lift my body off the bed. Abraham called me "beautiful and radiant," but it's hard to believe. I'll be happy when this child is born. I don't believe I can stand much more of this paunchiness.

Feb. 22, 1846, Washington's Birthday: Abraham took Bob to the festivities, then to the traveling circus. They had to leave early because the clowns frightened Bob! I delighted to have a quiet day to read and sleep. I slumber a great deal now, but it's hard without medication. Life is easier with laudanum.

Mar. 12, 1846: We have another boy, born on Tuesday, March 10, 1846. We wanted a girl, but this child is beautiful, and I know even now we will love him dearly. He almost looks like a girl, with perfectly straight eyes and the longest lashes I have ever seen! The birthing came off less painfully this time, and again I managed without medical assistance. But no more children for a few years!

"What will we name him?" Abraham asked as he rocked the baby.

I had predicted the question and decided the answer. "I chose Bob's name. You should name this boy."

He paused, looking down at his new son in the blue cotton blanket, then left the room. After a time, he returned, smiling broadly. "I'd like to name him after Edward Baker."

"Ned Baker? Not Joshua Speed like you wanted the first time? Why on earth would you...."

"Ned's a good, honest, handsome man, Mother. A good politician, and church going too, which should please you. I've always admired him."

"But he has been a political rival all your life."

"Yep, and a damned fine one. We don't have to call him Ned if you don't like it. How about Edward or Eddy?" So Edward Baker Lincoln it is.

Mar. 28, 1846: Abraham will leave Monday to try cases through April, but says he will come home for lunch on Easter Sunday. I can be patient for two weeks. We've moved Bob into the loft with Jane, and Abraham built him a small bed. The walnut–spindled cradle went to Edward, now called Eddy, and his little washtub warms before the fire in our room.

Apr. 12, 1846, Easter: A Mr. Nicholas Shepherd came to the church today to promote his new Daguerreotype Miniature Gallery near the square, and Abraham agreed we could be photographed. It cost a dollar each, but the daguerreotypes will be a lasting memory of this time in our lives when we're so happy and so much in love. We'll frame the images and display them on the parlor table next to the picture album and Bible. I wore the blue and gray silk I made last winter — with ribbons across the bodice, rosettes on the skirt, and white ruffles at the wrists, set off with Mother's cameo at my neck and a lace shawl. Hair in curls, parted on the side for a more regal, stylish look. I had no flowers to hold, and Mr. Shepherd asked me to remove my gloves to look more natural. I hesitated, because a gloved hand shows breeding and dignity, but did as he asked.

Abraham looked extremely handsome in his black suit. His jacket remained unbuttoned to reveal his striped waistcoat and high collar, and he had allowed me to trim his hair and grease it down. Bob squirmed uncontrollably until we gave him some stick candy, then sat still only because I threatened to take it away. We'll treasure these pictures forever.

Abraham rode off again tonight, campaigning for the House, and we may not see him for six weeks or more. I don't mind being alone when the goal is so important.

Apr. 20, 1846: Eddy is colicky most days now, and no one can lull him at night but me. I wish someone could calm me during Bob's temper tantrums, or him during mine. We do have some spats! Elizabeth says Eddy's sickness will pass — it comes with babyhood — but she says nothing about Bob's poor moods.

My days are full, but not of important things. I visit the grocer, haggle with the fruit peddler, and go to the pharmacist for my medicines, but I deal mostly with the children. I'm frequently queasy from the sour-milk smell of puddings and gruel. I long for the political arena and the days when I knew the inside secrets and could comment with authority on those in power. If it weren't for newspapers and the reports Abraham shares from his travels, I would be just a wife and mother with no knowledge of the country's positioning. I'm tired and bored.

May 3, 1846: Abraham has been announced as the Whig candidate! We celebrated in our own private style behind our closed bedroom door. Need I say more?

As expected, however, Springfield has not cheered his opposition to the war, and some have even turned against him. I advised him, "Ignore them. A man must stand by his convictions. If he doesn't, how will the people believe him when times are truly hard? Aren't you known as Honest Abe?" He agrees. We're putting enough effort into this election that I suspect we'll think the Presidential race an easy task!

May 12, 1846: I'm so nervous that I can't sleep. The house creaks and groans, and I recall the spirits Mammy Sally invoked to frighten me as a child. Jane sometimes brings her man into the kitchen after supper, and I remember the negroes who came to our barn in Lexington. I helped Mammy put a mark on our fence to show runaway slaves they would be safe on their way to the underground railroad. They always arrived very late, but she fed, clothed, and doctored them. I'm certain she still does. Father would be furious, but someone has to help.

I could have sworn a huge negro (or perhaps an Indian) attempted to come through the parlor window last night to rob and kill us. I saw him! I screamed for help and Mr. Gourley came running up the boardwalk from next door. He said it was only the sound of thunder and the reflection of rain seeping through a branch, but I put my head under the bedcovers and chanted Mammy's old prayer, "Hide me, oh my savior." Hurry home, Abraham!

May 15, 1846: Word has come that Mexican soldiers crossed the Rio Grande River and ambushed an American force at Ft. Texas. My dream of intruders has come true.

"You've got no need to be scared," my brave husband said as he held me in his lap. "Gen. Taylor is an apt military man and he's got a good army. They can handle the situation. It ain't close enough to us to be a worry."

I stood up and began pacing. "I'm afraid of so many things these days. Afraid of storms more than ever, afraid the children will die, that you'll sign up for the war, that you'll find a more worthy, less tempersome wife to...."

He rose up, slapped his hands against his legs, and bent down to meet me eye to eye. "Stop it, Molly! Your imagination is running amuck again! I'd never consider another woman. You're my whole life, you and the lads. Worry about the war if you have to, but never worry about my faithfulness."

He fixed me a cup of tea as my sniffles ebbed. I sipped and asked, "Are you scared of nothing, Abraham?"

He sat motionless, his head tilted as usual to the left. His voice seemed to come from another era as he said, "I reckon the only thing I fear is dying without making a difference."

May 17, 1846: President Polk has declared war on Mexico and called for 50,000 volunteer soldiers! "Will you go?" I asked Abraham at supper.

"No, I don't believe in fighting. And I certainly don't hanker to joining a war that tweren't legally begun on American soil or truly caused by an enemy. I think this war's mostly political and I don't want any part of it. I never could see much good to come from annexation in the first place, in as much as Texas was already a free republic. Besides, it will only increase slave territory, and I won't fight for that in any way."

I reached for his hand. "Opposing annexation won't be a popular decision."

"I reckon you're right, Mother, but a man has to stand behind his principles."

Most Whigs oppose this war, of course, though many are enlisting. Gov. Ford has appointed Cousin John Hardin colonel of the First Illinois Regiment. James Shields has resigned as Land Office Commissioner to become a brigadier general. Ned Baker has left Congress to lead a regiment. Who will fill out their terms? Abraham would be an ideal replacement for any of them, and it would be only a year early for him to take Baker's seat in the House. I'll seriously discuss the possibility with him.

June 14, 1846: The Senate finally ratified a treaty with Britain to split the Oregon Territory. Thank Heaven! We couldn't handle two wars at once. I credit President Polk for realizing compromise as the only way in this instance. We received the part of Oregon with the most valuable agriculture and fisheries, so it's a good treaty. The deal also added 800,000 square miles to our country. America continues to spread its wings!

Abraham's letters express concern over this vast expansion. The Whigs are worried about destroying the balance of free and slave states, just as many were concerned in 1789 when the US purchased Louisiana. Extending the Mason-Dixon Line in 1820 solved that problem and divided the land equally. Surely our wise men in Congress can do likewise.

June 23, 1846: I'm so upset with Abraham! We have no money to spare, hardly enough to make ends meet before feeding two babies, and he is wasting it! I purchased berries today from the peddler's sons. They asked 15¢, but the fruit was not luscious, so I offered less. They accepted the amount, proving that I was correct about it, but Abraham, with his generous spirit, followed them out into the street and gave them the full amount. More, for all I know! How dare he undermine my efforts at economy? Or allude that I'm not in control of the household?

"You embarrass me," he said after I threw a handful of ripe berries at him. "We don't need to scrimp so much. I made over $1500 last year, more than ever in my life, and you don't need to beg for anything. Do I ever ask what you pay or call on you to account for your allowance? No. You can afford to be fair with people. You can't bring prosperity to one house by cheating another. Fairness is the Lord's way, wouldn't you say?"

He has no idea how I scrimp to pay for our lifestyle and the trappings to keep us from appearing to be poor. I use only half what is truly needed to keep us in beans and bacon so the rest can be used to enhance our prestige. He made it clear before we were married that our income could disappear in a flea's heartbeat, and I will not go wanting.

"But Mother," he says in that quiet, calming tone he uses when I'm nettled—when his voice goes lower and deeper than usual. The melodious tone that soothes the stray animals that come into the yard and quickly turns them into pets. The tone that stills the wildness in my nature as well.

"But Mother," he says, "we've got funds now. I'm trying more cases than ever. We live in a grand house. You don't churn your own butter or grow your own fruit. You entertain a lot. We can afford help. We may not have a pocket full of diamonds, but we ain't destitute."

I watched him wipe blackberry juice from his chin. Then I said, "We would have more money if you didn't give half to your heathen law partner. I don't know why...."

He sighed and turned his back. "We're not talking about Billy Herndon here, we're talking about berries. You go on so about being poor, but we're not poor. Please don't mistreat the vendors and give us a bad name."

He just doesn't understand that the more we save here at home, the more we'll have to spend. I have lived with politicians all my life and know it's expensive to campaign. Bah!

June 24, 1846: We've made up. Our spats may last through the evening, but no matter how angry or nervous I am, or how uncommunicative he becomes, we seldom fall asleep without touching. And when we touch....

I'm smiling now to remember. His skin is so warm and his chest so strong. I fantasize that his bones are made of steel: unbreakable, unbendable. I love having my fingers in his long coarse hair—hair with no rules of which way to grow, no matter how much bear grease he applies.

My handsome husband brings out my desire just by looking at me in his special way, and his eyes twinkle with such glee when I have been satisfied. After the second time of the night, his chest expands like the cock of the walk. He is the only man I'll ever love and I'm truly sorry to upset him. It's just that he's gone so often, and it's so lonely without him. Our lovemaking takes away my feelings of abandonment. Until he leaves again.

Aug. 1, 1846, Bob's 3rd birthday: I made Abraham's favorite white almond cake for Bob, who immediately smeared it over his cheeks. Abraham thought that was the cat's meow. Sometimes I believe he allows the boy to act up simply to gain his love. Or perhaps to experience the childhood frivolity he himself never had?

Bob is now walking, but he still prefers not to wear shoes. He talks plainly too, and seems clever enough. I sometimes worry that he's one of the little rare ripe sort who will be smarter as a child than as an adult.

He and Abraham play outdoors in the warm evenings—games like hide and seek, horsy rides (on Abraham's back or knee), count the stars, and a sport apparently called "Who Can Scream the Loudest?"

The child clearly indicates a mischievous side—the sort of devilment that's the offspring of animal spirits, of which his father and I are certainly guilty! One bit of mischief he enjoys is wandering away from home, obliging a neighbor to bring him back. They all recognize the half-naked, bare-footed boy. I spanked him for straying a week or so ago, and to show me his willfulness, he simply ran off again. I had to summon Abraham from his office to collect his son.

Aug. 15, 1846: We dressed in our finery this morning and went to hear Peter Cartwright, who defeated us in 1832, make a campaign speech. He has been spreading rumors about Abraham, trying to win the House seat for himself and the Democrats. As usual, it quickly turned into a religious speech, but Abraham foiled him like a champion. Cartwright began to rant about being saved. He asked all to stand who wished to go to Heaven. Most did, but Abraham and I did not. So he asked those to stand who wished to go to Hell. No one did. Then he pointed at Abraham with his pudgy forefinger: "Mr. Lincoln, I noticed you did not stand at either question. If you don't wish to go to Heaven or to Hell, where do you plan to go?"

Abraham stood, drew himself up to his tallest countenance, and said loudly and clearly, "I plan to go to Congress." Then he sat back down beside me. Cartwright's congregation erupted in laughter despite his stern looks, and we received many warm wishes on the way out.

Nov. 10, 1846: The House seat is ours! Congressman and Mrs. Abraham Lincoln—at last! Abraham won by almost two to one, the largest majority ever in the district. The people's faith in him, like mine, remained too strong to be bothered by an ill-willer like Peter Cartwright, and Abraham has done too many Christian things to be considered an infidel whether or not he goes to church.

When I heard the news, I danced around the house like a mad woman, dragging Bob by the arms and lifting Eddy into the air. Then I realized Abraham was oddly silent.

"Why aren't you celebrating?" I asked.

"I don't rightly know, Mother. This election, though I'm mighty grateful for it, hasn't pleased me quite as much as I expected it to."

I stuck my tongue out at him. "Well, smile for my sake, Dear. We're on our way to Washington!"

Nov. 26, 1846, Thanksgiving: A wonderful luncheon at Elizabeth's. Abraham arrived home just in time for the festivities and will be here till year's end. No court in December this year because of the cold. I preened to introduce him to the guests as "My husband, the Honorable Abraham Lincoln." I often glanced at Ninian to see his reaction as I said it, and bit my lip to keep from saying I told you so!

"Congratulations again," Elizabeth said when she kissed me goodbye.

"Thank you," I replied with as much warmth as I could summon. "You know, of course, the next step is the White House."

"You've always wanted that, haven't you, Little Sister?"

"Yes," I answered proudly, "and I'll have it before your hair turns gray, I promise you! Our path is open and free. We're on our way. Make sure you mention that in your next letter to Father and Betsy."

Stephen Douglass, elected to Congress for the 3rd time, came to congratulate us, as did most of Springfield. He is moving to Chicago so he will be closer to the political front. He also confided his plans to marry and change the spelling of his name to "Douglas." I wish the best for my former beau and hope his life is even half as loving and fulfilled as mine.

As the Lincolns sat together later, watching the sun set through our parlor window, I realized how blessed we really are. The sky glowed with orange light, the kind Bob can stare at for hours on end. Soon we'll be in Washington. Will the sundown look any different?

Dec. 12, 1846: Goodbye again, Journal. I'm so happy. The courts called Abraham away again for a few days, but before he left, he asked what I would like for my birthday. My answer took no thought: the Presidency. He said he would bring a bottle of toilet water in the meantime.

<u>Dec. 13, 1846, my 28th birthday:</u> *I was galloping down a steep hill on a white horse. My hair was loose and streaming out behind me. A man was chasing me, and I eventually saw that it was Cousin John Hardin. I jumped a low bush and the horse's hoof caught on the greenery. John's horse cleared it easily and they passed as we steadied ourselves. He was wearing a black judge's robe, and I watched it flow behind him as my hair had done. He also carried a large silver pistol. I clicked my beautiful horse and it took off like lightning, but John was out of sight. I slowed and rode as if on a cloud into Washington, where the streets were filled with revelers. They were singing and dancing, but there was no sound coming from their open mouths. I looked left and right, but could not find John.*

I woke from this odd dream winded and a little scared.

In the evening, we left the boys with Elizabeth and went to the American House Hotel for a handsome supper. Abraham gave me a single-pearl necklace, which surely must have cost $3 or more! And he approved the new drawer chest I purchased. We must furnish the house slowly, but it's becoming a home to pride. The unexpected expense of another child has slowed remodeling somewhat, but Eddy is so beautiful that we hardly notice the sacrifice.

What a delight to have my beloved husband to myself for an evening. People speak to him constantly, however, and women stare brazenly. Worse, he smiles back! He says he seldom speaks to ladies while traveling, but he certainly seems more comfortable with them now than when we first met. No, I won't be distrustful! I will not doubt his fidelity, though dreams of such behavior often haunt me. His looks have softened over the years, he smiles more, and he's more attractive, but he would never betray me. I'll learn to be gracious too, for the good of the cause, and be as charming as

Dolley was in her role. She never fretted over her husband's friends. But then, James Madison was not as magnetic as Abraham Lincoln!

Dec. 16, 1846: I take a moment to record the scene before me. Abraham is sitting in the floor, legs spread out, feet in neatly mended black stockings propped on the newel post, shoulders against an upside-down chair, dangling and swaying our precious baby over him and making unintelligible noises. No matter how long they do this, Eddy keeps gurgling and laughing. Bob soured on this game quickly at Eddy's age, but this baby never tires of being held or petted. My heart beats with motherly pride. I will make them some hot chocolate!

Dec. 18, 1846: Bob found a black kitten today and we are feeding it under the porch. We call the cat Lumpy because, when fed the first time, the food made lumps in its belly! I don't know what we'll do with the animal when we leave for Washington. We'll have to find homes for all the cats, and old yellow Fido too. But for now, Abraham and Bob are enjoying the furry company. Abraham has always loved cats; they are a hobby to him and he brings them home quite frequently. I'm sure we'll have Washington cats very quickly.

We're beginning to pack up the house. There's a great deal to do, and my dear husband isn't much help with the storing and arranging. But such is a small price to pay for success.

Dec. 24, 1846: I've been thinking about visiting Lexington. Father hasn't seen Eddy, Betsy hasn't met either of our boys, and I haven't laid eyes on their last two babies. It would be good to go now amid our successes.

Besides, I miss the lilacs and honeysuckle in our sweet old garden. Even if the walk is still under a snow blanket, I could imagine Elizabeth and me strolling the path to the summerhouse as we did so often in our youth. Or frolicking in the cool spring rain showers and acting silly. I want my darling boys to also have such experiences, and they should know their family. I'll speak to Abraham about it.

Dec. 25, 1846, Christmas: We spent what may well be our very last Christmas with my sisters and all their sweet children. Next year we'll be in Washington, and I hope to never leave. Ninian took me aside after supper and said, "Mary, you need to prepare yourself for disappointment in the capitol city. Your vivid imagination has a tendency to exaggerate your position. Your husband is not Vice President, or even an ambassador. He's merely a congressman from the wilds of Illinois, and a Whig at that. He won't be taken seriously. His position on the Mexican War hasn't made him popular. If Cartwright hadn't been such a zealot, Lincoln might not have won at all. You'll be just another small state representative's wife, and you'll probably never see inside the White House."

I replied, "And you, Ninian, may never be invited inside the White House when we live there if you continue to berate us. You should learn not to underestimate your sister-in-law."

Jan. 1, 1847: A hundred or more people came to call today and Abraham remained at home as host. I took the buggy and the boys to call on neighbors. It was cold, but bearable, and we shared many cups of warm cider and cool punch. It will be a wonderful year for the Lincolns, our best yet, I know it! It will be a growth year for the US too. Iowa, a free territory, became the 29th state just before year's end.

Jan. 11, 1847: Abraham is gone this week and I was forced to ask Mr. Gourley to stay with us again and put another bolt on the door. It has been storming for several days, and I could no longer bear the thunder. Bob sleeps with me most nights, usually against his will. I could pay the neighbor boys to stay over, but they go to sleep too early and don't keep an alert eye. Besides, they ask for 5¢ a night!

Newspapers are filled with stories about robbings and lynchings. Why, a man was murdered this week at the Globe Tavern, just down the street. We might have been there for supper or visiting! It's no longer safe for proper people to stroll the streets at night.

Abraham will tease me about being frightened, but he'll be glad I called for help rather than staying alone in fear. He too still becomes uneasy in heavy rain.

Feb. 12, 1847, Abraham's 38th birthday: My wonderful husband just left for the market, and I delight to watch him saunter down the street. He walks loosely, with a skip in his step, his basket on his arm, his gray wool shawl wrapped around his neck. It gives me so much joy to see Abraham's boyishness and mirth remain as he ages. When he returns, we'll dine on fried prairie chicken, biscuits, and all the fixings. I made his special almond cake and a chocolate one as well. Bob drew a "picture" for his father and I signed all three of our names. Abraham will be pleased.

Feb. 25, 1847: Gen. Taylor was victorious in the battle at Buena Vista and pushed the Mexican troops from the north. But we incurred sadness too. Cousin John Hardin was killed in battle. Henry Clay and Daniel Webster also lost sons. Our old nemesis, James Shields, was shot through the lung at Cerro Gordo, and the Mexicans captured dear Cassius Clay after he saved a company of Lexington boys. Both, thank God, are still alive.

So many of our dear friends and relatives are gone forever. And why? Because a power-hungry President wants the US to become bigger than any other country during his term! Our men are dying for political reasons only. Polk should be impeached!

Mar. 2, 1847: Eddy has suffered a high fever for several days, and he is now coughing uncontrollably. Willie Wallace calls the condition diphtheria and prescribed emetics several times a day to induce vomiting, which makes the boy weak and lifeless. What to do? Two doctors in our family, but no one seems to know how to treat my son. I have added my own remedies: balsam on his chest, oatmeal gruel and rice jelly when he will eat. Uncle John says he will outgrow it, but he said the same about Bob's eye and it remains crossed.

Watching Eddy in such misery reminds me that I am also useless and lifeless. Abraham has all the glory, even though we have worked out much of his political strategy together. I have only sick children and chores to occupy my time. When he's riding from town to town, eating in nice boarding houses, and laughing with cronies, my life consists of housework and baby work.

How do women manage a large family? Elizabeth has servants and Fanny has her German girls, but we have no help. Cassie left several weeks ago for a family who would pay more. It's hard to find a good domestic, and the daily housemaids are no account. Abraham says they are afraid of me, but I'm a tolerant, understanding woman when people do their share. Today's domestics are rude and impudent. They work when they want, and do precious little even when the mood strikes them. Why pay them a high price to do less well what I can do myself? They have no understanding of what we go through for the money to pay them. Cassie broke my lovely china swan and then had the audacity to say I didn't respect her, that I spoke to her as though she had no feelings, that I "barked." Abraham says I should mind my tongue with people, but I won't take sass from a maid!

Everything must be done properly for Abraham. I couldn't bear for him to sleep in a bed not correctly made, eat a meal not well prepared, or wear a shirt not adequately pressed. Abraham isn't a finicky eater, but I don't believe he would be pleased with half-cooked potatoes. And if I have to redo a girl's work, why pay her at all?

Mar. 10, 1847, Eddy's 1st birthday: This precious child has an angelic glow that attracts people like moths to candles, and he is always in high spirits. His laugh is contagious and his eyes light up when he sees something he likes. Our home is filled with cats, dogs, rabbits, and all sorts of other "critters," as Abraham calls them, and Eddy likes them all. My biggest boy Abraham brings them home, and my littlest boy Eddy ensures they have enough love to stay. Bob's fondness for animals faded when the snake bit him several months ago.

Mar. 11, 1847: Stephen Douglas has outdone us once more! Just when we thought we were catching up, he resigned his seat in the House and was elected to the upper chamber. He assured me when we were young that once he won a Senate seat, he would stay there forever. Will we never best this adversary?

Abraham says Stephen's move is not important. "We are who we are, Mother, and we've achieved what we've been working for. I promised to stay in the House only one term, you know. You mustn't forget that we'll be plain old Abraham and Mary Lincoln again next year, practicing law in Springfield and covering the circuit."

"No Sir," I answered. "I'll find a way to the Senate. I want what I want...."

"I know," my beloved husband said as he put his arm around my shoulder, "and you aim to have it, the devil be damned!"

Apr. 18, 1847: I wrote to Abraham that I would like to travel with him awhile, because I'm extremely restless. He responded that it's impossible. I know Sarah Davis took her son and traveled with Abraham and Judge Davis after her youngest child died. But the trip was unbearable for him with young George in the buggy, and he refuses to even consider our joining him. He's right, of course; traveling with a poor disposition like Bob and a squirmer like Eddy could be tiresome. But we could be helpful to him as well, especially in the evenings when he's alone. My heart races to even picture us in a strange bed together.

July 1, 1847: I haven't been writing much; Bob and Eddy keep me constantly busy. Abraham left on the stage today for Chicago to speak to the delegates at the River and Harbor Convention. He asked me to go but I declined. I would have to take the boys, as we have no nursemaid now, and we would be in his way. He needs to freely mingle with other politicians and stay up till all hours if he wishes so he can pave our way into Washington. If he had asked before Cassie left, I would have gladly agreed, but he doesn't need my silly jealousies, or the boys' welfare, on his mind at this moment.

July 4, 1847, Independence Day: I hitched up the buggy and took Bob and Eddy to see the festivities. Bob is becoming harder to handle; he's more independent and prone to disobey. Eddy, my good boy, is easier to manage. He was awed by the bright flags and hot air balloons. Bob and I ate our picnic—boiled ham sandwiches, sharp cheese, lovely summer tomatoes, and gingerbread—right on the ground. The boys played little games and sat on the small ponies. Even without their adored father, they enjoyed the day. I hope there are no stomach aches tonight.

Aug. 1, 1847, Bob's 4th birthday: Bob is growing nicely. Perhaps a bit fleshy, but he will lose weight as he spurts up. I have begun to teach him bits of poetry and French. His father still spoils him. Last week, I saw Abraham carrying Bob in his arms and said, "Put that boy down. He's too big to be carried."

Abraham replied, "But don't you think his little feet will get too tuckered?" Bob is a smart child. He adamantly nodded that, yes, he would get too tired, and off they continued as though I had not spoken.

Abraham has arranged to lease the house so we won't have to sell when we move. Cornelius Ludlum has agreed to pay $90 a year, beginning on November 1st, and we'll keep the north bedroom to store our furniture and other belongings so we won't have to dispose of it all.

Sept. 20, 1847: The Whigs have officially decided to nominate Gen. Zachary Taylor for President, even though our beloved Henry Clay was once again interested. Also in line were Gen. Winfield Scott, who fought so valiantly in Vera Cruz, and Daniel Webster.

Because President Polk kept his word about not seeking office again, the Democrats are bandying around the name of Gen. Lewis Cass, who opposed the slavery-limiting Wilmot Proviso of 1846 and expansion in Mexico. The anti-slavery group favors Martin Van Buren. He was a Democratic President, but now he will run as a Free-Soiler.[3] The chameleon knew he had no chance with the Democrats again, so he simply switched parties. I believe it's unprofessional to change ideals so easily.

Oct. 1, 1847: We're going to Lexington on the way to Washington! We will stay at least three weeks and be there for Thanksgiving! We'll also be able to visit with Speed and Fanny in St. Louis on the way. Abraham is still riding the circuit in his buggy, but soon he'll turn his files over to Herndon and we'll be ready to leave. Oh what a wonderful adventure this will be. I'm so proud to be traveling in style as a congressman's wife!

Nov. 3, 1847: We arrived here in St. Louis on the 25th and are staying at Scott's Hotel. We'll dine with Fanny and Speed tonight for another evening of reminiscences. Tomorrow, on our 5th wedding anniversary, we leave for Lexington! We should be there in a week, first by steamboat down the Mississippi to Cairo and the Ohio River—over 500 miles! Of course, we'll

---

[3] Free-Soilers were a combination of the Abolitionist/Liberty Party and NY Democrats who split from the main party and pledged to prevent the spread of slavery.

have our own cabin for the four of us. Then onto the Kentucky River to Louisville and then Frankfort. From there, it's only a short railroad trip!

Nov. 8, 1847: I knew Bob would enjoy being on the boat, but he's taken to it as a cat to preening. He runs constantly around the deck, frequently hanging off the railing and scaring his poor mother out of her wits. I scream at him to be careful and he runs down the stairs into the galley. He loves to put his ear to the deck and listen to the huge engine turn and grind under the ship. He stares at the paddle wheel as it turns and splashes water in all directions. He hangs off the back of the boat and tries to catch the wake in his hands, looking pleased as Punch when he gets soaking wet.

Abraham has taken control of him, because I can't manage it. Regrettably, "control" to my husband often means scampering <u>with</u> Bob up and down the stairs and listening for the whistle that warns of black smoke rising from the stacks. Then Abraham scoops him up and runs onto the deck, both of them hoping to become covered in soot! The other passengers shake their heads in either amusement or annoyance. At least Bob isn't scowling and refusing to be with anyone at all. We're blessed that the passengers don't recognize one of these ruffians as their new representative.

Nov. 11, 1847: We arrived in Lexington this morning and have been rejoicing since. When the carriage reached the front gate, the family stood there with open arms, and the servants were peeking through the kitchen door. Being enfolded in Mammy Sally's fleshy black arms made me feel at home again. She crowed over all I have accomplished and assured me that Mother is smiling proudly from Heaven.

My greatest joy comes from seeing Emilie. It's difficult to believe how grown up she is at only 11. I described her so well to Abraham that he recognized her immediately, and picked her up right in the foyer! He calls her "Little Sister." The other children are also delightful: Martha, David, Aleck, and the babies Elodie and Kitty. Aleck is the same age as Bob, so they have become fast friends. Bob's dark coloring and Aleck's flame red hair and bright freckles remind me of raspberries and blackberries in a bowl waiting to be doused in cream.

Nov. 14, 1847: Last evening we went to hear Henry Clay speak at the courthouse. Abraham, though he has admired Clay for many years, had never met him. Afterward, Betsy invited Clay home for tea and sherry, and we talked for hours about Whig policy and the future of Mexico. Clay calls the war one of "unnecessary and offensive aggression." He agrees with me that the US should not attempt to appropriate Mexico and govern it. We're a sovereign nation, not a sovereignty!

I finally went to bed and left the gents to their conversation. Abraham came in long after sunrise, and said this one evening made the entire trip worthwhile.

Nov. 17, 1847: Betsy and Father hosted a supper for us and many friends and relatives attended. What a joy to see them and introduce our new congressman. And such splendor in the house! Betsy used her finest china and damask cloths; served the choicest roast beef, oysters, hens; poured tea from China and coffee from Columbia. She's never shown me such respect before.

Abraham displayed his best behavior. He was all dressed up, though he pleaded not to wear a full suit. I wore the dress I sewed on all last summer: white satin with blue marabou feathers at the neckline, skirt fluffed out with feathers at the hem. No one could tell I made the dress from remnants; I looked as well attired as any lady in the room.

When Abraham saw my costume, he said teasingly, "Fine feathers, Mother. Enough on you to make great birds of us both. Those ones on your dress are the color of your eyes." What a surprise! When I married him, he didn't know blue from red, or feathers from flapjacks for that matter!

He has taken some quiet time to himself while here to read law books and congressional records. He wants to be prepared when we get to Washington. He also brought along *Niles' Weekly Register* and the poetry book I gave him. He read Emilie a poem by Cowper on slavery, but she listened only from behind a pillar where her huge blue eyes stared in wonder. He now sits in a rocker happily reading the autobiography of Frederick Douglass, the negro abolitionist. Imagine a negro writing a book, and one about himself at that!

Abraham says it's well written and effective: "If every man would read this book and feel the pain Douglass describes, we wouldn't have to worry about slavery dying out in time. Anyone with a twinge of humanity in his bones would voluntarily eliminate it the next day."

He also goes downtown with Father to read the books in his law library. All in all, I believe he's enjoying himself. We're sleeping in my childhood room and memories flood my heart each time I enter it. Nothing much has changed in the Todd home. Everything is about to change in the Lincoln home.

Nov. 19, 1847: Bob is actually having fun! He's happy to have the diversion of his Cousin Aleck so he can avoid being with strangers. With Mammy Sally's nephew to watch over them, the boys daily explore the coach house, stable, and servants' quarters. They hold fishing poles in the stream behind the house and throw rocks at the ducks. As an added benefit, these activities keep him from being cruel to Eddy. On the trip, he took joy in teasing his little brother: hiding his shoes and socks, pinching him on the arms and legs, taunting him. This new attitude of goodness must be the result of keeping company with his cultured relatives.

Nov. 21, 1847: Abraham finished Douglass' book and asked to see a slave auction. We walked up to Cheapside and watched for several minutes, all the time either of us could bear. The slave pen, as usual, displayed adults and children ranging from light brown to the darkest ebony. Some were tied, some were shackled, many were bleeding and almost naked.

After the first sale, Abraham pulled me from the crowd. We trudged in silence. When he finally spoke, he echoed my thoughts: "This can't be allowed to continue. Men ain't property. Mothers shouldn't be separated from their children for the love of money. We've got to fight this evil; it must not spread."

I held his arm tightly. "We will, Darling, we'll fight it from this moment till both our terms as President have ended. I'll do all in my power to help you stop it." In one short exposure to the horrors so vividly described in Douglass' book, I sense that Abraham has progressed from non-extensionist to abolitionist. I pray it's true, but only time will tell.

Nov. 25, 1847, Thanksgiving: Most of my family came today for the afternoon meal. Brother Sam, who attends college in Danville, is a handsome young man, much taller than I, and like our father in appearance. He called me "Mrs. Congressman" the entire evening. He taught Bob to call him "Uncle Sam," though none of the youngsters understood the reference. Even Eddy's eyes followed him around the room.

My other brothers did not come. Levi lives in Lexington with his wife Louisa and manages Father's cotton mills, but he won't dine at Betsy's table. George, who is going to medical school, also won't acknowledge Betsy or her children as family, and Father says George drowns his burdens in alcohol. Mother has been dead 22 years; it's time to accept Betsy as Father's wife. It's true that Father waited less than a year to remarry, and it's true that he brought Betsy and her children home with no warning or prior meeting, but that was a lifetime ago. If I, who loved our mother best, can finally open my heart to Betsy, the others should also be able to do so.

All the children love Abraham, as I knew they would. Because of their attention, his face has lost some of its previous strain, his appetite has improved, and he laughs—great yowlings from his innards—at nearly everything the little ones do. They are envious of Bob and Eddy because Abraham is so unlike their own father. I doubt if Father has ever given piggyback rides or crawled like a snake on the floor. He certainly wasn't playful in my childhood, and his interest in Mother's children all but disappeared after Betsy's began arriving.

My sisters frown at Abraham's behavior, and Father says, "Lincoln, get up off the floor and stop acting like a tyke yourself." For once, I don't mind his lack of public decorum.

Nov. 26, 1847: This afternoon, after the long steamer ride to Winchester, Virginia, we boarded the Winchester and Potomac train to Harper's Ferry. We're all tired and dirty, but there are tubs on board. In a few days, we'll change to the Baltimore and Ohio rail line to Maryland, and then finally to Washington. The trip will take approximately a week. Congress convenes in two weeks, and we'll stay in a rooming house until we're settled.

Dec. 4, 1847: Mrs. Sprigg's boarding house overlooks Capitol Park on First Street and the iron railing around the park comes within 50 feet of our door! Our room is in the back, on the second floor, and has an adequate fireplace. The inn is much like the Globe, but our room is larger and we have two of everything: beds, wardrobes, washbasins. It also costs twice as much.

Meals are served in the dining area, which has wide windows facing the park, so it's bright and relaxing. The diners are mostly congressmen: four other Whigs, several abolitionists, and too many Democrats. Though two wives are expecting, ours are the only children in the house.

Washington is dirtier than Springfield, and filled with all sorts of odd men. Carriages and hackneys flourish about constantly. The streets are muddy, and rubbish sits out in plain view. Sidewalks are overrun with animals — pigs, geese, chickens, horses, even cows — that eat the garbage. Few streets are paved. The north side of Pennsylvania Avenue is brick from the Capitol to the White House. New streetlights also stand, but they are dark now because Congress is not in session.

Dec. 5, 1847: We explored the White House grounds today. So impressive, just as I always knew they would be. The Capitol, with its old wooden dome, sits at the end of Pennsylvania Avenue, and is surrounded by a smelly marsh and cowsheds. The State Department is in a small two-story house; the War and Navy Departments are only one story. A much larger treasury building is being constructed, for the current government's vast riches, I suppose. A foundation has been laid for what is being called the Smithsonian Institution — a museum of sorts, I believe. History is made in these buildings!

Because of the slave pen, perhaps half a mile away and visible from the Capitol, Abraham won't be able to forget his vows to help the oppressed. The pen is a wretched hovel surrounded by a wooden paling perhaps 15 feet high. It resembles a livery stable, where droves of negroes are kept until taken to southern markets, precisely like horses. It's constructed so the outside world can't see the human cattle shackled there. I've been told it's the largest slave market in North America.

Washington is an odd combination of magnificence and squalor. Nevertheless, we're here and Congress convenes on Monday!

Dec. 6, 1847: A Whig caucus last evening and the opening session of Congress this morning! I went to the Capitol with Abraham to hear his oath from the red and gold visitors' gallery. He drew from a basket to determine his seating position and it's dreadful—in the back row. Luckily, Abraham doesn't disappear no matter where he sits.

He looked so handsome, Congressman Abraham Lincoln, in his black suit, white shirt and collar, and silk stock. He allowed me to oil his hair and comb it back from his brow. His sideburns are now down three quarters the length of his ears and he looks quite cosmopolitan.

The scheme of buying only black socks, when I can find them large enough, has worked. At least I know his feet will match. He wanted to wear his Conestoga boots today, but I convinced him that Springfield casualness is not appropriate for such a prestigious place as the House of Representatives. Thank Heaven he listens to me!

After putting the little rascals to bed, Abraham said, "Well, Mother, looks like we made it after all."

"Of course," I answered. "I never had a doubt. You looked perfectly appropriate there today. You'll be a favorite, and someday you'll lead this great nation."

Dec. 8, 1847: Sen. Stephen Douglas stopped to see us with his new wife, the former Martha Reid. She is a lovely southern belle and has brought about great changes in our old friend. He no longer imbibes or smokes. Though they reside in Chicago, they are here for the term. It's nice to know we have friends in the city, even if we're at political odds.

Abraham is the tallest man in the House and Stephen is the shortest man in the Senate. If they should they ever team up, they would be the political long and short of it. And what an intellectual pair they would be! I can't imagine anything their minds could not conquer if they were to work together.

Dec. 12, 1847: The boys and I have been touring the city, visiting the sites, and looking for a rental house. While neither child is as disruptive to the boarding house as Bob was when young, we need our own home. A place to socialize and return entertainments with other politicians, to show the city that not all Illinoisans are rustics, to make plans for our next advance.

<u>Dec. 13, 1847, my 29th birthday:</u> Will my negligent husband never learn to tell time? We were supposed to go to dinner with the Douglases, but once again he stayed too late on the Hill. He carries his old pocket watch, and often winds it absent-mindedly, but he doesn't consult it.

He finally appeared with news of being appointed to the Post Office and Post Roads Commission, with four other Whigs and four Democrats. Since he was postmaster in New Salem, this will be a good place to distinguish himself. Oddly, he was also appointed to the Commission on War Department Expenditures, which means he will be reviewing and preparing documents about Mexican War expenses. No doubt his every vote in this committee will be negative.

He is especially pleased to have the Supreme Court library at his disposal. He enthused, "How wonderful, Mother! All those books available free, and I can study them anytime I want. We'll have to try to get elected again someday, because I'll never be able to read them all in just a year."

I smiled. "If we plan to be re-elected, we need to start now. You must start making yourself known and letting those around you, and the people of Illinois, know you want to be elected. I see no reason to leave Washington at all."

He shifted in his rocking chair, a prediction of bad news. "I meant elected at some other time. You know I promised to stay for only one term. Steve Logan is the front-runner for next time. He's already campaigning."

The time had come to be strong. "Yes, but each of you—John Hardin, Ned Baker, Abraham Lincoln—had a term. The agreement is complete and the office is open for anyone. Why should you wait another year and give someone else time to become entrenched when you're already here? The only reason I agreed to that silly plan was because you would be the last, and therefore the most easily re-electable, when the scheme was over. You must make your position known. Soon. Your advocates will help you. I will help you. I can write letters to get additional supporters, and entertain the appropriate people. We can do this!"

He nodded. "It's pleasant to believe there's others who want me in this race. I wouldn't personally object to another term, though I think it'd be quite as well for us if I returned to the law. I agreed not to run again more from a wish to deal fairly with Hardin and Baker, and to keep the district from going to the enemy, than for any personal cause. So you win. If nobody else wants to be elected, I won't refuse. But my word and honor forbid entering myself as a competitor."

I went to him and held his head to my breast, knowing what reaction it would cause and relishing the anticipation. "You silly old coot. Do you think the world will just come to your door if they don't even know where you live? I'll do the electioneering then. I'll begin by writing to the Illinois leaders and asking them to nominate you against your will. The newspapers will receive anonymous notice that you will consider running if urged, and we'll see what happens from there."

Dec. 14, 1847: I ask Abraham each night what he did to distinguish himself this day, and his answer to date has been nothing. "I'm biding my time, Mother. A man can't jump into a cold lake all at once. He has to warm up to it."

"Well, My Dear," I responded tonight, "I do hope you'll begin warming up quickly. A house can't catch fire if it's not lit at some point."

Dec. 18, 1847: When I asked Abraham tonight if he had spoken up for anything, I received a high surprise. "I'm dismayed about opening up," he said.

I ran to stand near him. "What? Abraham Lincoln doesn't fear anything, certainly not a room of puny men!"

"No," he said, "it ain't the men who frighten me, or even the speaking out. But you know I've had no training at politics. I served four terms in the legislature without doing anything remarkable. You say I've got to defend some issue, but I'm nervous about picking the wrong battle to fight, the wrong statement to make. I don't want to become known as a whiny ne'er-do-well."

We spent an hour thinking about issues and discussing several worthy topics. Finally I said, "Why not talk about the war with Mexico?"

He raised his eyebrows and stroked his hair. "What do you mean?"

"I know how strongly you feel about expansion with slavery attached, and you've said many times that you believe American troops actually started the war under the President's direction. Why not talk about that?"

He nodded in quick jerks. "I do believe it, yes. I don't believe Polk ever gave Mexico a chance to compromise, and I'm convinced the first shot went out on Mexican soil rather than American, but saying so won't make me popular."

"No, but it will make you famous. And you must have recognition to move up. Success requires determination, perseverance, and remembrance. You know that's true."

So he agreed. At the right time, he'll speak his mind. May God send the time soon.

Dec. 19, 1847: Abraham finally pulled his long legs out from under him and spoke up. A small presentation at best, and based solely on a post office question, but the cat no longer has his tongue.

"Were you frightened?" I asked.

"No," he answered, leaning back in his rocker to put his feet on the hearth. "I felt about as badly scared, and no worse, as when I speak in court. I reckon I'm getting the hang of it."

I'm getting the hang of it too. Eddy has a chest cold and Bob a sore throat, but I feel pluperfect for a change! Washington agrees with me!

Dec. 22, 1847: Abraham invited me to the House today to hear him challenge the President. I wore my finest day dress: the saffron-colored frock with the high neck and ribbed bodice, topped by the silk cabriolet bonnet with brown flowers filling its bowl. I wanted to look my best in case other wives attended or the assembly turned to check for my presence. I also wanted Abraham to be proud if he became nervous and glanced at the balcony. He says I'm his calming strength.

His "spot" resolutions, as they were immediately dubbed, were to the point and well presented. With ardent respect, and just as we had rehearsed, he accused President Polk of ordering troops into land belonging to Mexico, and requested that the President be forced to answer eight specific questions about the particular "spot" where the first blood was shed. He was magnificent!

I'll send copies of his speech to the newspapers. The five Whig papers will be pleased to get the text, I know. But I'll send them to all the major papers. We must be heard to be recognized!

Dec. 25, 1847, Christmas: We took Bob and Eddy to see the decorations today. They enjoyed the snow on the Capitol grounds. Bob went sledding later with Mrs. Sprigg's serving girl while Abraham and I worked on our campaign. We shared a lovely dinner downstairs and were in bed very early.

Jan. 1, 1848: New Year's Day in Washington is even finer than in Springfield! All the powers—President, Vice President, Secretary of State, etc.—held a reception for the congressmen in the White House. I wore my white velvet with ermine fixings, my best pearls, and golden side bands woven through my hair. Abraham dressed in canton crape trousers, black swallow-tailed coat, and white linen shirt with formal collar. We had to look our best!

We hired a coach to drive us through the snow and were overwhelmed by the sight: hundreds of people on the lawns; dozens of carriages coming and going; foreign ministers standing on the portico in their bright colors; and a main room, filled with chandeliers and mirrors, in which the Marine Band played loudly and aggressively.

President and Mrs. Polk greeted everyone who forbore to stand in line, and I found them quite agreeable. Mrs. Polk is not nearly so beautiful as Dolley Madison, whom I desperately hoped to see. Though the papers say she was there, it was not to be. That would have been the last jewel in my crown! We didn't stay long, as we saw hardly anyone we knew and no refreshments were served. But we were invited to the White House, something Ninian said would never occur. I will write to Elizabeth tomorrow!

We have been planning and rehearsing Abraham's next speech. He decided to remain firm on the Mexico issue rather than tackle something else. I would like to see him address more than one matter so he won't be considered a "one-drum" candidate, but he is impregnable on this. As he paces around our room practicing, his words become stronger and his grammar improves dramatically. He writes so eloquently. How curious that his lack of education shows only when he speaks, not when he writes. If he could deliver the presentations exactly as we write them, he would be even more acclaimed!

Jan. 5, 1848: Abraham presented his ideas to the House about forcing the Postmaster General to allow railroads to carry more mail. Not a large battle, but an important one.

And now he has taken to the sport of tenpins. He frequently meets other congressmen for a game behind Mrs. Sprigg's or at James Casparis' bowling saloon. I'm told he looks rather comical with his long arms and legs flailing down the lane. He plays solely for exercise and amusement, but I know they must talk about his lack of skill behind his back. They criticize his speech pattern, hair, and stories, and now he's given them a way to criticize his awkwardness. How can we prove we're not rubes from an unsophisticated western state if he continues to act this way? I spend hours preparing his clothing, teaching our children to behave as best I can, and reading newspapers so I can speak with confidence at the supper table. He talks about sending letters via rail and thrashes about in a bowling arena! Bah!

Jan. 12, 1848: Abraham has more openly attacked Polk in reference to Mexico. He said straight away, "The President unnecessarily and unconstitutionally started this war." Then he vividly explained why the Whigs are so opposed to the entire situation. An excerpt from the records:[4]

> I carefully examined the President's message and found that he falls far short of proving his justification for war. I believe he would have gone further with his so-called justification if not for the small matter that the truth wouldn't permit him.
>
> He's a bewildered, confounded, and miserably perplexed man. I more than suspect he's deeply conscious of being in the wrong and feels that the blood of this war, like the blood of Abel, is crying to Heaven against him. That originally having some strong motive to involve the two countries in a war, he plunged into it and was swept on and on until, disappointed in his calculation of how easily Mexico might be subdued, he now finds himself he knows not where. How like the half-insane mumbling of a fever dream is the whole war part of his message!
>
> As to the mode of terminating the war and securing peace, the President is equally wandering and indefinite. His mind, taxed beyond its power, is running hither and thither, like some tortured creature on a burning surface, finding no position it can settle on and be at ease.

Feb. 2, 1848: The peace treaty with Mexico has given the US 500,000 square miles to the west. The papers say gold has been found in California, so many families will likely seek their fortunes there. The treaty was ratified, but still without the Wilmot Proviso that would prohibit slavery in the new territory.[5] Polk called the proviso mischievous and foolish; he will never approve it.

The weather is not desperately cold, certainly not as frigid as February in Springfield, so house hunting isn't a terrible chore. The boys are happy to

---

[4] All records, newspaper, and speech reprints are authentic.

[5] In 1846, David Wilmot introduced a bill providing $2 million to negotiate a territorial settlement with Mexico. He later proposed an amendment stipulating that none of the territory acquired would permit slavery. The amended bill was passed in the House, but the Senate adjourned without voting on it. In the 1847 session of Congress, Wilmot again proposed an antislavery amendment. This bill passed the House, but the Senate drew up its own bill and excluded the proviso.

be bundled up outside, especially if we can play an hour with their boats and kites. Abraham doesn't know I am searching for a house. I'll tell him when I find the perfect place, just as he did for me in Springfield.

We have visited the historic spots, memorials, museums, and libraries. I stood before Dolley Madison's home in Lafayette Square and tried to find the courage to knock on the door. We gazed as a family at the area where the monument to honor George Washington will stand, and I have dreamed at night of a finer one — the Lincoln monument.

Washington is seething with talk of emancipation, pro and con, from all levels of people. I have never seen slavery more in evidence, even in the Lexington pens.

Feb. 5, 1848: Abraham had another horrible nightmare last night. He moaned and bellowed so loudly that Eddy began to cry and Mrs. Sprigg knocked on our door to ask if everything was all right. Abraham opened the door in his long yellow nightshirt, soundly asleep. I climbed from bed and led him back, all the while trying to assure Mrs. Sprigg that he is not a madman. As usual, he can remember nothing.

Today the rains came and the city is a morass. Men stand knee-deep in mud outside our windows, and Abraham says the Capitol floor is covered in muck. The boys and I can't go to the square or search for suitable housing. Thank Heaven I have so many documents and papers to read for Abraham. Such keeps me busy.

Feb. 12, 1848, Abraham's 39th birthday: Because it's Saturday, Abraham didn't have to spend his birthday on the Hill. It was too nasty to go outside, however, so we stayed in and played games with Bob, tended Eddy's fever, and chatted with the other residents in the parlor.

He felt the need to work on post office matters most of the evening, so we celebrated in our favorite way after the lads were asleep. I never tire of my longing for him, or he for me. We have to be more careful in the boarding house, but we have found ways to indulge and not shake the building. I predict we'll recommence our true animal ways when I find a house.

Abraham is not keen to move. He enjoys Mrs. Sprigg's. He walks to the Capitol with the other congressmen each morning, and sits in the parlor with them after supper. He says we'll only be in Washington for a year, and we don't need to pay high rents for such a short time. He is learning the political world, but will he ever understand what it takes to be on the society list? A home is a necessity.

Feb. 15, 1848: Abraham says a new senator from Mississippi — I believe his name is Jefferson Davis — is talking up war with England to take all of

Mexico. He even petitioned Congress for regiments to garrison Mexico. In addition, this madman has begun to lobby for splitting the Union. Unfortunately, he is not alone in this quest for separation.

Apparently our friend Stephen Douglas is quoting Frederick the Great to make his point about Mexico: "Take possession first and negotiate afterward. That is precisely what President Polk has done." As in his youth, Stephen believes it's easier to get forgiveness for wrongs done than permission to do wrong.

Abraham is in touch almost daily with Henry Clay or Daniel Webster; he could not have better advisors. With Clay's years and experience, Webster's way with words, and Abraham's vigor and drive, the Whig planks will prevail.

Feb. 18, 1848: A horrible thing happened right here where my children and I now live in fright. White men tied, gagged, and dragged a kindly negro man to a slave jail right before our eyes. The negro was buying his freedom from Mrs. Sprigg, but he will never see it now. He had a good heart, and played frequently with our precious angels. Now he may be tortured or killed. The incident so terrified me that I had to take double laudanum and go to bed. Mrs. Sprigg's hired girl watched Bob and Eddy until Abraham could come home. I don't believe I can stay here; it's not safe for us.

Feb. 23, 1848: John Quincy Adams died today on Capitol Hill. Abraham said he collapsed in his House seat. Adams spent his entire adult life fighting the spread of slavery. He said to the end that the Mexican war was instigated by slaveholders who wanted to extend our borders for their own means. The nation has lost a fine man.

On a more positive note, Abraham was asked to serve on the funeral committee. The Birthday ball was postponed, so we ventured to the theatre district and saw Mrs. George Jones at the Olympian. Magnificent!

Mar. 3, 1848: Abraham was on the Hill as usual, so the boys and I went alone last evening to hear the Slomans, a father and two daughters who sing while playing the harp and piano. A delightful evening, and so good to get outside. Abraham and I have actually been invited to many soirees this season, but he stays too busy and it is not proper for me to go alone.

I found a nice house on F Street. The rent is affordable, but Abraham will not hear it. "Who will you entertain?" he asked, his arms folded haughtily across his chest.

"Senators and representatives, past Presidents, Dolley Madison, Henry Clay when he comes to the Supreme Court, the Douglases, the Bentons, the Dixes, Mr. Buchanan, everyone. The best families in the District. We can't expect to show our status in a boarding house. We must have a place for society to come to us."

He grunted. "We don't have any status. Washington's run by a group of high-horse southerners who don't want anything from a junior member they never heard of. Being a Whig ain't what it used to be, and I'm not a society man. Besides, best I know, less than ten members rent houses and they're permanent members. Why can't you ever be content?" So we will have no house in Washington—this term at least.

Mar. 11, 1848: Eddy felt much better yesterday, so he was able to enjoy the small birthday party arranged by Mrs. Sprigg. I had such a fearful headache I couldn't tend to him all day. I felt as though wires behind my eyes were being pulled from their receptacles and set afire. Eddy tottled upstairs several times to kiss me and say, "Mama, I wuv you." How precious and dear he is.

My pain has lessened enough now to jot these words, but my stomach is still so ill I can hold nothing down. The only ease is chloral hydrate and complete darkness. I only wish the dreams would stop.

Mar. 12, 1848: Herndon sent an envelope filled with horrible clippings:

> *Belleville Advocate:* The meeting in Pinckneyville of patriotic Whigs and Democrats agreed that Abraham Lincoln authored the "spotty" resolutions in Congress against his own country.
>
> *Springfield Register:* Out damned spot! We denounce Lincoln for failing to support the war effort and backing a Presidential candidate who won battles in a war Lincoln claims to condemn. Those who try to render their own government odious deserve to be regarded as little better than traitors to their country.
>
> *Clark County meeting report:* "Spotty Lincoln" has placed a stain on the patriotism and glory of Illinois.
>
> *Morgan County News:* This Benedict Arnold of our district shall be known here only as the Ranchero Spotty of one term.
>
> *Ottawa Free Trader:* It's a damned shame that an Illinois representative has broken the state's united and patriotic front.

In addition, Stephen Douglas made a speech in the Senate against Abraham's stand, and Henry Clay and his supporters have ostracized us for causing "a deep and mischievous wound on the whole Whig Party." Bah! Damn them all!

The worst part is that the "spots" Abraham so diligently called for have not been revealed. That leg has been chopped off and now he has none to stand on. He has taken to leading the Whig attack against the war's constitutionality.

Mar. 15, 1848: Zachary Taylor has finally made a statement about his politics, but it makes little sense. He declared himself "a Whig, but not an ultra Whig." How can a man be one and the other at the same time? And what in blazes is an "ultra" wig? Using a modern slang term doesn't make him intelligent in my eyes. I assume he means he won't stand behind his party in all things—abolition perhaps being one!

He also said, "If elected, I would not be President of a mere party. I would endeavor to act independently of party domination. I should feel bound to administer the government untrammeled by partisan schemes." Such big words, such little meaning! I wouldn't vote for Taylor if I could vote, even if he is James Madison's cousin, and I'll encourage Abraham not to vote for him. A man who speaks from both sides of his mouth is not to be trusted! And his lack of political experience is bound to be a detriment, even though Horace Greeley calls him "the noblest work of God: an honest man." If the Democrat papers are correct and Taylor has never voted for a single Whig, we are in a serious dilemma.

Mar. 25, 1848: We have been invited to visit Father, and Abraham agrees it will be good for me to go. I am consumed with dread and headaches, and Eddy cries a great deal. A holiday will do worlds of good for us all. We have little to do in the winter, and socially we're not advancing. Bob and Eddy are restless in this single room and I'm serving no purpose. Without a house in which to entertain, I can be of little help. We will leave early next week via rail.

Apr. 12, 1848: A wonderful letter from Abraham says: "In this troublesome world, we're never quite satisfied. When you were here, I thought you hindered me some in attending to business. But now, having nothing but business—no variety—it's grown exceedingly tasteless to me. I hate to sit down and direct documents without your help, and hate to stay in this old room alone. I purchased, as you requested, some plaid stockings to fit Eddy's dear little feet; I think you and him will be pleased. Also bought a large whistle for Bobby. Don't let the blessed fellows forget Father." He says he saw Mrs. Arthurson sing *Verdi* at Carusi's. I'm envious.

Apr. 18, 1848: The *Washington Post* reports that a man named Daniel Drayton attempted to smuggle 76 slaves on his ship from DC to NY. They say the slaves belonged to "41 of the most prominent families in Washington and Georgetown," and were valued at $100,000. He was arrested and the slaves returned. The article said at least one negro belonged to Dolley Madison, and others to President Polk. I'm hurt to know Dolley would still own slaves, but perhaps the paper reported incorrectly. We have long suspected slavery in the White House, and this is the proof we need to make it illegal in DC forever. This is not the image our government center should portray to the world!

Apr. 23, 1848, Easter: Such a wonderful day at church with my sisters. I have savored this unexpected time with them and with Father, who thinks Eddy is especially adorable. The minister asked him where his father was today and Eddy said, "Papa hadth gone to the tapila," his best version of "capitol."

I have been free from headache since arriving, and feel like a lass again. I even went horseback riding! It's the first spring I've been completely well since before my marriage.

May 1, 1848: Abraham's latest letter sounded lonely: "I miss you dearly, but want you to enjoy yourself in every possible way. If you want to return at any time, I'd be mighty pleased. I'm proud to hear you're free from headaches. But I'm afraid you'll get so well as to want to marry again, and that'd be a very bad thing for old Lincoln here in Washington." He could talk a cat out of its whiskers.

He asked me not to affix "Honorable" to his name when I write to him. Is he becoming displeased with the recognition it brings? He said we have funds and need not worry about postage, from which the designation frees us. It amuses me to hear him talking so like a man serving on a post office committee. But cost isn't the reason I use his official title. I'm amazed he wouldn't easily discern that I use it because of the prestige. It's important in our goal to be recognized by the mail carriers and residents where we live. They are all future voters!

I will write him immediately that I want to return to Washington. How I wish that, rather than writing, we were together tonight. Though I've enjoyed my visit here, I long to caress him. He is the world to me!

May 4, 1848: The Locofocos — Democrats — have finally nominated Gen. Lewis Cass of Michigan, whom Abraham calls an evil doughface. He is an ardent expansionist, a northerner who agrees with southern principles of slavery, and Abraham wants to fight this man with all he can muster. The Democrats have vowed to block any attempt to bring the slavery question before Congress.

May 29, 1848: Wisconsin has been admitted to the Union as a free state, again balancing the congressional votes. This tiny state was ripped from its own territory and the part remaining is larger than the part admitted! How peculiar! Surely this will be the last state; 30 is enough.

June 1, 1848: Abraham writes that I should return to Washington "as soon as possible." He said, "Having got the idea in my head from your last letter, I'll be impatient till I see you. Come along just as soon as you can. I want to see you and our dear boys very much. Those in the house you were on good terms with send regards; the others say nothing. Everybody here wants to see Eddy."

June 10, 1848: Abraham now writes that he is extremely busy. Though I long to see him, I have no desire to spend every evening in our room at Mrs. Sprigg's without him, so we'll stay here a while longer. Bob and Eddy are becoming more rambunctious, and it's harder to handle them alone. At least here in Lexington I have assistance. And Bob is enjoying himself more this summer. He's made some friends and is constantly in their company. If I were to go, perhaps I could leave him here and take only Eddy? Or even go alone? It's worth considering.

June 14, 1848: I have decided to wait and join Abraham in Philadelphia or Chicago after his term, so I leave with my family tomorrow for Buena Vista, the Todd summer home. Bob and Eddy can spend their summer days in the woods and fields rather than in a muddy city street or a cramped hotel room. I'll spend two or three weeks out there, and then perhaps travel to Philadelphia with Uncle James Parker, who is also visiting with us.

June 23, 1848: A letter from Abraham has angered me. Those dratted Democrats are now attempting to amend the Constitution and provide for federal assistance in internal improvements. We must not begin changing the Constitution! Certainly no slight occasion such as this should tempt us to touch it. Abraham agrees and took a stand against amendments in the House: "As a general rule, I think we'd be much better off to let the Constitution alone. Better, rather, to accustom ourselves to considering it unchangeable. New provisions would introduce new difficulties and thus create and increase appetite for more change. New hands have never touched it. The men who made it have done their work and passed away. Who can improve on what they did?" Such an elegant speaker!

July 4, 1848, Independence Day: My lonely husband is urging me to return. His recent letter said, "I expected to see you and the dear codgers sooner. But let it pass. Stay as long as you please and come when you please." Perhaps I'm not being fair to him? He seems somewhat lost without us. Maybe independence is not so enjoyable after all.

July 6, 1848: Oh how I wish I had listened to Abraham and returned to Washington. The President and Dolley Madison presided on the Fourth at the laying of the Washington Monument cornerstone! How I would love to see my idol in her famous wig pieces and turbans, and Abraham could have arranged a meeting. How is one to know about such historic events beforehand? Bah!

July 10, 1848: Newspapers report that the women's suffragettes Lucretia Mott and Elizabeth Stanton have formed a convention in New York to plot for better education, better access to jobs, and the right to vote. The *Tribune* is calling the group "mannish women like hens that crow" and implying they are unhappy only because they are unmarried and without children. I wish I could join them. I believe in their cause, just as both my grandmothers did, but I have another battle to fight and another goal to achieve.

July 30, 1848: Abraham spoke for a full hour this Thursday on the floor! He said he would have gone longer, but time ran out. The *Baltimore American* quoted him at length and concluded that he "kept the House roaring." Hoorah! He has begun editing the *Whig Battery* and is working hard on the Taylor campaign. Perhaps my constant advice about "being seen and heard" is taking hold.

Aug. 10, 1848: The Free-Soilers have nominated John Frémont for President, with John Q Adams' son, Charles Francis Adams, for VP. This new party is coming on strong, though Abraham says they are like the pantaloons the Yankee peddler offered for sale: large enough for any man, small enough for any boy. He's right; they have no platform and are trying to fit everyone's needs. Their slogan is the most memorable element of the campaign: "Free Soil, Free Labor, Free Speech, Free Men, Frémont." Abraham believes a vote for the Free-Soilers might be a vote for the evil Cass by weakening the Whigs. How I wish I could vote!

Aug. 14, 1848: Last day of Congress for this session and Abraham is blue. He feels he has not made a serious impression and the Whig leaders do not take him seriously. I don't doubt it, with the way he clowns for them every morning before session and entertains them with his hijinks at the bowling alley. These men deal in ideas and graft, not in humor and witticisms. In Springfield, being homespun leads to elections; in Washington, it leads only to laughter. Tomorrow he leaves alone on "our" long-awaited trip east to campaign for Taylor. I'll meet him in October in Chicago.

Sept. 1, 1848: Thinking it would be most natural for the newspapers to be interested in presenting at least some of Abraham's House speeches to their readers, we made arrangements to have the *Globe* and *Appendix* regularly sent to all five Whig papers in Washington. And yet, with the exception of one speech, which only two papers published, I haven't seen even an extract. I'll venture the *State Register* has thrown more Locofoco speeches before its readers in a month than all the speeches Whig papers printed during the entire session. How can we become known if our own press doesn't support us?

Sept. 15, 1848: Abraham has been speaking on Taylor's behalf for the last week: New Bedford, Boston (with the governor of NY), Chelsea, Cambridge, Dedham. On the 12th, he spoke in far-away Worcester, Massachusetts, where he was very well received and covered in the *Boston Advertiser*. Comments from other papers are much better than the last clippings we received from Horrible Herndon.

Lincoln soon had his audience in a spell. I never saw men more delighted. His style was the most familiar and offhand possible.

Lincoln's awkward gesticulations, the ludicrous management of his thin, high-pitched voice, and the comical expression of his countenance all conspired to make his hearers laugh at the mere anticipation of the joke.

Sept. 20, 1848: Daily letters from Abraham. How I miss him! He and Thurlow Weed, the political head in NY, went to Albany to visit with Mr. Fillmore, the Vice President Elect. I insisted that Abraham ask Fillmore to recommend him for a Cabinet post! He always hesitates to speak up for himself, but this is an opportunity not to be missed! He promised to do so if possible. Oh that I could accompany him—there would be no "if possible" for this task!

Sept. 28, 1848: Abraham has left Buffalo for Chicago. While in NY, he visited Niagara Falls. He described its beauty and charm in such detail that I'm sorely disappointed not to have seen it with him. He wrote: "Niagara Falls calls up the indefinite past. When Columbus first sought this continent, when Moses led Israel through the Red Sea, even when Adam first came from our Maker's hand, Niagara roared here. It's as strong and fresh today as 10,000 years ago. Magnificent! Still, I wonder where all that water came from."

Tomorrow, the boys and I begin our journey to Chicago. Some women don't feel comfortable away from home, but I'm not one of them! Travel is a gift for the cultured.

Oct. 6, 1848: Abraham spoke rather impromptu in Chicago last evening. A high success, though still not as smooth as I would like. The crowd was so large that they had to move from the courthouse to the public square. The *Chicago Daily Journal* called the speech "one of the very best we have heard or read since the opening of the campaign."

Oct. 10, 1848: Rousing speech in Peoria, but the *Democrat Press* wrote, "Lincoln blew his nose, bobbed his head, threw up his coat tail, and delivered an immense amount of sound and fury." Abraham has convinced me of Gen. Taylor's merit, but how I wish he would learn to stand still when delivering his sound and fury!

Oct. 15, 1848: We're still canvassing Illinois, and have stopped in at least ten towns on our way home. An exciting life! Bob and Eddy never tire of it, nor do I. The only weary one is the man in the stovepipe. Perhaps if he would learn to keep his notes in his coat pocket rather than his hat, he wouldn't have so much weight to carry!

Nov. 4, 1848, our 6th anniversary: How nice to be back in our own house on this special day! We spent the afternoon bringing our belongings downstairs and rearranging again. Being in our own place has also renewed our passion! Perhaps this old bed contains magic? It was certainly magical this afternoon!

Nov. 7, 1848: Election day is filled with uneasiness. Abraham has been canvassing for Taylor the last few days in Petersburg, Jacksonville, Tremont, and Pekin. Will it be enough? Additionally, Abraham's name was proposed for a second term in the House, but there was little force behind it. Even one without my intuition knows that if a man won't campaign for himself, few others will take the gauntlet.

Nov. 10, 1848: Zachary Taylor won the election, but only by a mild margin, and only because the Free-Soilers took votes from the Democrats. Van Buren and Cass split the Democrat vote, causing Taylor and Cass to have the same number of electoral votes. But Van Buren took New York and those electors went with Taylor! No one has seen Mrs. Taylor—they call her a "phantom."

Ned Baker, who moved to Galena, won Abraham's seat. That's acceptable; he's a good hand to raise a breeze. James Shields won a Senate seat. Abraham Lincoln won zero. Still, if Taylor wins, we may not lose everything. He will appreciate all Abraham did for him during this campaign and bring us into the inner circle where we can be noticed. If we fight hard enough, we can be elected to the House next year, then the Senate in '50! We must begin planning soon. Should I accompany him back to Washington for the second session?

Nov. 27, 1848: We decided that the boys and I will not return with Abraham next week. It's too hard on us all, and I can manage his pronouncements just as well from here. So Abraham kissed us goodbye this morning and trained to St. Louis. He will visit quickly with Speed and then go on to Washington. Congress opens on December 4th, but he will not arrive until December 7th. He stayed longer to be with his family. He told me, "The House can wait. My term will be up in three months, but my family will never end."

"I'm pleased you feel that way, Darling, and your family will be with you when you return for the 32nd Congress next December as a senator."

Dec. 10, 1848: Abraham's letter says his first session went well. He sent the day's *Congressional Record* and promises to also send newspapers each day. He has three months to make himself known! He promises that I'm not missing any social events in Washington, because Mrs. Polk offers none.

In my return letter, I asked him to speak with President Polk about being appointed to the land office. Abraham believes an Illinoisan should get the position, and he is interested. I hope he will make his wishes known, but I won't hold my breath.

Dec. 12, 1848: It has been a roller-coaster year. We've won and lost battles, traveled, loved, and grown politically and professionally. Eddy's health has improved, Bob's attitude has picked up, my headaches have lessened, and Abraham's hypo has all but disappeared. I'll spend my winter months planning a campaign for the Senate.

<u>Dec. 13, 1848, my 30th birthday:</u> My mirror lies! I don't feel old, but the strands of gray show proof. My face is rounder and my girth wider than 10 years ago. Such happens with childbirth. But my eyes are bright and alert, and my teeth are good. Perhaps 30 is not so ancient after all.

As a gift to myself, I wrote Abraham a long love letter I hope will never be seen by another person, telling him about the physical acts we could do if he were here. We understand each other thoroughly, and he looks beyond my impulsive words and manner. He knows I'm devoted to him and his interests. In only 10 days, we will see how much of my fantasy we can turn into reality.

<u>Dec. 19, 1848:</u> Since Abraham didn't ask President Taylor for the land office as we discussed, I have written to him myself. The position pays $3000 annually and requires residence in Washington. It would be one more footprint toward our goal, and I know Abraham would like setting policy for land distribution. I also wrote to prominent Whigs asking them to support us for this office. The President will simply offer Abraham the position and he will never know I arranged it. Taylor is indebted to us because of the hard work on his campaign, and surely he will make appropriate restitution.

<u>Dec. 25, 1848, Christmas:</u> Abraham arrived late last night, too tired to even wake the boys. They have been expecting him, however, so Eddy was in our bed early this morning, jumping and squalling in delight at seeing his beloved father. Bob is more reserved, but it's clear he looks forward to Abraham's return.

He brought more gifts from Washington: a periphaniscope with animal pictures inside for the children and pink limerick gloves for me (two of my most favorite things, kid gloves and pink). Also books on European travel ordered from London and Paris!

"What does this mean?" I asked with great hopes.

He smiled absently and stroked my shoulder with his long fingers. "We'll not be tied down much longer, Mother. In a few months, I can have the practice running smooth again and we can leave it with Billy Herndon while we visit some of the sights you've always wanted to see. Eddy can stay with the Todds, and Bobby will learn a great deal, I reckon, being on the Continent." Europe! Hoorah!

Dec. 26, 1848: Congress resumes on Wednesday, so Abraham left tonight. This visit was so quick, he could have simply slept in his clothing and not bothered to bring a valise. No, he looks wrinkled enough most of the time. Sleeping in his suit would just make it worse. Heaven only knows how he is dressing for sessions without me there to guide him.

Jan. 1, 1849: We welcomed the new year without Abraham. Another trip this soon would be too much on our pocketbooks and his constitution. He is due back on the Hill in only three days. He will bowl with his comrades, I suspect, or go to the horse races if the weather holds. His letters say he wishes we were with him, but it will only be two more months. I am busy, meanwhile, planning for our next office and writing letters to the newspapers. I have listed all the important people we need to entertain when Abraham is back, and am trying to meet up with them beforehand and get their commitment.

Jan. 10, 1849: In his wanderings today, Bob came across a little puppy, and as soon as Eddy spied it, his tenderness broke forth. He made us bring the dog inside and he fed it bread and milk with his own dear hands. He was so delighted over this poor, straggly creature that I said it could stay. What is one more animal in our zoo?

Feb. 12, 1849, Abraham's 40th birthday: Abraham spent his day alone in Washington. Of course, he is never truly alone, is he? He's happy at Mrs. Sprigg's, and I'm sure he didn't mind being with the boarders on his day. Like most men, he has never cared much for birthday celebrations. He's studying law cases to be ready to practice again next month, and says he has memorized *The Pilgrim's Progress* in his free hours. I imagine he's not sleeping or eating much.

Feb. 22, 1849, Washington's Birthday: A big celebration in Springfield, but surely less spectacular than in Washington. Abraham will enjoy the fireworks and shindigs. He has been included as a manager for President Taylor's inaugural ball! How clearly I remember the soirees we attended before we were married, and how uneasy he felt. He still can't dance well, and normally stands against a wall with his hands clasped behind him, afraid to hold a glass or plate of food. He has yet to learn the social niceties of conversation or paying compliments. Putting him on a ball committee is like putting Frederick Douglass on a committee to re-elect Andrew Jackson!

Mar. 3, 1849: Last day of Congress, so my adored husband will soon be on his way home. He will stay in Washington to see Old Zach inaugurated, make sure the ball runs smoothly, and then ride the rails back to his family in time for Eddy's birthday. We are giddy with anticipation.

Mar. 7, 1849: The Honorable Abraham Lincoln has been admitted to practice before the US Supreme Court! I have nagged him since our marriage to apply for this appointment, and he saw fit to do so only after he secured a case. Much to our dismay, however, he didn't win it. On the positive side, he was paid highly for the attempt, so we continue to add to our White House fund!

Mar. 10, 1849, Eddy's 3rd birthday: A more wonderful child has never been seen. He can speak simple French words most excellently, has a wide-open heart, and laughs at anything and everything.

In light of Abraham's recent experience with gala events, I suggested that he organize Eddy's party, but he wasn't amused. He related his adventures at the inaugural ball: "I went with Elihu Washburne and some other men friends, and spent the evening leaning against the back wall. I tried to memorize all the frocks and music for your enjoyment, but my head can't spit them out now. We didn't leave the shindig till four in the morning! There was more wealth there than I've ever imagined. Flub-dub dresses with diamonds or such sparkling under the huge chandeliers, military men in brilliant uniforms, foreign ambassadors speaking languages I couldn't identify. I was peedoodled! I never wanted you by my side more than at that shindig." I made him tell the story twice.

He brought a most unusual present for Eddy: a boat he whittled as a model for a real one. It's equipped with buoyant chambers attached to sliding spars and pulleys. If the boat were to run aground, the pulley system would cause the chambers to fill with air and the spars would force the boat into the water! He also made a larger, more functional version, which he took to the patent office while in Washington.[6] Perhaps it will become a ecessary machine and we'll be rich overnight! Or we will never see a penny.

---

[6] Lincoln is the only president to hold a patent, #6469.

Apr. 8, 1849, Easter: We went to services and then took the boys to the egg rolling. Eddy won a small gold cross as the toddler finding the most eggs, and says he will keep it forever.

While I couldn't convince Abraham to buy a summer suit, he let me fix him up, and all the church folks were happy to see him. Once a congressman, always a congressman, and the title brings honor. Additionally, he's responsible for federal patronage in this district, which has added to his political importance.

After lunch, we sat quietly on the swing. I knew something was seriously wrong because his lips were pressed together and he was not laughing at the children ambling down the green hills. Then he broke my heart. "Mother, I've decided not to run for the Senate."

I tried to interrupt, but he held his hand up for my silence. "I committed political suicide in the House, and I won't be easily accepted again. I reckon we should wait a few years and let my poor record fade. My one history-making attempt, the bill calling for gradual emancipation in DC, met disdain from all sides. I don't think I'll ever see the day when people will rightly grasp the cause nearest to my heart and when I can truly render any service to my country. If I ran now, I'd be knocked into a cocked hat."

I said nothing. My disappointment was too near the skin. I simply rose and went to check on Eddy. But I won't let him quit. Just because Fate sent a great man to Washington and they didn't have the sense to recognize him doesn't mean we should give up. The world needs Abraham Lincoln, and I am determined it will have him! Bah! Must go now—those horrid colored glows are beginning to form before my eyes.

May 5, 1849: In his role as federal patronage recommender, Abraham has begun a letter-writing campaign to get Ned Baker appointed to the Cabinet, Willie Wallace to pension agent in Springfield, and Abner Ellis to Springfield postmaster. He's also working diligently to make sure a Springfield man is appointed as General Land Office Commissioner, so I had to tell him about my letter to President Taylor last winter, in which I requested the position for him.

His face hardened and turned an odd shade of green. The corners of his mouth curled slightly upward as he said, "My child-wife who wants so much to live in Washington will get us in hot water yet with her impatience. You've got to learn to control yourself, Mother. If this position is offered to me, it will be more from my work in the election than a letter written by an aspiring wife. Still, I'd as soon have the office myself as see any other Illinoisan get it. Butterfield will likely be appointed unless prevented by strong and speedy efforts. He's not on yet only because Taylor hangs fire.

Maybe you were right to want it for us, but you weren't right to take the reins and write to the President. I can beg for my own chitterlings."

Little does he know how much I do without his knowledge or consent. We have to keep up our momentum.

May 25, 1849: Abraham has gone to tell President Taylor that he will accept the land office if offered. He will only be gone three days. I packed his linen duster—it won't wrinkle badly and will show to his advantage in the oppressive Washington heat. I know Taylor will reward us for our efforts. We also wrote at least 50 more letters asking for support. We're going back!

June 7, 1849: Abraham brought two goats home from the feed store. One he and Eddy named Nanny, the other they tried to name Billy, but I wouldn't allow it. How would I ever know if Abraham is referring to his law partner or his goat? To me, they're about one and the same personality. So the goat is Doogie. Eddy loves animals as much as Abraham, and we now feed 2 goats, 3 dogs, 5 cats, 3 rabbits, and at least 6 chickens, plus the necessary animals like cows, horses, and pigs.

July 5, 1849: The papers report that President Taylor brought at least 15 slaves from Louisiana to the White House. Again we're made to look as though owning other human beings is a way of life in the entire US. What must the Europeans think of us? Slavery is an albatross around the nation's neck!

July 18, 1849: My blessed father died two days ago from the cholera that's ravishing Lexington. Only 58 years old, campaigning for the Kentucky Senate, and still so handsome. Betsy is devastated. I would like to be with her, but I haven't the strength. Funerals depress me deeply, and I need all my energy at home. Father died in the same month as Mother—the month of independence. I pray they are happy together once again.

July 20, 1849: Death has come again. Dolley Madison has died in Washington at 80. I regret I never made the opportunity to meet her. I could have rung her bell. She would have welcomed me, but I hesitated, and now the chance will never come again. In his eulogy, President Taylor called her "America's First Lady." That is what I shall call myself—Mrs. President Lincoln, First Lady!

Aug. 2, 1849: As I write, I can see Abraham holding Eddy in his lap while the child holds the black kitten. The three of them have spent an enjoyable hour reading from *Aesop's Fables*. It puts joy in my heart to see such a vision!

Eddy played a clever prank on Bob's birthday yesterday. He knows how his brother fears spiders, so he somehow crafted a string spider and put it near Bob's lunch plate with a few little gifts. He ran screaming from the room, leaving Eddy behind in an attack of chuckles. I asked Abraham to discipline Eddy, but he had no heart for it. He did talk with Bob for some time, and bought his forgiveness with a dime.

Aug. 10, 1849: The land office appointment has gone to Justin Butterfield. We are devastated! I have cried until my skin itches from lack of moisture. Abraham has sat for hours with his chin sunk into his chest, hands tightly grasped between his knees, ignoring his sons' attempts to play. His left eye is fastened high in its orbit, and he hasn't spoken since we received the news. The quiet is maddening. We lost the best office to which our state lays claim, and now Abraham will go back on the circuit. He most likely will also want to stop campaigning for all offices now.

Sept. 15, 1849: A letter yesterday from President Taylor offering Abraham the Oregon territorial governorship at $3000 a year salary, same as the land office. Then, of course, he would likely be the first state governor from Oregon, which might lead to a Senate seat if Oregon were not then so strongly Democrat. Abraham wants to accept this position, but I won't have it! I plead my case:

"It's true that governor is a fine office and most of our Presidents have served as such before moving to Washington. But once in Oregon, we will forever be in Oregon, and it has no civilization! No stores, theatres, concert halls, or bowling alleys for entertainment, and it likely has no churches. And the papers say the territory is inhabited by Indians! Besides, what chance would a Whig have in politics there? None! With no party to support us, we'll vanish and never be heard from again. Just as Martha Jefferson refused to allow Thomas to become commissioner to Paris in 1780, I must refuse you this."

We bickered back and forth until I finally brought him to my side with Eddy's health. "If you won't consider me, think about Eddy. He's never been a healthy child. Oregon is thousands of miles away, across treacherous mountains, and he most likely wouldn't survive the trip. If he were able to make the journey and then became ill later, he would be far from the physicians who know his health. He could die a hard and lonely death in the wilderness, away from our family and friends, without proper medical attention. If you were in Washington, you would be days or even weeks away, and you most likely wouldn't be at his side. I won't make Eddy live there! If you go, you go alone!"

Being advisor to a future President is a good position and I enjoy it, as long as he continues to listen to me. At least President Taylor knows we are open to federal appointments!

Oct. 10, 1849: California has elected a governor and declared itself a free state without waiting for ratification. This action has disturbed the south because they see California as a stronghold for the north. How quickly the country is moving these days! Will we ever again have the calm pace and peaceful life of our past?

Abraham has immersed himself with a vengeance in his traveling law practice, perhaps trying to forget the election is near and other men are vying for the Senate. He has always said that work is a cure for melancholy. He writes to me about partition suits, foreclosures, justice court appeals, suits over dower rights, and debt actions. I'm not worried though. The money he earns now will help us when we return to Washington. I asked him again to raise his fees and to increase his share from 1/2 to 2/3, but he won't consider it. The old goat can be as stubborn as Doogie and Nanny!

Nov. 4, 1849, our 7th anniversary: I've been feeling restless lately, ready to move on, to restart our campaign. Abraham is still nearly mute and holding back in all efforts at politics and life. When he does come home, he is less talkative, and his shoulders form a semi-circle. His face is etched with wrinkles and dark pouches.

Instinctively, Bob and Eddy spend most of their day outdoors when their father is here, and play quietly before the fireplace at night. I talk to him about perseverance and the need to refocus and start again, to no avail. Even flapjacks don't interest him! I served mashed turnips with our catfish tonight to see if I could at least start a spat, but he simply pushed them about on his plate. Something must be done!

Nov. 22, 1849, Thanksgiving: We invited the Francises and Trumbulls to lunch and had a fine day. Abraham even seemed like his old self. I opened an account at the new market and purchased many delicacies to make our meal more festive: turkey stuffed with walnuts and pears, mashed yams, beans, maize, pudding, raisin cookies, pumpkin pie. I used more than 10 pounds of sugar! I have almost become accustomed to the new iron stove, and Abraham gave me many compliments on the fixings! I can't eat much of the desserts, however; eating sweets often causes me to feel faint.

Dec. 12, 1849: Goodbye again, Journal. Next year should be an exciting and possibly devastating one for the Union. President Taylor asked Congress to legally admit California as a free state and allow New Mexico and Utah to decide for themselves, whereupon some southern senators vowed to secede. Did we fight for independence in vain? Did our men suffer and die just to see the Union break apart? Abraham and I have been discussing the issue with Clay and Webster through the post, and we're afraid separation is indeed a possibility!

Unless Abraham changes his mind and returns to the political world, next year will be a dull one for the Lincoln family. He again disappears to the circuit in April, May, October, and at least a week in June, July, November, and December. Our boys continue to delight us and give us great peace, though I'm concerned about Eddy's cough. Our romance is like days past when we were first married. Life is slow, yes, but happy.

<u>**Dec. 13, 1849, my 31ˢᵗ birthday:**</u> Why must birthdays keep coming? I feel as stale as last week's corn pone. I asked Abraham after our lovemaking last night, "Have I changed too much?"

He held me closer, stroking my neck." You ain't changed a whit, Molly. You were as beautiful as a sonnet when we met and you're still lovely. Your bosom is full and strong even after two babies, and it still makes me randy. And I'd have to read the dictionary to describe the feelings stirred up by your pretty legs and dainty feet." He began the movement I love so well. "And you're a scrappier lover than you were as a girl," he leered.

I laughed. "A lady can never have too many compliments, and you, Mr. Lincoln, are about to see how much youth is left in your old wife!"

<u>**Dec. 20, 1849:**</u> Eddy's cough is not diminishing. He alternates between high fevers and exhaustion, and his breathing is laborious. Uncle John Todd and Willie Wallace, both fine doctors, come every day and force him to gargle with chloride of lime disinfectant or silver nitrate. Bob tells Eddy stories, and Abraham reads to him late into the night, but he has little interest in stories, food, or even his beloved cats. I fear the worst.

I am dosing all of us with Castor Oil and Cough Candy. Bob complains that the malady is preferable to the medicine, but I will take no chances at this perilous stage.

<u>**Dec. 25, 1849, Christmas**</u>: Eddy could hardly even open his package. Bob unwrapped both their gifts and shared with his brother, but the house does not echo with the usual Christmas laughter. I gave Abraham a painting of a standing horse for the parlor, which I purchased from a catalog in the fall, and a book entitled *Joe Miller's Jests*. When Eddy is well, they will enjoy

the jokes together. He gave me *Letters of Madame de Sevigne* to keep my French current. And a pure boggle: a note that the "national debt" — the money he has owed in New Salem all these years — is paid.

Jan. 15, 1850: The sad news came today that Grandmother Parker has gone to be with her daughter, my beloved mother, in Heaven. I wish for strength to mourn, but my heart is too heavy with closer burdens.

The doctors now call Eddy's illness consumption, and they are giving him large doses of emetics and purgatives. I sit in his room and helplessly monitor his pallid lips and pearly cheeks. Fears crowd my mind and push out the sanity. My desire to eat is gone, and I can't sleep without chloral hydrate. I cry continually.

Abraham goes to his office for an hour or so each day, appears in court when necessary, and occasionally takes Bob or the dog for a walk, but we are all chained by love to the bedside of our little son. I'm not sure I could survive if he should die. Abraham will go on, of course, because he has fortitude. My soul is in this baby.

Is this our fault? Were we too passionate in his conception? Is the Lord punishing Abraham for giving up his House seat? Or Bob for teasing Eddy so mercilessly? No, it can't be them; it must be me. But what have I done horrid enough to bring suffering to such a perfect child? Surely overeating or spending too much on trifles are not such despicable sins that God would allow our baby to die! As my tears seep into this page, I know I may never write here again. What do I have to journal except pain, suffering, and sorrow?

Feb. 12, 1850: Our greatest horror has come to pass. After 52 days of unbearable agony, our darling child was taken Home on Friday, February 1, 1850, aged 3 years, 10 months, 18 days. His little throat became paralyzed and the rest of his body soon followed, leaving his adoring heart no room to beat. As it must be decreed in some supernal book of sorrows, thunderous rain beat down on the roof as the angels took him from us.

I have been alone in my room since his passing, with the curtains tightly drawn, and Abraham insists that I quieten my remorse so as not to frighten Bob. How can life be so unkind? My sainted mother, my baby brother, my father, my grandmother, now my beloved child. I long to be with them, yet I'm trapped in this body by the terror of death itself.

People will think me terrible, but I could not attend the interment, could not bear to watch my baby put in the ground with dirt shoveled over his beautiful face, never to be seen again.

Surely God would not take my child without allowing some way of contacting him. I read that both Empress Eugénie and Queen Victoria consult spiritualists, so I will seek out such a person who can help me through this dark period and permit me to speak with Eddy.

I have seen Abraham only through my fog when he brings my powders or slips into bed beside me. He appears smaller, shrunken, sagging. His face is etched with desolation and his skin is the gray of goose down. He speaks little except to comfort me.

He showed me the poem he wrote and had printed in the *Illinois Journal*. I admired the last line so much I have asked him to put it on Eddy's headstone, with a carved angel, in Hutchinson's Cemetery.

Angel boy, fare thee well, farewell,
Sweet Eddy, we bid thee adieu!
The angel death was hovering nigh,
And the lovely boy was called to die.
Bright is the home to him now given,
For of such is the kingdom of Heaven.

Feb. 18, 1850: Abraham fixed eggs and flapjacks for breakfast, then lifted me from the bed, forced me into a robe, and carried me to the table. "Eat, Mother; we have to live on," he pleaded, his own loving spirit in deep hypo, his ashen brow lined with creases that will never vanish. As he settled me back into bed afterward, we found passion in our grief and were able to finally break through the heartache we held inside. Our physical release somehow freed a little of the torment as well.

Feb. 28, 1850: Abraham has returned to work with an intensity I've never seen. Lincoln-Herndon has so many cases that they can hardly file the necessary paperwork. He is working at this pace to avoid his sorrow, but his absence and silence only hurt me more severely. He leaves wordlessly each morning, often ignoring his breakfast completely. After supper, he lies on the floor and studies by candlelight, sometimes till dawn. He has read and reread the statutes and books of practice, devoured Shakespeare, and analyzed Euclid so diligently that he can demonstrate all the propositions contained in the six books.

He doesn't mention his agony to me and yet he walks the dogs several times a night, shovels the first flakes of snow, pounds the carpets on the line for hours at a time, and chops wood as though we might never see another tree. *Godey's* says women suffer more when separated from loved ones, but it may have been wrong.

For my sorrow, I browse the stores, sampling the edibles and feeling the various textures available in cloth, clothing, and even household items. Abraham never sees the trifles I purchase; I simply put them on the shelf for later use. When he asks if I ran up bills, I usually say no.

Mar. 10, 1850, Eddy's birthday: I made his favorite chocolate cake and left it on the counter. Then I went to town and bought a bolt of soft white Spanish silk. In fact, I purchased all there was so no other lady in Springfield can copy my designs. Sister Ann's husband, Clark Smith, agreed to defer payment again until extra money accrues. How lovely to have merchants in the family! The silk is wrapped in paper and hidden under the bed. When I am most lonely, I pretend the roll is Eddy and sing to it. It's comforting to hold the downy bundle in my arms.

Abraham kindly went to church with us this morning. It would have been embarrassing to attend so soon without him. He didn't complain at all—just dressed in his black suit and hitched Old Buck to the buggy. The congregants were delighted to see him, and few noticed that he slept through the service.

Afterward, we talked about Eddy's death for the first time. He said, "Mother, you believe even more than me in God's goodness. The Almighty's purposes are perfect and must prevail, and it ain't our place to understand them. God notes the fall of a sparrow and numbers the hairs on our heads, and He won't forget us if we trust Him. Eddy's had a joyous meeting with loved ones galore, up where the rest of us will someday join them."

Hearing him speak so surely about Eddy's redemption and our eventual reunion has slightly unstrained my soul. I will try to rally for his sake.

Mar. 13, 1850: Abraham has taken a small interest in congressional happenings again, but only because Henry Clay has started a vigorous debate in the Senate. Back in January, Clay submitted a compromise bill, trying to contain the secession threats and stop the slavery issue once and for all. Since then, John Calhoun and Daniel Webster have joined the fight. They are being called the Big Three.

These men are not strong enough to be our principal paladins. The papers say Clay is dying from consumption, just like Eddy, except he has already lived 70 years longer. Calhoun is so ill he can't even read his own speeches. Webster himself appears apparitional as he says, "Peaceable secession is an utter impossibility. Your eyes and mine are never destined to see that miracle. Who is so foolish as to expect to see any such thing?"

How I wish the American people would divest themselves of these relics and elect younger, more energetic representatives who could light fires under freedom and democracy. Representatives like the once-fiery Abraham Lincoln. He could chop wood for the Senate stoves and keep the entire Congress warm in winter!

Mar. 31, 1850, Easter: Odd that Easter falls in March when the weather is still so winterish. I miss seeing Eddy giggle over eggs and bunnies, but Bob enjoyed the day. Abraham went to church with us, and is gaining high regard for Rev. Smith, even discussing his own depression with the minister. He prefers to talk with Smith rather than me, fearing, I suppose, that I couldn't bear to talk about such matters at length. He may be correct, though I keep silent. We've invited the Smith family for supper next week. Perhaps he can change my dear husband's fundamentalist skepticism.

Apr. 1, 1850: I am not in control of my mind. Grief comes unexpectedly crashing over me like a tidal wave, leaving me broken and unearthly. Eddy beckons at my door as though he wants me to join him. All I have left is the small lithograph we had made in late '47. It sits next to my bedside so I can blink at his little face as I pray for sleep. Even in the darkest night, I can see his smile. What will become of this woefulness is impossible to divine, but I will survive. I only wish the rain would stop.

Apr. 5, 1850: We hired a black woman named Mariah Vance to come on alternate Mondays and help with the laundry and housekeeping. She once did the cleaning in Abraham's law office. She reminds me of Mammy Sally, which warms my heart. Even Bob likes her and her son Billie, who is about the same age.

May 15, 1850: I am again with child! It's a sign that Eddy is returning, and Rev. Smith says the Lord works in strange ways to end sorrow. Though we've prayed for a girl, this child will be a boy—Eddy coming back to us as quickly as he could. Abraham begs me not to believe our son is returning, but I know it's true. He says I'm in the family way because he consoled me so ardently, and because I so often wanted him beside me for comfort. But I am assured because I received the confirmation on a wonderfully sunny day, with just enough breeze to keep the gnats away. No rain, no thunder—only joy!

June 1, 1850: I employed a live-in maid to help until the baby comes, a nice 18-year-old Irish girl named Catherine Gordon. Bob seems to like her quite well and is on his best behavior when with her. It's harder to hire domestics now. They prefer to operate sewing machines in the new clothing manufactories. Having a career is more acceptable now, and it must be rewarding to make your own money. Perhaps I could also find employment there? No, I'm busy enough.

June 15, 1850: I visited the Lincoln-Herndon Law Offices today for the first time. A package arrived at home that I believed Abraham might need, so I strolled over. The office is on the 3rd floor of the Tinsley Building on the square opposite the State House, within a stone's throw of the capitol, the post office, and all the courts.

I battled spider webs and flies as I climbed the creaky stairs and walked down a dark hallway. When he heard my knock on the glass pane, Abraham said absently, "Come in then." Thank Heaven it was my husband's voice rather than Horrible Herndon's.

When I entered the room, I collided with unexpected disarray. (Abraham later said that Herndon does the cleaning.) The room's centerpiece was a T constructed from a long table and a shorter one turned in the opposite direction. Both were covered with faded green baize, looking rather like ancient billiard tables in an awkward battle position. Two dingy windows looked into a small, unmanicured back yard. An unpainted 5-shelf pine bookcase, containing about 100 law volumes, filled the space between the windows, and a larger bookcase covered much of a perpendicular wall, its doors opening out into the room. There were books on most every other flat space in the room. In one corner sat Abraham's old secretary with overflowing pigeonholes and a half-open drawer. A ragged sofa, a rusty stove, and several wooden chairs sat haphazardly around. I could see little visible order to anything in the room.

Abraham's silk plug hat sat on a stool, upside down, with his bankbook and sheaves of paper flowing from its insides. That hat is his desk and his memorandum book. I remember the time he had to apologize to another lawyer for failing to answer a letter. He explained, "When I received your inquiry, I put it in my hat, as is my custom. I bought a new hat the next day, set the old one aside, and lost sight of your letter for a time."

Next to his hat lay an envelope of money indicated as "Billy's half." Their bookkeeping system never fails to astound me.

This is what our home would look like if I would allow it! Have I taught this man nothing? How will he ever learn to keep the whole country organized? I suppose that will be my task. Perhaps, as Benjamin Franklin said, it's best to keep your eyes wide open before marriage, half shut afterward.

June 20, 1850: With Abraham out courting this week, I have begun remodeling the house for Eddy II's arrival. I'll add a small bedroom and another pantry. Catherine sleeps in the attic room, and Bob needs a room of his own for friends to stay the night. I'll also add a brick retaining wall out front and a stone walkway to replace the dilapidated wooden one. I bought wood stoves for the parlors and hired a man to install wallpaper in the sitting room. Though my negligent husband seldom notices changes, surely even he won't be able to ignore bright blue flowery wallpaper!

Abraham allowed no money for the remodeling, so I used the $1500 Father left me. Abraham would never deny me use of Todd money!

July 4, 1850, Independence Day: I finally feel well enough to seek daylight. One of those damned headaches has had me on my back for many days, and the child is moving forcibly. I'm easily alarmed and my heart flutters for no reason. I can barely doze through the perspiration drowning my bed, leaving me flipping and turning like a flounder on dry land. The storms of the past week caused heightened nervousness and Abraham rushed home more than once to comfort me. Now, as he readies in Chicago for a state Supreme Court case, I can turn only to medication to ease my nerves. I have taken all the doses of paregoric and laudanum Uncle John left and will soon need to ask Willie Wallace for more.

As if one could truly be calm amid all this talk of secession and war. The newspapers from Washington, NY, Charleston, and Richmond predict the unspeakable. I've also read about compromise, but who is strong enough to deliver it? Henry Clay? Daniel Webster? John Calhoun, who urges a southern convention? Horace Greeley, who urges secession but claims to speak for the north? Is no one left in Washington who will fight against southern independence?

The Senate has defeated Clay's compromise bill, as President Taylor requested. Passage would have meant sure victory for Clay as President in the next election, but now it's moot. Taylor's act showed his true Whig colors — transparent.

July 10, 1850: Does death have no end? President Taylor has passed away in the White House, reportedly from overeating on the Fourth. The Vice President, Millard Fillmore, has taken command, and the upcoming election will be a free-for-all. The good news is that Abraham was invited to deliver Taylor's eulogy in Chicago, so some benefit has come from his being there. We have another opportunity to impress the legislature with his oratory and wisdom. Dear God, please let him shine!

Aug. 1, 1850, Bob's 7th birthday: My absentee husband is finally home after two weeks in Wisconsin — just in time for Bob's day. I sense he is overworking himself to avoid his disappointment in the world around us. He efficiently hides his thoughts and intentions from others, but he can't veil himself from me. We're alike, we think as one. Even when we're at odds, he listens to my opinions and I seek his counsel. When my head aches, he holds me until I sleep or am calmed. When he drags his stooped body from room to room as though lost in his own home, I make strong black coffee and rub his cold feet until he finds his way again.

"Work's a cure for sad feelings," he says when I ask why he spends so much time away. A cure for him, perhaps, but what about his wife and son? Often I summon his young law apprentice, Gibson Harris, or Fanny's nephew, Stephen Smith, to stay with us. A male presence eases the anxiety Bob and I feel in the dark evenings alone. I worry constantly for unborn Eddy II, for those who have passed over, and for those still living as well.

Aug. 5, 1850: I ran from the house today to avoid yelling at Bob again. He receives enough scolding. Though not cuddlesome, he is our first-born and deserves to be loved. At 7, he's quite a young man and insists on wearing his finest garments whenever others will be present. I expect he inherited this peculiarity from me, so I wish he had more fine clothes to wear. Most of his breeches are patched and I can hardly keep his pantaloons in knees. I sense he's embarrassed at school where many of the children are more affluent. He'll be a discriminating gentleman one day like the Lexington Todds, and if he would only apply himself scholastically, we could have another politician in the Lincoln family. He prefers watching the stars to studying.

Sept. 1, 1850: President Fillmore has saved the nation! He has overruled President Taylor's veto of Henry Clay's compromise bill and declared in favor. According to the proposal, Texas will relinquish the disputed land back to the US—in return for $10 million! The other territories—New Mexico, Nevada, Arizona, Utah—will be organized without regard to slavery. The slave trade will be abolished in DC, though slavery itself will still be permitted. California will be admitted as a slave-free state. But—the worst part—the Fugitive Slave Bill has been included, requiring citizens to assist in recovering runaways. This addition is a high danger to all negroes, whether free or slave, and amounts to government endorsement of kidnapping. Men will more willingly enslave others where there's money to be made. They say Mrs. Fillmore urged her husband not to sign the bill, but she apparently doesn't have much influence.

Fillmore asked Stephen Douglas to chair the compromise movement. I know Stephen helped create the bill, but how is he qualified to hold the Union's fate in his pudgy little hands? If he manages to get New Mexico and Utah admitted without causing secession, he'll be the most popular man in the country. How could he have gone so far when we're still in Springfield in a dingy office with Horrible Herndon? Bah!

Nov. 4, 1850, our 8th anniversary: I miss my husband. He's staying very busy, having been away 165 days already this year. On the long weekends when he can visit with us, he goes to his office every day and occasionally even sleeps there, being too tired to walk the three blocks home. He refuses to talk with me about a Senate run. Why has he given up? We've beaten Stephen before and we can beat him again! Then we could finally have a real family life.

Nov. 28, 1850, Thanksgiving: We did no entertaining today, which pleased Abraham. He bought a pumpkin pie at Dickey's and covered it with ice cream he and Bob cranked outside in the freezing rain. They were happy to be out of the house because of my surliness. The continual headaches and nausea make it hard to be amicable. I try to make my mind control my mouth so I won't speak before thinking, but usually without success. Abraham says my tongue is the part of me that works "fastest and mostest." I throw myself on his amiable nature, knowing my shortcomings will be forgiven. I said to him today, "Will this pregnancy never end? It seems to be taking longer this time."

He replied, "A woman watches her pear tree day after day, impatient for the fruit to ripen. If she attempts to force the process, she might spoil both fruit and tree. But if she patiently waits, the ripe fruit soon falls into her lap."

The man has a story for everything. I believe he meant patience is a virtue, but I wonder. Perhaps it is true that things come to those who wait, but only the things left by those who hasten!

Dec. 12, 1850: Goodbye, Diary. I sense that next year will be tumultuous. If war comes, my family will fight for Kentucky, but we'll fight for Illinois. My brothers will be battling against my cousins and uncles, and our lives will be torn asunder. But we'll soon be parents again and perhaps, in our joy, we can overcome our pain from the past and our fear of the future.

<u>Dec. 13, 1850, my 32nd birthday:</u> *"Mrs. Lincoln, the children are here," said the White House clerk in my dream. He opened the door and 12 youngsters of varying ages came bounding in, all yelling and laughing.*

"Stop!" I bellowed, and they came to attention. "You live in the Executive Mansion and must behave as ladies and gentlemen at all times. Bob, you are supposed to be watching them."

"Yes, ma'am," Bob said as he stepped forward. "But there are too many, and Billie is black. I know you're the First Lady, but must you keep spitting out Presidential babies? Most women produce one at a time, but you never do anything small. Can't we send some of them to Africa or Bogotá? You always say African children are hungry, so these little terrors would fit right in."

I stamped my foot and pulled my face into a threatening grimace. "Where is your father?" I asked.

Bob gave me the strangest of looks and his breath caught in his throat. "Father is dead. Have you forgotten again? Have you been at the paregoric?"

I began to scream, "Noooooooo! You lie! He's alive! Why are you lying?"

I woke to another birthday, and the mirror confirmed that I'm larger than any human should be. I can't even see my feet! It seems like a whale has taken residence in my body and I'll never be able to walk again. But it won't be much longer before my beautiful Eddy will return to my arms. It is predestined. Much to my amazement, Abraham rented a pew at the First Presbyterian Church as a special gift to me. He hasn't agreed to join, says he "can't quite see it," but this is a first and fine step in that direction. And he's very much alive, thank Heaven!

Willie Wallace continues to come every day and frequently stays into the night. He's concerned about this birth and asked to deliver the child himself. I did well without a doctor during the last two, but I agreed and am secretly pleased. I would not have asked, but will feel much safer for the baby and myself. Willie's presence will also comfort Abraham, who has become very jittery.

Dec. 25, 1850, Christmas: Our gift this year is from God. Just as I predicted, a beautiful boy arrived on Saturday, December 21, 1850. I expected Abraham to finally ask for the name of Joshua (or, Heaven forbid, Speed), but he requested that we choose William Wallace or James Smith—a dedicated doctor or a devout minister. After much discussion, we've named him William Wallace Lincoln, because Fanny's husband is such a dear friend to us both and gave such loving care throughout this ordeal. The boy will be called Willie; I long ago stopped asking that our children be called by their formal names.

It was a difficult birth, and I felt more relieved than embarrassed when the screaming infant was pulled from me. Dr. Willie continues to gauge us both daily.

Baby Willie is a beautiful, responsive little boy whose sunshine has already begun to ease the pain in our hearts. He does uncannily resemble Eddy, but Abraham won't allow me to mention it. I'll be confined to bed for a time longer, but my family celebrated this day beside me.

Jan. 20, 1851: Abraham's father has passed away at the age of 73. I regret not meeting Mr. Lincoln, but Abraham never deemed it important. A letter from Abraham's stepbrother last year reported that Mr. Lincoln was ill, but then we received another that he had recovered, and then another describing illness again. Abraham said the claims were imaginings of his wayward sibling and, even if true, the reunion would be more painful than pleasant. At any rate, because of Abraham's crowded calendar this month (including three Supreme Court cases), we won't attend the services. He says we might visit his stepmother when time allows and I am healthier. I have been feverish, brought on by an infection in the torn birth canal, and the chloral hydrate causes me to sleep a great deal.

Feb. 1, 1851: Abraham believes my current bout of hysteria arose because of this date: the first anniversary of Eddy's death. He rocked me and Willie in his lap as he said, "I know something about black moods myself, and I loved Eddy as much as you did, but you have to control yourself. You've got two other sons who need you, and you ought to be pleasant around them. Your bursts of rage and crying ain't a good atmosphere for the tykes. I've learned to cope and forgive you, but our boys and the help don't understand. I know you can't control your moods and don't mean any harm, but you've got to get a grip on yourself or lose everything you love."

Yes, he's a wise man. I'll never forget the angel child who was so much a part of both his parents, but Willie has filled the void, and I must remember how blessed we are to have this new boy. He is beautifully endowed, sweet natured, and a near replica of his father, and I predict he will be very bright.

Feb. 9, 1851: We went to church this morning, and afterward had a lovely carriage ride in the winter sun to an Episcopal fund-raising lunch in the Supreme Court. I baked a sweet cake filled with sugarplum jelly to sell. Then we attended an evening ball at the courthouse. I couldn't dance, but the atmosphere was invigorating.

Abraham goes to church with us practically every Sunday now when he's home. The minister used to exclaim with delight over his presence, and now he exclaims with worry when Abraham is <u>not</u> present. Did God take Eddy to make religion a part of my husband's life? That doesn't seem quite equitable, but it's possible.

Feb. 17, 1851: After supper tonight, we went to see the Christy's Minstrels show. What a loud, laughing, gay event! The music was spectacular, the humor enough to make us laugh immoderately. I'm still singing *Nelly Was a Lady.* Abraham said it was his best time since Eddy's passing.

Feb. 22, 1851: I'm still abed much of the time, leaving Catherine or Mariah to prepare most meals and attend to Bob. I roused myself enough to visit with Bob's teacher this week, however. Bob has been fixating on a murder case in Boston, and said Mr. Esterbrook was teaching the pupils about the trial and the upcoming hanging. The tutor we previously employed would never have planted such thoughts in a young boy's mind!

"Women know nothing about such things," Esterbrook said when I spoke with him. My God! Men hide from educated women as though we had the plague. Women are supposed to only cheer and solace, strengthen and caress men. Bah! Women have made great strides in recent years, becoming stenographers, professional seamstresses, authors, poets. I sense that a woman will even sit in the President's chair someday! How will Bob ever become learned and fair-minded if the institutions won't teach him right?

The little rascal shows much resistance to learning anyway, and Esterbrook needs to be more forceful for Bob's own good. He's quite smart enough, just disinclined to apply himself to such matters as sums and letters.

Apr. 20, 1851, Easter: All the Lincolns dressed in their finest and attended church services today. In the evening, we all went to see the Robinson Family in *The Dumb Belle*, a comedy so youthfully produced that even Bob liked it.

May 21, 1851: Abraham has agreed I can take the boys and visit Betsy at Buena Vista next month while he's gone! Bob's memories of the Todd summer home are so fond that he too is counting the days. We'll leave on the 25th and stay through June. Must go, there's much packing and arranging to do!

July 1, 1851: Home from our long trip, tired and happy to be back in our own beds. But we all had a grand time! Betsy kept the house filled with roses and other garden flowers—a luxury we seldom have in Springfield. We must depend mostly on wild flowers if we have them at all. She had so many roses I could wear them in my hair every day. It's been a long while since I had money enough to weave roses in my hair!

Betsy and I spent hours in conversation about life, death, memories, loved ones, politics, slavery. We have finally become friends. We cried together and embraced each other tightly when we visited Father's grave.

I wrote down Old Chaney's biscuit recipe because it appalled him that Mariah can't make biscuits or corn bread. I doubt the recipe will help much, however, as it consists of "a pinch, a little bit, some sweetening to taste," and so forth.

Little freckled Aleck has become even more Todd than before, quick tempered and prankish. He and Bob were inseparable for the entire month. He taught Bob how to ride a pony, which terrified me because of Bob's poor eyesight. They romped with the dogs and goats, slid down the icehouse roof, and tried to out-act each other in every play plot they could dream up. Bob took his new checkers set with him, and they played every day. Now he's determined to outwit his father at the game. He could more easily bail out the Potomac with a teaspoon!

Abraham is delighted to have us here again. He picked up Bob and Willie and swung them around until they were dizzy. He dangled me a few times as well! I don't believe he has changed his apparel since we left, and Mariah says he has been dining in his undershirt—when he bothered to eat at all. How can such an independent man be so dependent on a little wife like me for sustenance, clothing, grammar, and manners?

While we were away, he gained an important new client: the Alton-Sangamon Railroad. On their behalf, he attends legislative sessions and reports on any railroad bills introduced. Because of this, he won't be going to the circuit courts this fall, and will remain at home until year's end! We've never been together so long in one continuous period. What if we find we don't like being together?

July 4, 1851, Independence Day: Bob and his friends put on a short minstrel show this afternoon for any interested parties, and received much applause at the end. Perhaps he'll become famous after all. And acting is a good trade for a politician. In fact, his father could learn a thing or two from Bob about playing a role!

Jenny Lind, the famous Swedish Nightingale, sang at the Independence Day celebration. I never imagined anyone could sing so beautifully—like a songbird! We're still humming her tunes, and Bob is singing them loudly, though no one can remember all the words. We also watched a singing group called the Ethiopian Serenaders, consisting of some incredibly beautiful negro women. We attempted to introduce Bob to them, but he hid behind my skirts, too shy to even say hello.

In Washington, President Fillmore laid the first cornerstone of the new Capitol and Daniel Webster delivered the dedication. Fillmore is doing an excellent job and I have become a great admirer.

Aug. 1, 1851, Bob's 8th birthday: His eyes are looking better, as though he may outgrow the condition after all. He's not happy in school, however, because the children call him names such as "cockeye" and "sissy." He has the Todd sensitivity to criticism. I continue to force him to peep through keyholes as Uncle John recommended. It seems rather silly, but Uncle says it will help in time.

Abraham told him, "My father used to say to me, 'Boy, if you get a bad bargain, hug it the tighter.' Ain't nobody can cause you to be unhappy unless you allow them, and your happiness don't depend on what other folks say. You've got a good mind, Bobby. Use it to help yourself and stop worrying about the others. Always remember that your resolution to succeed is more important than any other thing."

In addition to being teased, Bob says he's bored at school and has more interesting things to do. I've told him many times that he'll never be able to live well unless he obtains an education, but he seems to believe, even at this early age, that his Todd heritage will provide for his welfare and future. I regret that we let him spend so much time with the family last year. Had I envisioned what would be made of it, I would have thought better. A child must never feel entitled!

Abraham is more restless since taking the railroad position. In the evenings, he will often go to the Supreme Court library where the lawyers and legislators congregate. I hate being alone and am hurt that he would rather be with them than with me after the boys have gone to bed, but such is life.

Nov. 4, 1851, our 9ᵗʰ anniversary: We went to the theatre to see *Maid of Munster* and then celebrated in our most favorite way after the baby went to sleep. How I could question our happiness in being together every night is a peculiarity now. I forget that sometimes my precognition teases me with untruths. Our love life and our social life are as fine as they've ever been. Yes, I believe Abraham misses the circuit and is lonely for his comrades, especially in October when all the lawyers were traveling. But the railroad is a secure client and the money is welcomed. I am again crusading for the idea of Congress, but he's not eager. He has said more than once, "I ain't electioneering again, Mother. Just get yourself secure with my decision and leave it alone, dammit."

We hear rumors of Stephen Douglas for President in '52, but still Abraham won't fight back! I'm so frustrated with his lack of political drive! But I "ain't" giving up, Father, so just get yourself secure with my decision!

Nov. 27, 1851, Thanksgiving: Winter is forcefully making herself known. Snow and ice, ice and snow. Still, spirits are high in Springfield. Within the last three weeks, we've attended a grand fête almost every night, and some two or three are coming off this week. Abraham says we socialize too much and he will gladly see the season end. The boys, however, love the flavored ices we make with the snow to serve our guests and they enjoy seeing the fine horses and gowns.

Dec. 21, 1851, Willie's 1st birthday: Willie is fatherless on his special day, as I was on my day last week, and his eyes search the chairs for the man he loves so dearly. He's crawling now and remains a lovely, peaceful child, though he has been in bed for three days with colic. Abraham should be home tomorrow or the next day, at least in time for Christmas. These periods without him seem longer and longer. In his absence, I went to the Provision Store and purchased two pairs of shoes, a deep rose knitted shawl, and four pairs of gloves in white, cream, black, and pink! Shopping eases my loneliness. I love to hold the wares to my cheek and smell their newness. I regret my small fibs to Abraham about the amounts owed, but it never seems wise to open up.

Dec. 25, 1851, Christmas: I bought tickets to the Washington's Birthday dance in February, which will be held in the new ballroom over the post office! Abraham was bothered that I purchased ball tickets without knowing whether he will be at home. Silly man, that is exactly why I did it—to assure his presence! The county courts don't even meet in February. Does he think I don't know the circuit schedule?

Jan. 4, 1852: A lovely supper here on January 1st with 15 favorite couples. We hadn't seen many of these friends in a coon's age! Many had not met Willie yet and were impressed with his beauty and intelligence. We served barbecued beef, pork, and mutton; vegetables from my own garden, including roasted peppers; fruit plates; and desserts galore. Even Abraham over-indulged in the offerings. The Lincolns are entertaining in style again!

Feb. 1, 1852: To commemorate Eddy's passing, the boys and I joined First Presbyterian Church today. Abraham won't join yet; he's a strong-willed man. He believes in God, but has his own interpretation of the Word, and such version sometimes disagrees with the Scriptures. He says he can speak directly with God and doesn't need a minister to intervene. Though he respects Rev. Smith and has learned from him, he asserts that even Smith can't tell him what the Lord looks like, says, or thinks. Heresy? Even the minister agrees he may be right. Abraham says he frequently talks to God when he's riding from town to town, and God guides him about where to go and what to do. I wish I had someone to guide me. My strength is my own. Oh if only Mother were here to console and advise me. Why did she have to go so early? The hole in my heart will never heal.

Feb. 3, 1852: I'm still pushing Abraham to actively seek the Presidential election this year. If he's ever to do it, now is the time, because the Whig field is weak. He is stubborn on this point, and says the Whigs will nominate him if they want him—without any politicking. He doesn't understand that people need to be told what they want and need. If we don't make clear what Abraham can do for them, they will elect a weaker man, which will allow the Democrats to finally elect Stephen Douglas. I could not bear that after all these years of planning.

Stephen has come far in the last several years. Somehow he's become the Democrats' foremost leader at only 39 years old! He owns a mickle of land in Chicago—more than any other citizen, I suspect. The locals talk about his giving 10 acres to the University of Chicago—free! He rides in private cars on the Illinois Central, and the businessmen who want a railway to the Pacific cater to his every desire. If Stephen makes it to the White House, Abraham—who is far superior in intelligence, wit, and kindness—will be humiliated! I will not allow him to be second again!

Feb. 12, 1852, Abraham's 43rd birthday: Having taken a case in Supreme Court, Abraham will receive only a long love letter on his birthday. He promises to be home for the ball, but we will see. The boys miss him as much as I. Bob is still displeased with school, and Willie is sick again with colic. Being both mother and father is difficult, but living alone so much does at least give me time to visit my favorite stores and keep abreast of the latest styles in clothing and home necessities. For the upcoming ball, I made a gown from the white Spanish silk under the bed, with pink and yellow brocaded flowers scattered in garlands. I love the feel of it! I bought a headdress and covered it with white silk, then added peacock feathers. Very nice indeed. New eardrops from Mansk's to match, and my pink kid gloves. Surely Abraham will be proud of his wife and happy to be home for the festivities!

Feb. 14, 1852: I could no longer sit like a dowager with two children and wait for my moody husband to appear, so I entertained the Bodleys last night. When I tell Abraham about entertaining alone, he smiles absently and says, "Good, Mother, good; you need some company." Does he truly not understand that it's <u>his</u> company I need? Does he see nothing around him? Does he have the company of other women on his travels? The knowledge of such would kill me, but I often wonder.

Feb. 16, 1852: Abraham rode in late this afternoon. He was dirty and stank so bad that I sent him to the tavern for a hot bath. His clothes are still soaking in the washtub, including his old carpetbag. He obviously hasn't been immersed since he left, so my suspicions of other lovers are surely unfounded.

He also had a strange buffalo robe in the buggy. When I asked, "Where did you get the robe?" he looked at the garment like it had only just appeared in his hands.

"Well," he stammered, "I don't rightly remember. I vaguely recall a friend, maybe Henry Villard, telling me I was a damn fool for riding in a short overcoat on a snowy day. He must have lent it to me."

I shook my finger at him. "And why were you riding with the top down anyway?"

"I don't know, Mother, just never got around to putting it up, I guess."

So I'll probably soon have a husband fully laid up in bed, coughing and sneezing like the old coot he is. Even after all these years, I don't understand why he covers so much of the circuit. Other lawyers have trimmed their territory, begun to ride trains instead of buggies, and head for home after court rather than waiting till the next day. Other wives tell me that long absences no longer occur. Abraham savors being away from home. He loves his family, but he loves his work just as deeply, and he told me long ago that he was a wanderer.

Feb. 26, 1852: A spectacular evening at the Birthday ball, and the three nights after were even better. Abraham has lost none of the youthful drive and strength he had when we married. He's as handsome and virile as ever before. I still shiver when I think about his long bare legs. And when I close my eyes, I can see him leaning over me on his elbows, his hair soaking in perspiration, his breathing fast and gasping. Even mentioning it now makes me weak.

He did notice my beauteous new silk dress, but I fibbed that the material was on sale. I looked lovely, if I may be so bold. Wore my hair parted in the center and pulled back with a gold chain looped through the thickness at my nape. The very latest style!

Mar. 22, 1852: Abraham has left in his rickety old buggy for a 10-week circuit ride. I should be accustomed to it by now, but I always try to change his mind. "Why not let Herndon go?" I asked at breakfast. Apparently Herndon wants to be home with his family, but Abraham would rather be staring at a horse's behind! Damn them all!

Apr. 11, 1852, Easter: The lads and I attended services with the Francises. We took a long ride after church and then had a picnic on the banks of the Sangamon. They are happy Abraham is doing so well and are boggled at my disappointment that he refuses to seek office.

"Mary," Eliza said, "you expect too much. Abraham is a fine man and he works hard to give you a good life. You have a nice home, two handsome boys, and a husband who loves you and would never be unfaithful. You share all the same interests, except perhaps living in the Executive Mansion. Why are you never satisfied? Why must you nag him so?"

Fine questions, I suppose, with no fine answers. Father always said diligence and perseverance would pay off. I'm persevering as diligently as the dews of Heaven, but seem to be losing ground. Where is that aspiration I saw in Abraham back in 1839? Where is the drive I sensed? Could I have been so wrong?

June 5, 1852: The early summer heat has caused a headache from which I can't recover. I've been abed for days—I can't recall how long. I feel scorching daggers carving patterns through my brain and cry out to only a ghost's reply. My heart convulses in a jagged rhythm and breaths must be coaxed out. Will I ever be free of this pain? All around me, the world is in chaos, and though my beloved husband is again in the house, I feel frightened. I'm alone in a crowded room, and crowded when alone.

Abraham and Mariah are keeping the boys away and Abraham sleeps with Bob at night, but still I can find no relief. I can't even doze—I have slept too long. Willie Wallace has prescribed more powders, but they're as useless as the Pope's bull against the comet. Eddy comes to me in the shadows and sits in my rocker until daybreak.

I suffer through this writing only to direct that, if I should die, my remains are to be clothed in the pink silk day dress in my cabinet. Abraham hasn't yet seen that one and he will like it. I want my body to remain in the open for two days and checked with a mirror before closing the casket lid. And please don't lay me to rest during a storm! I want a solid rosewood casket, plain, with a silver plate bearing the inscription, "He grieveth his beloved sheep." Yea though I walk through the valley of the shadow of death, I shall fear no evil. Death seems inviting tonight.

June 17, 1852: Stephen Douglas has been defeated for the Democratic Presidential nomination by Franklin Pierce of New Hampshire! Stephen was not even chosen as a VP candidate, though Abraham believes he would have been a better choice.

Abraham himself would be a much better choice, even if he had to become a Democrat. I said to him, "The time will soon come when everyone will be Abolitionist or Democrat. Slavery or freedom is the demarcation."

He answered, "If that time comes, my mind's made up, because I believe the question can never be compromised. Slavery's incompatible with the ideals of the American Revolution. But for now, I'll keep campaigning for Gen. Scott. It'll be a pleasure to have a Whig to look up to."

Why can't he see that the Whig Party is in its final days? While it's true that Scott is taller than Abraham, so we must all "look up" to him, Old Fuss and Feathers is a vain, pompous puppet for slavery-loving William Seward. Why won't Abraham listen when I tell him what I know from reading the papers he now only glances at? He could quickly rise to the top of the new Republican Party, and I see little difference between them and the dying Whigs.

June 30, 1852: God be with us. Our beloved Henry Clay, the Great Pacificator, passed away yesterday noon, at his home, aged 75. All the country is mourning. Stores are closed and flags fly lowered. As the *Chicago Journal* said so eloquently, "Clay's career has been national, his fame has filled the earth, his memory will endure to the last syllable of recorded time." We attended services in the Episcopal church and a memorial in the House. Abraham was asked to deliver the eulogy in Washington.

July 4, 1852, Independence Day: For me as well. I have abandoned Willie's suckling because of the lactation sore mouth he has developed. I've enjoyed the last 18 months. Nursing allowed Willie and me to become close, and permitted unrestrained physical relations with my handsome husband. Perhaps it's a myth that suckling keeps a woman from becoming fertile, but it has worked well these past years. I'll have to talk with Abraham about the many other methods of birth control mentioned in *Godey's*. Abstinence is not an option!

July 16, 1852: Abraham did a superb job of condensing Henry Clay's long, successful life. He credited Clay with holding the Union together on many occasions and praised him for his efforts in the Missouri Compromise, the 1850 Omnibus Compromise, and the American Colonization Society.

Goodbye, dear Mr. Clay. Few men can claim so many victories or such an exalted place in political history. You'll always be in America's heart. I have long loved you and know you go now to a richer reward. You were never honored for your worth on this earth as you will be in the higher realm. My mother and father will greet you with love.

Aug. 1, 1852, Bob's 9th birthday: Thank Heaven the county courts are on vacation and Abraham is here to help with Bob's celebration. I have been feeling low-spirited and experiencing stomach sickness for several days. Though I've been tempersome, my patient husband has been kind. He takes me onto his lap and hugs me till my moods vanish. But then the father bird flies away and I'm left alone again in the nest with the chicks and the chores and the memories.

Aug. 15, 1852: Very uneasy lately, and a poor wife as well. If that were not true, Abraham would be here more often. He stays away because of my humours, I know it, preferring to play handball in the square with the other men. Horrible Herndon is likely poisoning him against home and hearth!

I'm also a reprehensible mother. My boys are loud and nettlesome to the servants and the neighbors, but I can't strongly discipline them. I know too well how short a child's life can be. I seem to be losing my strength and my goals. I still want Abraham to run for office again, but I can't seem to keep those thoughts alive and excited. The summer is heavily upon us and has sapped my strength and left me restless and irritable. I should take the boys to Buena Vista where there are breezes.

Sept. 1, 1852: Now I understand my recent temperament changes and sickness. Willie Wallace has confirmed that I am with child again. I pray for a girl this time. How I would cherish holding Dolley Elizabeth on my lap! Abraham said he's pleased about this event, but his eyes are worried. Willie is not even two yet, and we have little quiet to ourselves.

I hope Abraham will take a larger parental role with this child. He wants only to play with them—in the house, in the yard, even in his office, which Abraham says annoys his partner. That's the only part I like about their unruliness—bedeviling Herndon. I've been told that he calls our boys "brats." They are not brats, though they do become a bit rambunctious at times.

Abraham says, "Now, Mother, reason will shape their character better than switching, and the cubs will grow up the way they'll grow up anyway," but I'm not so sure. Bob often needs a good switching and I've been known to deliver one, especially in cases of thievery or perilousness. But Abraham is correct that boys will be boys. I suppose Elizabeth is also correct that we don't work very hard to control them. Abraham loses his temper occasionally, but it's usually with me, not with his "codgers." If we have a girl, everything will change. We'll be <u>required</u> to live with more sophistication and elegance to teach her properly!

Sept. 19, 1852: Abraham is gone until the beginning of November, and is writing little to us here at home. Perhaps he is busy, perhaps just indifferent. He has lately had no interest in the newspapers, or Stephen Douglas' raging speeches, or even Edwin Webb's nomination for governor. Abraham was appointed to the Whig State Committee on Resolutions and asked to help select delegates to the Whig National Committee, but even those events didn't make him smile. He drags his old bones around town as though his shoulders carry the weight of the world. He doesn't help with chores or children. His left eye is frequently off balance, his skin is dry and sallow, his hands appear beaten and leathery. Old Abe indeed. I die inside to see his state, but he won't listen to my ideas. Politics was so much a part of our lives, and now that it has vanished, I have little else to offer him. The lower he goes in his aspirations and demeanor, the more he pulls away. Even discussing the new child doesn't make him happy. He seems to have lost his passion for life. For the first time ever, I was glad to see him leave.

Oct. 25, 1852: The Whigs are dead now for certain, both literally and figuratively. The great Daniel Webster has joined his friend Henry Clay in death. They are together in a Heavenly campaign headquarters discussing politics and bemoaning that they did not recognize their finest Whig here on earth. Abraham could have saved their platforms, their buttocks, and their party if only they had been wise enough to promote him.

Nov. 4, 1852, our 10th anniversary: Abraham arrived two days ago, looking drawn and pale. He's still tightly wrapped in a cloak of gloom and anger, the omnipresent sarsaparilla twig shoved deep inside his cheek. He speaks only when addressed, and appears to have been fasting since he left. His garments fairly hang on his skeleton. I know it's a feminine concern, but I worry he is losing interest in me and our marriage. I know how many women cross his path. I asked him tonight, "Am I still attractive to you?"

He patted me absently. "You are, Mother. You're a fine woman."

Nov. 5, 1852: Franklin Pierce won the Presidential election by a vast margin, with William King of Alabama as his VP. King is a bachelor who has lived with James Buchanan for 20 years or so. The papers say he's quite tubercular and being treated in Cuba. Why would they elect him under those circumstances? And Stephen Douglas has been elected to the Senate for another term. The Whigs made hardly a showing at all, carrying only four states and a paltry 42 electoral votes. I pray Abraham will now see the writing on the wall. Whiggery is developing a bad odor.

Nov. 25, 1852: I've been reviewing books for Abraham, and he proclaims to everyone that he has no need to read a book after my synopsis.

He has overcome his hypo and stopped taking his blue pills again. I've tried faithfully to push him into our preconceived destiny, but he says that what is to be is to be and nothing we can say or do can divert fate. In spite of this, I always feel better when I fight whole-heartedly to get the best of destiny, and I've done so in this case. I wanted the White House for Abraham, but my ambitions were not his, though I never guessed as much in the beginning. I only wanted the whole world to see him with my eyes as the great and glorious man he is.

Dec. 13, 1852, my 34ᵗʰ birthday: I called for Willie Wallace's assurance again today that I am truly carrying only one child! This must be the way the whale felt after it swallowed Jonah—bulky, unwieldy, unattractive, and unable to breathe easily. Do all women feel like this at some point? How my dear husband can bear to look at me is more than I can understand. He stayed at home an extra day to be here for my birthday, but has left now to try cases for a week in this horrendous snow.

Dec. 21, 1852, Willie's 2ⁿᵈ birthday: Abraham cooked flapjacks this morning, allegedly as a special breakfast for Willie. He ate his small bowl of mashed cakes with his hands; Abraham and Bob devoured the rest with spoons. To be so thin, Abraham can certainly eat a mess of flapjacks! Without my help, the only additions the chef could manage were eggs and the bacon in the icebox, but it made no difference. Later Abraham and Bob scraped away snow to make a large circle on the rear porch and played marbles for over an hour, with Willie clapping his hands after each roll. Finally, when their hands were too cold to shoot, they came inside for hot chocolate. I can't say which of the three Lincoln males is the most childlike. I hope to soon have a girl to keep me company inside the house on blustery days.

Dec. 26, 1852: We had a wonderful Christmas at home! Snow was falling, but the night sky glows with stars and a full moon. I gave Abraham the new novel by Harriet Beecher Stowe, *Uncle Tom's Cabin*. I must admit I read the book before giving it to him. I was very curious, as it's being discussed in every newspaper and parlor. The story is so realistic and truthful in its depiction of the horrors of slavery that many fence riders have fallen to the abolition side.

Mrs. Stowe writes about a black Christ lashed by a Yankee Satan, much as I saw slaves beaten in my youth. The book ends with a prophecy: "This is an age when nations are trembling and convulsed. A mighty influence is abroad, surging and heaving the world as with an earthquake. Is America safe? Every nation which carries in its bosom great and unredressed injustice has the elements of this last convulsion."

Since *Uncle Tom's Cabin*, a man named Josiah Priest has published a book entitled *Bible Defence of Slavery*, which counters Stowe's allegations. Abraham, who knows the Bible almost by heart, says the claim is bunk — there is no defense whatsoever in the verses. He still believes it's possible to have a society of equals where every man has a chance. Though he believes slavery must ultimately become extinct, he won't condone immediate emancipation because of the confusion, and possibly even war, it could cause.

Abraham presented me a dedication certificate from the new town of Lincoln, Illinois, in Logan County. Imagine having a town named after us! I'll put this document in fine gilt frame and hang it on the parlor wall for all to see. I'll also send copies to everyone in my family. We're making our mark again. Stephen Douglas doesn't have a town named after him!

Willie Wallace came by to suggest that we ask the new German surgeon — Dr. Wohlgemuth, I think — to attend the birthing. Dr. Willie said he distressed over Baby Willie's birth because he's only a pharmacist, not a surgeon. Uncle John says he would also rather have a surgeon near. Abraham has agreed; he knows how much danger and suffering occurred last time. In all seriousness, however, he ended our conversation by exclaiming, "But we'll not be naming the child Wohlgemuth Lincoln, I promise you that!"

Jan. 1, 1853: Rev. Smith came almost at dawn and stayed all day. I could hardly separate the two men so Abraham could greet our guests. Since reading Mrs. Stowe's book, he hasn't stopped talking about the evils of slavery. He has a compatriot in Smith, who has also read both books, and of course himself wrote *The Christian's Defense*. They've had many discussions that saw the sun rise about how to rid the country of this transgression. Do you suppose a Presidential ticket of Lincoln and Smith would interest the Republican Party?

Dr. Wohlgemuth also came by. He looks rather like Moses, especially in his long black coat and wig, but appears to be a kind, understanding man, and I have great faith in him. He gave me a powder that attacks my pains much better than the one I've always taken. Laudanum works wonderfully on headaches, but not on baby pains.

Jan. 19, 1853: Attended a luxurious ball last evening for Elizabeth's 40th birthday! Everyone was there: Democrats, Whigs, Know-Nothings,[7] senators, representatives, judges! I was bold enough to go even in my 6th month. I should probably stay out of sight, but I don't take well to that rule. I'll stay inside for 3 or 4 months after the birth, but to stay restricted for 2 years as Elizabeth often does is unthinkable! Whoever decided that women in the family way must go into confinement? Everyone knows how babies are conceived; it should be a secret only to the nuns at St. Peter's. Why does pregnancy have to be so solitary? It should be 9 months of celebration, but instead it's 24 months of loneliness, isolation, and worry. Birth is a normal part of life—why should I be ashamed of the love my husband and I share? Besides, Abraham has never cottoned to going anywhere by himself just because it's not "proper" for me to go with him.

Feb. 1, 1853: Has it really been three years since Eddy was taken? I can still feel his delicate little eyelashes playing "butterfly" on my cheek and hear him giggling while I bathed him in the washtub. I remember like yesterday the toy spider he put at his brother's plate. How Bob squealed! Oh Eddy, you are sorely missed!

I understand the pain President and Mrs. Pierce must be feeling. They lost their 11-year-old son recently in a train wreck. Watched him die before their own eyes. At least God's kindness allowed their boy to go quickly. They say Mrs. Pierce is devoutly religious, so perhaps she can find peace.

Feb. 12, 1853, Abraham's 44th birthday: In honor of this day, the Illinois legislature has unanimously passed a bill making the new town of Lincoln the seat of Logan County! What a special gift. Even so, Abraham spent most of the day in his office. When I complained, he said, "At 44, a man's too old to worry about birthdays. Save the celebrations for the little codgers. I have everything I need already and the money is better kept than spent."

Instead of gifts, I made one of his favorite suppers: curried mulligatawny soup, fried chicken, biscuits, and cold potato salad. For dessert, aged cheese, crackers, his favorite cake, and strong coffee. He ate like a lumberjack! Bob said birthdays are his favorite days too because of the feasting.

---

[7] The American Party, an anti-foreign, anti-Catholic party popularly known as the Know-Nothing Party because members answered "I know nothing" when asked about their platform and beliefs.

Apr. 10, 1853: We have another son, Thomas Joshua Lincoln,[8] born on Sunday, April 4, 1853. Our first son named for my father, our last named for Abraham's father and the friend he promised so long ago. It's good and proper, because the doctors tell me I will never have another.

I have suffered dreadfully since the day after Easter. My pains came too soon and lasted too long. Then Thomas refused to be easily extracted, and Dr. Wohlgemuth said the birth canal was badly damaged this time. Our last child — what a sorrowful statement. I've always wanted a daughter, but I won't question God's decision. I'll just spoil my boys even more. Thomas is a beautiful child, very fair in complexion. Definitely not his father's coloring.

For now, I'm taking several powders a day to ease the pain. Since Abraham leaves soon for a month, he asked my sister Ann to stay for a few weeks to help Mariah watch over Bob and Willie. I must sleep now, it's almost feeding time.

Apr. 11, 1853: Abraham has given Thomas a nickname, as I knew he would, but it's not "Tommy" as I expected. He says the boy looks like a tadpole — a large head on a small body — and squirms like one too. So, over my objections, the baby is being called Tad, or worse, Taddie. Ann said a big head indicates big brains. I hope that's true.

We have also noticed that he has difficulty swallowing. When he nurses, milk often flows upward into his nose. Dr. Wohlgemuth calls it a cleft palate and says the boy may have some trouble speaking. I well remember how hard school was for Bob with his eye problem, and now we have another deficiency! Why does God continue to test us?

May 15, 1853: Abraham was appointed as a special prosecuting attorney at Pekin in a rape trial. Of course, with such a fine prosecutor, the victim will be vindicated. Perhaps we'll move toward more exciting cases now. Regardless, this one will create a great deal of publicity, which will be helpful when we resume our ambitions.

Eliza and Simeon have sold the *Sangamo Journal* to EL Baker, who plans to rename it the *Illinois State Journal*. The sale is disheartening for us all, but perhaps he can do better financially than the Francises.

July 10, 1853: Abraham is home unexpectedly — until October! The weather is just too hot to sit in a courtroom all day, so cases have been postponed all across the district until the heat subsides. What a brilliant idea! Why are they just now thinking of it? The temperature in Springfield rose to over 90 degrees yesterday!

---

[8] Thomas' middle name was never actually recorded.

He brought home the news that Stephen Douglas' wife and third son have died in childbirth. God be with their souls. And with Stephen. How well I understand his grief. I will send condolences immediately.

July 20, 1853: Abraham has been offered his biggest case ever! Champaign and McLean counties are assessing the lands owned by the Illinois Central for tax purposes. The legislature granted the railroad immunity from taxation and this case will test the law's constitutionality. The railroad will pay a $250 retainer, the kind of fee NY lawyers receive! I can finish remodeling the house and perhaps buy a new buggy!

Aug. 1, 1853, Bob's 10th birthday: As a special gift, we have given in to Bob's request to leave Mr. Esterbrook's school and enter the new Illinois State University under Dr. WM Reynolds.[9] The school has four instructors, and the classes are actually divided by subject. The cost of $100 a year is quite high, but if it will help his learning, it will be worth it.

Received a letter from Betsy saying Sister Emilie wants to visit Springfield later in the year! Of course, she's expected to stay on Aristocracy Hill, but I wrote immediately that she would be most welcome here. Emilie and I have always been close, and she loves Abraham like a brother. I hope she will agree to stay with us. I predict even Bob would be pleased with that arrangement.

Sept. 20, 1853: Tad—his nickname has stuck like dried honey—is weaning, and I'm learning new ways to feed a child. I have never faced such a challenge. I have to distract him with toys and songs so he will swallow quickly and the porridge will go down into his throat rather than up into his nose. Willie helps me divert Tad's attention. He loves his little brother more than any of our boys have loved each other so soon. Bob doesn't seem to care much for his brother, but then he doesn't care much for anyone. He studies Latin and Greek at school, but hasn't learned much about friendship.

Abraham is off to finish the year's cases. With $250 already in the bank, he doesn't really need to go, but he won't hear of staying. He said, "If it weren't for my reputation on the circuit, the railroad wouldn't have asked me to represent them in the first place. This is good politicking. You always tell me it's important for the right people to know me. I'm doing that." As usual, his point is well made.

---

[9] Although called a university, this was actually the first private preparatory (high) school in Springfield. It later became Concordia College, a theological seminary.

Oct. 10, 1853: Abraham's letter reveals that the railroad case is going well and he has been working long days. The lower court decided in favor of the railroad, but the verdict has been appealed to the Supreme Court. I try not to wonder what he does with his nights.

The older boys and I are filling our time with many of the traveling entertainments now in town. We heard the Swiss Bell Ringers and Blind Tom, the Black Mozart; saw Tom Thumb at Barnum's circus; visited the picture gallery; marveled at a ventriloquist and his dummy; and watched steamboats race on the river.

In the evenings, I often leave the boys at home with Catherine so I can visit Robinson's Athenaeum with various friends. We've seen some wonderful dramatists there.

Nov. 4, 1853, our 11ᵗʰ anniversary: Abraham is with me where he belongs on our special day, and we had a great adventure this morning. Bob decided to fix flapjacks for us while we slept and serve us in bed. Instead, we awoke to howling. We ran to the kitchen and found Bob and Willie sitting in a white mess on the floor, covered in flour. Willie was holding a squirming kitten.

Here's the story Bob recited: "I wanted to surprise you and didn't want to wake anyone to help me. I found the big mixing bowl in the cupboard and the flour in the crockery. I scooped flour into the bowl, but spilled some on the floor. I must have got it on my shoes when I got the milk and eggs from the icebox. When I poured milk into the eggs, some slopped out, and in a minute, I saw that there kitten licking up the spilt milk.

"I didn't know what to do next, so I woke up Willie. When we got back, the kitty was up on the table licking in the bowl, so I pushed it away, but my hand hit the rest of the eggs and they fell on the floor. Willie and me tried to clean it up, but he slipped and got all covered with flour. When the cat tried to run off, I went to catch it and I fell too."

We stood there looking at Bob, Willie, the kitten, and the mess, and we began to laugh. I giggled myself tired, and Abraham said he believed his ribs were shaken loose!

"Are you sore at me?" Bob asked.

Abraham threw the dirty boy up on his shoulders like he used to do when Bob was young. "No, Son, we're confoundedly well pleased. You tried to do a good thing, it just didn't turn out so well. Now help us clean up this mess so Maw can make us some rightful flapjacks."

As my sisters so often say, the Lincolns' biggest weakness is the indulgence of our children.

Dec. 8, 1853: Emilie has arrived! She is so beautiful, with her reddish blond hair, deep blue Todd eyes, smooth skin, and fine features. She resembles me at her age. Bob is smitten with her and Willie follows her everywhere. She holds Tad as though he were her own child, and even his palate backup doesn't disturb her. Thank you, God, for sending such a ray of sunshine into our lives!

<u>**Dec. 13, 1853, my 35th birthday:**</u> In wonderful spirits today! Excited, happy! Feel like I could fly into the clouds! Abraham went to Arthur's on his recent trip to Chicago and bought an expansive (and expensive!) hall mirror, painted in gilt. Harnden's Express delivered it right to the front door. How the neighbors stared!

The mirror shows the reception area and our visitors to their finest. We situated it between the large damask chairs, over the calling card table. For the same area, Emilie gave me a silver china cardholder—very costly, I think. I had hoped for a piano, but it's important to save for our campaign. We won't always be poor; someday we'll be able to afford anything our hearts desire.

I love Emilie! She is a true delight and reminds me of my youthful days in Lexington. We have been in a whirl of gaiety, going to the Odd Fellows Hall, the new salon in the Ives Building, and all the most respected places. We've attended parties and balls in quick succession, without Abraham to accompany us. Emilie is on display and holding up magnificently. With her in Springfield, I feel loved, unalone, and cared for. I wrap my arms around her and tell her I love her, and she responds. Abraham still doesn't understand why a response is necessary.

Since Emilie never has blue days, I seldom have them either. And because my time is filled with companionship, I'm not compelled to shop or embellish the truth of our lives, and am slowly reducing my accounts. I feel so balanced with her here. Even when we do patronize the stores, it's more to look at and feel the fabrics. She helped me pick out some material to re-cover the rocking chair cushions and to make new curtains for Tad's room, but we haven't gone onto credit.

Dec. 21, 1853, Willie's 3rd birthday: How fast time goes! Willie is a delightful child, and the brightest of all. He received an array of ball rattles, crackle boxes, and squeak toys, and he loves them all. I made his favorite cake, lemon with chocolate icing, and he pushed his little hands right into it! I do truly love this boy. I love all my family! Life is a joy!

Dec. 25, 1853, Christmas: Quite a commotion today. My sisters called on us, saying they realized the Lincolns usually go to Aristocracy Hill on this special day rather than their coming here. I believe they wanted to show Emilie how "loving" they are, and spend more time with her, but I won't question their motives today. I'm just happy to be surrounded with loved ones. With the 6 of us and the 12 of them, we were as thick as unshorn sheep in a pen.

Jan. 1, 1854: Friends galore came to call and most stayed the day. The favorite topic now is Sen. Stephen Douglas and his attempt to override the laws of history that have kept us free. Though more than half the states are now emancipated, we believe he will try to sneak a bill through Congress to force national slavery. He seems to have a magician's powers when it comes to Congress—the members fall under his spell and do what he asks. Lucky for me he didn't have that skill when we were courting.

Simeon said, in front of everyone, "Mary, you have an uncanny insight into the motives of men. Your intuitions are usually clear and strong, and you've predicted many a political outcome for us. What do you think about this issue?"

Proud to be asked, I replied, "I believe Stephen has changed for the worse since his wife's passing. I read in the papers that, by the time Congress reconvened last year, he had begun using alcohol and tobacco again and was tempersome and slovenly.

"Stephen has always believed in slavery. I've heard him say many times that he would prefer a black man only to a crocodile. I also believe he's driven by the financial opportunities of having a transcontinental railway depot in Chicago. If it's chosen as the northern terminal site, I'll bet the land will be purchased from the senator himself. And, of course, we all know the little giant wants to be the next President. A win of any kind, even if harmful to the Union, could give him that victory. I believe the people are wise enough to see that Stephen Douglas is not our friend and Abraham Lincoln could be our savior. But then, I may be blinded by love and hope."

Everyone laughed, as they so frequently did in Elizabeth's parlor when I was young and not fattened and wrinkled by age and four births. I felt appreciated again. Abraham later said he was proud of me, and I went to bed filled with happy memories.

Jan. 5, 1854: As feared, Stephen has struck again. The *Illinois Journal* reports that, as Chairman of the Territories Commission, he recommended that the Nebraska Territory be received into the Union with squatter's sovereignty. That's basically the same as popular sovereignty—the landowners will decide the slavery question. This is a mystery, because the territory is north of the Missouri Compromise line, so legally no question exists about its status. Everything north of the line has been free since 1820!

Abraham is angry about this and I'm glad to see his reaction. He's been passive and uninvolved for over a year. If Stephen's move can reheat my husband, I'll call on the senator with flowers!

"What is he trying to do?" I asked as we warmed ourselves before the fire.

"As you said the other night, Mother, this move's a result of his passion for national slavery. Douglas claims the compromises of 1850 established a new principle that requires repealing the Missouri Compromise. So all national territories would be open to slavery."

He continued, his left fingers emphasizing points on his right. "To argue that we rejected the Missouri Compromise with the new bills is no less absurd than to contend that, because we've so far chosen not to take over Cuba, we've rejected all our former additions and decided to dissolve the Union. He's saying that if I refuse to build an extra room on my house, I mean to destroy my existing house! He also says the Missouri line was only an extension of the line set by the 1787 Ordinance, so it'd be an extension of the Ohio River! I think this in itself is weak enough to prove all his claims shaky, but he says he's ready to raise a hell of a storm."

I moved over and nestled into his lap. "Why can't we just free the negroes?"

He bolted upright, dropping me on my feet. "Free them? All at once? And what next? Make them politically and socially our equals? My own feelings won't allow this. Even if mine would, we well know most white people won't."

"Is that feeling democratic?" I asked.

He turned away, but I knew from his sigh that he answered with closed eyes. "Whether it fits with justice and sound judgment ain't the sole question, if it's any part at all. A universal feeling, whether well or ill founded, can't be safely disregarded. It does seem to me that systems of gradual emancipation might be quickly adopted, but I can't figure out, as I think no wise man has figured out yet, how slavery can be eradicated all at once without producing an even greater evil to human liberty. I think it's our duty in the free states to let the other states alone. On the other hand, I think it's equally clear that we should never knowingly prevent slavery from dying a natural death. Or we should find new places for it to live when it can no longer live in the old. But I don't think it's time to worry, Mother."

He turned back to face me and, as usual, made his point with a story: "You know Father Benjamin, the old Methodist preacher?" I nodded that I did. "And you know Fox River and its freshets?" I nodded again.

"Well, once, while chatting with Father Benjamin, a young preacher said he was afraid a freshet in the river might prevent him from fulfilling his appointments. The Father checked him in his gravest manner and said, 'Young man, I've always made it a rule in my life not to cross Fox River till I get to it.'

"So," my learned husband continued with a slap of his arms to his sides, "I ain't gonna worry myself over the slavery question until the country gets to it."

Jan. 12, 1854: Held a reception last evening at home, which our friends called very agreeable. The crowd overflowed up the stairs and into the bedrooms, proving again that we need another parlor!

Abraham allowed me to spend freely on the decorations, food, and entertainment—knowing, of course, that I would be wise in my purchases. I served venison, wild turkey, and quail. No ham, no turnips! We also had cheeses of many sorts, pastries, and the most wonderful coffee flavored with hazelnuts!

Many guests talked about Stephen's Nebraska Bill and agree it's purely a bid for the White House. To my mind, pushing slavery where it has never existed and changing the intentions of the founding fathers is a mighty poor campaign strategy. Benjamin Franklin petitioned the very first Congress to free the slaves England sent here, and Thomas Jefferson began prohibiting slavery in new territories back in 1787. Now Stephen wants it to flourish! All the papers are reporting on this travesty. How far will he go?

Jan. 24, 1854: Stephen made his move yesterday by presenting a revised bill to the Senate. It divides the land into two territories, called Nebraska and Kansas, which will be admitted to the Union according to their own constitutions. The bill also stipulates, however, that the Missouri Compromise will be null and void, as though it ought never to have been! Such would allow both territories to be admitted as slave states if they wished.

This move has been like a fire bell for Abraham. I woke several times last night to see him standing at the window in his inexpressibles and bare feet, staring into his own heart. Once I said, "Father, at least put on a robe and slippers. You can't defeat Stephen if you come down with pneumonia."

I thought the comment would make him chuckle, but he had no reaction or reply. When I woke again, still before the sun, he sat in the parlor in front of a meager fire, fully clothed, with his gray shawl about his shoulders. I dressed and silently made him breakfast. Then he paced and mumbled for hours, back and forth, back and forth. He wouldn't share his thoughts, and demanded silence from us as well. Willie tried to follow behind, a tiny shadow of his noble father, with his little arms folded across each other on his backside, his head also hung toward the floor.

Occasionally Abraham muttered through clinched teeth and tightly drawn lips. I repeatedly heard the words "why," "illegal," wrong," "divisive." I understand. If Stephen's bill becomes law, the entire country will be vulnerable to slavery.

How did Stephen become so powerful? He seems to hold not only the Democratic Party, but also the entire federal government, in the palm of his hand. The papers say he has lost the extra pounds, given up drink and tobacco, and become his previous charming self. But his prior self was never charming enough to destroy our entire democracy!

Feb. 12, 1854, Abraham's 45th birthday: My husband is back on track; energy and ambition flow from his eyes! If he had possessed this political passion and fervor for the last two years, we would be in the Senate by now. We would be making law, not Stephen Douglas! His enthusiasm renews my hope that we will be involved in politics again very soon. He goes every day to the State House library to study the Constitution, the Northwest Territory Ordinance, the Missouri Compromise and its debates, the 1850 compromises, and the census returns. He has sworn to find a way to defeat Stephen's bill. I don't know how, nor does he, but I believe in him. If passion can sway, Abraham can move the world!

Clasping his hands between his knees in the posture I know so well, he said, "Even if God gave me the power, I wouldn't know what to do about the existing slavery. But I've always known that to extend it is a crime against God and man."

I applauded. "An excellent phrase, Father; write it down for a future speech. Do you really believe slavery will move north?"

He ran his fingers through his hair as if to keep his head from unconscious movement, and said, "What's to stop it? Not climate. Delaware, Maryland, Virginia, Kentucky, Missouri, and DC are all north of the Missouri Compromise line and they contain more than a quarter of all the slaves in the nation. Not boundaries. Slavery pressed itself completely up to the old western boundary of Missouri, and when part of that border recently moved out a little more west, slavery followed right on up to the new line. When the restriction's removed, what's to stop it from going still farther?"

He shook his head from side to side in spite of himself. "Slavery's profitable, Mother, for slave traders and for plantation owners. It's figured to take only a year of slave work to make up for the price paid. And, unfortunately, so long as money can be made by selling and owning human beings, they will keep on being chattel."

I detest slavery and hate that I like the zeal being created over it. I would be ashamed to admit out loud that I enjoy Springfield's current atmosphere. But people seem alive again, filled with passion—Saint Elmo's fire come to earth. I'm also reveling in the vitality of our own home. Abraham's determination brings back the days we spent together at the *Journal* fighting other wrongs. I am no longer the only one here who moves quickly and talks rapidly. Thank Heaven we finally have more to discuss than Bob's poor learning skills, Willie's animal friends, or Tad's cleft palate. We talk late into the night about important issues: slavery, the Union, independence, the future. Such conversation arouses more than political interest in our hearts and bodies. It has been too long since I felt his heat, and we're alive with ardor every night. Abraham is once again the man I married, and the future is bright!

Mar. 4, 1854: We are doomed. In spite of all the efforts to stop him, Stephen has negotiated his bill through the Senate. Hundreds of newspapers vehemently opposed it, including the three largest—*Tribune, Times,* and *Evening Post.* It was protested in nearly every city, and thousands of objection letters were sent to Congress, but it passed just the same. To our amazement and consternation, the Illinois legislature voted unanimously to back the measure, and for the first time, we're ashamed to call this state our home. I pray the House will not be as susceptible to Stephen's power as the Senate.

Apr. 4, 1854, Tad's 1st birthday: Our sunshine boy's lip may be damaged, but his eyes are shiny and his mind is quick. I made him a small red velvet ball stuffed with old crinoline material that still makes noise when squeezed just right. He loves bright colors and is thrilled with it. Bob and Willie were timid at this age, but not Tad. He shows no fear of human, animal, or insect. Even thunder doesn't alarm him. Willie is trying to help Tad learn to crawl by running faster and faster as Tad chases on his knees. They bump into the furniture and each other. It's quite a sight!

Willie Wallace says Tad's upper lip will be pinched all his life and he will probably lisp when he talks, like my brother George, but that just causes us to love him more.

Apr. 17, 1854: People all across the nation turned out yesterday for Easter prayers, and the papers report a continual rise in church attendance.

This is good. We need invocation more than ever now that Stephen's bill has passed through the House and will soon become law. How this could happen, with millions of people lobbying against it, I'll never understand. The newspapers are saying no one can stop him now; he will win the next Presidential election and our country will become a slave nation.

Abraham is circuiting this month, spreading the word that we need a strong anti-slavery Illinoisan in the Senate. He swears loyalty and promises to stump for any man who will campaign. I know who should run and wonder why he is blind to it. Only by standing face to face with Stephen as a senator can Abraham stop this dictator.

May 5, 1854: Last evening I invited for supper one of Springfield's most eligible bachelors, Ozias Hatch. I miss having an intelligent man with whom to talk and it's so nice to be attended and appreciated. I have no interest other than invigorating conversation, of course, and Bob remained in the room at all times.

We talked intensely about Abraham's chances for public office. Hatch says the new Republican Party, which he has joined, needs strong, honest men, especially those with potent oratory skills. He believes Abraham would have a good chance for the Senate in the next election if he were to switch parties, and promised to personally support us. I'm peacock proud of myself for this strategic meeting. If Abraham won't campaign for himself, his wife will continue to do so in her own way here at home.

May 30, 1854: God help us! President Pierce has signed the Kansas-Nebraska Act into law! Not only will slaves be allowed in, the Indians will be pushed out! If only Henry Clay and Daniel Webster were alive. That oratorical duo could easily make Congress see the folly of repealing the Missouri Compromise.

I thought Cassius Clay was also an orator to be respected, but the Secretary of State must believe differently. He refused to allow Cash to speak in the State House rotunda. And Democrats profess to be anti-partisan! So Cash held a public forum in Mather's Grove, and Abraham and I listened enraptured.

Afterward, I invited Cash to our home for supper. It's been too long since we saw this old friend, and he could be a strong political advisor. Though retired, he's still well known and can offer Abraham's name into many important circles.

During supper, Cash brought up the Republican Party. It has become stronger since its formal charter in February, and has already met in two conventions this year. I asked if Cash knew Ozias Hatch, and he thinks Hatch a fine man with whom to become associated. "We already have an acquaintance with him," I said. "He's been to our home!"

"Ah," Cash beamed at Abraham, "so you're already considering the Republican Party, Lincoln?"

"No," Abraham said, tilting his head toward me, "I'm being instructed to consider it. I ain't met Mr. Hatch myself, but my little wife seems to be intimate with many high political minds." How embarrassing. No, I admit it here only—I was thrilled to be acknowledged for my forward thinking!

June 5, 1854: We continue to debate the merits of the Republican Party. I have been clipping articles for Abraham to read about the powerful men who are endorsing it. The time to fall in is when the party is new. And they will need a senatorial candidate from Illinois. They will also need Presidential and Vice Presidential candidates, though we may be too newly involved for that.

"But, Mother," Abraham said, "that group itself is a johnny-come-lately. And made up mostly of abolitionists. I've never been a reformer. You know how I feel."

"Yes," I replied, "but I also know how that scene with the manacled slaves on the Ohio River steamer has tormented you since you visited Speed years ago. And how the auction in Lexington pierced your heart."

He wrung his hands together and then rubbed them down the front of his trousers. "Yep, you're right. The thought of slavery makes me miserable, but I still think abolition will cause division and likely war itself. Also, now that I'm thinking politically again, I don't want to lose the support I've worked so hard for. I reckon I'll stay with the Whigs a while longer." Stubborn old goat!

July 4, 1854, Independence Day: A grand celebration in Springfield! I know the anti-slavery men have little joy, but I believe everyone in town turned out just the same. The flag seems to have more stars each year it's unfurled.

The best news is that Abraham agreed to run for the Illinois House in the fall. Not the office I wanted, but I'll gladly settle for any active politics at this point. Also not the party I think wisest, but his mind can't be changed. He has promised to help Richard Yates run for re-election to the US House as Illinois' one Whig representative. Abraham would be happy in the Illinois House for eternity; he believes it's the highest office for which he is qualified!

Emilie left earlier in the week, because she wanted to be with Betsy again. She's a kind-hearted girl and I'll miss her terribly. Willie will also pine for her; he's learned much about the art of checkers from her wise hand. I gave her the locket Father presented to me so many years ago. I hope it will help her always think lovingly of her sister.

July 6, 1854: Woke with a violent headache this morning and could not pinpoint its cause. Then, as I scrambled eggs for breakfast, I remembered. It's the 29th anniversary of Mother's death. Each year it becomes harder to count how much time has passed since she left me, and yet I recall the day itself so clearly. I've been so busy this month that I forgot to mourn, and God reminded me with that dreadful headache. I'm sorry, Mother; it's not that my grief has lessened, only that my responsibilities have grown. I have three lively boys to attend and one large, moody husband who undergoes bouts of enthusiasm interspersed with anger and boredom. My responsibilities would be much easier if he would just stay on track! Perhaps I've pushed him too hard. Perhaps my own shifting moods and jealousies cause his anxieties. But I know his possibilities and his capabilities, and I won't settle for less.

Sept. 1, 1854: Abraham has been called to Bloomington for a case, and while there, he plans to publicly challenge Stephen Douglas to a series of debates on the Kansas-Nebraska Act. We have planned the arguments carefully, working night after night on our strategy and retorts since the courts recessed in July. We have honed his words, he is ready to roll up his sleeves and spar, and he's eager to confront this particular opponent. My Lancelot rides again!

Stephen is being hissed, booed, and burned in effigy across America. In New England, 3000 clergymen protested the Act. Churchmen in Chicago and other northwest areas have followed suit. Congregations are separating and churches are being burned. People are rioting and killing. The Know-Nothing Party, until now a small joke, has begun to attract people from other political parties who are against the Act but want to remain secret, including several longtime Democratic leaders. When asked what they stand for, members answer, "I know nothing."

Sept. 7, 1854: I'm so eager for the Kansas-Nebraska Act to be rebuked and condemned that I have written to several Democrats who are also against it. I wrote, in essence: "How painful it must be for an honest, sincere man like yourself to be urged by his own party to support a measure he believes to be harmful. I don't expect you to do anything that may be wrong in your own judgment or injurious to yourself. But perhaps you're having a severe struggle with yourself, or have already determined not to swallow the wrong. Wouldn't it be beneficial for you to state your reasons in a few public speeches and thus justify yourself? Mr. Lincoln and I wish you would." I haven't mentioned these letters to Abraham; he has enough on his mind just now.

Sept. 15, 1854: Abraham's case went well, but Stephen refused to debate and pouted as he did when we were young and things didn't go his way. He replied to Abraham, "This is my meeting; the people have come to hear me and I want to talk to them by myself." Damned coward!

Oct. 3, 1854: The fair opened today and the main attraction was to be a speech from the "revered" Sen. Douglas. Our family toured the fairgrounds early; visited the livestock and poultry exhibits; gaped at the displays of mowers, reapers, and thrashers, which look like something from another world; ate funnel cakes and ice cream; and cheered for Elizabeth's quilt in the bee. Then the rains came, as they often do on Fair Day, and the speech was postponed and moved to the State House.

We took the boys to stay with Mariah and made our way, with 2000 other citizens, into the sweltering State House, where Stephen paced across the dais. He hasn't changed much since we were swapping riddles in Elizabeth's parlor. His hair is grayer, as is mine. Even with more fullness to his body, his head still looks misplaced and too big for his frame. Perhaps <u>he</u> should be called Tad!

He still captivates an audience as purely as he did in the '40s. I understand now why he has become so powerful. People will flock to a strong shepherd even if he leads them into the flaming pits of Hell. What he has done with the Kansas-Nebraska Act is illegal and immoral. It will ruin our peace and likely destroy our Union, and we won't be able to survive in disunion. England, or worse Mexico, will overtake us state by state until we are a monarchy once again. United we can stand against other powers, divided we will fall.

Abraham said, "Nearly all men can stand under adversity. If you really want to test a man's character, give him power." We saw Stephen's character today as he proclaimed, "My message is clear: The time has not yet come when a handful of traitors can turn the great state of Illinois into a negro-worshipping, colored-equality community."

When Stephen finished speaking, to great applause and approving hoots, Abraham did something very unusual. He stood at the doorway as the crowd streamed out, imploring them to return at noon tomorrow and hear him reply. Some smiled, some hid their faces, some nodded in anticipation.

"Do you think they will come back?" I asked Abraham.

His eyes danced. "Yep, I bet they will, if just for the fun of hearing Douglas skin me in his rebuttal."

We worked on Abraham's comments after supper. He had dozens of paper scraps in his hat and even a draft of the speech itself, written back in Bloomington. We reviewed his points and syntax. I played devil's advocate and pretended to be Stephen, refuting Abraham's comments. He did well. Our major points are unfrosted: The Missouri Compromise is the only thing that has kept the states from warring with each other; slavery is morally and Biblically wrong; the Constitution and Congress have always had the right to limit slavery's extension; slavery is illegal. Must make ready for bed now — the moon is sinking and tomorrow will be a long day.

Oct. 4, 1854: An endless day. We rose after only three hours sleep and began work again on Abraham's speech. For one of the few times in their lives, the boys were not allowed to romp among the papers and pens. Bob and Willie were strongly advised to play in the barn, and oddly enough, they obeyed.

I wrote Abraham's new words, and some of my own, as he paced and spoke, his toes digging grooves in the carpet, his hands wringing in front of and then behind his torso. He rubbed his nose, ran his hands through his hair, cracked his knuckles. I wanted to take him to our bedroom and demonstrate how proud I am of his renewed energy. I wanted to taste this new passion, test its authenticity, feel it pounding beside me. But I went to work instead.

We need not have worried about drawing an audience. I believe even more than 2000 showed up, thanks to Simeon Francis' handbill and the gossip mongers. A group of Republicans was also meeting in Springfield and they came to hear the celebrated Whig orator who is rumored to have an eye on the Senate. As Abraham prepared, I met with them and secured their choice seats.

Abraham stimulated and uplifted us — as glorious as I've ever heard him. I tapped my feet as Stephen became smaller and more obscure in his seat. Gov. Matteson and Sen. James Shields (another old Democratic "friend") also seemed to shrivel as the mighty orator progressed. Abraham paced, he perspired, he mopped at his forehead with a checkered handkerchief, he combed his hair with his hands, he filled the hall with white heat. He kept his temper, even when taunted. As he discarded layers of clothing, concluding in only his shirtsleeves and suspenders, so did the men in the audience. The ladies fanned for all their lives and often squeaked "Oh" in unison. He could hardly continue over the deafening applause.

Here is a newspaper clipping quoting the essence. What is left to utter? My beloved husband said it all.

The repeal of the Missouri Compromise is wrong. Wrong in its direct effect, letting slavery into Kansas, and wrong in its prospective principle, allowing slavery to spread to every other part of the wide world where men can be found to take it.

I can't help but hate this declared indifference because I believe it's a covert zeal for the spread of slavery. I hate it because of the monstrous injustice of slavery itself. I hate it because it deprives our republican example of its just influence in the world, enables the enemies of free institutions to taunt us as hypocrites, and causes the real friends of freedom to doubt our sincerity.

I hate it especially because it forces so many good men into an open war with the very fundamental principles of civil liberty, criticizing the Declaration of Independence and insisting there's no right principle of action but self-interest. What natural right requires Kansas and Nebraska to be opened to slavery? Isn't slavery universally granted to be a gross outrage on the law of nature?

Oct. 9, 1854: Simeon Francis woke us early today with the voting results. Abraham and Cousin Steve Logan have been elected to the state legislature!

The big shock is that the Know-Nothings have elected mayors in Philadelphia and Washington, and the governor and legislature in Massachusetts, which will give them a senator. They also made a very proper showing in New York. Republicans elected the governor in Maine and carried every congressional district in Iowa and Vermont. Anti-Nebraska men elected a congressman in every Ohio district and all but 2 in Indiana. Pennsylvania elected 21 anti-Nebraska congressmen and only 4 pro-Nebraska. All in all, 70,000 votes against Stephen Douglas!

I asked Abraham after the excitement had subsided, "What will you do now about a political party? Everyone says the Republicans are absorbing the smaller anti-Nebraska parties. The *Tribune* says the 21 congressmen from Ohio were designated as Republican rather than Whig. Even Horace Greeley said he considers the Whig Party a thing of the past. And, after all, Republican <u>was</u> the name of Thomas Jefferson's party!" [10]

He grinned. "Well, Mother, if we are un-Whigged, I reckon we'll have to consider becoming Republicans."

Oct. 17, 1854: An unexpected visit today from the Republicans, almost as many as were at the State House when Abraham spoke. They came to plead with him to join, but he had left right after receiving the election returns and was today in Pekin. Did he anticipate they might call? I'll have to ask him outright.

---

[10] Jefferson headed the Anti-Federalist (or Federal-Republican) Party. It became known as the Republican Party for a time, but finally settled on Democratic-Republican Party. Jefferson was elected under this banner in 1801, as were the next three chief executives. By the time Andrew Jackson ran for president in 1828, the word "Republican" had been dropped and party members were known simply as Democrats, although they were popularly called Jacksonians.

Simeon is concerned, however. He says alignment with the new party could lessen Abraham's opportunities for the Senate as a Whig. I wonder why Simeon thinks Abraham might consider the Senate? My husband has not talked seriously with me about this option. Has he been sharing our hopes with others? Or has Simeon heard wishful rumblings from Illinoisans themselves?

Oct. 22, 1854: Cousin Steve Logan asked to nominate Abraham for the US Senate! He says Abraham is the strongest Whig voice in a decade and his recent election to the House gives him needed visibility. Was I wrong in wanting him to switch parties? No matter, nothing can stop us now! First Abraham must resign from the Illinois House and then we begin our campaign for the Senate. I will have many speeches to write now!

Oct. 24, 1854: Stephen has finally agreed to debate, probably to discredit our Senate possibilities. Abraham will leave again in the morning to follow Stephen from town to town, city to city, answering his points and convincing Illinois to strike against slavery by voting to repeal the Kansas-Nebraska Act. His ambition has fully surfaced!

Oct. 28, 1854: The Peoria paper printed the speech Abraham gave this week, after Stephen had spoken for three hours! I can close my eyes and see the way my husband sighed, shrugged his shoulders, smiled slyly, and suggested the crowd go on home for supper and return in a hour with their bellies full and their minds ready to listen for another three hours! And, as music to my ears, is the revulsion I hear for the horrible institution itself. It's not enough to be against slavery, we must be for emancipation.

Before proceeding, let me say I've got no prejudice against the southern people. They're just what we in the north would be in their situation. If slavery didn't now exist among them, they wouldn't introduce it. If it did now exist among us, we would not instantly give it up. Doubtless, some individuals on both sides wouldn't hold slaves under any circumstances and others would gladly introduce slavery anew if it were out of existence. We know some southern men do free their slaves or go north and become tip-top abolitionists, while some northern ones go south and become most cruel slave masters.

When southern people tell us they're no more responsible for the origin of slavery than we are, I acknowledge the fact. When it's said the institution exists, and is very difficult to get rid of in any satisfactory way, I understand and appreciate the saying. I surely won't blame them for not doing what I would not know how to do myself. If all earthly power were given me, I wouldn't know what to do about the existing institution.

My first impulse would be to free all the slaves and send them to

Liberia, back to their own native land. But a moment's reflection would convince me that whatever high hopes there may be in this solution, its sudden execution is impossible in the long run. If the slaves all landed there in a day, they would all perish in the next 10 days and there's not surplus shipping and surplus money enough to carry them there in many times 10 days.

What then? Free them all and keep them among us as underlings? Is it quite certain this betters their condition? I think I wouldn't hold a person in slavery at any rate, yet the point is not clear enough for me to denounce people who do.

Little by little, but as steadily as man's march to the grave, we've been giving up the old for the new faith. Near 80 years ago, we began by declaring that all men are created equal; but now, from that beginning, we've run down to the declaration that for some men to enslave others is a sacred right of self-government. These principles are as opposite as God and Mammon, and whoever holds to the one must despise the other.

Nov. 4, 1854, our 12th anniversary: Abraham is still following Stephen through the state, and his speeches are being printed in the papers and distributed over the region. The finest anniversary gift we could receive is being presented to us every day. All the papers are crying, "Lincoln! Lincoln!" He is headlined in Whig papers, Republican papers, and even Anti-Nebraska-Democrat papers. I began a scrapbook for him and am scanning every issue I can buy or have sent. My daily activities have truly changed, and I must stay politically alert and ready to assist my husband at any moment.

Nov. 8, 1854: The results have been reported. The Democrats won only 41 of the 100 congressional seats! We immediately listed all the congressmen to study. Who will back us for the Senate? Will James Shields, whose seat is the one available? No, that's unlikely after the old Rebecca duel. But will he harm our chances?

I have shared my concern with Julia Trumbull. Though her husband is also considering the seat, she heartily opposes his action. He has no chance of success, and at any rate, Julia can be trusted to keep our feminine secrets. We've been friends for many years.

Sister Emilie is coming to Springfield again, bringing her fiancé, Ben Hardin Helm, the son of a former governor of Kentucky! I'm so proud of her choice: a West Point and Harvard Law graduate who served in the Kentucky General Assembly and is pursuing a legal and political career. He's also kin to me through the Hardin family. They should be here in time for Thanksgiving!

Nov. 12, 1854: We're engaged in an agony of maneuvering for the Senate and are writing letters by the bundle, many to new congressmen, asking for support. Of course all the letters are signed "A. Lincoln," but we are collaborating and I'm writing many—this time with Abraham's knowledge! If my involvement were known, people would call me "ambitious," or even "a meddling deviant," as they call the suffragettes. I would not hurt Abraham's chances by having my role in his campaign become public, though in my dreams I am lauded for it.

I worry, however, that we're not being aggressive enough. One letter says, "It has come round that a Whig may be elected to the US Senate, and I want the chance to be the man. As a member of the legislature, you have a vote. Think it over and see whether you can do better than to go for me." Not the way I would state it! If Abraham would allow me, I would ask directly for the vote and not mention the Whigs at all. I'm also displeased with the wording of "See whether you can do better than to go for me." What degree of gumption and confidence does such verbiage show? The nation is ready for a strong leader, one who says, "I want to be US senator and will appreciate your vote!" I wish he would go back on circuit and let me finish the letters by myself.

Nov. 23, 1854, Thanksgiving: I'm thankful for so many things on this special day: I have a wise, loving, ambitious husband; we will surely soon win our bid for the Senate and move to Washington; our boys are precious and well behaved (perhaps a bit of wishful thinking); we're going to make a difference in the country; and we're finally on track to the White House!

I'm also thankful for the large fees Abraham brought in this year. One slander case brought a $3000 verdict and a bodily injury case returned a $2,000 verdict! We're allowed 10%, which of course is split with Herndon, though he does nothing to help. Thank you, God, for all your glory and blessings!

Nov. 28, 1854: What a strange feeling. I've worked all our life together to ensure that Abraham stays in an elected position, yet today I watched him resign from the Illinois House of Representatives! How odd that seemed. But it's the only way. He can't campaign for US Senate if he sits in the state legislature because that body nominates the candidate. This strategy worked for Stephen Douglas back in 1847, so it must work for us! Our designation looks promising, but we face a robust campaign. Many letters to write and people to entertain. Now is the time for shopping!

Dec. 12, 1854: Goodbye, Diary. The Lincolns are rapidly moving forward. After our hard campaign, Abraham has been recognized as the Senate favorite from Illinois. We receive dozens of letters daily from citizens and legislators who vow support, votes, even money. Lyman and Julia Trumbull are frequently here, strategizing and planning for our respective trips to Washington. Our only concern is that this contest may come to blows and bloodshed before it concludes.

Dec. 13, 1854, my 36th birthday: Between the continual parties, to which we are now thankfully invited, and our campaign, we have no time to ourselves. We have hardly time for lovemaking, which we miss in all parts of our minds and bodies. I won't complain, however; there will be time later.

Dec. 15, 1854: Unfortunately, there is still time for arguing. Abraham can get angry over the tiniest things!

Dec. 25, 1854, Christmas: Today I received one of my most desired possessions—a piano! A small Steinway upright with cast-iron frame—the kind I've dreamed about since I left Elizabeth's! It's not new, but it's in fine condition. I played tunes all day, and Abraham says I purchase some sheet music next week. My sisters came to see it and we sang together for hours, like we used to in Lexington! I'll teach Willie and Tad all the French hymns I learned at my sweet mother's knee, and Abraham says he may want to learn too! I am hugely blessed.

Ben Helm still comes to visit Emilie about once a month, and they always spend time with us. Though Ben is 23 years younger, Abraham has taken quite a liking to him. He has a sharp literary mind and a great taste for politics, and he has been an inspiration to Abraham's thinking. Ben is extremely comely: six feet tall, deep blue eyes, massive brown hair. Very handsome indeed!

Jan. 1, 1855: Much calling about today. We're electioneering now, so every moment and every handshake counts. We hosted three soirees in December, and our first political goal is soon to be achieved! Now that we're

Senate-bound, our home is always filled with highly important people—
beauteously attired beaus and belles dancing and eating (at separate times,
of course). Such a cultured way to entertain! This is the life I've dreamed
of—the Lincolns in high society. See, Ninian, I told you success would
come! We may not live on Aristocracy Hill (yet), but we're loved and
respected. No more loneliness or insecurity.

Jan. 10, 1855: We're imprisoned by a blizzard like Springfield hasn't
seen in 40 years! This is hampering us greatly, as the legislature is to
nominate its senatorial candidate next week and we're unable to campaign.
We fill our days by weighing our chances and measuring our favors. There
are 41 Democrats, 37 Whigs, and 19 Anti-Nebraska Democrats in the
legislature, and we expect the vote of most. We have 17 years of circuit court
cases behind us—surely we have the history to win.

But Abraham is concerned about Gov. Matteson's being a clandestine
candidate. He told me, "Matteson's been a prospect for a coon's age, though
he's not on the ballot. All the members round about the canal are anti-
Nebraska, but nearly all are Matteson's friends. His plan's been to privately
impress them with the belief that he's as anti-Nebraska as anybody else, or
at least could be so with the right instructions. I'm scared of his backstairs
operations. If anybody can beat us, it's Matteson." No! Surely God is finally
on our side and won't allow that to happen.

Feb. 8, 1855: We lost. Our hopes are ruined. God turned His back on us
again. Will all our successes be met with heartbreak?

We had 45 votes on the 1st ballot, needing only 51, and my spirits were
high. James Shields had 41, Lyman Trumbull only 5. Elizabeth and Emilie
sat with me (and Mrs. Matteson, smiling like a hyena) in the gallery and
held my hands with anticipation. We gained 3 votes on the 2nd ballot, but
lost 4. At the supper break, after the 6th ballot, Abraham sought me out and
said he planned to throw his votes to Lyman! My toes curled under in my
shoes and my stomach turned sour.

"But why?" I asked. "You're still leading, you can still win. Why would
a man with 45 votes surrender to one with 5 votes? It makes no sense
whatsoever! Lyman should give his votes to you! What about Norman Judd,
who claims to be your friend? Why is he voting each time for Lyman? Can't
you change his mind? We've worked too hard to quit now. You can't do
this! I won't allow it! I thought you wanted the Senate as badly as I."

He took both my hands in his, and his eyes told me I couldn't win.
"Please don't cry out so loud, Mother. Do you want the whole place to hear?
I won't win this race. Yes, it's hard to surrender my votes, and a less good-
humored man might not consent to it. I can't, however, let the whole
political result go to smash on a point merely personal to myself. I've got to

stand behind the party. At least Trumbull's against the Nebraska Bill. If we keep taking ballots like this, a Democrat will become Illinois' next senator. Do you want that? Can't you be consoled that the Democrats will be worse whipped than me?"

I fear I acted childishly by turning my back and leaving the chamber without staying for the final ballots. This forfeit reminds me of losing my promising little Eddy. Even to this day, I don't feel sufficiently submissive to that sacrifice...or this one.

With humiliation and anger, I attended Elizabeth and Ninian's "celebration" event, originally planned for the Lincolns but instead showing off Sen. and Mrs. Trumbull. Though Abraham offered his hand to Lyman, I could not do the same. I believe Julia knew of this scheme all along, even as I told her about our plans. She is no longer a friend. She's a walking corpse, a traitor, a besieger! She should not have allowed her husband to accept Abraham's offer. She should have convinced him to throw his votes to us. By not intervening, she harmed our quest. Not defeated it, I swear that, but harmed it. From this point on, the Trumbulls are invisible to me. I pray they soon discover the fate of liars and hypocrites. Damn them all!

Feb. 10, 1855: We have finally had time to discuss the election. I can hardly mention it without a handkerchief. "I still don't understand, Father. Why did we give up our votes?"

He explained again, "It was Matteson's work, as I feared. The Nebraska men weren't for him in the beginning. But when they found they couldn't elect an avowed Nebraska man, they decided to let Matteson take as many of our votes as he could, by whatever means possible, and ask no questions.

"On the 7th ballot, right after you left, the signal went to the Nebraska men to turn to Matteson. Next ballot he had 46, then 47. In the meantime, our friends, hoping to stop our bolters, had been turning from me to Trumbull till he'd risen to 35 and I'd been reduced to 15. Those 15 would never desert me unless I said so, but we couldn't prevent Matteson's election if my friends stayed on me. So I decided to strike at once, and advised my remaining supporters to go for Trumbull.

"That's the way it happened, Mother. I think you'd have done the same under the circumstances. Sure I regret my defeat, though not so much as you do, but I ain't nervous about it. I'll get back in when the time's right. I could have headed off every combination and been elected if it hadn't been for Matteson's double game, and his defeat pleases me more than mine pains me. On the whole, it's probably as well for our general cause that Trumbull got elected. The Nebraska men hate that worse than anything else that could have happened. It's their own damn fault. They had plenty of opportunity to choose between Trumbull and me, but instead forced it on me to decide between him and Matteson."

I swallowed the lump in my throat and said, "I know you're wise, and I apologize for leaving so impatiently, but politics shouldn't be a game. You were meant to win that election—you!" I went to bed alone.

Apr. 8, 1855, Easter: The entire Lincoln family went to church this morning, dressed in our finery and pretending all is well. But all is not well. Abraham is having horrid nightmares again and I wake to find him staring sightlessly out the window, his lips and arms preaching to the moon. I often have to call out several times before he wakes. Last night he dreamed about singing negroes carrying caskets up a mountain on their bare shoulders. He asked them, "Where are you going?" They answered, "Going home, Father Abe, going home." The premonitions are frightening for us both. He comes to bed very late and lies with open eyes and clinched fists because he doesn't want to dream. As a result, he's colorless and sallow. Apparitional.

We no longer talk about our future, and our physical love is negligible. People have stopped calling and we've been to no entertainment since the travesty. My headaches seldom subside completely, and Tad's speech is unintelligible. It's hard to keep our goals in sight, and I dream of falling into bottomless crevasses.

Apr. 15, 1855: Abraham has left and I've begun adding to our home again. I had to do something big or go mad! Mr. Gourley helped me secure a firm to raise our house to 2 stories, 12' high, in the new Greek Revival style. I'll add siding to match the original walnut clapboards. Then I'll create 5 bedchambers. Robert will have his own room, Willie and Tad will stay in a room together, there will be a small room for a nurse or maid, and Abraham and I will each have our own. He reads so late into the night that I'll be pleased to have his light shut away behind a door. When I'm in the throes of a headache, he's reluctant to read, or even to turn over, and I'm afraid for him to do so as well. Besides, sleeping in the same bedroom is so provincial! It denotes a lower financial class, and we can't afford to appear pinched at this point in our career, even though we may be. The rooms will adjoin, so we can easily and frequently cross the threshold.

I also bought him an oversized mahogany bed. Not the 9' bed I've always promised, but the largest I could find. For the first time in his life, his feet won't hang off the end (if he lies diagonally). He will be so pleased, and what fun we'll have in it—so much extra room to play in!

I'll create a rear parlor in our old bedroom, making a double salon, with folding doors between the rooms and a stairway to the second floor. Bob will no longer need a ladder to reach his bed, and we'll have more open space downstairs for politicking! The back stairway and enlarged dining area will absorb a good bit of kitchen space, so we will have to eat in the "banquet area" like proper people. Perhaps Abraham will now give up that disgusting habit of eating in minimal clothing.

Apr. 20, 1855: What an event today! I was speaking at the fence with Hannah Shearer about the construction, and so wasn't watching Willie for a few moments. Hearing his screams from the back yard, I ran to find him inside the privy, holding on to the seat boards for dear life. He tried to use the outhouse without assistance and nearly fell in! After ensuring that he had not ingested lime from the waste, like Bob did when small, I sat down and laughed until I was gasping. I should have whipped him, but he learned this safety lesson by himself, and now his tale grows larger with each telling.

June 1, 1855: Summer has wrapped its sticky arms around us. Thank Heaven the construction is finally complete. Two months, four days, and $1300, but meriting every cent and malediction I put into it! Though the workmen might disagree about the maledictions.

When Abraham came home tonight, he knocked on our front door and said to Mariah in a voice loud enough for me to hear, "Excuse me, Ma'am, do you know where Lincoln lives? I thought this was his house, but I must be mistaken. He could never live in a palace like this!"

I ran down the stairs. "Shut up, you old goat, can't you see James Gourley on the street? He'll think I've spent your fortune behind your back!"

Abraham doesn't need to know how much I invested. He wouldn't care anyway, because I used Todd money, but some things are best left unsaid. Our home is now lovely, but not pretentious, with a wide hall through the center and parlors on both sides for entertaining. Mariah helped me plant flowers in the front yard, as Abraham has never seen fit to plant shrubbery. I hope they will survive the hot summer and the dogs' diggings.

June 4, 1855: I have finally completed the summer cleaning of home, rugs, yard, and privy—drudgery beyond words. I would never be able to accomplish it twice a year without Mariah. The bugs have begun their annual trek indoors, and Abraham has no time to fix the broken windowpanes. We have boiled many bucketsful of pokeberry and molasses to entice the cockroaches and bedbugs to their death.

June 14, 1855: I am soul sick to see Emilie leave. We had much fun, and I feel so very close to her. How wonderful to be loved, hugged, held, appreciated. We went for long drives, gathered wild flowers, embroidered the new seat cushions, renewed our French, and talked for hours on end.

How I dread going back to my everyday routine. I will miss her dearly, especially after Abraham leaves tomorrow.

Aug. 24, 1855: We dined on Aristocracy Hill last night, and Ninian asked, "Well, Lincoln, with the Whig Party in rapid decline, what will you declare yourself in the future?"

Abraham shuffled in his seat before replying. "I still think I'm a Whig, but Mary and others say there ain't no more Whigs. Some call me an abolitionist, but I don't oppose anything but the extension of slavery, so I can't be one of them. I'm not a Know-Nothing, that's certain. How could I be? How can anybody who loathes the oppression of negroes be in favor of degrading classes of white people? I think our degeneracy is pretty rapid. As a nation, we began by declaring that 'all men are created equal.' We now practically read it 'all men are created equal except negroes.' If the Know-Nothings get control, it'll read 'all men are created equal except negroes, foreigners, and Catholics.' When it comes to that, it won't matter what you call me. I'll consider heading to some country where they make no pretense of loving liberty. To Russia maybe, where tyranny can be taken without the base alloy of hypocrisy."

Russia, for Heaven sake! Once Bogotá, then Oregon, now Russia! My God! Next he'll be aiming toward the South Pole!

Nov. 4, 1855, our 13ᵗʰ anniversary: We're beginning to focus on our goals again. The Democrats are losing their hold on Illinois, and Abraham is coming round to the Republican Party. He's still disappointed about the Senate race, but he battens down his politician's smile and pretends it doesn't hurt. It does hurt, and we will be vindicated, I vow it!

Abraham's cases are increasing, which is a blessing because he refuses to stop accepting poultry in payment or raise his fees. Why, he charged only $35 in the Dungey case, and Cousin Steve said it was worth a hundred! Even Judge Davis accuses him of beggaring the entire legal profession with his paltry fees. The man has no financial sense at all, and would probably work for free if I would allow it!

Dec. 12, 1855: Except for the deceitful election, this has been a good year. Abraham's practice is better than ever. He has tried a great variety of things, including business offenses, fraud, divorce, riot, even murder. I know I complain, but my heart realizes God has been good to us.

Dec. 13, 1855, my 37th birthday: Abraham gave me *Early Engagements*, a romance by Mary Frazear, and I have read it half through already. The boys gifted me white silk gloves trimmed in lace. Of course their father purchased the gift, but it's nice to receive something "from" my sons. I have many, many gloves, but I love them dearly. I long ago discovered that a tiny gloved hand can charm any man.

We are busy planning our next moves. Abraham says I have become an astute political counselor. My primary task is collecting and reviewing articles from the many newspapers we buy each day. It's an interesting and rewarding chore.

Dec. 21, 1855, Willie's 5th birthday: We gave him Bob's old train cars and Abraham fetched railroad timetables from the depot. Willie has learned all the schedules by heart—what days and times the trains go to Alton, Lexington, even Cincinnati. Like his father, he has an infallible memory. Like Bob, he can't get enough of trains. He's the most lovable, sweet-tempered child I've ever known, except perhaps for his brother Eddy. He is calmer than at this time last year, more mature. Soon he'll go to school and his mama will be forgotten. Or, as with Bob, she'll be considered an embarrassment. He says I try too hard to impress people, and I talk too much. Children can be cruel.

Dec. 25, 1855, Christmas: My perfect gift was much-anticipated floor coverings: two Belgium flowered carpets for the new parlor, bought from Lauderman's in St. Louis, and two rugs to replace the worn-out ones in the old parlor. The lads received pantaloons, penny toys, and a velocipede. For

Bob, board games to challenge his mind: chess, checkers, backgammon. For Abraham, a world globe and a Petroleum Nasby joke book. All were appreciated and will be used!

Jan. 1, 1856: I'm still beaming over our new trappings and tried to tactfully ensure that everyone who visited today saw all our lovely things. Then to the Bowery Theatre for supper and a show. Happy New Year to all!

Jan. 10, 1856: Abraham has won a fee of $5000 from the Illinois Central Railroad! They had refused to pay his fee of $2000 for saving them millions in taxes, so he sued in Supreme Court and won $5000! Of course we have to give half this fee to Herndon. Abraham refuses to change the inequity, even though Herndon is little more than a clerk.

Jan. 26, 1856: The *Boston Liberator* reports that Congressman Joshua Giddings has proposed a resolution for disunion:

> Mr. Giddings says he looks forward to the day when a servile insurrection will rise in the South; when the black man, armed with British bayonets and led by British officers, shall assert his freedom and wage a war of extermination against his master. Upon his urging, the Massachusetts Anti-Slavery Society has passed a resolution in favor of disunion.

Disunion proposed by a legislator? It can't be! We couldn't survive as two countries; we need each other. The south needs our industry, we need their agriculture, we both need the security of partnership. Why don't the men in Washington put a stop to this? If I were President, I would hang those who preach disunion. They are traitors to the nation and don't deserve its glorious freedoms. If they dislike the Union as it is, let them leave! I have written Giddings a letter expressing my feelings that he should be expelled from Congress and the country itself!

Feb. 12, 1856, Abraham's 47th birthday: To celebrate his day, Abraham purchased spectacles! At this age, a man's eyesight begins to wane and Abraham needs to read his speeches clearly. The eye doctor says he is "myopic." My comic husband says he is "near-sighted, but never short-sighted." He looks rather dignified in the thin black wire rims. Abraham was advised to wear the glasses regularly, but he plans to keep them secret as long as possible so as not to give the younger candidates something to poke at.

He also required a visit to the chiropodist for his aching corns and bunions. He goes without shoes whenever possible; says he likes to give his "big old bumpy feet" a chance to breathe.

Feb. 14, 1856, Valentine's: We entertained Willie's little friends today with a heart-shaped cake, ice cream, and lemonade. Children are so adorable at this age. Willie is the image of his father, even walking and talking like him. Abraham gave the littlest tots piggyback rides, carried beautiful little Josie Remann around on his shoulders, and bounced the children up and down on his long foot for hours. I can see when he plays with Josie how much he would like to have a daughter, but not less than I. It's another loss that I couldn't bear a girl to make our family complete. We must depend on Josie Remann and Delie Wheelock to be our surrogates.

Dr. Henry stopped by during the party (much to his discomfort, I believe, being with 20 children). He urged me to make peace with Julia Trumbull, but I told him, "No, I won't honor the conniver with my blessings. In fact, I cross the street to avoid her cold presence. I don't initiate disagreements, you know, especially this one. I merely respond. This subterfuge was done deliberately, and I won't suffer for her cruelty more than I have to date. She could have stopped Lyman from stealing our election, but she chose to stab us in the heart. I hear she has become unpopular with the other town ladies as well, finally showing the true colors first revealed to me, though I loved her as a sister. Bread cast on the waters comes back. Abraham says I harbor grudges and take offense at slight criticisms, but if I do, it is only to protect my home and family. My husband, our sons, and our future are all that is important to me, and Julia Trumbull doesn't matter a hill of beans."

Mar. 10, 1856: Abraham actually noticed the little changes I've made, especially the new blue curtains in his bedroom! He said, "Mother, you're a right-out genius, and you've done howling good things with this old house." I'm so pleased. The boys are also happy now, with their own rooms. Even Bob likes his accommodations! Abraham enjoys his new bed too, but he did not sleep there last night!

We have a wonderful life and a marriage that lightens the rooms in which it blooms. Surely love based on deep friendship is the best kind, because physical love will someday fade into companionship, though not for many years, I pray. If a couple does not respect each other in their older years, what will they have left?

Mar. 23, 1856, Easter: Attended church with the Melvins, Wheelocks, Shearers, and Francises, and learned that Rev. Smith has resigned. We will all miss him dreadfully. He and Abraham have become quite close, and I believe Rev. Smith has helped my husband find his spiritual core. Uncle John Todd and some others would like to engage Dr. Brown, our minister in Lexington. Although he and his wife appear pleasant, I don't think either would suit the people here. Rev. Smith is talented and beloved, and would stay if the congregation would increase his salary. But even though many of the church members are wealthy, most are very close with their money.

Apr. 4, 1856, Tad's 3ʳᵈ birthday: Tad loves his birthday gifts and is pushing the new little cart around by himself. I wish he could talk as well as he can walk! His lip is still misshapen and I'm afraid we'll have to cut it. He asks many questions, but the words don't sound right. "What" is "whadth," and "father" is "fodder." I'm very worried about that.

And because he can get around so well, we can barely keep him from skittering off. Abraham sometimes takes the boy to his office, and he gets into everything at once. "Why do you allow him to run wild?" I asked.

Abraham responded lightly, "He's a lad, he needs to be free. There's time enough to get pokey." He wouldn't be so permissive if he spent as much time as I chasing the one running free!

May 1, 1856: Thunder! My God, how I hate thunder! It causes rumblings in the back of my mind, like a train that can't be stopped before it destroys all that we are. My body shakes with the noise of the invisible track. In my nightmares last night, Eddy stood at the track's far end, calling my name. I answered, but he couldn't hear me. I tried to run to him, but my legs were frozen. As the train ran him down, I woke to rain pounding on the windows and wished, oh how I wished, that Abraham were next to me. When he holds me, the dream fragments fade and I can slumber again. It will be days before I attempt sleep now. I look in the mirror and see the toll my maladies are taking. If not for my beloved husband and sons, I wouldn't care. As I wouldn't care to live.

May 10, 1856: Horrible Herndon has accidentally done a wonderful thing! When the county convention selected delegates to the Republican state convention last week, Abraham was not here. So Herndon put Abraham's name on the list without asking permission. Cousin John Stuart rode here immediately after hearing the news and demanded an explanation. I had none, so he confronted Herndon and found that Abraham's name had been presented in absentia. "Signing up for that abolition call has ruined your husband's future," John huffed, but I disagree. Abraham was livid, but finally came round and agreed to go.

May 21, 1856: Violence has come to Congress! Rep. Brooks beat Sen. Sumner almost to death because of his recent anti-slavery speech. Senators who claim to be Christians stood by, countenancing the act, and even applauding afterward! Even Stephen Douglas sat within helping distance, yet let the murderous blows fall unopposed.

At the very time Sumner was being attacked, Lawrence, Kansas, was being destroyed for the crime of freedom. Papers report that "pro-slavery border ruffians, posing as a posse," invaded Lawrence, burned the hotel, wrecked the newspaper presses, and pillaged private homes. It seems that the most prominent stronghold of liberty in the state must now give way to slavery in order to survive.

In retaliation, an anti-slavery zealot named John Brown brutally killed five unarmed pro-slavery men. Only two months ago, a bill was proposed to prevent civil war and restore peace in Kansas, but it stalled. My God, what are we coming to? I want the White House as dearly as I always have, but am glad we're not dealing with this conflict and enigma. I'm afraid the controversy over Kansas will rip the country apart.

May 29, 1856: I have decided to enhance the house again: an iron railing to the upstairs porch and a wall to separate the kitchen and dining room. I will also redesign the exterior to resemble a Swiss cottage. Only another $300 and the work will be completed before Independence Day! I'll also buy wallpaper for the entire house now, to put up later. Buying in quantity endears one to the vendors. And keeps me busy.

Abraham writes that he made a powerful speech at the Republican convention in Bloomington. I'm eager to read the papers and his notes. Because he continues to stand up for the rights of the slave states as guaranteed in the Constitution, however, his opponents are calling him half-hearted and two-faced. I wrote to him, "Tell them that's silly! If you had two faces, would you truly choose to wear the one you do?"

June 1, 1856: Abraham is home, with $500 in fees, and entertained us with stories from Bloomington. All kinds of humanity were there for the state convention: Whigs, bolting Democrats, Free-Soilers, Know-Nothings, Abolitionists, Lyman Trumbull, Leonard Swett, David Davis, Norman Judd!

Abraham spoke up loudly and helped nominate William Bissell, who was highly decorated in the Mexican War, as the Republican gubernatorial candidate and Richard Yates as the House candidate. He also helped choose the rest of the slate, ending with John Frémont as the Presidential candidate over William Seward and Salmon Chase. Frémont is Thomas Hart Benton's son-in-law and a former senator from California.

Their platform includes saving Cuba for US annexation, constructing a railroad to the Pacific, and outlawing polygamy and slavery. All fine goals with which we are proud to be associated.

To hear Abraham talk about his speech gives me excitement like in years past! Normally reticent to extol his own greatness, my modest orator admitted to his success. He said men were jumping to their feet and shouting in the aisles. Previously he has simply argued the slavery question on grounds of policy, without reaching the question of rights. In Bloomington, as we had decided, he stood up for all men. The *Illinois Journal* printed his speech in full. Here are some of his points, with the editor's comments:

> We're in a trying time, for unless a change is made in our present course, blood will flow because of Nebraska, and brother's hands will be raised against brother! *[Uttered in such an earnest, impressive, tragic manner as to make a cold chill creep over me.]*
>
> I was deeply moved by Mr. Emery's statement about the wrongs done to free-state men. I think it just to say that all true men should sympathize with them and be willing to do any needful thing to right their wrongs. But we mustn't promise what we ought not, lest we be called on to perform what we can't. We mustn't be led by excitement and passion to do something our sober judgments wouldn't approve in our cooler moments. *[Applause]*
>
> We're here to protest a great wrong and to take measures to make that wrong right; to place the nation, as far as it may be possible now, back as it was before the repeal of the Missouri Compromise. The plain way to do this is to restore the Compromise, and to demand that Kansas will be free! *[Immense applause]*
>
> I once read in a law book that a slave is a human being who is legally not a person but a thing. If the safeguards to liberty are broken down, as is now being attempted, when they have made things of all the free negroes, how long do you think before they will begin to make things of poor white men? *[Applause]*
>
> The immortal Declaration is being called "a self-evident lie," and "a string of glittering generalities." Thomas Jefferson solemnly declared that he trembled for his country under slavery when he remembered that God is just; while Sen. Douglas, with an insignificant wave of the hand, says he don't care whether slavery is voted up or voted down. The framers of the Constitution were particular to keep out the word "slave," because they knew slavery would ultimately end, and they didn't wish to have any reminder that human beings were ever prostituted to slavery in this free country. *[Applause]*
>
> We must reinstate the birthday promise of the republic; we must reaffirm the Declaration of Independence; we must make good in essence, as well as in form, James Madison's avowal that "the word slave ought not to appear in the Constitution." We must make this a land of liberty in fact, as it is in name. *[This was the climax, though not quite the end; the audience rose to its feet, applauded, stamped, waved handkerchiefs, threw hats in the air, and ran riot for several minutes. Lincoln, the arch-enchanter who wrought this transformation, meanwhile looked like the personification of political justice.]*

June 10, 1856: The Democrats met in Cincinnati and selected James Buchanan of Pennsylvania as their candidate, just barely over longtime politicians Franklin Pierce, Lewis Cass, and Stephen Douglas. John

Breckinridge of Kentucky is his running mate. Buchanan is definitely the wisest choice for them, being the only one who did not offend the north or south by taking a stand on the Kansas-Nebraska Act. But he's hindered by the fact that he's never married. No President has ever been unmarried. Widowed, yes, but never a bachelor. Marriage makes a candidate seem more stable and trustworthy. They call him a "nancy" and "affected," and his opponents chant, "Who ever heard in all his life…of a President without a wife?" They say he kept company with William King, Pierce's VP, who died last year.

Also in the race, representing the Know-Nothings, is former President Millard Fillmore, with Andrew Jackson's nephew, AJ Donelson, as his running mate.

June 20, 1856: I learned from the *Chicago Press* that the Republicans nominated Abraham as the Vice Presidential candidate! He received 110 votes on the first ballot! Though he lost to William Dayton, a former senator from New Jersey, he remained one of only two on the last ballot, from a start of 15. I have never been happier! Surely the party will endorse him for another high office! The Republicans will most likely not win this election anyway, as they are so new. Abraham says it's impossible for Frémont to best Buchanan, but we're moving quickly.

But what if Abraham had won instead of Dayton and then the Republicans had won the election? We would have moved directly to the White House and had four years to learn the ways of Washington before making our bid for President! I would have been content as Mrs. Vice President. Abraham's comment was typical: "I'm sure it ain't me. There's a great man named Lincoln in Massachusetts, and I reckon he's the one. Nobody knows me."

I hugged him tightly. "Maybe not, My Dear, but they soon will!"

June 29, 1856: Our lives are overflowing with excitement and joy! People are calling and writing in droves. Even Ninian sent his congratulations on the nomination and the visibility! The little rascals don't understand it all, but they love the atmosphere. Finally we will show all those people who looked down on us—my naysaying stepmother who said I would never amount to a hill of beans, the women who said I was marrying a nobody, my relatives who said my husband was white trash, the men who snickered behind his back. Now Abraham is one of the most recognized Republicans in the state. Other state newspapers also write about him, print his likeness, and record his speeches. And Abraham is enjoying the stature as much as I. His ambition is soaring!

July 1, 1856: New clients are coming from all across the district. In May, Abraham represented the Rock Island Railroad and charged $1000. In

June, he worked with Edwin Stanton in a patent case for McCormick Reaper in Chicago District Court. Although Stanton treated Abraham as incapable and inferior, we still received $2000. He's now representing a woman in a land dispute and will be paid $1000. He even represented the wife of a murdered man and the killer went to prison!

July 4, 1856, Independence Day: The wind reeks with whisperings of vote-buying and personal favors. Some abolitionists have become disunionists, and even northerners like William Lloyd Garrison, JB Swansey, and Horace Greeley, editor of the *New York Tribune*, are advocating secession. They say Buchanan will let slavery spread into the territories if he wins. Stephen Douglas is spouting publicly that he was right about the Kansas-Nebraska Bill.

Abraham is stumping all of Illinois for Frémont, though he still doesn't believe we can win. He writes about bands, fireworks, rallies, parades, banners, and audiences in the thousands, whether inside a structure or outside in the rain. Other speakers on the Republican platform are Ralph Waldo Emerson, William Cullen Bryant, and Henry Wadsworth Longfellow. Abraham is in good company! If the Republicans should win this election, we can run for the Senate in 1858, and with the visibility and experience we are gaining now, we will surely win!

July 13, 1856: Abraham came home last night, for only the weekend, but it was glorious to see him drive up. Old Buck came prancing into the yard, knowing he would get a hay bale in his own stall, and Abraham came prancing into the bedroom, knowing he too would get his favorite treat in his own stall!

We did have a small argument about the extra $300 for the new decorations. He just doesn't understand how important appearance is for a politician. He quetched and sulked for several hours, especially after he spoke with the storekeepers about my charges, but we made up when I promised to ask his permission from now on. And I'll certainly try.

July 18, 1856: Abraham writes from Chicago about being carried off the platform on the shoulders of singing men. It becomes clearer every day that the issues he raises are of great concern to the nation, and people are responding to him as a child responds to its mother—with trust, warmth, and need.

But the political climate itself grows hostile. The Democrats charge that Frémont was an illegitimate child, favors the Catholics, and had some shady deals with a banking house. Most frightening, however, the southern papers say that if he is elected, the south will secede immediately. His name is not even on the southern ballots. I hear rumors that the Democrats spent half a million dollars to influence the election in Pennsylvania. The Republicans don't have that kind of money behind them, or even near them! Why is it that politicians must be rich to succeed? Wouldn't a poor man be closer to the people he must govern?

Aug. 1, 1856, Bob's 13th birthday: He is growing taller and more robust, has begun running for sport and so has slimmed down, and is actually quite comely. He still resembles the Todds more than the Lincolns, and reminds me of his Uncle Levi.

Bob and Abraham have extended the brick wall around the house and topped it with a white picket fence. It was nice to see father and son working together. The little ones were not much help, but not for lack of trying!

Though I'm happy to have everyone at home, I spend many hours in my room. The dizzy spells are increasing, and I sometimes fear I won't survive. My head often pounds away my vision, my chest thuds until I lose balance, and my gullet becomes blocked. Then Eddy appears and tells me to hold on to life for a while longer. He is so beautiful, and I'm thankful for his visits. Occasionally he brings Mother with him and we hold hands quietly until I can breathe again. Why can't I feel well? Am I losing my sanity? Abraham grows weary of my complaining, so I try to hide my pain, but it's difficult. Perhaps one of the new spiritualists in Springfield can help me find peace. Abraham leaves again soon, so I can visit the medium without reprisal.

Sept. 15, 1856: Abraham arrived home tired and excited. He has made more than 50 speeches since late June, and tried some important cases. He was asked to speak many more times than he accepted, even as far away as Wisconsin, Iowa, Indiana, and Michigan! His prominence is exceeding his availability! Thank Heaven for the new rail lines—no more horse and buggy for his long travels.

His voice is becoming lower, probably from shouting over full houses and making overly long speeches. He can't stop just because his time is finished. Afterward, he stays up till all hours talking with the townsfolk, trying to win votes any way he can.

"How are we doing in the state?' I asked.

"Well," he said, "we're still racing uphill. The Democrats are calling us a 'sectional party,' and some southern states, led by South Carolina and Virginia, have promised to secede immediately if Frémont wins. A Virginia congressman, James Mason, is appealing for 'immediate, absolute, eternal separation,' and Virginia's governor instigated a conference of southern governors to discuss sticking together. Kansas is still fighting itself and 55 people have died there already. The Union may be in trouble."

Loving Mr. Lincoln:

Sept. 16, 1856: Abraham admitted that southern heathens sometimes boo when he speaks. He said to the hecklers in Galena, "Who are truly the disunionists? We in the north don't want to dissolve the Union, and if you attempt it, we won't let you. We have the purse and the sword—the army, navy, and treasury—at our command, so you couldn't do it. This government would be very weak indeed if a majority with a disciplined military and well-filled treasury couldn't preserve itself when attacked by an unarmed, undisciplined, unorganized minority. All this talk about dissolving the Union is humbug and folly. We won't dissolve the Union and you shan't."

My family is torn asunder for the first time. Cousin Steve Logan is with Abraham for Frémont, Cousin John Stuart is speaking loudly for Fillmore. Ninian was for Douglas and now backs Buchanan, who is definitely the nut to crack in this race. Fillmore has no true chance, so every ballot taken from Frémont and given to Fillmore becomes a vote for Buchanan. With the splintering, Buchanan will likely carry the south and Frémont will win only New England and New York. Pennsylvania, Indiana, and Illinois are the deciding states.

Oct. 1, 1856: Hugely ashamed of my behavior today. About noon, Willie showed up with another whelp to tend. "Look, Mama, he's lost. I'll take care of him."

"No, young man, you will not bring another animal into this house," I said more harshly than intended. I wanted to stop ranting, but couldn't. It was as if a dam burst. I cursed the dogs and cats, rabbits and pigs, turkeys and goats. Damned Fido for traipsing through the house with muddy paws and scratching at the door at suppertime. Blasted Old Bob for being swayback. Blamed Abraham for not replacing the broken pane through which the chipmunks and other rodents climb. Cursed our past, our present, and our future. Poor Willie was terrified, his face colorless, his legs wooden. When I said he could go, he bolted as fast as his little legs would carry him, holding the spotted dog in his arms. He scampered all the way to Abraham's office and hid under the desk all afternoon. Tad was napping, so he was spared.

Why is this happening to me? I don't want to carry on like this. I want to be a perfect, loving mother. I need to talk with Willie Wallace about my moods—they're affecting everyone. Abraham has begun to call me "Contrary Mary," and the boys prefer to play elsewhere. I feel helpless and fatigued, but I can't stop. There's too much to do. I would cherish a slow day.

Nov. 4, 1856, our 14th anniversary: Our anniversary falls on election day. The news, though expected, is grim. Buchanan carried Illinois,

Pennsylvania, Indiana, and New Jersey, assuring his win. Fillmore did very poorly. Frémont captured all but four northern states, so the Republicans are making some headway. We'll try again in 1860.

Better luck on the local. William Bissell became governor by a vast majority and Republicans won all the state offices. But Illinois voted two to one for a Democratic President. How strange voters can be. How does a candidate know how to please them?

Nov. 29, 1856: A telegram from Stephen Douglas announced his marriage in Washington! I didn't even know he was betrothed. Her name is Adele Cutts and she is a grand-niece of Dolley Madison. Of course, he would tell me about the connection to cause me envy. His love of competition never stops. But I'm truly pleased for them. He has been alone too long and I, of all people, understand how hard that is. While I hate to lose the small advantage in the polls (married men win more often), Stephen has always been a friend and we would never deny him happiness.

Dec. 10, 1856: Every day, my beloved husband becomes a stronger politician and a more compelling speaker. His knowledge of right drives him, and he will not see the Democrats win again. I sense Abraham will have the VP nomination in 1860 and Republicans will win all round. Some of his associates from the House, most notably William Seward and Thurlow Weed, have also joined the party.

Dec. 13, 1856, my 38th birthday: Here I am, well into middle age. I will ask Madame Bigorati when I'm next in town how much time remains for me on this blessed earth. I'll also learn about my health, our future, my darling child in Heaven, and what he's trying to warn me about. Some may think my quest strange, and Abraham says spiritualism is poppycock, but the papers say both Empress Eugénie and Queen Victoria practice the ritual, so there's no harm in it. I know Eddy lives; he comes to me many nights with his adorable little pucker. My brother Robert is sometimes with him, and often my mother. Never my father.[11]

Jan. 1, 1857: Much flourishing about in the city today, calling on friends and neighbors, being invited for all sorts of gaiety. Tomorrow Willie begins attending a private school operated by Miss Corcoran, and he is hugely excited. He loves learning as much as his father, has excellent ability in math, and writes fair poetry. He's also a most peculiarly religious child. I wish Tad could learn as well. Like Bob, he doesn't care about attaining knowledge.

Jan. 10, 1857: Willie adores his school and his teacher. He chatters constantly about his studies and his friends. Perhaps he will follow in his

---

[11] Mary Lincoln was not the only First Lady who believed in spiritualism. Jackie Kennedy and Nancy Reagan were quite open about their beliefs in Heavenly guidance, and Hillary Clinton admitted speaking with Eleanor Roosevelt. Reagan and Florence Harding consulted a psychic shortly before their husbands' elections. Jane Pierce wrote letters to her dead son and hosted a séance in the White House, as did Julia Tyler. Julia Grant dreamed complete versions of her husband's upcoming battles and gave him military advice based on them.

father's footsteps and become an attorney. Maybe they will go into business together as Lincoln and Lincoln or Lincoln and Son. Abraham will soon need to bring home a simple law book for him to read!

Feb. 1, 1857: Abraham has symptoms of consumption or ague: coughing, sneezing, perspiring, fatigue. I worry so about him and the children when they are unwell. He has both chills and fever, and can't seem to get warm. He can hardly lift his head off the pillow. I simmered a peck of horehound for tea, and Dr. Willie gave him a mixture of turpentine, treacle, vinegar, and laudanum for his symptoms.

Feb. 5, 1857: I regret to admit that my husband and I had a broil about the new Republican paper. I don't want to waste money on insignificant rags when we so badly need to follow the papers from Chicago, New York, and Philadelphia, which are expensive. Abraham did not tell me he subscribed to this paper. In fact, he said he would not subscribe, but I found it on the doorstep. I asked him, "Are you going to take another worthless little paper?" He averted his eyes and muttered, "I didn't direct the paper to be left here."

From this answer, I assumed (rightfully, I still believe) he had not ordered it, so I wrote to the editor demanding that it not be delivered here. Lo and behold, he called on Abraham in rage and the story came out. My husband, while recovering from his recent illness, had indeed ordered it sent without telling me. He said he felt it a duty to review one copy. "Is Honest Abe honest only with others these days?" I demanded. "Why did you lie to me?"

His face lengthened. "Because you're too hard to reckon with, Mother. Everything I do is wrong, everything I read is unacceptable, everything I say is questionable. You're jealous of invisible women and worry me to death about politics. I asked them to deliver one issue to my office, so I didn't fib to you. I said I hadn't directed it to be left here, and that's the truth. Please stop whining and trust my judgment for once."

Now this story about our misunderstanding has appeared in the newspaper and Abraham is embarrassed. The Democrats are asking how he can possibly keep peace in the nation if he can't keep it in his own home. What is happening to us? What have I done? Why must I be so quarrelsome? I assume the paper is now being delivered to his office; he wouldn't cancel it under such circumstances.

Feb. 12, 1857, Abraham's 48th birthday: Time has borne changes on its wing for him as well. His temples are turning gray, and white hairs push out waywardly from his brows. But he's as handsome and loving as the day we met. It's good that he has the patience of Job, because we're not an easy bunch to handle. But then, he's not always a saint himself!

We had a special supper, followed with pudding in warm pastry shells. The boys drew pictures for him and built wooden frames so he can display the drawings in his office or study. When Willie showed Tad the picture he drew, Tad wrinkled up his nose in mock dislike. Abraham said to him, "When I was a tadpole, my maw told me if I made an ugly face, it would freeze and stay like that."

"Weel, Papa," said our little precious, "you than't tay thee din't warn you." His father's humor or his mother's sarcasm?

Feb. 14, 1857: We have argued again. My head was not responding to the many medicines I had offered it, and I don't even remember what I said that brought on the broil. All I recall is opening the front door and yelling, "Well, go on then! Just disappear to your office as you so often do and leave your family alone. We're by ourselves so much we have grown accustomed to it. Go see your fancy ladies or whatever it is you do until the late hours. Go on, see if I mind!"

"No, Woman," he shouted back in his old high-pitched voice, grabbing my shoulder and pushing me toward the door. "You make the house intolerable, dammit! You get out!" I was crying hysterically, babbling whatever came to my mind, and the argument continued in the foyer. Our neighbors were in their yards and I know they heard. It will be weeks before I'll be able to go out again. Abraham is in his own room now and the door is closed. Should I go to him? No, not tonight. I'm so sorry.

Feb. 15, 1857: Abraham was gone when I woke this morning, but he came home for lunch. I met him at the door and he took me in his arms. No words were needed. We could not survive without love, because we're as different as night and day. I need his constant physical and intellectual presence in my life, but he's frequently distracted, forgetful, or uncentered. I know I try his patience with what he calls "my theatrical attempts" to get his attention, but sometimes when I talk, he shuts his ears. I beg for warmth, he returns a chilly presence. I'm driven toward success, he'll take it if it comes. I try to savor every day, he broods over the mysteries of man's personality. He prefers silence, I like to chat. He would be happy in a log cabin, I want splendor. We both toss back and forth quickly from laughter and joy to melancholy and anger, hardly knowing when to expect it from the other. Yes, we're both hard bargains.

Feb. 26, 1857: Winter has certainly passed most rapidly. Spring, if we can call March such, is nearly here. The first part of the season was unusually quiet because of so much sickness among our friends and neighbors. Several families endured scarlet fever, and two or three children were swept away. But within the last four weeks, we have been to a party almost every night. The grandest was at the fire station, raising money to purchase an engine from Boston!

Mar. 4, 1857: Inauguration day in Washington for our unmarried President. Some cheering and crowing in Springfield, though the Whigs are quiet. Buchanan promised peace and union, but showed his true colors when he passed the slavery question to the courts. He said the issue is now a matter of little practical importance, which the judicial system will speedily and finally decide. Damned coward!

Better news is that the Kansas governor pulled in US troops and effected peace. What day is so dark that no ray of sunshine can be found to penetrate the gloom?

Mar. 10, 1857, Eddy's birthday: Desperately low today. Abraham took the boys to his office, because I couldn't keep my nerves from showing. I slept and cried, cried and slept, until it began to rain. At the second loud thundering, all of them came rushing into my room, dripping, and climbed into bed with me. They had left for home as soon as the thunder started, knowing I would be frightened all alone! Abraham cradled me until I steadied. The little angels lay their heads on my legs and patted me gently. "Dun't cwy," begged Tad. "Papa will make the thunder thop. Make it thop, Papa."

Mar. 15, 1857: The Supreme Court, made up of mostly southerners, ruled that the negro Dred Scott, who sued for his liberty, is still a slave even though he resided in free territory for much of his life. They ruled that, by voluntarily returning to a slave state, Scott lost the right to be free. Once a slave, always a slave; property is just property. Worse, the Court also declared the anti-slavery provision of the Missouri Compromise unconstitutional because it contradicts the 5th Amendment guaranteeing protection of private property! From now on, no restriction exists against owning other people. The Republican platform of "no extension" now has no substance. Nor does the Democratic platform of popular sovereignty, because the choice has been removed. The decision is just another calculated step in the plot to legalize national slavery, and we're both outraged. I just can't understand how honorable men can allow such. Our biggest worry is that the court will next decide that the Constitution does not permit a state to exclude slavery at all.

Abraham says that, though the Declaration of Independence does not literally extend full freedom and equality, the authors meant to set up a standard of free society for people of both colors. And he plans to fight.

"The Supreme Court has often overruled its own decisions," he asserts. "Though we'll not resist this one, we'll do everything we can to have it reversed."

Apr. 4, 1857, Tad's 4ᵗʰ birthday: Our littlest trouble-maker has learned to outsmart his parents with the best weapon possible: words. This evening, Willie begged to play with one of Tad's birthday toys and Abraham said, "Give it to him, Tad, to keep him quiet." Tad looked up at his father and said, "No, thir, I need it to keep mythelf quiet." Tadpole won another round!

June 12, 1857: Stephen Douglas spoke here this week on the topics of Kansas, Dred Scott, and Utah. We listened to the speech at the courthouse and then purchased a copy to study. He has adjusted his popular sovereignty ideas to conform to the Supreme Court's recent decision, and his opinions contradict and assail all of our own. He stated emphatically that the Declaration did not intend to include negroes, and claimed that Republicans want the right to live with, work with, and marry blacks.

Now Abraham constantly paces back and forth across the parlors, muttering to himself, then calling to me to test the phrases. "What will you say about marrying a negro?" I asked.

He paused for a moment. "I'll tell them I protest the counterfeit logic that concludes it. Because I don't want a black woman for a slave certainly don't mean I want her for a wife. I needn't have her for either; I can just leave her alone. In some respects, she certainly ain't my equal, but in her natural right to eat the bread she earns with her own hands, without asking leave of anybody else, she's my equal and the equal of all others."

"I believe that will cover it," I said.

Stephen also claimed, "No man can vindicate the character, motives, and conduct of the signers of the Declaration except on the hypothesis that they referred to the white race alone, and not to Africans, when they declared all men to be created equal. That they referred to British subjects on this continent being equal to British subjects born and residing in Great Britain, and so they were entitled to the same inalienable rights. The Declaration was adopted to justify the colonists in the eyes of the civilized world for withdrawing their allegiance and dissolving their connection with the mother country. The Declaration was written by white men, for white men."

I've heard words of that sort from him for many years. What a mangled ruin his sentiment makes of our Declaration. "They were speaking of British subjects on this continent being equal to British subjects in Great Britain." Bah! According to this, not only negroes but white people outside Great Britain and America were not mentioned in the Declaration. The

French, Germans, and other white people of the world are all gone to pot with Stephen's "inferior" races!

Abraham said, "I thought the Declaration contemplated progressive improvement in the condition of all men everywhere, but no, it was merely 'adopted to justify colonists in the eyes of the civilized world.' Since that object was achieved some 80 years ago, apparently the Declaration is useless now—just old wadding left to rot on the battlefield after the victory is won. Douglas is a pompous ass!" Well said, My Dear.

June 14, 1857: Abraham plans to rebut Stephen's remarks, and we've been very busy preparing for the evening of June 26th. I suggested he enumerate Stephen's points one by one: "I begin with Kansas.... I speak now about the Scott decision...." This would keep the issues straight and help the audience follow more smoothly. We're considering basing the speech on Abraham's question: "If those who wrote and adopted the Constitution believed slavery to be a good thing, why did they insert a provision prohibiting the slave trade after 1808?"[12]

June 16, 1857: Still hard at work on the points Abraham needs to make. I believe this will not be the last debate between these men and we want to begin strong. To be worked in now is the election in Kansas. The anti-slavery men refused to register to vote, so pro-slavery men were elected. Abraham fears they will draft a quick constitution and be received as a slave state. The records indicate that only about 1/6 of the registered men actually voted. Don't they understand the importance? Worse, not more than half of the rightful voters were even registered. Abraham says this is the most exquisite farce ever enacted. So much for the legality of popular sovereignty!

June 28, 1857: Abraham was magnificent! He gains power every time he speaks. He now also looks like a leader. He is using his height to his advantage rather than leaning over as he once did, like Father Time in December, and has lowered his voice. He also combed his hair, had his suit pressed, and polished his shoes. He finally listens when I assert that he can't go up against rich men by looking poor.

The *New York Times* has printed Abraham's entire speech, with the recent photograph he had taken. We are nationally recognized! Our scrapbook grows thicker every week. Here is an especially poignant excerpt:

---

[12] Article 1, Section 9: "The migration or importation of such persons as any of the states now existing shall think proper to admit shall not be prohibited by the Congress prior to the year 1808, but a tax or duty may be imposed on such importation, not exceeding ten dollars for each person."

Sen. Douglas does not directly assert, but plainly assumes as a fact, that the public estimate of the black man is more favorable now than in the days of the Revolution. This is a mistake. In some trifling particulars, the condition of that race has been improved; but as a whole, the change between then and now is decidedly the other way, and their ultimate destiny has never appeared so hopeless as in the last three or four years. In two of the five states that once gave the free negro the right of voting, the right has since been taken away, and in a third, it has been greatly abridged. It has not been extended, so far as I know, to a single additional state, though the number of states has more than doubled.

In those days, masters could free their slaves, but since then such legal restraints have been made on emancipation as to amount almost to prohibition. In those days, legislatures held the power to abolish slavery in their respective states, but now it's quite fashionable for state constitutions to withhold that power. In those days, by common consent, the spread of the black man's bondage to new countries was prohibited, but now Congress decides it won't continue the prohibition, and the Supreme Court decides it couldn't if it would.

In those days, our Declaration was held sacred by all, and thought to include all; but now, to aid in making the bondage of the negro universal and eternal, it's assailed, sneered at, hawked at, and torn until its framers couldn't recognize it.

July 4, 1857, Independence Day: Abraham spouted wisdom from the dais today:

You're preparing to celebrate the Fourth, but what for? The doings of this day have no reference to the present; and quite half of you ain't even descendants of those who are referred to today. But I suppose you'll celebrate, and may even go so far as to read the Declaration. Suppose, after you read it once in the old-fashioned way, you read it once more with Douglas' version. It'll then run like this: "We hold these truths to be self-evident, that all British subjects who were on this continent 81 years ago were created equal to all British subjects born and then residing in Great Britain."

And now I appeal to all, to Democrats as well as others: Are you really willing for the Declaration to be frittered away and left no more than an interesting memorial to the dead past? Shorn of its vitality and practical value and left without the germ or even the suggestion of individual rights in it?

July 8, 1857: The most wonderful news! Abraham has been called east for the Illinois Central Railroad and says I may go along! The client is paying the expenses and we'll be gone almost two weeks! Our honeymoon at last, though I believe we'll take Bob with us. It has been so, so long since I've been on a jaunt! I'll have to buy a few new things, of course. A woman can't go traveling with her important husband in old clothing. Abraham says this "paid" trip will probably cost him a small fortune by the time I have outfitted us! We'll visit New York, New Jersey, and even Canada!

July 15, 1857: We leave tomorrow. I've lost weight, packed enough for two weeks for us all, said goodbye to the neighbors, gotten the tykes settled at Elizabeth's, bathed like a courtesan, and rose watered. I am ready.

July 28, 1857: Arrived home yesterday, weary and happy, but more determined than ever to succeed in life and travel regularly. When I saw the large steamers at the NY landing, I felt inclined to sigh that poverty is our portion, and teasingly told Abraham that I am determined my next husband will be rich. Instead, I'm a staid matron and mother of three noisy boys. No matter; someday we will have it all!

NY is the cat's meow. I love it like no other place. We went to several plays, including *The Merchant of Venice, Hamlet,* and two operas. We picnicked in Central Park, took a ferryboat to Staten Island, moseyed along the piers, ate food from street hawkers, and shopped on Broadway and Fifth Avenue. I bought so many wonderful things, because the stores had discounts unheard of in Springfield. They even remain open in the evenings! Niagara Falls was the wonder of all. So much water. "Where does it come from?" Bob kept asking people, just as his father once wondered.

Sept. 22, 1857: A letter from Emilie saying she is now a happy mother. Katherine (not Mary as I had hoped) was born on September 2, 1857. Emilie will make a wonderful mama.

The *Washington Post* writes that Stephen Douglas denounced President Buchanan because he favored Kansas' pro-slavery constitution. If this is true, it's a feather in our cap. The Republicans were defeated last year because they were split. If the Democrats are split in '58, we have a mighty good chance of winning. If, as I suspect, the Senate race will be neck and neck between Lincoln and Douglas, perhaps we have an edge. We're eager for the next election to favor the Republicans on as many fields as possible. Abraham lost nearly all the working part of last year to the canvass; we are altogether too poor to lose another year.

Sept. 26, 1857: My blessed husband arrived home early from Chicago! I prepared a special supper, including Cornish hens purchased at a discount, and we talked by the hearth till he drifted off on the floor. We retired to our own rooms, but he crept in about dawn. He is almost insatiable when he has been gone so long.

While in Chicago, he had a photograph made in his white linen suit so the lawyers at court could purchase copies if they wish. The likeness is extremely good, and it will make a wonderful campaign picture. I'll frame the original for the parlor wall.

Sept. 29, 1857: Can't we stay ahead for even a short while? Rather than splitting the Democrats as we hoped, Stephen's lambaste of Buchanan has caused the Republican papers to mention him as a Republican senatorial candidate, and they are calling Abraham "the most unfortunate politician who ever attempted to rise in Illinois." It does seem that whatever we undertake, we are soon overtaken. Abraham is disheartened and talking about giving up. "We must never give up," I continue to say. I hold his head to my breast at night and hope he'll sleep without nightmares, without sleepwalking, without moaning unintelligibly.

To counter the slap, we're planning a magnificent event at Brown's Hotel, presumably to celebrate our wedding anniversary, on Saturday, November 14th. I'll invite all of Springfield, most of Lexington, and many in between. I'll hire caterers and musicians, cooks and servers, liverymen and butlers. I'll dress to show our prominence and make sure the men in this household also fig up. We'll show Illinois that we are cultured, solid, affluent, and ready for the Senate.

Oct. 10, 1857: We have addressed invitations to over 500 people, including the new state officers, legislature, judges, and most of the lawyers in Illinois (not including Herndon, though Abraham and I argued heavily about it). We also invited notable Republicans from other states who have expressed favor for Stephen Douglas, so they can see the error of their decision.

Nov. 16, 1857: I'm still recovering from the fatigue of our very successful entertainment on Saturday. Owing to unexpected snow, only 300 attended, but it was a smash. The boys were perfect gentlemen, weaving between people's skirts and canes, bowing politely when acknowledged, and singing on cue. A young man there with the Simpsons praised Abraham's oratory as we spoke, and remarked that my husband is well liked in the eastern part of the state. "Yes," I answered, "he's a great favorite everywhere. He will be President of the United States some day, so you may want to ask for his signature. If I had not thought so, I would never have married him, for you can see he's not pretty. But look at him—doesn't he look like he will make a magnificent President?" The young man agreed, laughed heartily, and ran to tell others what I said. I will keep this Presidential wheel in motion!

Nov. 26, 1857, Thanksgiving: We have so much for which to be personally thankful. Though the country is hurting financially and many people have no work, Abraham has many clients. Another Senate race next year, much politicking going on, many parties, the respect of our neighbors. The noblest, purest, most talented sons ever given to parents. Love in both body and spirit. We have aged well together and forgotten the sorrows and fears of the past in the enjoyment of the present. I rejoice at this physical and mental evidence of our affection. Our nerves and health fail us occasionally and we have spats, but we never stay in a pet, and once we get it behind us, the trouble is over forever.

Dec. 5, 1857: Why does the *NY Tribune* constantly eulogize, admire, and magnify Stephen Douglas? Have they concluded the Republican cause can be best promoted by sacrificing us here in Illinois? Abraham complains silently, but I have written a dozen letters to the editor in rebuttal. How dare they treat us like commoners! Damn them all!

Dec. 12, 1857: This has been a fluctuating year. I hope the next will be more steady. We're confident of our Senate win, though we'll have a hard race if Stephen is our opponent. Adele Douglas is a young beauty and I'll need to be especially careful with my appearance, demeanor, and political maneuverings. She travels with her husband everywhere, but Abraham isn't in favor of that idea for us, so I'll have to work on a new way to convince him.

Dec. 13, 1857, my 39th birthday: We are preparing for the race of our lives. We have good notice that Abraham will be named to represent the Republicans in the Senate contest. I hold my breath and pray. Perhaps growing doddery won't be such a burden after all.

Dec. 21, 1857, Willie's 7th birthday: Almost 50 children graced our home with their laughter and goings-on today. I made Willie's favorite lemon cake and filled it with custard as a treat. He beamed! He received a new train car, which Abraham whittled, and a few inexpressibles he dearly needed. His little friends brought numerous versions of squeaking toys: dogs, lions, fish, birds.

Dec. 25, 1857, Christmas: Willie is not feeling well. Tad is upset at having to be still and quiet, and the weather is too harsh to go outside. Bob is sulking because he is Bob. We were forced to cancel our plans with Elizabeth and Ninian, so we dined on leftover pork roast and played with the lads' new toys. Merry Christmas to all!

Jan. 1, 1858: Several hundred guests attended the governor's reception at noon today. What splendor! What food! What riches! I am so envious! But this will be a grand year for the Lincolns, and we will have our own splendor by year's end when we head for Washington as the new senator from Illinois. I hear rumors, though, of a political scheme to ensure Stephen's re-election. Lyman Trumbull, still in the Senate himself, tells us Sen. William Seward is behind Stephen, not only for the Senate but also for the White House in '60. Worse, the Republican leader himself is backing Stephen, and the *Lexington Observer and Reporter* says the remaining

Kentucky Whigs are unanimously for him. If this is true, my entire family has deserted us.

Feb. 1, 1858: Good news to offset the "Elect Douglas" campaign. President Buchanan seems to have set out to wreck Stephen's chances. He is pledging legislative candidates to oppose him, putting anti-Douglas men in new positions, and ousting pro-Douglas men from old positions. I regret speaking out against Buchanan. Perhaps he's a wise man after all.

More good news: Abraham's cousin, Harriet Hanks, is coming to spend time with us again. She's a nice girl, though not so much "girl" now, and she's good with youngsters. The last time she stayed with us, in '44, we had only Bob. She never knew our precious Eddy, who passed on 8 years ago today. I love you, Eddy.

Feb. 12, 1858, Abraham's 49th birthday: He's in Chicago consulting with Norman Judd, head of the Illinois Republican Committee. I believe our nomination is secure. Lyman Trumbull has turned out to be an advocate, working closely for us behind the scenes. I may have to be cordial to Julia again, but I won't jump just yet. Harriet has arrived; she looks happy and healthy.

Feb. 22, 1858, Washington's Birthday: Abraham is home for the celebration and delivered a small speech on patriotism while Bob and the other Springfield Cadets stood behind at attention. Bob looked like a strutting cock in his dark blue, gold-trimmed coat; white pants; and glazed cap—the proud uniform of a 4th Corporal! Being a cadet has been good for his confidence.

Apr. 4, 1858, Tad's 5th birthday: Because Willie had a large birthday party, Tad insisted on one as well. His friends from around the neighborhood were invited and stayed several hours over lemonade and pastries. Tad is so handsome—a boyish face, with fine hair that won't stay in place. His eyes seem to understand that life is not always for the young, and his patience is remarkable. Yet his movements and mind are quick. At 5, he's already showing signs of high imagination, sensitivity, and emotion. He will be a great comfort to us in our waning years.

Apr. 12, 1858: Abraham spoke today in Bloomington on "Discoveries and Inventions," but it wasn't particularly well received. He talked about "man and his progress" over the years in machinery, arts, and sciences. I have told him repeatedly that this topic won't help his political career and he should focus more on the issues of the Senate race, but he so enjoys talking about inventions. He speaks often about the machine he patented in '48 and apparently those in his audience enjoy hearing the details.

May 2, 1858: Abraham has begun a murder trial in Beardstown! The son of his old friends in New Salem, Hannah and Jack Armstrong, was accused of bludgeoning another young man. Abraham used to dangle the Armstrong boy on his knee, and doesn't believe the lad can be guilty. Another youth has in fact already been convicted and sentenced for the crime. Unfortunately, Mrs. Armstrong is a widow now and has no money to pay, but a murder trial, if we win, will be wonderful press!

May 12, 1858: Today I attended the final day of the Duff Armstrong murder trial. He was acquitted. The major witness, Charles Allen, claimed to have seen young Armstrong strike the victim with a large piece of metal fastened to a strap late one night. Abraham sat through the morning with his head leaned back on his shoulders, his eyes fixed on one spot of the blank ceiling. He seemed in a daze, oblivious to the events around him, sphinx-like.

Then in cross-examination, he brutally attacked Allen's testimony that the full moon allowed him to see the event. Suddenly and with a lashing jerk, Abraham asked the sheriff for an 1857 almanac. To my delight and surprise, the almanac reported that the moon on said night had barely passed the first quarter and had actually disappeared before 11pm. Allen could not have seen the act. The jury declared Armstrong innocent on the initial ballot. Because Abraham believed in the boy, the jury believed in him.

Though people are now saying Abraham has more politics than law on his mind, this trial will do much to help us win the nomination. He has been practicing law regularly and successfully for more than a year now since his return, and his state Supreme Court cases are numerous. He wins most suits and is well liked by lawyers and judges. With Abraham at the helm, the Republican ship will outsail its rival and dock in Washington!

May 15, 1858: We have been assured that Abraham will be chosen as the senatorial candidate! His old hat fills up with scraps of writing as he crafts his acceptance remarks for me to see later. We have discussed using as his basis the phrase we first used in 1843: "A house divided against itself cannot stand." I sense it's a statement to make him famous, but he's concerned.

"Is it a wise comment to make at such a fragile time?" he asked. "It's true, of course, and it served us well when campaigning for the House, but will it be labeled radical in the slavery issue? Will it drive away voters?"

"Perhaps you're correct, My Dear, but it's a universally known idea that will ring sound in the minds of modest men, especially now, and clarify the peril for all who hear it. I believe you should use it."

He smiled. "Well then, Mother, by all means I must use it."

Some Republicans, including Burlingame, Wilson, Cameron, and Greeley, now back the idea of running Stephen, but I don't believe it will happen. The *Chicago Tribune* writes about the rumored switch unfavorably:

> There seems to be a considerable notion in the eastern political brains that the barbarians of Illinois can't take care of themselves. To support Douglas would be to destroy the Republican Party in Illinois. We will deal with Senator Douglas in our own way.

June 16, 1858: Celebrations tonight, especially in the Lincoln home. We were unanimously chosen as the Republican candidate! Unanimously! The convention sent round its resolution: "Abraham Lincoln is our first and only choice for US senator, to fill the vacancy about to be created by the expiration of Sen. Douglas' term." Hurrah! Of course, incumbency is difficult to overcome, but we'll run the obstacle with patience. We also face the impediment of having little money, but still we'll persevere and win! We know Stephen, we have fought him for 20 years, and now we'll give him the challenge of his life. As expected, Abraham was called on to make an acceptance speech, and he said the words we have rehearsed time and again:

> If we could first know where we are and where we're heading, we could better judge what to do and how to do it. We're now far into the 5th year since a policy was initiated with the promise to put an end to slavery agitation. That agitation has instead constantly increased. In my opinion, it won't cease till a crisis has been reached and passed.
>
> A house divided against itself cannot stand. I don't believe this government can permanently endure as half slave and half free. I don't expect the Union to be dissolved; I don't expect the house to fall; but I do expect it'll cease to be divided. It'll become all one thing or all the other.

I was right. "A house divided against itself cannot stand" is now on the lips of every Republican, and will soon be in every newspaper in the land! I sense these words will be remembered long after our earthly bodies are passed to the great beyond.

Against my wishes, however, Abraham also claimed a conspiracy for the extension of slavery ranging from Douglas to Buchanan to Pierce to Taney. He predicted another Supreme Court decision declaring that the Constitution does not allow a state to exclude slavery: "A decision like that is all slavery needs to become lawful everywhere. Welcome or unwelcome, such a decision will soon be on us unless the power of the present political dynasty is met and overthrown." This conspiracy tact may backfire. I pray I'm wrong.

June 20, 1858: The Democrat papers have reprinted Abraham's acceptance comments, and some, rather than focusing on "a house divided," have concentrated only on his inference of conspiracy and labeled him a radical and a fanatic. Even Ninian wrote an article expressing this opinion, which broke our hearts. Why must my family continue to upbraid us? It's been 16 years now; why can't they see that I made the right choice? What must we do to be good enough in their eyes?

July 2, 1858: Abraham is home! Imagine my amazement as he rode into the yard on Old Buck, both covered in dust and grime, both panting, both looking pleased as Punch to be surprising us. The little angels were as excited as I to see him. Of course, he brought three legislators and his campaign advisor, Norman Judd, with him. They were fed supper and bedded in the parlors. They will be on their way after breakfast tomorrow. Our sitting room has now been converted into Lincoln headquarters and strangers tread its carpets day and night.

Our conversations, both outspoken and whispered later in the night, were adamant and energetic, sensual and political. I remember Abraham saying to me, "You've convinced me I'm good enough for the Senate. But, in spite of it all, I say to myself every day, 'It's too big a thing for you, Lincoln, you'll never get it!' Then I hear you telling me years ago that I could be a senator, and President too! So I'll go on with the race."

July 4, 1858, Independence Day: Abraham and I talked strategy at the fair as the boys went from exhibit to exhibit. "I need an edge," he said, "a way to outshine the Democrats and Douglas. He's making speeches now, calling me inexperienced and countrified. He's justifying slavery and rewording the Constitution. I need a way to get ahead of him and make him declare his real sentiments about the slavery issue."

"Why not a debate?" I asked. "You're the best debater in the country, and you certainly took the prize last time you went against him. People will come out just to see if you can do it again."

His bushy brows shot up over wide eyes. "Another debate? We ain't done that since '54. It's an interesting idea, Mother, an interesting idea indeed."

July 6, 1858: Abraham has left again, heading south this time toward Jonesboro, then back up to Chicago to hear Stephen open his campaign. He said before he left that he is seriously considering my idea of challenging Stephen to debate. I'll write him even tonight and encourage him to do so.

July 11, 1858: Today's letter from Abraham says Stephen made a grand showing at the Tremont House. An "unrestrained and wild" demonstration greeted his appearance, so he's not losing his popularity as I had hoped. He said to his own followers: "The Republicans have nominated a very able and honest man. Lincoln is the strong man of his party—full of wit, facts, dates—and the best stump speaker, with his droll ways and dry jokes, in the west. He's a kind, amiable, intelligent gentleman; a good citizen; and an honorable opponent. If I beat him, my victory will be hard won."

Then he strongly attacked our house-divided doctrine as being radical and plead for states' rights in domestic concerns. He repeated the words that make me cringe: "Our laws were made by white men, for white men, to be administered by white men." My wise husband has always said Stephen can compress the most words into the smallest ideas of any man he ever met.

Abraham spoke the following night to a crowd as large as Stephen's and "five times as enthusiastic." He, of course, defended our house-divided message as a prediction only, not truth or wish, yet he said clearly that "slavery must be put on the path to ultimate extinction." His close was strong: "Let us unite as one people throughout this land till we once more stand up declaring that all men are created equal." Very elegant!

Aug. 1, 1858, Bob's 15th birthday: We celebrated without Abraham. He is somewhere in the wilds of eastern Illinois, following Stephen's stump path to take advantage of the crowds already assembled (the crude Democratic papers say this is the only way he can draw an audience). He finally challenged Stephen to a round of debates, which was accepted. The arguments will be based on questions from one to the other, and will be held in each district except Chicago and Springfield. The contests should be most interesting, but no concern, because Abraham is much stronger on his feet. The first is in Ottawa on August 21st.[13]

Aug. 25, 1858: Letter from Ottawa: "After speaking one after the other in Bloomington, Clinton, Beardstown, Havana, Lewistown, and Peoria, Douglas and I finally crossed swords here on Saturday. The fire flew some and the dust rose both metaphorically and in reality, but you'll be glad to know I'm still alive. Probably 10,000 people were present. The event lasted more than three hours, with Douglas' one-hour opening, my 90-minute

---

[13] No other political contest, except perhaps the one between John Kennedy and Richard Nixon in 1960, has seen debates like these. They were not prearranged discussions like the televised ones we see today. These were wide-open, no-holds-blocked slugfests. Douglas and Lincoln questioned each other with the intent of destroying the other's campaign, surprising him with unforeseen issues, and hurling red herrings.

rebuttal, and his half-hour closing. I'll be the open and close in Freeport on Friday and will go on with the questions you and I planned."

I worry about one of the questions he plans to ask: "Can the people of a US territory, in any lawful way, against the wish of any US citizen, exclude slavery from its limits before executing a state constitution?" In other words, is the Dred Scott decision a good law? Can a slaveholder take his slaves into Kansas if the people of Kansas want to keep him out? We've discussed this question many times recently. I said, "If Stephen answers that question smartly and noncommittally, his answer alone will make him senator."[14]

"That may be," Abraham replied, "but if he takes that shoot and goes against the Supreme Court, he never can be President, and I'd give up this whole gig for a win in the bigger event. I'm killing larger game. The big battle in 1860 is worth a thousand of this race to the Republicans." Finally he sees himself in the right role!

Aug. 27, 1858: Abraham continues to stump between debates. He receives invitations from almost all quarters beyond the actual debates, sometimes making several speeches a day. Stephen's schedule was printed in the papers and people know Abraham is not far behind. We recognize that the race will be won in the center of the state, because the north is declared Republican and the south is truly Democrat. Abraham debates today in Freeport. We at home are hot and very lonely.

Aug. 29, 1858: Abraham's report on the Freeport debate: 15,000 people, including many ladies, in the rain! A thousand torches carried by men, women, and children! Stephen threw mud in great handfuls. His language was so disgusting, including repetition of the term "Black Republicans," that the crowd hushed him three times from the ground.

Abraham writes, "I was mortified at the end of my talk when supporters picked me off the platform and carried me on their shoulders all the way to the hotel — like an old log plank, laid out horizontal, though I squirmed to get down. As if I don't have the feet to walk myself." I would like to see him flailing about in such a position! Next debate is Jonesboro on September 15th.

Sept. 14, 1858: Abraham writes about daily speeches and long ovations: Monticello on the 6th, Clinton on the 8th. He enclosed a wonderful clipping of his September 11th speech, from the *Edwardsville Reader*:

---

[14] Lincoln did ask this question in Freeport, and Douglas basically replied that it didn't matter which way the Supreme Court decided because the people had the right to decide as they please. The Southern papers immediately labeled Douglas a traitor because he had repudiated the Supreme Court verdict.

> When you've succeeded in dehumanizing the negro, put him down and made it impossible for him to be but as the beasts of the field, extinguished his soul in this world and placed him where the ray of hope is blown out as in the darkness of the damned, are you quite sure the demon you've roused won't turn and rend you? What constitutes the bulwark of our own liberty and independence? It ain't our battlements, our bristling seacoasts, our army and our navy. All of them can be turned against us without making us weaker for the struggle. Our reliance is in the love of liberty God planted in us.
>
> Our defense is in the spirit that prizes liberty as the heritage of all men, in all lands everywhere. Destroy this spirit and you've planted the seeds of despotism at your own doors.

Sept. 15, 1858: I'm as mad as a poked hornet! Stephen and his wife, the "beautiful and accomplished belle of Washington" (I quote from the *Philadelphia Press*), ride in a private railroad car decorated with flags and streamers, donated by George McClellan of the Illinois Central Railroad. Secretaries, reporters, and servants travel with them. Bands playing the *Star-Spangled Banner* and *Hail Columbia* meet them in each town. Stephen even carries his own brass cannon on a flatcar behind his train to announce his arrival.

But we can't afford a railroad car! We can hardly provide for an ox-drawn or a coach. Abraham says he feels like royalty when he can take a rail car at all. I can't possibly travel with him. We couldn't impose on Harriet or Mariah to watch the boys, and even if we did, we don't have funds for the extra lodgings, food, and clothing. Oh the distress of being poor beats deep in my soul. Once I could have asked Ninian to lend us money, but I would never darken his door in the name of politics now. So we wear mended shoes and patched unmentionables while the Douglases strut about in expensive finery. Bah!

Sept. 20, 1858: Abraham writes about bands, military companies, and cavalcades escorting him and Stephen to the dais before the Charleston debate. 5,000 people in attendance! Fireworks, rockets, and cannons marked the ending of the events. They drove Abraham in a wagon, covered with bunting and flowers, containing approximately 32 young girls, each carrying a banner with a state's name inscribed thereon.

He seems to be losing his patience. I hope he's not also losing his determination. The papers describe how, in answer to Stephen's never-ending harp on the Mexican War, Abraham grabbed Mr. Ficklin (who served with him in Congress) from the audience and made him confirm that Abraham always voted for supplies to sustain the troops! I know my husband so well—this is a sign of irritation, and his irritation leads to loss of calculation and eloquence. I write to him every day, urging him to persevere, stay strong, count to 20. I remind him of our goals. He writes less these days and I know this battle is debilitating him. He's a peacemaker, not a warrior.

He's also still speaking every day between the debates at crossroads, fairs, picnic groves, and courthouses; kissing babies (oh that he could kiss me); declining rides in air balloons; staying with strangers and eating meals at a voter's table; trying to put a little life into the Republican campaign for the legislative candidates. Those are the men who will take him to Washington, and we need each of them.

Sept. 24, 1858: Apparently my beloved husband is still feeling crushed. He recently used the words "fraud" and "forgery" to refer to Stephen's statements. The *Illinois Journal* printed Abraham's Charleston debate comments about equality, and I can sense the anger and fatigue lurking beneath his humor and gentleness:

One of Lincoln's most personal statements: "I am not, nor have I ever been, in favor of bringing about the social and political equality of the white and black races. I am not, nor have I ever been, in favor of making voters or jurors of negroes, nor of qualifying them to hold office or intermarry with white people.

"There is a physical difference between the white and black races that will forever forbid them living together in social and political equality. And in as much as they can't so live, there must be the position of superior and inferior, and I, as much as any other man, am in favor of having the superior position assigned to the white race."

Senator Douglas, in his closing remarks, pointed out that this statement of Mr. Lincoln's did not square with his previous statement in Chicago that we should "discard all this quibbling about this man and the other man—this race and the other race—being inferior, and unite as one people throughout this land."

Sept. 27, 1858: Abraham arrived yesterday—worn and agitated, but still filled with excitement and pride for the result. How I love his exhilaration! It always translates into desire for me after the boys have gone to bed. I treasure those moments!

We have talked a great deal about Stephen's attacks and the Democratic papers' untruthful reporting. He's calmer now, ready to fight again. We'll change our strategy for the remaining debates from constitutional law to moral law. I asked, "What's the main difference between the Democrats and the Republicans now?"

"Why, the slavery matter, of course," he replied.

"What about it?" I pushed.

"Republicans believe slavery is wrong in all cases; Douglas and his people believe it's right if someone wants it."

"Then let's argue that difference in the last debates," I said, moving to sit on his lap and smooth the hair now overflowing his ears and neck. His silent caress told me I had reached him.

Later, around noon, the Republican Club came to the house with a band and a thousand cheering admirers. The musicians played outside our door and all the neighbors came to gawk. The boys ran and frolicked, pretending to carry instruments of all kinds, and they sang at their highest capacity. Bob and I watched from the upstairs windows, waving at the crowd when they saw us. Abraham spoke for a few moments from the porch. I'm so glad we enlarged the house and added the lovely veranda for all to see. How embarrassing our former house would have been! Finally the world is beginning to see what I have known all these years. Abraham Lincoln is the man to lead our country to peace and prosperity.

Oct. 7, 1858: Abraham spoke on October 1st in Pittsfield over in the west, two days ago in Tazewell at a "Grand Rally of Lincoln Men," last night in Petersburg, tonight at Knox College in Galesburg. I hope it's not as raw and damp there as in Springfield. I feel for those poor people standing outdoors for three to four hours at a time in the sleet as I sit here cozily by my own fire with my children and dogs at my feet. My soul is peaceful for a change.

Oct. 10, 1858: Abraham writes about Galesburg (15,000 people) and heading on to Quincy. I no doubt will read his speech in the papers before I receive his letter describing the results. How strange that situations can be seen in so many different ways. The Republican papers, including the *Chicago Tribune*, praise Abraham and say he is decidedly trouncing Stephen. The Democrat papers, including the *Chicago Times*, say just the opposite. When his admirers carried Abraham from the platform on their shoulders, the Democrat papers said he was "so used up in the speech that his knees trembled and he was too weak to walk." This double-sided coin is much the way people see slavery. It does seem that truth would be truth, but it becomes more evident every day that even this statement itself is not accurate. Abraham once told about a man who had such great regard for the truth that he spent most of his time embellishing it. I believe newspapers do the same.

Oct. 13, 1858: Abraham's letter from Petersburg says he spoke for only 60 seconds! Can you imagine? It takes longer than a minute for him to get warmed up. How I would have enjoyed hearing that short speech! Perhaps he will deliver it for us when he arrives late tonight after the debate in Quincy.

Oct. 14, 1858: Abraham is home, but only long enough for me to wash his clothes, clean his hat, polish his shoes, and pack for myself and Bob to go to Alton for the last debate. The Alton-Sangamon Railroad is offering a half-price fare from Springfield, so we can afford to attend. Bob will take part in the ceremonies as part of the Springfield Cadets, and we couldn't refuse. I wouldn't have allowed him to go without me to chaperone, though I'm sure I will hardly see him after all the boys arrive. This is his junior year at school, and he is asking to go on to Harvard University, up near Boston, where John Q Adams was educated! If we're in the Senate, perhaps we can afford to let him go. Otherwise, he'll have to learn from books by himself like his father did.

Oct. 15, 1858: We left early this morning on the train for Alton. Though a cloudy, dark day, hundreds were on the cars and thousands followed us on horseback and in all means of equipage. We shook many, many hands on the trip, being allowed no solitude at all. Merritt's Cadet Band was also on the train, so we were constantly endowed with music and merriment. Both groups were practicing for their events and trying to outplay the other. Though four hours long, it was the most exciting trip I have ever taken! How glorious to be recognized, spoken to with respect, admired.

Finally Mrs. Douglas won't be the sole wife in the debating audience. The voters will see that Stephen is not the only candidate with a cultured, well-dressed wife. A shade older perhaps, but still in her prime. I chose my outfit with care: the purple dress with white flowers on the hem and my white beehive bonnet with purple trim.

We arrived to Democrat fizzlegigs and fireworks, making Bob giggle and Abraham shake his head in wonder. He has never understood that part of campaigning. He says these are serious occasions, not fluffery, but I see a twinkle in his eyes when the mayor asks him to be honored on the platform, or when his supporters surround him with chants of "We love Honest Abe."

We were invited to dinner by Mr. and Mrs. Gustave Koerner, the Republican state legislator I met many years ago in Transylvania. He is more hopeful than I at this moment about our chances. He says we will likely not carry Alton, but we will carry Illinois and are "tolerably certain of carrying the legislature." I pray Abraham will soundly trounce Stephen in tomorrow's debate. I'll be so proud to see him sulk off the dais into the arms of his beautiful weeping wife.

Oct. 16, 1858: The debate was the most magnificent performance I have ever witnessed. Flags appeared in every direction and two dozen men sat on a large dais: 12 for Abraham on the right, 12 for Stephen on the left, facing approximately 3000 people. Stephen opened. He was obviously ill, because he resembled an old toad: bloated, haggard, and furrowed. He was also hoarse and at times the crowd could not hear his words. He stopped often to clear his throat or nose. His emphasized points frequently sounded barked rather than emotionalized.

Abraham spoke after lunch and what a sterling performance! He was filled with truthfulness and sympathy, even though his voice was sometimes shrill and quaked, and he occasionally gestured wildly. By bending his knees, crouching slightly, and then rising quickly up on his toes to make a point, he appeared eight feet tall. A world of meaning passed from the bony fingers of his right hand as he plotted his ideas on the minds of his listeners. He followed the path we charted on his last trip home and received long revels of applause. Here is a clipping from his speech, as reported in the *Boston Globe*:

> The real issue here is the sentiment on the part of one class that looks on slavery as wrong, and of another class that don't. The Republican Party says slavery is wrong. It's the sentiment around which all their actions and arguments circle, from which all their propositions radiate. They look on it as being a moral, social, and political wrong; and while they contemplate it as such, they nevertheless have due regard for its actual existence and the difficulties of getting rid of it in any satisfactory way, and to all the constitutional obligations thrown about it.
>
> That's the issue that'll continue in this country when these poor tongues of Stephen Douglas and myself are silent. It's the eternal struggle between right and wrong throughout the world. The one is the common right of humanity, and the other the divine right of kings. It's the same spirit that says, "You work and toil and earn bread, and I'll eat it." No matter what shape it comes in, whether from the mouth of a king who seeks to bestride the people of his own nation and live by the fruit of their labor, or from one race of men as an apology for enslaving another race, it's the same tyrannical principle.

The crowd laughed, cried, applauded, whistled, threw flowers, and hardly stood still after the first ovation. His speech was clear, succinct, logical, and emotional. He used Stephen's hoarseness against him, accusing him of "garbling" his stand on slavery. He repeated the idea I have heard so many times: "These two principles of right and wrong have stood face to face in an eternal struggle from the beginning of time. And right always wins in the end."

Stephen closed the debate. He had received high applause after his opening, but hardly anyone stirred after his close. The people had heard the master and the little giant was slain.

We suppered at the Franklin Hotel with our supporters, including Lyman Trumbull. Also included were *Chicago Tribune* reporter Horace White and the Hitt brothers. Bob Hitt invented the new shorthand process all the papers now use to record the debates. I invited him back to Springfield with us, but he said he wouldn't call at our home until we live in the White House! I assured him that would not be too long.

We arrived home very late and fell asleep rapidly. I woke twice to the sounds of my own moaning. My dreams were about growing old in the small, dingy office Abraham shares with Herndon. I roused Abraham once and asked him to hold me, but he was barely aware. We can't lose this election, not now, not after all our work. Surely Stephen will not best us again. I don't want to be a small-town lawyer's wife for the rest of my life! I want more—for my family even more so than myself. I want the world to see my husband's greatness. I want Elizabeth, Ninian, and the other Springfield socialites to come on their hands and knees asking for forgiveness. Am I so horrible a person?

Oct. 17, 1858: Our home vibrates from sun up to moon down. So many well-wishers, so many hopes and dreams, but none as high or heartfelt as my own. We were visited by the likes of Salmon Chase, Thurlow Weed, Simon Cameron, Carl Schurz, even Horace Greeley. They reviewed each point Abraham made, and I heard quotes from his Quincy speech that I had not heard before:

"Does Sen. Douglas mean to say the territorial legislature can nullify a constitutional right by withholding necessary laws or passing unfriendly ones? Does he mean to ignore the proposition, so long and well established in law, that what you can't do directly, you can't do indirectly? The truth about the matter is this: He has sung praises to his popular sovereignty doctrine till his Supreme Court, cooperating with him, has squatted his squatter sovereignty out.

"Douglas has at last invented this sort of do-nothing sovereignty—that people can exclude slavery by doing nothing at all. Ain't that running his popular sovereignty down awfully? Ain't it got down about as thin as a homeopathic soup made by boiling the shadow of a pigeon that's starved to death?" What a clever man, my husband!

Oct. 25, 1858: I dreamed last night of sex and slavery:

I was gone from Abraham's life, presumably dead, and he, like Thomas Jefferson, took a slave into his bed. Then he married the negro woman, with our sons at their side. He looked into her eyes and said, "I will love you until day and night are one, until life itself has ended. And then I will love you even beyond." She read the inscription inside her ring: "Love is everlasting."

Their sexual union was vivid and multicolored. I recognized Abraham's embraces and heard his deepest moans. Even in my death, I sweltered with jealousy.

I recounted the nightmare between sniffles. Abraham brushed it off. "Don't get worked up, Mother. You're simply responding in your sleep to Douglas' never-ending nagging about us being white negroes. Don't go giving yourself one of those three-day collapses."

"Could you ever love a black woman?" I asked.

"Now you sound like a Democrat. How would I know the answer? I ain't never really thought about your not being here, and never considered finding another wife of any color. And I ain't got time to keep a woman in the barn. I've lived till my 50th year without having a negro woman for a slave or a wife, and I think I can live another 50 years—50 centuries for that matter—without having one for either. Stop fretting over my feelings for you. I'm not leaving, no matter how dotty you get."

Oct. 30, 1858: Abraham's final speech was tonight at the closing Republican rally here in Springfield. 63 speeches since August 12, more than 85 hours of speaking, a traveling distance of 4200 miles. The papers say Stephen spent more than $50,000 during the debates. We spent almost all we had saved—a little more than $250—and about the same in loans and donations.

This speech resonated much like the others, strongly punctuated with ardor, earnestness, pacing, and perspiration. The crowd of approximately 15,000 was loud, and I wonder if they heard a word he said for the screaming and stomping. He began by calling them friends: "I stand here surrounded by friends—some political, all personal I trust."

He ended by saying, "I claim no insensibility to political honors. But today, could the Missouri restriction be restored and the whole slavery question be replaced on the old grounds of toleration by necessity where it exists, with unyielding hostility to its spread, I'd gladly agree that Douglas should never be from, and I never in, an office, so long as we both or either live." It was very well received and we're in fine spirits this evening!

Nov. 1, 1858: It has been raining all day—a dark, icy rain. I don't like the omen. The mud is knee-deep and may keep voters away. I have a stabbing pain in my back and a worse one in my heart. My stomach churns. I worry that all our work and plans have been for nothing. Abraham's gloom permeates the house and hides only dimly behind his weary eyes. He drags around in his ancient gray shawl, buckskin slippers on his throbbing feet. The weather hurts his joints and makes him sniffle. Please, Lord, don't allow us to lose. Oh God, please....

Nov. 2, 1858: It continues to rain, inside my soul and outside the house. The Democrats have taken control of the legislature and Stephen Douglas will be the next senator from Illinois. Even though Republicans received 4,000 more votes, because of something called legislative apportionment, which I believe is highly illegal, the Democrats have the majority. Something is very rotten in Denmark! How could we lose when we had the most votes? This is one aspect of democracy I just don't understand, and I'll never trust the cheating government again.[15]

Though disappointed, Abraham says he had a word from God as he walked home from the telegraph office. When I asked why he came in so soiled, he said, "I fell in the mud. The path was pig-backed and slippery. My right foot slewed, knocking my left out of the way and leaving me none to stand on. As I rose from the puddle, I heard a voice in my head say, 'It's a slip, not a fall, Lincoln, a slip and not a fall.' Let's believe that, shall we?" Bah!

Nov. 4, 1858, our 16th anniversary: The Lincoln home is still quiet and bleak, but Abraham shows little outward emotion. When I mentioned his lack of disappointment and asked if he was still breathing, he said, "You ain't the only one who's hurting, Mother. I wanted the office too, with more than merely a minor, selfish interest. Inside, I feel like hell—like a flat failure. But Douglas managed to be supported as the best instrument both to break down and to uphold the slave power. He has the high distinction, so far as I know, of being the only person in politics not to declare slavery either right or wrong. Almost everybody says one or the other, but Douglas never does. It was a coup, but it won't last. No ingenuity can keep this deception forever. But some other man will have to fight it next time. I'm done. My political career is over."

I know Abraham wanted to win, but I put even more effort and prayer into the race than even he and don't understand how I could have been so wrong. My senses never lie. I haven't felt this empty since losing my darling Eddy. Why must we continue to lose everything?

Nov. 15, 1858: Stephen invited us to a grand fête, but I refused to go. I won't be humiliated again. He and his lovely wife can just go to hell! We've received many condolence visits and letters, but I want none of it. Abraham

---

[15] In those days, there was no popular vote for the Senate, and neither name appeared on a ballot. Instead, the voters elected state representatives who elected the senator. Technically, Lincoln won, because Republican legislative candidates received more votes than Democrats. But, with the holdovers in the legislature, Democrats maintained a 54-46 majority and assured Douglas' election.

is slowly becoming jovial again, calling himself "convalescent but not terminal." He said, "Get out of bed and stop sniveling, Mother, and you'll feel better. We had great sport in this contest. Another blow-up will come someday and we'll have fun again." I don't understand how he can take life and loss so lightly. This is not fun.

Nov. 25, 1858, Thanksgiving: We received several invitations for supper, including Elizabeth and Ninian, but declined. I'm in no mood to hear my sister dwell on the merits of her fair daughters and talented son-in-law. I'm also too ill to be seen and too hoarse from crying to be heard. My eyes are blotchy. No amount of tint will put color back into my cheeks or cover the darkness under my eyes. Abraham told one caller he felt like the boy who stubbed his big toe: "It hurts too bad to laugh and I'm too big to cry." Bah! I don't mind admitting my pain.

I heard Abraham tell Mr. Gourley, "This loss has given me a hearing on the great questions of the age, which I couldn't have gotten any other way. Though I'll now sink from view and be forgotten politically, I believe I made some marks that will help the cause of civil liberty long after I'm gone. I reckon we've fairly entered on a durable struggle as to whether this nation is to ultimately become all slave or all free, and though I fell early in the contest, it's nothing if I contributed, in the least degree, to the rightful result. I've got an abiding faith that we'll beat them in the long run. Stroke by stroke, the Democrats' objectives will become too obvious for the people to stand them."

How noble and philosophical, My Dear! Have you read this quote from the *Chicago Times*? It should bring you back to earth.

> Lincoln put up a good fight, but was no match for the little giant. From all accounts, he is much in need of money, but he has taken his defeat in a good-natured way, and is again practicing law. It is most likely the last we will hear from him as a politician and the Republican Party may die a quiet death before the next election.

Nov. 28, 1858: Norman Judd came by to console us again today, but his smile is as counterfeit as mine. He said, "Hard as this loss is, Lincoln, the Republicans have to go on. Trumbull has to be re-elected to the Senate next term, and you have to make it clear that you aren't ambitious for his seat."

Abraham replied, "I won't be in nobody's way for any of the places. I've enlisted for the permanent success of the Republican cause and I'll be fighting in the ranks. You can count on it." But don't count on it too heartily, Mr. Judd, for Mrs. Lincoln did not make such a promise.

Dec. 12, 1858: How quickly life changes! A month ago we were lost from all political hopes; now the *Illinois Gazette, Chicago Democrat,* and *Olney Times* have recommended Abraham for President! Can this really be true? For so long, I've waited and dreamed, planned and schemed, prayed and pleaded with God. Will any other state come out for us?

Goodbye, Journal. Next year I'll either be electioneering for President or be back to the life of a poor circuit lawyer's wife. We've been on expenses for so long without earning anything that we're absolutely without money now for household purposes. I'll be forced to return everything I purchased this year and hope Abraham doesn't discover that accounts are still due. We'll go to the wall for bread and meat if he neglects his business next year as he did this, because Herndon still doesn't help.

Still, if we can get more support for the Presidency, we'll be back on top. Even if we don't achieve the supreme position, the Vice Presidency will give us the White House! I'll pray very hard.

Dec. 16, 1858: I visited a spiritualist this week and asked about our future. The answer: "A strong future and a rebound very soon. But you must always be careful what you wish for; sometimes when the gods want to punish us, they answer our prayers." I wonder what that means?

Dec. 25, 1858, Christmas: Bob has asked again to attend Harvard University. I would truly die from the separation, but he's a willful child. When he wants, he wants desperately, and refuses to give in. His interest in higher education may have been advanced when his friend John Hay entered Brown University, because John's letters intrigue with fun, people, and excitement.

Abraham is concerned about the expense. We put so much money into the campaign, and those traitors in the Republican committee have actually asked us to send more! They should be sending money to us! Where are those generous, wealthy Republicans up north? Why don't they come forward and help their standard-bearer? It's not right! Still, we promised another $500. Abraham says we could sell the house, but I'll give up all else first.

I secretly wonder if he is more concerned about the money or the "snobbery" involved with Harvard. He argues that Bob should remain stable, especially as he is only 16.[16] But our son will never gain the prominence of which he is capable if he stays in Springfield. The schools are too easy, his ambition is not stoked, and there are not enough quality educators to train him for the life he wants and deserves. He wants to live

---

[16] Most young men, if they continued into higher learning at all, did so in their early teens.

like Elizabeth and Ninian, not counting pennies like his own parents. Who can blame him? And if he does go, Ninian will no longer be able to peacock strut about his son going to Yale!

Dec. 27, 1858: Jesse Fell, a most reliable man from Bloomington, has confirmed that Abraham's name is being bandied in other states as a Presidential candidate: New York, New Jersey, Pennsylvania, Ohio, Michigan, Indiana. Though Fell has little faith in our final success, he believes Abraham will be a good choice because of the reputation and following gained through the debates. Fell has strong ties in his native state of Pennsylvania and wants to support us there. Even if we lose this time, we will be invincible in '64! Abraham says he doesn't want to be President, but realizes that campaigning for the position might give him a better chance at the Senate next term if he decides to run, and would widely publicize Republican principles, so he's considering the opportunity.

Mr. Fell asked Abraham a question I have never heard him asked: What is democracy? My husband laid his fork on the table and perched his elbows next to his plate. He looked toward the ceiling, clasped his hands together in a prayer-like position, slowly cleared his throat, and replied, "It's simple to me. As I wouldn't be a slave, so I wouldn't be a master. This expresses my idea of democracy. Anything different from this ain't democracy. I go for sharing the privileges of government with those folks who assist in bearing its burdens. Labor is the common burden of our race, and the effort of some to shift their share onto the shoulders of others is our great curse. As Daniel Webster and William Lloyd Garrison both so eloquently said, a democratic government is a government of the people, by the people, and for the people."

Feb. 6, 1859: What a fête we hosted last evening, the grandest since 1857! Everyone of political prominence convened in our home, including all the legislators. A rainbow of dresses, musicians playing till dawn, food catered to perfection. We have shown Springfield that we're in the swing again!

Feb. 12, 1859, Abraham's 50th birthday: Old Abe, my foot! Young, virile, and insatiable! This morning, we enjoyed predawn passion seldom equaled since our youth. How I love these cold winter dawns between the comforters, waking up to roosters crowing and turning over to touch my adored husband's strong thin frame. I never cease to be aroused by his awakening, and am thrilled each time he touches me with his lips or caresses me with his hands. We are too busy during the day to show the affection we once had leisure for, but before the house is awake, life is all ours and we revel in it.

Feb. 15, 1859: Abraham asked a gentleman of his acquaintance to publish the recent debates in book form, but was refused because "no one would want them." We also asked Simeon Francis, who similarly declined. How wrong men of limited sight can be! We will rebound; I will see to it. I don't know how or when, but we'll be on track again soon.

Feb. 28, 1859: Tad is quite sick. He passed a bad, bad night and I don't like his symptoms. Willie Wallace thinks he may have a slight case of lung fever. I summoned Ozias Hatch, who leaves for Chicago this evening, and asked him to find Abraham there and tell him to come home immediately. I am at my wits' end. How am I supposed to manage all these troubles alone?

Mar. 4, 1859: Abraham arrived at noon, just in time to hear Dr. Willie say that Tad has pneumonia. I am terrified. If I should lose another baby, I could never walk this earth again. He is so precious that God could never create another like him. Abraham sat with Tad the rest of the day while I tried to rest, but it's impossible. Even with extra medication. When I tire enough to close my eyes, Eddy's spirit takes my hand. While I could probably sleep in his presence, I don't want to lose sight of him. He says he's not ready to receive Tad just yet, so I'm more confident of the outcome of this illness. Abraham says my visions are wishful thinking, not prescience or prediction, but I know Eddy is with me and I believe his words.

Mar. 6, 1859: Tad is finally improving, so Abraham will leave again tomorrow. We have had little time together, being always at our son's bedside. Willie also proved a good tender for his brother. As Tad breathes easier, so do we all. What a fright! Perhaps I can doze a bit tonight.

Mar. 28, 1859: Though Abraham is working diligently at his practice and bringing in funds, I wish he were out in public making speeches. I don't want Stephen Douglas to watch us fade from sight, nor do I want to lose society's recognition. In town, I'm greeted so cordially: "Good morning, Mrs. Lincoln," "How are the boys, Mrs. Lincoln?" "Is it true your husband will be nominated for the Presidency, Mrs. Lincoln?" Yes, I admit I enjoy the admiration of others and don't want to lose it because of a few wayward voters!

Apr. 4, 1859, Tad's 6th birthday: We spoke tonight about sending Tad to Miss Corcoran's school, as he is the right age, but the boy is not eager. In fact, he ran screaming from the room at the mention, even though Willie enjoys his time there and Tad questions him each afternoon about his "thool" activities. Abraham said, "Let it be, Mother, he's got plenty of time to grow up." I wish he never had to grow up and could remain my baby forever, but I know it cannot be. A boy needs education and social skills.

I believe Tad's reluctance is influenced by his lisp. We are the only ones who can understand him now without difficulty, and the neighborhood children hardly try anymore. They laugh and call him "Twad Winkum." Yes, I'm sure that's it. His embarrassment would be even worse with strangers. I'll continue to teach him myself till he's more prepared to tackle the outside world.

Apr. 8, 1859: A horrible blow for my beloved husband. He drove to Bloomington this morning to deliver his Inventions speech, but so few attended that the engagement was cancelled. He wears a wounded face and refuses to talk about it, or anything at all for that matter. I tried to humor him out of his hypo. "Don't!" he commanded as sharply as I have ever heard. "That plagues me." He is difficult to be around. Though truly a minor defeat, this has hurt him worse than our political loss. I will never understand his priorities.

Apr. 15, 1859: The worse news possible: My dear friend Hannah Shearer, whose poor husband has contracted tuberculosis, is leaving me to move to Pennsylvania. What will I do without her to share my soul? She often stays with me when Abraham is away, and shares my shopping sprees, and I enjoy her company immensely. If only I had a daughter with whom to share my life, entrust my hopes and dreams, open my heart. If only....

Apr. 18, 1859: Hannah and I could not resist going to town one last time. I was in such a high, gay mood that I purchased another 16 yards of plaid silk, and 11 yards of cambric, 14 yards of grenadine, and 16 yards of cashmere. Also assorted ruches, chenilles, buttons, stockings. Abraham would be angry at the total of $40, but Clark will keep my credit silent till I can pay it from the household funds. The final outfits will be so exquisite that my frugal husband won't be able to resist me when he's home again.

Apr. 24, 1859: Abraham spent this beautiful spring day playing ball and spinning tops with the boys while I lounged in the parlor and mended socks, trying to keep broth and biscuits inside my stomach. Oh how I tire of torn toes and heels. With four men in the house, I have a never-ending supply of holes!

Apr. 26, 1859: Abraham delivered the Inventions speech again at the courthouse. I attended to hear for myself why this talk, unlike all others, is not well received. I knew immediately. It's his lack of fire, his lack of passion. He loves inventions to be sure, and he has studied long and duteously for this presentation, but the topic doesn't set his heart aflame. Nor anyone else's. People just don't care enough about the issue to jump to their feet. No, it's a good thing he has politics and slavery about which to make speeches. He is not an orator who can speak on mundane things. Abraham himself says he won't attempt this topic again.

When we arrived home, we learned that the gray tabby cat had died and the boys were inconsolable. I churned peach ice cream for dessert.

May 8, 1859: Abraham accepted my suggestion that we purchase the weekly German newspaper *Staats-Anzeiger*, which Theodore Canisius has been trying to sell for some months! How I used to treasure being at the *Journal* with Abraham, setting type and reading drafts, laughing at silly ideas and comments. Remember the Aunt Rebecca letters? Oh we did have some grand experiences!

When I approached him about it, he said, "Why on earth would you even consider such a purchase? And where would we get the money?"

I was prepared. "It's a fine paper, Father, and the Republicans need the backing of the German neighborhood. It will cost only $400 for the type, press, mailing lists, and all equipment. I spoke to Jacob Bunn at the bank and he says we can use our Iowa land as collateral. Mr. Canisius says he will continue as editor if we buy it. We can both write articles touting the Republican platform. We can also run all the 'Lincoln for Senate' or 'Lincoln for President' ads we want. No one needs to know we own the paper, and we can sell it after the election if we choose."

"But," he protested, "we don't speak a word of German!"

"Of course we do. *Kaufman* means merchant, *schneider* means tailor, *wahlstimme* means vote, gloves is *handschuhe*, love is *liebe*, and money is *geld*. What else do we need to know?"

He chuckled at my logic. "Well, My Dear, if you think it's a good idea, I reckon I'll have to go along. There's no stopping you when your mind's made up."

May 10, 1859: Abraham has been invited to the Republican convention next week in Kansas. "May I go with you?" I asked after reading the letter, using the conversation as an excuse to stop mending for a while.

"I ain't going, Mother. They'll probably adopt a platform and I'm afraid they'll lower their standards to gather recruits. That'd be a serious mistake and open a gap that more would pass out of than in."

"Why do you feel this way?" I inquired.

He unconsciously balled up his fists. "They're fighting Douglasism and the southern opposition element. Giving in to either would surrender our whole objective of stopping slavery's spread and nationalization. If this goal is surrendered, the party will go to pieces."

I looked into his eyes. "What if they place a southern man on the ticket instead of a northerner?"

He went to the window, dragging his fingers through his hair. Will I now have to cut his hair as I do the boys' because he won't take time to visit the barber? He replied, "I've got no problem with a southern man on the national ticket. There's many in the slave states I could cheerfully vote for, either for President or Vice President, if he promised safety for the Republican cause and wouldn't let down our standards."

I hesitated, then barged on. "What if they should decide to nominate you for President?"

He smiled. "Such likely won't happen, but if it does, somebody will come tell me."

Just then, Willie arrived home from school and began to race Tad through the kitchen, two hounds following in hot pursuit. Abraham grabbed Tad in midair and held him at arm's length, laughing as the boy tried to kick him in the chest. "Your legs ain't quite long enough, Boy!" Abraham squealed.

Tad clenched his fist in much the same way Abraham had done a few moments earlier and shook it at his father. "Thus jud wade, Papa, thus jud wade. Thumday I'll be bidder!"

May 21, 1859: Alone again. Before he returns, Abraham will speak in Wisconsin, Iowa, Ohio, Indiana, and Kansas. The Republican committee met last week but finalized only policy and plank, not candidate. Head runners are handsome Salmon Chase of Ohio, unremarkable John McLean of Ohio, rich William Seward of New York, and beloved Abraham Lincoln of Illinois. I'm too scared to be excited. Do I truly want this? Perhaps Abraham is right, perhaps the Senate would be enough. No, it would never be enough, so why waste another 10 years waiting? My predictions were correct from the beginning. My senses never fail me.

May 25, 1859: I thought the worst had happened when the Shearers and the Wheelocks moved away, but now my dearest friend of all is leaving me. Eliza Francis, who has been my mother stead for so many years; who reconciled me with my beloved; who has stood by us, loaned us money, tended our children, witnessed our family births and deaths. She and Simeon are moving to Oregon. I don't believe my heart can bear it. Eliza means more to me than my sisters. I have no friends or confidantes left in the city. I'm alone again, so I must try even harder to arrange the promotion that will take us to Washington. Oh my God, how would I go on if we were to lose the nomination? No, I won't think about it.

June 1, 1859: I made a wrong stitch somewhere in the silk dress and can't see how to correct it. Perhaps I should consider spectacles like Abraham's. Aging is a miserable condition. I engaged Mrs. LaBarthe, the

Irish dressmaker, to finish the outfit and also make up the plaid one. They will look like they were made in NY! With all the work I've already completed, both will cost only $38. I despise worrying about money, but Abraham will probably not deny me, especially since I began them on my own.

<u>June 5, 1859:</u> Abraham has to go to Chicago again next week and asked if Willie could go along. How wonderful for them both to spend some time together! As dearly as Willie loves trains, I fear he will be too excited to eat and will return home emaciated. They will stay at the Tremont, a superb hotel. I admit here only that I'm envious of the time Willie will get to spend with his father.

<u>June 8, 1859:</u> A letter from Willie, clearly indicating how much his mind functions like Abraham's: "Chicago's a beauteous place and the weather is very, very fine. We have a nice little room to ourselves. There's 2 pitchers on a washstand – the smallest one for me, the largest one for Papa. We also have 2 towels, 2 beds, and 2 washbasins of the same size. Me and Papa went to 2 theatres the other night and have also been to an exhibition."

<u>June 26, 1859:</u> We have had a continual round of parties. Last week, we ourselves hosted a strawberry company for about 70, and an even larger dinner party for the men who helped Abraham this and last year. We must be certain they will help us again. We spent five evenings out this week and I'm happy to simply savor this quiet day of rest.

Julia Trumbull attended the Remanns' dinner, looking as gauche and ungainly as ever. Though she has been in the city 10 days, and her husband has been mentioned as a nominee for President, this was the first notice taken of her by the papers. It's unfortunate, I suppose, to be so unpopular, but she brought it on herself by exposing her ignoble heart. Her name and tongue have become well established, and others hold grudges more than I.

<u>July 28, 1859:</u> Jesse Fell called again, still trying to convince Abraham to make himself available for the Presidential nomination. "Why are you hesitating?" Fell asked over raisin scones. A question I've been asking for weeks!

Abraham chewed silently for a moment and then answered, "I very much regretted two things the Republican convention in Ohio did: the repudiation of Judge Swan and the plank for repeal of the Fugitive Slave Law. Many good men consider these in disregard of the Constitution itself. I won't agree to be in nomination, even if they should have me, if these are included in our next national convention. I can't stand behind them and won't have them stand behind me."

He sipped his coffee before continuing. "Another thing our friends are doing that gives me some uneasiness is leaning toward Douglas' insidious popular sovereignty idea. I've got some substantial objections to this. First, no party can command respect by sustaining this year what it opposed last. Second, Douglas is the most dangerous enemy of liberty we face today, but still his Republican friends magnify him and his humbug. How can I stand with men who stand with Douglas? But chiefly, I oppose his idea of popular sovereignty, now almost accepted by the public mind as a just principle because of the way he has spun the issue. I won't be even narrowly associated with it." Fell left empty-handed.

Aug. 1, 1859, Bob's 16th birthday: Tomorrow he leaves for Harvard, all the way across the country! We will miss him dreadfully, and I can hardly write about it now. We'll simply have to travel north more frequently.

Bob carries with him a letter of introduction from our friend and enemy Stephen Douglas. My senses tell me Stephen's recommendation regarding the "son of my dear friend" is all that allowed Bob's acceptance into such a prestigious institution. That and a bond for the annual dues signed by Judge Julius Rockwell, Judge David Davis' brother-in-law, who knew Abraham in Congress. The promise of an unknown lawyer from rustic Illinois did not suffice to ensure payment at Harvard. They have never heard of Abraham Lincoln. Not yet. We will change all that soon, I vow it. Someday young men will come to <u>my</u> husband for introductions to high places.

Aug. 6, 1859: Because of Bob's departure, I suppose, I developed a throbbing headache and wasn't able to train to Cambridge with him. I tried not to embarrass him by dissolving into tears on the platform as we said goodbye. To himself, he's a grown man, but to me he's another baby lost. Abraham also left today to view land in Council Bluffs that Norman Judd wants to use as security for a debt. How nice that someone owes us for a change! Abraham will make a speech while there and meet with Republican leaders.

Aug. 15, 1859: Terrible news from Bob. He failed 15 of his 16 entrance exams and will not be allowed into Harvard. How could such happen? I tutored him regularly on those subjects. He's a rare bird, my son, who hears only what he chooses to hear. That trait he gets from his father. Upon the recommendation of Harvard's president, however, Bob was accepted into Phillips Exeter Academy, in New Hampshire, for a preparatory year.

Aug. 20, 1859: Bob is home, and seems more mature and determined to succeed. He has resolved not to retire beaten from education. Abraham said to him, "It pains me that you're in this position. And yet there's very little in it if you won't allow discouragement to seize and prey on you. You can enter and graduate from Harvard when your spirit and mind are ready."

Bob said he felt demeaned at Harvard, as though people from Illinois are wild, uncivilized, and not good enough to walk its hallowed halls. We will change that opinion when we return to Washington in our exalted position.

Aug. 25, 1859: Bob has left for Exeter, and I worry I shall never see him again. I have had two dreams of violence and mayhem in which he was brutally stabbed—murdered in the prime of his youth. If these visions continue, they will drive me mad. Sometimes I wish I were not so sensitive to the dangers around me. I'll consult a spiritualist as soon as possible to confirm his safety.

Sept. 14, 1859: Because Stephen Douglas is pulling some Republicans to his side, the party leaders are opening their moth-filled purses a bit! They provided the funds for Willie and me to train to Columbus with Abraham tomorrow to refute Stephen's recent comments and speak out against popular sovereignty once again. If Ohio elects a Democratic legislature, the Republican Presidential candidate will have no chance. Abraham will speak on the 16th and we will return on the 19th. I had already invited Miss Corcoran to spend some weeks with us, so she will move in today and keep Tad while we are traveling.

Sept. 16, 1859: Though the crowd was small, Abraham's speech was a marvel. I am so, so proud of him. Stephen sat in the audience, and to my amazement, he now wears a full beard! It's a strange look for one with such a large round head. Here are some of Abraham's speech excerpts from the *Columbus Times*:

> The chief danger to the Republican Party just now ain't revival of the African slave trade, or passage of a congressional slave code, or even a second Dred Scott decision that would make slavery lawful in all states. The most imminent danger now is that insidious Douglas popular sovereignty. I say the "Douglas popular sovereignty," for there's a broad distinction between that article and genuine popular sovereignty. I believe there is a genuine popular sovereignty and a definition would be this: Each man shall do precisely as he pleases with himself, and with all those things that exclusively concern him.
>
> Applied to government, this principle would mean that a general government shall do all those things that pertain to it, and all the local governments shall do precisely as they please in respect to those matters that exclusively concern them. I understand that this government is based on this principle; and I'm misunderstood if you

think I've got any war to make on it.

This slavery thing is a durable element of discord among us, and we'll probably not have peace in this country till it either masters the free principle in our government or is so far mastered that the public firmly believes it's going to end.

Sept. 17, 1859: Abraham spoke today in Dayton and Cincinnati. Here is an excerpt from his speech to the southern faction:

The issue between us is that I think slavery is wrong and ought not to be outspread, and you think it's right and ought to be extended and perpetuated.

There's abundant history to show that the framers of the Constitution expected the African slave trade to be abolished at the end of 20 years, to which time their prohibition against its being abolished extended. But, while they so expected, they gave nothing for that expectation, and they put no provision in the Constitution requiring it should be so. They were that sure of its natural extinction. As to this planned extinction, the Republicans, and others who oppose slavery, intend to stand by our guns, to be patient and firm and, in the long run, to beat you on this issue.

When we do beat you, maybe you want to know what we'll do with you. We mean to treat you, near as we possibly can, as Washington, Jefferson, and Madison treated you. We mean to leave you alone, and in no way interfere with your institution; to abide by every compromise of the Constitution, according to the examples of those noble fathers. We mean to remember that you're as good as we; that there's no difference between us other than the difference of circumstances. We mean to bear in mind always that you have good hearts in your bosoms and treat you accordingly.

I've told you what we mean to do. I want to know now what you mean to do. I often hear it intimated that you mean to divide the Union as soon as any Republican is elected President. I want to know what you're going to do with your half of it? Are you going to split the Ohio down through, and push your half off a piece? Or are you going to keep it right alongside of us outrageous fellows? Are you going to build up a wall some way between your country and ours, so that certain movable property of yours can't come over here anymore? Do you think you can better yourselves by leaving us here under no obligation whatever to return those who do come over?

You've divided the Union because we wouldn't do right with you, as you think, on that subject. When we ain't under obligations to do anything for you, how much better off do you think you'll be? Will you make war and kill us all?

Why, gentlemen, I think you're as gallant and as brave any men alive; that you can fight as bravely in a good cause, man for man, as any other people living; that you have shown yourselves capable of this on various occasions. But, man for man, you ain't better than us, and there ain't as many of you as there are of us. You'll never make much of a hand at whipping us. If we were fewer in numbers than you, I think you might whip us; if we were equal, it would likely be a draw; but being less in numbers, you'll make nothing by attempting to master us.

Sept. 19, 1859: Home again, fatigued but happy. We saw some other portions of Ohio and had several warm visits with political friends and distant relatives. I do so love traveling about!

Tad developed a cough while we were gone and can't stop spitting up long enough to ask his thousands of questions about our trip, but he has come to love Miss Corcoran!

Sept. 21, 1859: Norman Judd brought a letter from Iowa promising to fully support Abraham for VP and partially support him for President! We agree that Vice President will be an acceptable title in '60 (with Salmon Chase as President), then President in '64. My stubborn husband's head is finally facing the White House!

Oct. 10, 1859: Abraham left again today to attend court in Clinton, having been home only a few days in total. With Bob also gone, I feel even more unsettled than usual. I am wild to see my son, though he has been gone barely six weeks. What will I be like in a year? I miss having him to protect me when Abraham is gone; I felt secure when he shared my bed. Now I depend on Willie to be the little man and guard his mother. Both boys often sleep with me, and I sometimes allow them to spend the night in Abraham's big bed. With the door open, I can hear them breathe and know I'm not truly alone.

Dec. 9, 1859: To my delight, more newspapers, many in the midwest, are suggesting that Abraham would be a wise candidate for the Republicans to consider, and Norman Fell asked him to write a biography to help the accepting newspapers spread our name and accomplishments. Fell says Abraham needs somebody to "run" him, like Thurlow Weed is running William Seward in New York and Thaddeus Stevens is running John McLean in Ohio.

Finally someone sees our true potential. Abraham certainly does not. "Just think of a sucker like me as President!" he laughed when I showed him the endorsement from the *Chicago Tribune*. I am, My Dear. I have been thinking of little else for nearly 20 years.

"And why not?" I asked him over roasted pig and mashed potatoes.

He put down his fork. "I reckon I ain't the fittest person to answer that. When a man who ain't very great begins to be mentioned for a very great position, his head's likely to be a little turned. I can surely do better in that profession, though, than as an Inventions lecturer. But it won't go. You know I ain't got a chance against the likes of Seward, Chase, Bates, and the others who are so intimately associated with the party principles. Nobody knows me at all except through a few speeches."

I took his hands in mine and felt love and protection coursing through them. "I told you many years ago that the whole world would soon know you. I've always believed in you. And I sense that your time is almost here. Yes, you're unknown, but that will work for us, because you're marked as neither radical nor conservative. Because you've been in Congress only once, you have no record that can be used against you and you have few enemies, except those who also want the prize."

I released his hands so he could continue eating. "What the Republican Party needs is a man of simplicity, one with a deep soul who is committed to fight inequality and the atrocities of slavery. Seward and Chase have both made radical statements and backed unpopular causes. They have made enemies and I believe our strength is in their weaknesses. People have come to love you, Abraham. You have attacked no man, hardly even Stephen Douglas in open debate. You cause men's brains to think and women's heartstrings to mourn. You're destined, just as I always sensed. We will see the White House in 1860—perhaps as second in command, but that will be all right. You write the biography Mr. Fell requested, and quickly. We have no time to waste. Then we'll talk to David Davis and Norman Judd about running you."

He wrapped his arms around me. His heart raced even into his legs, as though he had been playing handball. I looked up, expecting to see a flushed complexion, but he was placid, his eyes closed in thought, his head barely nodding in agreement.

Dec. 10, 1859: Abraham showed his "biography" to me and I could hardly restrain my laughter. This is what he thinks will get him elected President:

- Born February 12, 1809, in Hardin County, Kentucky.
- Education, defective.
- Profession, a lawyer.
- A captain of volunteers in Black Hawk War.
- Postmaster at a very small office.
- Four times a member of the Illinois legislature and once of the lower house of Congress.

When I questioned its unnecessary brevity, he responded, "There ain't much of it for the reason, I suppose, that there ain't much of me." Rather than his writing and my editing, we will change roles.

<u>Dec. 12, 1859:</u> Another year has sped by like the newest train. We accomplished a great deal, though our future is still uncertain. Like the engine, we're moving forward. Unlike it, I don't know our destination. The unending sleet has chilled our bodies, but not our internal flames. Our political fires once again stoke the fires of our desire, and we approach the new year with the heightened passion of young people in love and on a mission. Abraham hopes for a secure future, and I won't counteract his expectation with needless spending or nagging. I ask forgiveness for my tantrums this year and for demanding so much from my husband as he travels this unknown and frightening road. I may lose my position as his advisor to men more politically wise, like Fell and Judd, but I won't harp. Abraham needs all my support. I beg God's help in this endeavor.

Dec. 15, 1859: Abraham is still backwashing. He refuses to believe he has an iota of a chance to become President, even though his supporters proclaim it constantly. He believes this nomination is simply a maneuver to bring his name to national attention so he can be unchallenged in the next Senate race. Or perhaps he keeps his bigger dreams silent.

"Seward will beat me easily, Mother, and if he don't, Bates is in the wings. Hell, I may vote for Bates! How could I even hope to be nominated for President, much less win it? I've never held any national office except one term as an unnoticed representative. I've never served in the Cabinet, never been nominated as governor or mayor, nothing. I wasn't even born in one of the original colonies and no President has ever been elected from outside that area. I'm an untended garden with a few cabbages sprouting forth here and there to support me. I'd do better, and enjoy myself more, in the Senate. I can probably take Douglas' seat next time, but I don't have a black rabbit's chance of being elected President. A bird in the hand, you know. No, I'm going to just keep working behind the scenes, unless the party assigns me a different position, which I don't think likely unless they're lacking a VP. That position wouldn't be so bad, would it? There's just some fleas a dog can't reach, and he ought not to waste time scratching."

Dec. 18, 1859: I have rewritten Abraham's biography, lengthening it greatly, and he has edited it to his liking. We'll send it to Fell this week. We have heard that Stephen Douglas' baby girl has died, his wife is very ill, and he has left Congress to go home. I pray for them. He may be our rival, but he has always been our friend too.

Dec. 20, 1859: Norman Judd has entered the governor's race and I sense Abraham wishes he had also done so. He could easily win as governor. Since that would be the end of our dreams, I avoided the topic each time he brought it up. Judd, though our adversary in the '54 Senate campaign, has been our friend for some time, and promises to support our Presidential efforts, but I'm uneasy about him. Something in my soul tells me he won't stick with us. I saw him conversing on the street with Herndon, which bodes poorly. We know for truth that Herndon has been passing untrue and unjust statements about me, and Abraham has spoken to him about this embarrassment. He, of course, denied the charges. At least Abraham has learned to be more cautious in what he shares with that snake and agreed to keep him from our affairs as much as possible. For that I am grateful.

Abraham is spending much time at the library, pouring over the *Congressional Globe, Annals of Congress, Debates on the Federal Constitution,* and I can only imagine what other tomes. He has not worked so hard on a speech in many months. This one will be delivered in NY.

Dec. 23, 1859: The Republican National Committee requested permission to publish the debates scrapbook! We worked very hard cutting, pasting, and organizing the book, and now Abraham will be a published author! This will surely be persuasive material for people on the voting fence!

Jan. 1, 1860: What a glorious day! Hundreds came, many bringing food, books, toys for the children, scarves and gloves for me, umbrellas and totes for Abraham. I have never eaten so much in one day or shaken so many hands. Willie answered the door till he completely exhausted himself and had to be put to bed. He now says he would enjoy owning an inn and greeting guests all day. This is the life I've always wanted, and I am savoring every moment! Just to have Abraham at home each night makes our toils worthwhile.

Jan. 2, 1860: Received an invitation from Gov. and Mrs. Matteson for a large entertainment on Wednesday evening. Abraham gave me permission to go, but declined for himself. Though I'll never forgive the scoundrel for the Senate results in 1855, I do love grand parties! I would like to attend, but will also probably spend the evening at home.

The cow is very sick and I sense we will need a new one very soon. For once, I'm glad it's so intensely cold; I can save the meat.

Jan. 15, 1860: The *Chicago Press and Tribune* has emphatically endorsed Abraham for President, reprinted parts of the debates book, and called

Abraham "a man of the people, a champion of free labor." The *Illinois Journal* has done likewise, adding, "It is a most delicate and expressive compliment that the name of 'Old Abe,' the leader of the great Republican army of the northwest, has become a name of power and might." A name of power and might! How I love phrases of that sort. They will look good on candidacy posters.

Feb. 9, 1860: The attacks are now starting in earnest, which means the other men on the Republican horizon are running scared. These foiled assailants are extremely bitter, and we fear they may lay to the Bates egg in the south and Seward in the north, squeezing us out in the middle. We're writing a dozen letters a day asking our supporters, and those who have not yet proclaimed, for their help in winning this nomination. We have heeded John Wentworth's admonition to watch for prominence. Now that it appears none of the prominent candidates can be nominated, it's time to move.

Feb. 22, 1860, Washington's Birthday: Abraham refused to speak at the festivities. He said it would not be fair to the other candidates! This man has no idea how to win a political race! We stayed as much in the background as we could, but were often trailed and pointed out. I heard constant whispers: "Look, Mr. Lincoln and his family are here! Come see, he may be our next President!" I could not restrain my happiness and gleamed at everyone we passed.

The weather was bitterly cold, and I'm retiring early. Abraham will feed the boys and, if his behavior continues as it has for months, I won't feel his presence in my bed tonight. He reads, I believe, till he sees the sun begin to rise and only then does he lay his head on the pillow for a few moments of rest.

He leaves for Manhattan soon. I haven't seen him this concerned about a talk in many years. Since the group is paying his expenses, he is going on to Exeter afterward to speak at the academy and visit with Bob. He has been trying to get north for some months, because we're both concerned about our oldest son and his progress. I have a large package prepared for Bob with shirts, shoes, books, his favorite almond cookies, and a warm robe— New Hampshire is under five feet of snow!

I also prepared a valise for Abraham containing his black broadcloth suit, carefully pressed; black stockings; crisp white shirt with rounded collar and pearl buttons; black silk tie; black galluses; his best silk hat; and soft leather pull-on boots that don't hurt his bunions. He must look his best!

Mar. 1, 1860: According to the *NY Tribune*, that fair city had not seen a larger assemblage of intellect and mental culture at a speech since the days of Clay and Webster! Despite a violent snow, 1500 people attended, including many ladies. Editor Greeley reported that Abraham convincingly proved that 21 signers of the Constitution, together with all of Congress, favored federal control over slavery. He then threw Stephen Douglas' words back at him: "Let all who believe the fathers of the republic understood this question even better than we do now speak as they spoke and act as they acted on it." I sense this speech will ensure us the nomination, though William Seward is still favored.

The *Herald* also wrote favorably about Abraham's words at the Cooper Institute, but I saved the following article from that paper to remind him that northerners must be addressed with more formality than our Illinois friends. How many times I have mentioned it!

> Mr. Lincoln is a tall, thin man, dark complexioned, and apparently quick in his perceptions. He is rather unsteady in his gait, and an involuntary comical awkwardness marks his movements while speaking. A peculiar characteristic of his delivery was a remarkable mobility of his features, the frequent contortions of which excited the merriment that his words alone could not well have produced.

He's still traveling through New England and will speak later in the week at Exeter. Will Bob be pleased? Will he even attend? He has always been embarrassed by his father's rustic mannerisms and speaking style. Will his opinion change now that Abraham is a contender for the most important position in the US? He plans to take Bob and George Latham traveling with him for a few days so he can spend more time with his first-born. I pray for success. Both Willie and Tad are quite sick, but their illnesses are not threatening. I watch them constantly, ever alert to a change in prognosis.

Mar. 2, 1860: I believe Abraham's Cooper Union speech has been reproduced in every newspaper with a telegraph machine, and they have nothing but praise. Here is a portion from the *NY Times*. The comments are directed toward the <u>southerners</u> in the audience.

> You say you're eminently conservative while we're revolutionary, destructive, or something of the sort. What is conservatism? Ain't it adherence to the old and tried, against the new and untried? We stick to, and contend for, the identical old policy adopted by our fathers who framed the government we live under; you reject, scout and spit on that old policy and insist on substituting something new.
>
> If a Republican is elected President, you say you will destroy the Union. And then, you say, the great crime of having destroyed it will be on us! That's cool. A highwayman holds a pistol to my ear and mutters through his teeth, "Stand and deliver or I'll kill you, and then

you'll be a murderer!"

To be sure, what the robber demanded of me—my money—was my own, and I had a clear right to keep it. But it weren't no more my own than my vote is my own. And the threat of death to me, to extort my money, and the threat of destruction to the Union, to extort my vote, can scarcely be distinguished in principle.

If slavery is right, then all words, acts, laws and constitutions against it are wrong and should be silenced and swept away. If slavery is wrong, all laws against it are right. This is our thinking and not yours. Your thinking it right and our thinking it wrong is the precise fact this whole controversy depends on. Thinking it right, as you do, you ain't to blame for desiring its full recognition; but thinking it wrong, as we do, can we yield to you? No!

We won't be slandered from our duty by false accusations against us, or frightened from it by menaces of destruction to the government or of dungeons to ourselves. We'll have faith that right makes might and, in that faith, we will, to the end, dare to do our duty as we understand it.

Further, the *Chicago Press* has printed an editorial saying Abraham can be elected President on the Republican ticket, but Seward can't! How wise the man who wrote the piece. Perhaps they do read my anonymous letters!

Mar. 4, 1860: A letter from Exeter says Abraham has completed his tour. He and Bob got along like brother chums, even sleeping in the same room. Last Thursday, they went to Concord, where Abraham spoke in daylight, and back to Manchester, where he spoke at night. On Friday, they went down to Lawrence, and then back to Exeter. Abraham went alone to Dover, returned on Saturday, and went to church with Bob on Sunday. I'm glad he's showing a good model. He seldom goes to church with me these days, but it's wise to insist that our children learn about the Holy Book.

According to the schedule, he spoke at Hartford yesterday, today at Meriden, tomorrow at New Haven, Thursday at Woonsocket, Rhode Island. Then he will start home. If the trains don't lie over Sunday, he should be here tomorrow week. How keenly I anticipate his arrival.

William Seward is speaking in Abraham's footsteps, as Abraham once did with Stephen Douglas. Seward now says he is opposed to conspiracy, ambush, invasion, and force; and he favors reason, suffrage, and the spirit of Christianity. I believe he's blowing in the wind.

Mar. 12, 1860: My husband will be home tomorrow! Already my heart shouts with anticipation and my body perspires with eagerness. I have for him a copy of the *Chicago Tribune*'s pamphlet reproducing the full Cooper Union speech. It is mighty handsome and Abraham will be humbled. Though the booklets sell for a penny each, the editor sent us a package of free copies, and I have sent one to all our close friends and relatives, including Betsy and Elizabeth. People must continue to see what strides we're making and how our possibilities are enhanced. Abraham's stepmother will be most pleased of all to receive it; like myself, she has always been proud of him.

Mar. 13, 1860: This trip took a toll on Abraham, though he delighted to see our son doing so well. He had a fine time in Bob's room with a large group of young men — talking, telling stories, and listening to one boy play banjo.

"Why was this trip more difficult than the others?" I asked as I sat rubbing his swollen feet next to the fire.

He sipped his coffee, thinking carefully. His eyes were closed as he spoke. "It was drudgery. If I'd foreseen the hardship, I think I wouldn't have gone at all. The speech at New York, being within my calculation before I started, gave me no trouble whatever and went off passably well. The difficulty was to make nine other speeches before audiences who'd already seen all my ideas in print. In the old days, my words were new if people hadn't heard them before. Now they read everything I say before I get there. I'm not sure that's a good thing. And this slavery issue is about to wear me ragged. I get so soured on defending freedom and shooting at the popular sovereignty thing. It's dragging me down. I don't know why we can't just let slavery alone."

I kissed his toes. "I'm so sorry, My Dear. Can you just ignore the issue in your next address?"

"No, the people wouldn't let me. The truth is, we can't help dealing with it. The country has to do something about it. We can't avoid it no more than a man can avoid eating. It's on us; it attaches to the body politic as closely as natural wants attach to our bodies. As Thomas Jefferson said, we've got the wolf by the ears and we can't hold it or safely let it go. We've got to kill it."

"Why?" I knew the reason. I asked only to hear him answer.

Instead, he got up and went to the window, grasped his hands behind his back, and cleared his throat. "Here's the way I put it in New Haven. See what you think. I said, 'If I saw a venomous snake crawling in the road, any man would say I should grab the nearest stick and kill it. But if I found that snake in bed with my children, that'd be another question. I might hurt the children more than the snake, and it might bite them. If I found it in bed with my neighbor's children, and I'd bound myself not to meddle with his family under any circumstances, it would become me to let that particular mode of getting rid of the snake alone. But if a bed was newly made up where the children were to be taken, and someone proposed to take a batch of young snakes and put them with the tots, I don't believe any man would question how I ought to decide!

"That's just the case here. The new territories are the newly made bed where our moppets are headed, and it lies with the nation to say whether they'll have snakes mixed up with them or not. It don't seem there could be much hesitation on what our policy should be!'"

He turned toward me. "That's what I said. I believe it's the naked front and aspect of the measure. Do you see?" I had to admit I had never heard it stated more plainly.

Mar. 16, 1860: Now I know we're in the running; electors are beginning to bedevil us for funds! Abraham would not give them money even if we had it to give, but I understand the value of money in a political race. I saw it for many years in the Whig races of my father and uncles. It's part of the game, but Abraham is an honest man. It doesn't matter, though; we have none and can get none. Our long struggle has included great financial loss. But it's temporary; someday we'll have it all!

I also know we're in the running because John Jay, now a force in the party, came this week to ask Abraham to seriously consider accepting the nomination. Abraham said he would think about it.

"Will you consider it?" I asked later.

"I will, Mother," he said honestly. "The taste sits in my mouth a little. Jay has made me more confident." He sipped his cider, smiled like a youth on his first date, and said quietly, "Well now, I've considered it. If the party seriously asks, I'll go for it."

Mar. 20, 1860: This week I visited Mrs. Roonamen, the spiritualist, and asked about our future. She believes we will win the office but also saw unhappiness ahead. She warns of disunion and grief, both personal and political. I'll have to find another sensitive; I don't like her extra visions.

Mar. 30, 1860: I asked Abraham today about the possibility of war and the disunion Mrs. Roonamen predicted. "Seward keeps predicting an 'irrepressible conflict,' implying battle between north and south. Can it happen?"

Abraham wagged his head. "We're a whole lot less inclined to war than countries in the past. Americans don't want war with anybody, certainly not each other. It's just a ploy to scare the north and intimidate us to give up things. The south is threatening to destroy the Union unless they're allowed to construe and enforce the Constitution as they please on all points in dispute. They want to rule or ruin. They just don't want a northern President, and they think this taunt will cause us to back down with our tails between our legs. Southerners have been threatening to secede since you were a girl, Mother. They used it against Frémont in the last election too, remember? I've heard it till I'm nearly deaf to it now. Like Thad Stevens once said, 'We've saved this Union so often I'm afraid we'll save it to death.' It's all wolf cryings."

Apr. 8, 1860, Easter: I used Abraham's Exeter church visit to coerce him into going with us today. He enjoys Easter more than regular Sundays because there's more music and a picnic afterward. He was embarrassed by all the attention, but I cherished each well-wisher. This afternoon, the famous photographer Mathew Brady arrived to photograph Abraham for the campaign ribbons in Chicago! I am floating on air!

Apr. 21, 1860: The Democratic National Committee will meet in Charleston in two days, and we expect Stephen to be nominated. It's only right that this biggest contest of our life to date will be against him. We have opposed no one else seriously for many years. The learned opinions are quite conflicting—some are very confident Stephen will win the nomination, others that he won't. He hasn't been as well received this time, so perhaps my anxiety is based on habit rather than reality. We'll soon see. I want to win more than I've ever wanted anything.

May 4, 1860: The news from Charleston is confusing, and the Democrats have no candidate yet. According to the papers, they finally adjourned after 10 days and 57 ballots! Apparently the southern Democrats withdrew because the others advocated a platform apology for slavery. The southerners insisted that, rather than apologize, the party should declare slavery morally right, advocate its extension, enact congressional protection for it, and publish a clear renunciation of popular sovereignty. They refused to back Stephen Douglas under any platform; he has lost their favor since the debates and his break with President Buchanan.

The Charleston paper reported that William Yancey of Alabama said to Stephen's "drawn, sallow" face, "The proposition you make will bankrupt the south. Ours is the property invaded, ours the interests at stake. You would make a seething caldron of passion and crime if you were able to consummate your measures."

Sen. Jefferson Davis reportedly told the convention that if Stephen wanted the nomination, he would have to abandon the popular sovereignty doctrine, agree to a territorial slave code, and constitutionally protect slavery in all territories. Stephen refused, so the southern faction withdrew. Under the rules requiring 2/3 of all delegates to vote, rather than 2/3 of those in attendance, Stephen could not be nominated.

May 9, 1860: The Illinois Republican convention begins today in Decatur. Our managers, headed by Judge David Davis, will be hard at work. I'm amazed at the internal workings of this sudden campaign. Abraham goes tomorrow to meet with this committee and speak to the convention.

We talked about our probabilities. Abraham said, "Well, I think the Illinois delegation will be unanimous for me at the outset, but no other delegation will. A few individuals in other delegations would like to go for me at the start, but their colleagues may restrain them. Some men who ought to know tell me Indiana might not be difficult to get. I certainly ain't Ohio's first choice, but I don't know of anybody making positive objections to me either. It seems to me the same is true everywhere else. So I guess, if my men can handle it, we've got a shot."

May 14, 1860: As I knew he would, Abraham returned home with the Illinois Republican Committee's full backing for the Presidency! The convention is now underway in an immense new building called the Wigwam, and our managers are working night and day, hardly sleeping or eating at all. They are busily conferring with friends from states other than Illinois, trying to spread Abraham's legend, likeability, and electability. I'm glad Abraham chose to stay here with me; I'm not sure I could stand the anticipation alone.

We're writing to everyone we know who might have a vote or influence one, asking him to speak to one of our men. A telegram from Nathan Knapp said, "Your chances aren't the worst. We're laboring to make you the second choice of all delegations where we're unable to make you first."

May 16, 1860: Telegram from David Davis said, "We're quiet but moving Heaven and earth. The hearts of the delegates are with us." I can hardly breathe this afternoon, and our home is filled with people as we await more news. Telegrams arrive every hour. Our men write that 30,000 people fill the hall where the nominations will be made and spill out into the streets. Norman Judd, as head of the delegation, placed Abraham's name in nomination. Seward seems to be still favored, but our men are confident. Davis and Abraham have come to words over concessions, however. Davis and Judd want authority to offer promises or positions to those who will be swayed to vote for us; Abraham is adamant that he will authorize no bargains and be bound to no one. I say hold firm, Judge Davis, with a chain of steel. Don't let this victory slip from our hands no matter what you have to bargain. Abraham is not there, so you and Judd are in charge.

May 18, 1860: We won! Thank God in Heaven, we won, and it took only three ballots! In the end, the vote was unanimous. The first precious telegram from Knapp read, "We did it! Glory to God!" The next, from Lamon, said, "God bless you. We are happy and may you ever be." From Fell: "City wild with excitement. From my inmost heart I congratulate you." Davis' telegram said Seward's men were "so overcome by the defeat they cried like heartbroken children. Tears flowed like water among the vast throng." I will keep these messages forever.

I'm trembling too much to write! I hold the telegrams and watch them blur in and out. This is what I have wanted forever, my childhood vision fulfilled, my dreams come true. Abraham is somber and somewhat unbelieving, but happy; I can see the sparks in his eyes and feel the excitement in his embraces.

The party paired Abraham with Hannibal Hamlin, a senator from Maine who was also briefly considered as a candidate. Abraham once heard Hamlin speak in the Senate, and remembers him as being a strong voice against President Buchanan's policies. He helped devise the Wilmot Proviso, and strongly opposed the Compromise of 1850 and the Kansas-Nebraska bill. Davis said Hamlin was chosen because he is an easterner; he's against slavery, drinking, and hanging; and, as a former Democrat, he'll balance the factions.

Abraham will remain in Springfield till election day. There is much to do, and he believes in the old style of campaigning—invisibility. He says he can tell the people nothing he hasn't already said and he won't "stoop" to electioneering for himself and "embarrass the canvass."

I disagree with that sentiment, because I understand the value of self-promotion. Stephen also understands and is still barnstorming the country, even though the papers say he's quite ill. He is maligning Abraham, saying a Republican victory will bring secession, and calling for immediate acquisition of Cuba as a slave territory. To his credit, though, he is urging continued unity and asking the southern states to abandon secession plans. The *New York Tribune* said that "no other candidate for President has ever played his hand so openly and boldly." I sense Stephen is frightened now, using all means to stay afloat and be nominated, but I won't sleep easily till the final ship has reached shore. We're headed for the White House! Robert Todd, are you proud of your daughter now?

May 19, 1860: A huge crowd formed in front of our house tonight, even some avowed Democrats, filled with excitement and noise! Abraham spoke to them from the front step and then invited them inside. I apologized as best I could for the small size and someone shouted, "Don't apologize. We'll get you a larger house on the 4th of next March!" Yes, the house I have always wanted!

May 20, 1860: We have carefully crafted our reply to the men who will cross our doorstep tomorrow and officially tell us that Abraham has been chosen to represent the Republicans in the race for President of the United States. It's clear and strong:

"Deeply and even painfully sensible of the great responsibility that is inseparable from this high honor—a responsibility I could almost wish had fallen on one of the more eminent and experienced statesmen whose names were before the convention—I will consider more fully the resolutions and platform, and without any unnecessary or unreasonable delay, respond to you in writing, not doubting the platform will be satisfactory and the nomination gratefully accepted."

So many hours spent on so few sentences. So many years of hope, work, sacrifice, and waiting for one moment. Patience is indeed valuable. God bless us and keep us safe.

May 24, 1860: The Republican Party has united behind us! Seward, Chase, Bates, and all the others have spoken out in endorsement and vowed their support. I wasn't certain they would be so honorable. This will darken the Democrat feuding even more in the voters' eyes. In our honor, the cannon is fired several times a day, a demon to my sensitive head. Requests for pictures and signatures arrive, dozens at a time, several times a day. Abraham can hardly hold a pen anymore. His fingers draw together and fold toward his palm.

Our joy is marred somewhat, however, and Abraham is visibly vexed because his men didn't honor his directive on offering no bargains. They promised the Interior Secretary position to the Indiana chairman and the Indian Affairs Commission to another from Indiana. They promised the War Department to Simon Cameron of Pennsylvania and the Treasury to Salmon Chase.[17]

May 27, 1860: I never tire of reading descriptions of Abraham, especially when he's compared to Napoleon's generals! From *Harper's Weekly*:

---

[17] This campaign was one of the dirtiest yet conducted. Not only did Lincoln's men make promises and grant positions without authority, they purchased votes and counterfeited admission tickets. Norman Judd, a lawyer for the Rock Island Railroad, brought trainloads of men to Chicago and printed fake tickets so they could fill the Wigwam, leaving no room for the Seward delegates. Every time Lincoln's name was mentioned, these men shouted their approval and stomped their feet. Of course, the other side was also making deals, promising government grants of up to $600,000 in exchange for votes.

"Old Uncle Abe" is long, lean, and wiry. He has a great deal of the elasticity and awkwardness that indicate the rough training of his early life, and his conversation savors strongly of Western idioms and pronunciation. His complexion is about that of an octoroon; his face, without being by any means beautiful, is genial looking, and good humor seems to lurk in every corner of its innumerable angles.

He has dark hair, tinged with gray, a good forehead, small eyes, a long penetrating nose with nostrils such as Napoleon always liked to find in his best generals because they indicated a long head and clear thoughts; and a mouth which, aside from being of magnificent proportions, is probably the most expressive feature of his face.

As a speaker, he is ready, precise, and fluent. His manner before a popular assembly is as he pleases to make it—either superlatively ludicrous or very impressive. He employs little gesticulation, but when he desires to make a point, he produces a shrug of his shoulders, an elevation of his eyebrows, a depression of his mouth, and a general malformation of countenance so comically awkward that it never fails to "bring down the house." His enunciation is slow and emphatic and his voice, though it has a tendency to dwindle into a shrill and unpleasant sound, is sharp and powerful.

June 13, 1860: Our beloved nephew, Edgar Smith, passed away yesterday from typhoid fever and was buried this afternoon. Only 10 years old! He had been sick for weeks, and I have been staying with Ann and Clark for a few days. The poor boy—I hope never to witness such suffering again. I'll stay here a while longer, as I know how devastating the loss of a child can be. The family is inconsolable. I myself am quite unnerved, as this event assaults my mind with memories of darling Eddy.

June 18, 1860: More unrest and dissention in the Democratic Party. The northerners have regrouped in Baltimore and, by changing the 2/3 rule to meet their needs, have finally nominated Stephen Douglas, with Herschel Johnson, a Georgia Unionist, for VP. I have never heard his name before.

Here at home, people knock on the door day and night: newspaper reporters, biographers, photographers, sculptors, party men, campaign contributors, even people just asking for money or other special favors. Often as many as 100 a day! Someone is always encamped in the guest bedroom, sometimes 5 and 6 people at a time, with more sprawled within our parlors.

We all must be fully groomed and dressed in our Sunday best when the sun rises, for these visitors know no hours. Even Abraham now dons a clean shirt each day, a miracle unto itself. The delivery boy has worn a path from the telegraph office to our door.

June 20, 1860: Abraham goes to the Capitol every day now with his new secretary, a young German named John Nicolay, who worked for Ozias Hatch when he was Secretary of State, and Bob's friend John Hay, who serves as Nicolay's clerk. Our parlor has been designated as additional headquarters. Everywhere are newspapers, diagrams, plans, speeches old and new, names of delegates, mountains of letters to be answered—as many as 50 a day! I must always have coffee, sandwiches, and cold chicken ready for the men who drop in at all hours. I wish Abraham would talk more with me, but he prefers the counsel of those who mingle with the voters.

We had to borrow money to hire additional servants, and the Springfield Republicans raised $5000 for our expenses. Mariah's days have been increased, and Frances and Mary, known to be faithful and trustworthy maids, have returned. And a ripened negro named William answers the door and escorts the visitors, a duty I have tried to wrest from Abraham for all our years together. At least William wears shoes and a jacket. I would have long ago dismissed Abraham, the poorly dressed doorkeeper, if he weren't so precious to me.

No fewer than five artists have asked permission to paint us, but we have no time now. Abraham did sit for two photographers, however, because he had so few suitable likenesses to supply the press, and one print is now being sold for $3! I have allowed but one photograph of myself; I don't like the images they produce. The lithographs represent me as plump and aging. My hands always appear bigger in them and I seem overly stern. I also won't permit a picture of us together, because our dissimilar heights cause us to look freakish. I won't allow posterity to believe we were anything but beautiful, so I pass judgment on all portraits and other images.

Several times a week, I plan and execute a formal dinner party for a visiting governor, senator, or political leader of some ilk. It's all very exciting, but sapping as well. I hoped for assistance, or at least moral support, from my sisters, but it doesn't come. Ninian, and therefore Elizabeth, is for Stephen; Ann and Fanny are distant. Only Cousin Lizzie Todd comes to help when times are busiest.

June 23, 1860: I'm still secretly collecting my own mentions from the newspapers. One of my most favorite is from the *Daily Republican*:

> It's often not in good taste for visitors to bring ladies in before the public, but I shall be proud as an American citizen when the day brings Mary Lincoln to grace the White House. She reminds one of Dolley Madison.

And a special mention in the *New York Tribune*:

> Lincoln's wife is amiable and accomplished, vivacious and
> graceful, a refined hostess and a vivacious talker. She is very
> different from President Buchanan's niece, Harriet Lane. Her house is
> neat without being extravagant. An air of quiet refinement pervades.
> One would know instantly that she who presides over that modest
> household is a true American lady.

So much better than the visitor in my own house who asked too loudly upon my entrance, "Is that Lincoln's old woman?" I suppose I'll get used to the negative comments in time, but they are hard to swallow. I'll simply try harder to look more youthful.

July 1, 1860: A book has been published about Abraham and how he achieved the nomination. My stubborn husband is hair-pulling mad and won't allow me to preview a copy because he didn't approve it.

This is frightening. In our present position, we must communicate even more often with the public. How will we manage if we can neither write nor speak a word without sending forth hundreds of pages that our adversaries can use to make points?

Terrible things are being said about our entire family in some papers. They call Abraham white trash, a third-rate country lawyer who uses improper grammar and delivers coarse, clumsy jokes. They say he is out of proportion, with a dull, heavy, repellent countenance. The worst says he descended from an African gorilla. They call our home low Hoosier style and badly decorated. They refer to our entertainments as "serving food of the worst and most cloying kind, consisting of an old-fashioned mess of indigestion." They call our boys rambunctious brats with no manners. They mock Willie's little speeches to the neighborhood children and Tad's urging on the front steps to "Boat pore Ode Abe." Damn them all!

July 4, 1860, Independence Day: The most exciting parade I have ever witnessed! Thousands walked past our house with five-foot-high depictions of Abraham and Hamlin! The boys are so excited they won't be able to sleep tonight, though Willie is not yet free of the remnants of scarlet fever. They don't understand all the hoopla, but they are well aware that we're about to make an important change in our lives. They stand on the balcony in their little bare feet and play their toy instruments as the parades pass, marching to the beat, waving their scribbled "Old Abe for President" signs. Bob wrote that he plans to celebrate by reading the Declaration of Independence at a jamboree near Exeter. Perhaps he is finally becoming more social!

Aug. 1, 1860, Bob's 17th birthday: John Henry Brown, a Philadelphia artist, has been here for a week painting a miniature of Abraham on ivory.

The result is striking — no fault or defect whatever. I will be pleased to see it in print instead of the horrible caricatures now being published by the Democrats!

We received a letter from Bob telling us of his acceptance into Harvard. He's now doing well in his studies and is determined to get a dependable education. He has suddenly become the most popular boy in school and the others teasingly bow or salute each time he passes. I sense he's proud of his father, perhaps for the first time.

Aug. 8, 1860: A parade of people on floats and horses passed our house for a full 8 hours today on its way to the fairgrounds for the Republican rally. The people carried broadsides saying "Old Abe, the Rail Splitter." The crowd sang and danced to many made-up tunes about Abraham. It was a good thing we didn't want to leave; we couldn't have gotten out. Abraham stood outside and waved most of the time. The boys and I, many neighborhood children, and the servants watched from the upstairs windows. Abraham spoke only a few words, promising that the fight for the Republican cause will go on long after he is dead and gone. I pray that will be a century from now.

Aug. 15, 1860: More talk about secession, though we receive assurances that no formidable effort to break up the Union will truly be made. Abraham told me, "Secession is the essence of anarchy. Southern people have too much good temper and sense to attempt to destroy the government rather than see it administered as it was by the men who made it. Even if we win, the Democrats are sure to remain in control of Congress, and they won't allow such a travesty. It's just another bushwhacking contrivance! At least I hope and believe so." I hope so too, My Dear, though my sense is not as strong that such will be the case.

The damning slurs continue unabated. The *Illinois Eagle* printed an invented speech in which Abraham traduced his paragon, Thomas Jefferson. Our friends will denounce it as a forgery, of course, but what about the rest of the country? What about the southerners?

We're all weary and nettlesome. Abraham also has symptoms of scarlet fever, and my throat is sore. How would we go on if we're all stricken? God, please grant us respite and health.

Aug. 30, 1860: Bob is home for a few days before joining the Harvard class. He brought with him a letter of recommendation from an Exeter trustee: "Bob has behaved himself as the son of Abraham Lincoln would be expected to do. He stands at the top of the ladder as a scholar and is a singularly discreet, well-behaved, brilliant, and promising young man. He is frequently tested by the attention he now receives, but he stands it all."

Abraham said to Bob over supper, "Having now been accepted, Son, you've got to succeed at it. You must whet your mind. You can't fail if you resolutely determine you won't. That's what your mother told me back in '42, and she's surely been right."

Bob said firmly, "I will not fail, Father, I promise you I won't."

Sept. 25, 1860: Vermont and Maine have voted early and we were victorious! But I won't get overly stirred. Pennsylvania, Ohio, and Indiana vote next month. Then I'll get excited!

Abraham returns tonight after a speaking tour through Ohio, Indiana, Wisconsin, and Illinois. I anticipate his arrival with great physical longing, though he may be too fatigued to appreciate such a welcome. I asked him in a recent letter, "How many lectures can you deliver without giving out?"

His reply was typical: "I reckon I'll speak up for freedom as long as the Constitution guarantees free speech, till everywhere on this wide land the sun shines, the rain falls, and the wind blows on no man who goes to unrequited toil." He's a magnificent writer, but he could have simply said, "About a dozen more."

Oct. 17, 1860: Abraham has boggled me again. At supper tonight, he asked what I thought about his growing a beard. I was stunned, because he's never considered the idea so far as I know. I replied, "Well, it would be a first. No President has ever worn a beard. Why is this on your mind after all these years?"

He reached in his hat and pulled out a slip of pink paper. "A month or so ago, I received a note from some earnest Republicans suggesting that my dignity and Presidential appearance would be enhanced with some hair. I dismissed the idea till today when I received this letter from a little girl in New York. She writes, 'Dear Mr. Lincoln, I have seen your daguerreotype in the newspapers and recently received your lithograph as a gift. I admire you with my whole heart, but I think your appearance would be much improved by cultivating some whiskers. It's all the style now. The ladies like whiskers and they will then encourage their husbands to vote for you because you will be so much more handsome. Forgive me for being ambitious. Your friend, Miss Grace Bedell.'"

I ruffled his hair, then ran my fingers along his bare chin. "Since you've never worn facial hair in your life, don't you think people would call it silly affectation if you began now? And you propose to do this because an 11-year-old girl wishes it? Do I have a reason to be concerned about your fidelity?"

He grabbed me up in his arms. "I'll show you about fidelity, Wife!" he growled into my hair as he carried me quickly up the stairs. Thank you, Grace Bedell.

Oct. 19, 1860: A letter from Hannah Shearer reminded me of how coolly I once took the matter of politics. She wouldn't think so if she could see me now. Fortunately, the waiting time is rapidly ending—a little more than two weeks will decide the contest. I scarcely know how we would bear up under defeat, and trust we won't have such a trial. Hannah feels quite apprehensive for us, as we do for ourselves. She enclosed a linen collar and an easy book for Tad. Many friends are now sending gifts, a custom I find quite nice.

Oct. 20, 1860: Pennsylvania, Ohio, and Indiana have gone for us and I trust other doubtful states will follow in their footsteps. We are almost assured of victory! I will begin a gown with the dressmaker immediately. Abraham holds his excitement till November.

Oct. 26, 1860: We received notice that the officers at Ft. Kearny have vowed that, if the Republicans prevail, they will take themselves and their arms south to begin resistance to the federal government! Abraham believes this is a humbug, but I'm frightened. I was raised a southerner, and know how they treasure their independence and their word. If a southerner says he will do something, he will try mightily to do it. I sense the aggression is real, but don't want to spoil our mood by speaking about it.

John Nicolay told me that, among the many things visitors say to Abraham at the State House, is nearly always the hope that he will not be killed off by foul means or die from the cares of the office like Presidents Harrison and Taylor. I have the same thoughts and premonitions, but keep them to myself.

Nov. 1, 1860: Once again, I asked my exhausted husband, "Will we win?"

I know he tires of my need for reassurance, but his answer soothed: "I don't rightly know, but I do know that what we've done, and will continue to do, will eventually win freedom for all men. There's a higher aim here than mere office. I've not allowed myself to forget that Great Britain's abolition of the slave trade started 100 years before its success. That measure also had its open fire-eating opponents, 'don't-care' opponents like Douglas, religion and good-order opponents, dollar-and-cent opponents, inferior-race opponents, and negro-equality opponents. All those resisters got offices and their adversaries got none. But I also remember that, though the slavists blazed like tallow candles for a century, at last they flickered and died out. I'm proud, in my passing speck of time, to contribute a humble mite to that end, even though my own poor eyes may not last to see it. As Henry Clay once said, 'I'd rather be right than be President.'"

Nov. 4, 1860, our 18ᵗʰ anniversary: What more could I want for our anniversary than the White House? Our next anniversary will be spent in posh surroundings. We'll also have time to celebrate then. Now we're in turmoil and confusion, with hardly a peaceful moment to call our own, and the anxiety is wearing on us both.

Abraham dreamed recently that, while lying on a sofa in his room, he glanced at his reflection in the mirror. Looking more closely, he saw himself at full length, but his face had two distinct images, one nearly atop the other and much paler. He rose and went to the mirror, but the vision vanished. He lay down again and it reappeared, even plainer than before. I described the vision to the spiritualists and they told its meaning: He will win the upcoming election, and then a second term as well, but he won't complete the latter. For the first time, I pray they are wrong.

Nov. 5, 1860: Tomorrow our future will be decided. No, I won't allow myself to think about defeat. We've done everything right. All our plans for recognition, perseverance, and support have paid off. I have recited this mantra for so long, I don't know if I will be able to let it go. My body is wracked with nervousness. My skin itches, my stomach churns, my words come rushing out without pause. Abraham paces inside or shoots marbles with the boys outside, but the game never lasts long. He can't keep his head or his feet in one place for more than a few minutes. God go with the voters.

Nov. 6, 1860: The day was uncharacteristically warm and sunny, a good omen. After being awakened by rousing cannon blasts at cock crowing, Abraham went to his office for several hours, though I imagine he played handball rather than practicing law. In the early afternoon, he cast his ballot at the courthouse, then home for lunch, then off to the telegraph office where he remains while I wait alone for sleep to tempt me. The old coot cut his electors' names off the ballot so it would not be said he voted for himself! How silly! Who better to vote for than oneself?

The boys are down the street at Mrs. Bradford's, for I just couldn't stand their noise today. I have tried to sew or read, but concentration avoids me. I know this contest will end correctly. We have not fought this long for nothing. I must try to sleep. My ink, like my patience, is waning.

Nov. 7, 1860: Midnight had passed when the cheers erupted across Springfield last night. I heard them from my bed and knew we had won. Guns were discharged, flares filled the sky, noise permeated the air. I was outside, dancing on the balcony in my woolen robe and slippers, when I heard Abraham running home from the telegraph office, shouting "Molly, Molly, we're elected!" I thought he would stay in town for hours to make speeches, but no, he immediately headed home to me!

"Of course I came straight away," he grinned. "Without you, none of this would have happened. You alone believed in this old sucker and prodded me to this point. We won, Lady President, we won!"

I have never known such joy. My pen trembles while seeking the words to express this overwhelming feeling of jubilance, triumph, completion, and hope. I can't erase this wide smile from my face or stop my heart from dancing, and I'm reveling in the good wishes already pouring in. Julia Trumbull and the other snakes will never again spoil our garden. They are likely discussing, even now before sunup, how to appear unsurprised and elated when they see us.

Nov. 10, 1860: Mercy has come to visit for a spell! I am so, so happy to have my dearest friend here at this wonderful time. The rest of the world has also been to our doorstep. So many people that their faces are blurred in the swirl of activity and excitement. But all the visitors are not so welcome. Office-seekers from practically every state in the north, and some from the south as well, invade our parlors every day. Everyone in Springfield now claims to be our long-loved friend and has some idea of who should be appointed to the Cabinet. Bah!

Nov. 12, 1860: Why must bad always accompany good? Word has come that an effigy of Abraham was hanged in Florida. The *Charleston Mercury* banners that "the revolution of 1860 has been initiated" and advocates war. The senators from South Carolina have resigned their seats in anticipation of secession. We have even experienced small anti-Lincoln protests here in Springfield! How long will this defiance and menace continue?

Nov. 17, 1860: Abraham is exhausted. He greets as many as 175 people a day at the State House, taking only three hours at midday to himself. Visitors come from all over—men and women, young and old, Republicans and Democrats. People who want to shake his hand, get his signature, or tap him for money and other favors. Then they come to our home, leaving us no private time for supper or conversation. They are ill mannered and rude— touching our belongings, taking pinches of this and that. Damn them all!

Nov. 27, 1860: We have returned from a horrible 5-day trip to Chicago with a small group of friends to meet VP and Mrs. Hamlin. Democrats filled the train and we were scorned and cast ridiculing looks. I don't like this part of the office we have won.

Once there, we toured the Wigwam, and I felt a great sense of excitement seeing where we were nominated. My hands and feet still hurt from the reception we attended. I changed into 10 pairs of gloves by the end! Abraham doesn't look well either. His hand is swollen and bruised, and his head has throbbed for two days. No, this was not our best trip ever, but we were thrilled to meet up with Speed and Fanny, also visiting there. They are both well, and married life continues to bless them. Abraham offered Speed a position in the Cabinet, but he declined, saying he couldn't afford the decrease in wages.

We were also pleased with Hamlin. He is tall, though not to Abraham's shoulders, and somewhat fattish, with brown eyes, dark skin, and receding black hair. His manner is courteous and friendly. He seems to be a strong-willed man who can get things done, and he's well connected in the Senate. Although he apparently didn't want the office of VP, he promises to give his best. "I neither expected nor desired it," he said, "but it's been made and, as a faithful man to the cause, I have no alternative but to accept it." His "cause" is abolition. His wife, Ellen, is also affable, and they have several children.

Abraham wants to hold a balance between former Whigs and former Democrats in the Cabinet, and asked Hamlin to choose the Navy Secretary from New England. He selected a former Jackson Democrat, Gideon Welles, now an editor in Hartford.

They also discussed William Seward, with his hawky nose, bushy eyebrows, and incessant foul cigar, for Secretary of State. My senses tell me this is an unwise decision. Seward was pro-slavery before joining the Republicans, and he tried to harm us in many ways during the election. Abraham nods at my ranting, but says Seward will bring in the power of NY and the Free-Soil Whigs. I believe he will bring interference and adversity. He has never proclaimed true allegiance to us, and would seize the office without a moment's hesitation.

Dec. 12, 1860: My life is complete. I could die now in total happiness. In just a few months, I will be Mrs. President of the United States! Abraham will seldom have to leave our beautiful new mansion, we will have money to spare, and our lives will be as entwined as I have always wanted.

<u>Dec. 13, 1860, my 42nd birthday:</u> I have what seems to be a new husband. His name is "President-Elect." He stands straighter than my previous spouse, has a more affirmative and authoritative voice, is more social, and is almost fully bearded from hairline down across chin. It's difficult to keep this new growth neat and close-cropped. Like the hair on his head, the chin bristle is wiry and goes in all directions. It's odd to see a furry critter in the bed beside me; the sight often causes a quick gasp before I'm fully awake. Not that he comes to my bed regularly now; he consults with his advisors till all hours. I've asked him to allow half a day on Saturday or Sunday just to be with the boys and me because we feel ignored. At least I have no more dreams of trysts with other women. Even my somulent brain knows there is no time available.

Abraham has much to worry about. The south still moves toward secession and many people are advocating war. Seven senators and 23 representatives have urged secession, 2 senators and 2 Cabinet members have resigned. It's too terrifying to conceive! Wise men in both north and south are seeking compromise. Even Stephen Douglas says our country is in more danger now than at any other moment in his public life. He professes to every audience—even, I'm told, the Senate—that the election of a Republican is no justification for secession, and has proposed several compromise bills. We could have used his assistance much earlier!

I am also terrified by the death threats we receive—horrible telegrams, effigies, baskets of poisoned food, voodoo dolls, dead animals on the doorstep, blood-stained notes slipped under our door in the dark of night. Many promise that Abraham will never be inaugurated, some threaten to keep him from ever leaving Springfield. There are even letters addressed to me, some covered with skulls and crossbones, advising me to counsel Abraham to withdraw. I am very concerned, but Abraham says the threats only reflect the baser soul of politics. With his assurance, we go forward.

Dec. 15, 1860: Abraham has begun to worry about the danger, as well he should. He has never had real influence before, and now he confronts the entire country with his version of right and wrong. In the end, it all comes back to him. He has hardly any seasoned advisors. The Republican Party itself has never been in power, and so has no experience with Cabinet appointments and things of such ilk. Now we must chose men to supervise the appointment of several thousand others in federal offices and bureaus.

He decided to honor Davis' word and appoint Simon Cameron to a place in the Cabinet. From what I hear, Cameron is ambitious and radically anti-slavery. He will do nothing but wage war on his own if given half a chance. I am not the only one opposed to him. We received a strong letter from Joseph Medill, editor of the *Chicago Press and Tribune,* against the appointment. I know the sentiment made an impression on Abraham, but he did not waver. What good are advisors if he won't listen? I'm not completely fond of his newfound independence!

"What else has Judge Davis promised?" I asked as we bickered over the Cabinet.

He adjusted his spectacles and stared at the floor. "They've gambled me all around, bought and sold me a hundred times. I can't begin to fill all the pledges made in my name." But we both know we must try.

Dec. 21, 1860: My God! South Carolina has seceded! Now we are two nations, soon to be fighting with all our economic, cultural, and political strength to overtake each other. Why hasn't President Buchanan attempted to stop this? Is he sitting still, smoking cigars, and waiting to turn this horrible matter over to us? When SC became defiant in 1832, President Jackson immediately threatened military intervention. What has Buchanan done? Not one blasted thing to prevent or counteract secession or to protect federal property. Post offices, banks, and even military posts in the south are left open to sabotage behind enemy lines! Buchanan's Cabinet is resigning like frightened mice—some because he does nothing to help the south, some because he does nothing to help the north. This is his Gordian knot, not ours. Please God, stop this insurrection before we take office.

I asked Abraham this morning as he dressed, "John Crittenden and Stephen Douglas talk about compromise. Why not? Why can't we come to an agreement?"

He chewed his bottom lip before answering. "I won't go for any agreement that involves denial or rewording of the Constitution. Crittenden proposed a compromise to extend the Missouri line to the coast and allow slavery south of it. But Buchanan 'don't have time' to pass it, so the due would fall to me, and I won't permit any extension. If they get the southwest territories, they'll want Mexico. And then they'll want something else. And if they don't get that, they'll threaten us again. I don't like being menaced, Mother, and I ain't giving in to bribery. The Republicans were elected on a platform opposing extension and I won't waver from it. My word is my bond. Besides, like I said before, this crisis is all artificial! It's got no foundation in facts. If we let it alone, it'll go down by itself. I've still got confidence the Almighty will bring us through this."

Dec. 22, 1860: I visited Mrs. Roonamen today because last night's terrifying dream ended with Abraham in a hangman's noose, his feet in chains, his body tarred and feathered. She foresees men traveling with us who are not trustworthy, but says he won't be killed on a journey. She also had a vision of kidnapping, so we must still be diligent on our way to Washington. When Abraham heard the warning, he first shooed me for visiting a seer at all and then said, "Well, Mother, I've died many times on the platform. If they shoot me, at least it'll be the last time I expire." I don't see much humor in that response.

Dec. 25, 1860, Christmas: Not a very joyful day. We received another telegram from Stephen Douglas urging compromise: "SC had no right to secede, but she's done it. The rights of the federal government remain, but possession is lost. Are we prepared in our hearts for war with our own brethren and kindred? I confess I am not." Nor am I, Stephen, nor am I.

Then we received news that the rebels demanded surrender of Forts Sumter and Pickens. Buchanan finally refused them and organized expeditions to protect the garrisons.

Abraham is still working on his Cabinet. Against my strong advice, including some overly loud battles, he asked even more of his former rivals to serve with him. That seems doltish, but he won't be swayed. I have also talked, cried, and even hurled a frying pan to dissuade the appointment of southerners. "Mother, you're too suspicious," he admonished. "I give you credit for good sense, but you tend to magnify trifles, and you hold eternal grudges for things that weren't real in the first place. You can't keep people in a noose forever." Bah! One should never sleep with the enemy!

Dec. 29, 1860: After gunfire forced a US ship to surrender, the rebels seized Ft. Moultrie and Castle Pinckney in SC. Federal buildings were confiscated in other areas as well, and Maj. Anderson has moved to Ft. Sumter. Abraham says the government must reclaim anything taken, by force if necessary. I've never seen him so military-minded. I'm accustomed to living with a negotiator, a mediator, a peacekeeper, and I've never glimpsed this side of him.

Jan. 1, 1861: What a year we have to anticipate. As soon as the threat of war is resolved, we'll have the life I've always envisioned. Imagine, Madam President, First Lady, Queen Mary. I must make sure the world sees us as cultured, educated people, and will go to NY soon to buy the necessary apparel. Though we live in a rural state, we mustn't present ourselves as ruffians.

I'll be aided in my effort to show elegance by the diamond necklace I received from Isaac Henderson, publisher of the *NY Evening Post*. All he asked is that I speak to my dear husband about a position as a naval agent in the Customs House. Abraham was not pleased, and he called me "mulish." But he finally agreed to the appointment when I flatly refused to return the necklace. I have never owned jewelry this fine.

Jan. 7, 1861: Salmon Chase and his daughter Kate were here for supper with the Hamlins. I suppose his Cabinet appointment is secure, but I sense the placement will cost us! Chase is like a bluebottle fly, laying his eggs in every rotten spot he can find. He hasn't given up the idea of being President himself, I know it! Nor has his most charming offspring, who is so obvious in her desire for my position. Damn them all!

Jan. 10, 1861: Shots were fired on a US supply ship yesterday in Charleston Harbor! Is war soon to be a reality? "Just as surely as the sun will rise tomorrow," Mr. Hamlin said earlier this week at dinner.

Jan. 15, 1861: Though it was dreadfully cold and damp, Bob and I had a productive trip to NY, and brought back Saratoga trunks of fine apparel for the entire Lincoln family. The stores offer so much to choose from when money is no object. All I needed to say was, "I am Mrs. Abraham Lincoln," and people bowed to my every wish and need. Credit was never questioned, nor the ability to pay, so I'll worry about the funds later. All the boys, Abraham included, will grouse over having to wear such formal outfits, but they must look the part. No more bare feet, white socks, open shirts, rough textures. Only silk, linen, velvet—fabrics to be stroked and admired.

We received the same type of regal treatment at hotels and restaurants for the entire trip. Some presented no tab at all, declaring it an honor to serve the "new President's" wife and son. We were entertained nightly by people I never expected to meet, and I myself hosted a lovely tea at the Astor. Women bestowed small gifts. Men asked powerful, deep questions about politics, the possibility of war and secession, Cabinet choices,

Abraham's opinions, foreign policy. I yearned for my wise husband's presence, but had no lack of attention, and felt comfortable with my conversational skills. I was far too exhausted at night to dream about anything but tomorrow. Some people will no doubt call my behavior "unladylike," but I took precautions to give information only to the right people. I have always been an astute judge of character and my prescience seldom fails.

Bob will stay for our inaugural journey to help protect his father. The threats continue, and rumors prevail that southern militias are planning to capture Washington. Alabama, Florida, and Mississippi have now joined South Carolina in secession.

Jan. 22, 1861: Abraham is considering Norman Judd for the Cabinet, but I no longer trust him. I'll never forget that he continuously voted for Lyman Trumbull back in the Senate race of '55. And now, if Wall Street testifies correctly, his business transactions do not bear inspection. Further, the former Whigs will not go for him. I overheard some men at breakfast one morning in NY laughing at the idea of Judd in the Cabinet in these times when truthfulness is so important. As Abraham is almost a monomaniac on the subject of honesty, I know he and Judd would soon come to blows.

Abraham grunts, but doesn't truly listen when I speak about this. So I have written to Judge Davis and asked him to intervene. Abraham respects Davis, and his opinion will have an impact. I asked him not to mention my letter, so Abraham won't suspect my involvement.

I have planned a farewell gala for January 26th, inviting over 1000 people to the American House. Abraham is already occupied with Presidential matters, so the arrangements are left to me alone. I don't really mind; it's all so exciting!

Jan. 27, 1861: Approximately 700 people attended our goodbye gala last night! Guests spent 20 to 30 minutes in line before reaching the door where we greeted them. Someone would escort them through the parlors with a glass of cider and out the back door to allow more to enter. Bob, Lizzie, and Mariah helped me fill glasses and offer cakes. Willie and Tad led people to the exit. The Springfield ladies gave me a Wheeler-Wilson sewing machine as a going-away gift; I am touched and pleased.

Abraham leaves tomorrow for Coles County to visit his father's gravesite and say goodbye to his stepmother. His dreams portend that he won't see her again; Mrs. Roonamen confirms it.

Feb. 1, 1861: Lucius Tilton has rented our house for $350 a year. It's hard to see the items we love go into storage or be placed aside for sale, so we are storing many, many boxes in a spare room not being leased out.

Abraham tried to persuade me not to accompany him and Bob on the inaugural train to Washington, but rather to follow in a few days with Willie and Tad. Of course I won't allow it. I planned this office for him, and I will not be excluded from such a prestigious journey. Nor will I set my beloved husband and son out to be slaughtered alone, if such is to be the case. We've had some harsh words over this but, as Abraham so ineloquently said, it's difficult to make "Contrary Mary" do anything she doesn't want to do.

Feb. 5, 1861: The Union is dwindling daily. Georgia, Louisiana, and Texas have seceded, although Kansas was admitted as a free state. Thank Heaven Virginia and Kentucky have not withdrawn; to lose either would be disastrous.

We have begun work on Abraham's inaugural address. He is studying Henry Clay, Thomas Jefferson, Daniel Webster, Andrew Jackson, the Bible, and the Constitution for inspiration. When he finishes his draft, we'll go over it together and discuss the merits of each point. From now on, his speeches must be finely polished! I will be very busy.

Feb. 10, 1861: We leave for Washington tomorrow! We sold the *Staats-Anzeiger* back to Mr. Canisius for just what we paid, so we have a little money in the bank with which to start our new life. We have also sold much of our furniture and packed our necessities to be sent. Mr. Tilton will care for the horse, cow, and dog. The small animals will find new homes in time. Abraham has left his practice to Herndon, though he instructed the "Lincoln and Herndon" sign to remain until our return.

I hope we're doing the right thing. Abraham never really wanted to be President in the early years. Back then, he wanted nothing more than a Senate seat. But I kept pushing and prodding. Have I given him over to a life he will hate? Will he learn to despise me for doing it? Only God knows. I just hope it stops raining before we leave.

Feb. 12, 1861, Abraham's 52nd birthday: The wind is as bitterly cold here in Indianapolis as in Springfield, so we are wearing our heaviest coats and woolen shawls. Despite the rain and sleet, thousands gathered in Springfield to say goodbye yesterday, and most wept openly. When we pulled into Indianapolis, we were greeted by 34 firing guns. What a headache that caused!

The train is magnificently decorated with flags, festoons, and signs blazoned with the silly moniker, "Abra-Hamlin-Coln." I had to study the word for several seconds before realizing its meaning. The car's walls are covered with crimson plush and heavy blue silk studded with silver stars. The furniture is carved black walnut with horsehair upholstery. There is even an extended sofa for Abraham. Willie and Tad are enjoying themselves immensely. They love the engineers, the people trotting alongside holding banners, the bands that play as we pass, the men with Union flags every mile or so, and the speed. I like the ride as well. It can hardly be felt, much unlike the old days. Bob stays mostly in his compartment, reading I suppose, though I spied him once at the liquor bar. I didn't mention it because, in truth, I was somewhat envious.

The newspapers captured Abraham's unplanned speech from the station in Springfield and I have preserved it here. It may be the best talk he has ever given. Our friends, neighbors, and loved ones will be pleased to see us return in 8 years.

> My Friends, one who's never been placed in a position like mine can't understand my feelings at this hour, nor the oppressive sadness I feel at this parting. For more than 25 years I've lived among you, and during all that time I've received nothing but kindness. Here the most cherished ties of earth were assumed. Here my children were born, and here one lies buried. To you, my friends, I owe all I've got, all I am.
>
> Today I leave you to assume a task even more difficult than that which devolved on General Washington. Unless the great God who assisted him will be with and aid me, I can't prevail. But if the same almighty arm that directed and protected him will guide and support me, I'll succeed. Let us pray that God won't forsake us now. To Him I commend you all. Permit me to ask that, with equal sincerity and faith, you'll all invoke His wisdom and goodness for me.
>
> With these words, I've got to leave you, for how long I don't know. Friends, one and all, I wish you an affectionate farewell.

For his birthday, I gave him a bag of sarsaparilla, in case it's not available in Washington, and 2 books: Walt Whitman's *Leaves of Grass* and Hinton Helper's *Impending Crisis of the South*. One for his heart, one for his mind.

He has appointed another rival to the Cabinet: Edward Bates as Attorney General. Perhaps he wants another beard close by? At least he's anti-slavery. The last appointed, Montgomery Blair as Postmaster General, is one of his better choices. Blair is judicious and astute. Abraham says he wishes the roles could be reversed—that he could serve as postmaster and let Blair be President. I replied that I would then have to divorce one and marry the other.

So his Cabinet contains 2 men from the west, 2 from the border states, 3 from the east, none from the south. Men who are, or have been, Free-Soil

Whigs, Conservative Whigs, and Independent Whigs, as well as
Independents, Jacksonians, and National Democrats. My husband is wise.

Feb. 15, 1861: We stopped today in Pittsburgh and once again the
people bombarded Abraham with questions about the crisis. And again he
refused to talk about it. I like the way he phrased his silence this time:

> In every crowd I've passed through lately, some allusion's been
> made to the country's distracted condition. It's natural to expect I
> should say something on this subject; but to touch on it at all would
> involve an elaborate discussion of a great many questions and
> circumstances, requiring more time than I've got, and might
> unnecessarily commit me on matters not yet fully developed. When I
> do speak, I hope I say nothing in opposition to the Constitution's spirit,
> contrary to the Union's integrity, or inimical to the liberties of the
> people or the peace of the whole country.

Feb. 13, 1861: The train continues through snow, rain, and deep mud.
We met the Ohio governor in Cleveland, President Fillmore in Buffalo, and
young Grace Bedell in Westfield, NY. Abraham stepped out onto the
platform, his gray scarf blowing wildly about his head, and called for the
girl in a voice strained to almost soundlessness. When she came forth, he
kissed her cheek and showed off his new beard. I personally think it looks
quite handsome.

He is white with exhaustion, with dark circles around cavernous eye
sockets. I hope he can last till we get there. If we make this trip without
being shot, I would hate for him to die next week from pneumonia as
President Harrison did! I sent a courier out in NY to purchase a heavy
broadcloth overcoat and elegant silk hat—Abraham was wearing his shabby
ones. The press noticed and remarked on it:

> Since then Mr. Lincoln has looked 50% better. If Mrs. Lincoln's
> advice is always as near right as in this instance, the country may
> congratulate itself upon the fact that its President-Elect does not
> reject, even in important matters, the advice and counsel of his wife.

Thank Heaven we've had no trouble thus far to mar the trip's pleasure.
We have been met at every stop by the whole population of the areas we
passed through. And the *Home Journal* has begun referring to me as the
"Illinois Queen." I rather like the title and hope it catches on!

Feb. 18, 1861: Sen. Jefferson Davis has been named President of the
Confederate States of America, with Alexander Stephens as VP. The pictures
of them in the press are not kind. Davis appears to be about 55, thin,

wrinkled, and apparently blind in one eye. His first wife was Zachary Taylor's daughter; she died early in life and marriage. His current wife's name is Varina; people say she is lovely and less than half his age. He is friends with President Pierce and is one of the southerners Abraham considered for his own Cabinet.

Stephens is an odd-looking little man, weighing about 90 pounds, with a pale face that reeks of consumption. He served with Abraham in the House as a Whig, and Abraham admires him. They communicated in writing late last year when Abraham promised that the Union wouldn't interfere with slavery where it now exists. I hope this prior relationship bodes well for a compromise. If it doesn't, I'm dreadfully concerned. Davis is a West Point graduate, has military experience, and was formerly Secretary of War. Abraham has always said that his combatant experience consisted of fighting mosquitoes and leading a charge on an onion patch. I wonder if Mrs. Davis is as frightened as I?

Feb. 19, 1861: I have had such fun riding the train and being greeted by the crowds (some quarter million people in New York City). When we stop long enough, I book a room in a large hotel and invite the local ladies to a reception. When I told Abraham about my joy in being so well recognized, my humble husband admonished me. "Don't suppose for a moment that these demonstrations are for us personally. They're for the Union, the country's institutions, and the perpetuity of our liberties. It ain't for us, Mother, it's for the office. You'd do well to remember that."

Bah! For the office, yes, but we are the office holders and I won't subdue my enthusiasm. I have waited and planned too long to be cheerless.

Feb. 21, 1861: We dined with Hamlin last evening. I like him. He's a chunky little man, but carries himself well and speaks intelligently. After supper, we attended the new Verdi opera, *Un Ballo in Maschera*. We bedded down slightly after midnight and left NY early today for Philadelphia. En route, we were warned of an assassination plot in Baltimore, just as Mrs. Roonamen predicted. Abraham is not concerned, but I am numb! Thank God for my medicines.

Feb. 24, 1861: I am so angry I could spew nails! Because of the threat from Baltimore, they (I'm not allowed to know who "they" are. Security, military, managers, advisers. Abraham's circle no longer considers me important.) "They" decided late Friday night that Abraham would leave the train in Philadelphia and disguise himself on another line. So we weren't allowed to arrive together on the journey for which we've worked our entire lives. They were not even going to tell me about the switch, but Abraham insisted.

Hill Lamon, whom I trust, was with him. So was Allan Pinkerton, the security man. Otherwise, he faced his assassins alone. The throng in Baltimore threatened to overturn the train when they learned Abraham was not there to speak! Too upset to write more. Welcome to the Presidency, Mrs. Lincoln!

Feb. 26, 1861: Confusion and sadness overwhelm me. I dress early each morning to receive callers, but no one comes. Even Harriett Lane, President Buchanan's hostess, has not paid respects, which is a blatant breach of protocol. Where is the White House "sorority" I read about? Many men have come to meet with Abraham, but none have brought their wives, and few women have called on their own. Such poor manners! Doesn't this town understand proper etiquette? Surely they know to welcome the President's wife! I have always tried to secure the best wishes of everyone I associate with, so I don't understand being ignored and discounted in this way. Perhaps I'll write an anonymous letter to the press in my own defense and urge the gentry to visit — as is proper.

Though Washington has grown way beyond its borders, the city is no better than I remember it. And I recall I could stand it for no more than a few months! But I was not as mature then, and had two babies to care for. Willie and Tad now think this move is quite the adventure, so I'll have no trouble from them. Bob is his usual gloomy self, but he'll return to Harvard soon.

This move is hard for Abraham also; he is already toiling and not even sworn in yet. He has no voice and can hardly lift his hand from his lap. Since we left Springfield, he has spoken 35 times, in 28 cities, including glorious places like New York and Philadelphia, and little places like Steubenville, Peekskill, and Fishkill Landing. We have only just arrived and he is as peaked as an albino frog. What will he be like in 4 years?

Feb. 28, 1861: The Missouri Line Extension Compromise failed in the Senate, but Abraham said he would have vetoed it anyway. Congress has, however, sent a proclamation to the states forbidding any federal interference with slavery where it now exists. A harbinger of peace?

I didn't realize how fully surrounded we would be by southern sentiments and troops. Even though DC is considered to be in the north, the population seems intensely southern, and very few profess to be Republicans. Maryland is Union in name only, and Virginia has always had a southern heart.

Mar. 1, 1861: Stephen Douglas came to see us again! Though he spent most of his visit with Abraham behind closed doors, he took time to have tea and chat with the boys and me. He's trying to convince Abraham to attend the peace conference being held in Washington. I hope Abraham will lean on him for advice. They both nettled me that my husband plans to be sworn in as "Abe" Lincoln, and I pitched a cat fit before I realized they were teasing. They chuckled heartily as I ranted and argued against the idea. I was not amused.

Mar. 3, 1861: A most wonderful gift arrived today: an elegant barouche with four black horses from NY merchants who hope I will shop there, which I certainly shall. Although Abraham says it's improper, I see no problem accepting. The staff told me that Mrs. Tyler accepted hundreds of gifts, including a magnificent Arabian steed!

In his final address to Congress, President Buchanan said states have no right to secede, but in his back-and-curve way, he also said the federal government can do nothing to prevent it. Then we learned that President Tyler has donned traitor's boots and joined with the rebels. What must George Washington be thinking as he looks down on us?

Mar. 4, 1861, Inauguration Day: The day I've waited for my entire life, though it wasn't quite what I saw in my dreams. Abraham was sworn in this afternoon, surrounded by cannons, military men in uniform, cavalry at every intersection, riflemen on the rooftops, and dozens of disguised security. He and the others on the platform were encircled with a wooden fence. Behind them stood the unfinished Capitol, with a huge crane swinging from the scaffolding.

Though somewhat cold and cloudy, approximately 30,000 people attended—those who would harm us and those who would protect us from harm. Some of my sisters, brothers, nieces, nephews, cousins, and dozens of Springfield friends attended at our invitation and will stay in the mansion for a few days.

Abraham's men ludicrously suggested I should stay inside, but I wouldn't hear it. Dolley Madison began this tradition by attending her husband's inaugural in 1809, and I would not be deprived of the right. I watched from a guarded area a stone's throw from the platform. Dolley also hosted the first inaugural ball, so I will certainly follow suit.

Our friend Ned Baker eloquently made the introduction. Abraham had hardly adjusted his spectacles before he addressed the slavery issue: "I've got no purpose, directly or indirectly, to interfere with the institution of slavery in states where it exists. I believe I've got no lawful right to do so, and I've got no inclination to do so."

He also reminded them that the Constitution advocates a perpetual Union, and promised to fight to protect it. He plainly said, "No state, on its own mere motion, can lawfully leave the Union."

Today was the first time I've heard him use the term "civil war":

> In your hands, my dissatisfied countrymen, and not in mine, is the momentous issue of civil war. The government won't assail you, so you can't have a conflict without being the aggressors yourselves. You've got no oath registered in Heaven to destroy the government, while I have the most solemn one to preserve, protect, and defend it.
>
> We're not enemies, but friends. We must not be enemies. Though passion might of strained, it mustn't break our bonds of affection. The mystic chords of memory, stretching from every battlefield and patriot grave to every living heart and hearthstone all over this broad land, will yet swell the chorus of the Union when again touched, as surely they will be, by the better angels of our nature.

Despite the perilous atmosphere, he ended by pleading for friendship and assistance from all parties and all states. Then Judge Taney administered the oath! I was glad for my veil, because tears cascaded like Niagara down my cheeks.

It was odd to see Adele and Stephen Douglas in the audience. I know how much they both wanted to be in our position. I was amazed when Abraham absent-mindedly handed his hat to Stephen as he took the podium, and I delighted to see Stephen nod vigorously in favor of Abraham's comments. They have become chums again, and Abraham actually consulted Stephen about his inaugural speech. Stephen is still a strong Democrat, of course, and has proclaimed loudly to the Senate that he has no political sympathy with our administration and expects to oppose it with all his energy on those principles that separate our parties. But, he added, and for this I bless his soul, "On the question of preserving the Union with a peaceful solution of our present difficulties, I'm with Lincoln." I believe Abraham will offer Stephen a Cabinet post in '64—perhaps even the VP position.

I also thought President Buchanan's last words to us were odd: "If you're as happy to be entering the White House as I am to be leaving it, you're the happiest people in the world."

Abraham replied, "I'm tired of it already."

Mar. 5, 1861: What a magnificent ball we had last night! I have never been forced to shake so many hands. I wanted to sit and nod at the passersby like Mrs. James Monroe and Lovely Lady Tyler did, but Abraham wouldn't allow it. His own hands are too lame to even sign documents today.

He danced with me a great deal. I also danced with many former Presidents, ambassadors, and politicians. Abraham extravagantly praised my royal blue silk mantua—highly hooped—worn with pearls, gold bracelets, new diamond rings, one perfect feather in my hair, and blue satin shoes. I looked like the pictures of Empress Eugénie recently shown in

Godey's! Abraham did ask me to keep the shawl about my shoulders to avoid making the other women envious of my bodice. He had eyes for no one else!

I remain quite upset, however, that I was forbidden ("they" are still making the rules) to enter the ball on Abraham's arm or dance the first round with him. Seward said it wasn't proper. They who have ignored all protocol so far now tell me the rules! I am the President's wife and should lead with him. And yet he must offer his arm to another lady, making her primary and placing me second. I won't endure this backward custom again! Thank Heaven Stephen was with us; I didn't shrink from his arm.

Perhaps my senses are off balance, but I did not feel the deference we should have. The women didn't honor my presence, the men didn't bow. I even heard whispers of "unattractive" and "middle class," though the young girls liked Bob well enough. Surely this is just the newness for us all. We'll become accustomed to each other soon.

Mar. 6, 1861: Cousin Lizzie and I (with Willie and Tad underfoot) explored the mansion from top to bottom, 30 rooms in all. Abraham's office is in a large suite on the east side of the second floor with the other offices. The family quarters are just down the hall in the west wing. Our bedrooms join with a door as they did in Springfield. Willie and Tad will bunk together across the hall. Hay and Nicolay, Abraham's secretaries, will also live in two of the many guest bedrooms.

The Executive Mansion is not much of a mansion. It's yellowed, dusty, and declining, though not quite as "seedy and dilapidated" as Lizzie dubs it. The years of visitors and staff treading through it and clipping pieces as souvenirs has done much damage. I don't know how I will manage to even clean it. Didn't Buchanan have servants to care for it? Yes, but Miss Lane, the "Democratic Queen," preferred entertaining to redecorating and maintaining. What a shame to allow the ruination of such a historical and important residence!

The state rooms are not horribly bad, but the private accommodations aren't fit for the humblest farmer, much less the President. The furniture is of poor taste, scarred, and broken. Some pieces look as though John Adams himself brought them in; we left better behind us in storage. Perhaps, like the Hardings, we should have brought our own furnishings. Abraham will be pleased, however, with the upstairs library, which was begun by Mrs. Fillmore. I'll decorate it like his study at home and add to it as much as possible. I borrowed the large book entitled *Canons of Etiquette to be Observed by the Executive* for us to review.

Lizzie agreed to stay and help me assemble a staff and begin the refurbishing. I promised to take Willie and Tad to Boston and NY as soon as

I receive funds from Congress. I'm told that every President since Harrison received at least $20,000, but can't tell where any was spent. Shopping with no worries about money will be so good for my morale and well being! I'll buy only the finest for the mansion!

Mar. 7, 1861: Another excitement in so many—the *New York Herald* praised our inaugural reception:

> Mrs. Lincoln is more self-possessed than Lincoln himself, and has accommodated more readily than her taller half to the exalted station to which she has been so strangely advanced from the simple social life of the little inland capital of Illinois.

Some people, however, didn't find Abraham's speech as palatable as our reception. Here are some of the disgusting and unintelligent headlines:

> *Arkansas True Democrat:* If declaring the Union perpetual means coercion, then Lincoln's inaugural means war!
>
> *Montgomery Weekly Advertiser:* War, and nothing less than war, will satisfy the abolition chief.
>
> *Charleston Mercury:* A more lamentable display of feeble inability to grasp the circumstances of this momentous emergency could scarcely have been exhibited.

Mar. 8, 1861: I have learned that I'm expected to host a regular Friday evening event, a ladies' reception every Saturday afternoon (the first is in 4 days), and receptions twice a week in winter and spring. What a glorious hostess I'll be, just like Dolley. And very well dressed now that I've secured Elizabeth Keckley, the famous mulatto dressmaker. She formerly worked for Mrs. Jeff Davis, but chose to stay in Washington after receiving freedom. She has already begun on a bright rose-colored moiré-antique gown for me and a blue watered silk for Lizzie.

Mar. 9, 1861: Disrespect did not take long to rear its ugly head. The papers have begun printing scorn and contempt, calling us "Lincoln and his northern myrmidons." They mock Abraham's arrival in Washington, using words such as "skulking," "slinking," and "sneaking." I have been referred to as "the new administration's kitchen Cabinet." Though I know the term refers to my influence with Abraham, I don't like it at all. The cartoons are too hurtful to even read. How will the negativity affect our public reception tomorrow?

Mar. 10, 1861: The remaining Union states have met and drafted a compromise plan. As Abraham feared, it agrees to extend the Missouri line to the coast, and applies the free-soil doctrine only to regions the US already possesses. It says no new territory can be acquired without the consent of senators from both sides, meaning that slavery is still possible in new states. Abraham is furious, but still says there's no need for bloodshed and war.

We have learned the identity of the Confederacy Cabinet members, and the results frighten me because the men seem so qualified. Jefferson Davis has also assembled an army—not a difficult task for a former War Secretary!

Mar. 11, 1861: What an exciting day! First, Mathew Brady came to take photographs of us all. I normally don't like such occasions, but he's such a charming man. I chose my most flattering dress: heavy white silk with 60 velvet bows and thousands of black dots. White roses and jasmine on my bodice and hair.

I didn't realize until I saw Abraham posing how skeletal he has become. I expect he has lost 30 pounds or more since last fall. His new beard covers minimal flesh. What will he look like when we leave this place? Will he be run beyond his distance?

Mar. 19, 1861: Willie and Tad both have the measles! What else can happen to anguish us? The doctor says they have only a mild case, over in a few days, but they are cranky and bored, so they must be attended. Thank Heaven they enjoy Elmer Ellsworth's company, for he too has contracted the disease. Since he must stay a while longer, he has time to read to the boys and play checkers. Their tutor, Mr. Ambrose, will not come near them in this condition! I must admit that it's peaceful to be free from their continuous jokes and pranks. Our rascals believe the Presidency comes with a license to frolic!

I have so many obligations of my own to handle, including tomorrow's reception, that I have no time to myself. I suppose the crowd will soon leave the city, and then we may hope for more leisure. Though if the upcoming ladies' receptions go as well as the last, I'll soon be the talk of Washington!

No matter what else goes on around me, my favorite moments are the few spent with my beloved husband in the lovely black barouche after supper. I so fear for his life that I'm peaceful only when holding his hand. He still refuses to meet with the Confederate representatives.

Mar. 22, 1861: I have retained a secretary for myself, an older man with jowls like an old hound dog. His name is William Stoddard, but he is called "Stod." I sense we will get on well. His first duty was to transcribe my letter to Seward requesting the appointment of our friend Col. Mygatt to the

Honolulu consulship. Abraham is constantly encouraging me to be quiet and stop asking for favors and appointments. But the positions I request are only small ones with which he should not trouble himself. So many people ask for approval, and his goodness often allows imposition. He has always placed great confidence in my knowledge of human nature, because he little understands the seedier side of men.

Mr. Brady has returned the ambrotypes and I have instructed him to destroy all but one of me. The only picture at all passable is the one standing with my back almost turned, showing only side face. The others make me look dowdy and fat. It's the crinolines that are portly, not me. I will cut back on them.

Mar. 23, 1861: The *Richmond Examiner* continues its mission to incite the southerners:

We must capture Washington at all and every human hazard. The filthy cage of unclean birds must and will be purified by fire. Our people can take it, and Scott the arch traitor and Lincoln the beast can't prevent it. The just indignation of an outraged and deeply injured people will teach the Illinois Ape to retrace his journey across the borders of the free negro states still more rapidly than he came.

Mar. 27, 1861: Our friends have all left. Only Cousins Lizzie and Lockwood, Sister Peggy, and her dear Charles remain. It was so good to have family with me again. I'll be soul sick when Peggy and Charles leave, but Lizzie agreed to remain longer. I'm finally beginning to feel at home, but need her friendship to overcome the loneliness for those left behind. Though the grounds are still guarded, we do get out for pleasant drives, but it would be no fun alone. Last week, we were able to visit Mt. Vernon, George Washington's home in Virginia. To my delight, Abraham found time to go with us!

My favorite area here is the Buchanan conservatory, with its open glass dome and fish tank. I find peace there when I have a moment. So many choice blooms: camellias, roses, jasmine, all the flowers I love so much. I send a bouquet to someone every day to show appreciation, court favor, or simply say hello, and take many bunches to the military hospitals. The mansion is replenished regularly with fresh flowers, and I have thrown out those horrid artificial blooms that sat for decades on all the tables! They also grow fresh tomatoes in the greenhouse. How I love having tomatoes on my plate each and every day!

The Marine Band plays for the public every Wednesday and Saturday on the front lawn. I enjoy listening from the south balcony, especially when Abraham can be enticed to sit with me. They play all the songs of my youth, in addition to some new tunes. Tad also loves this music and usually marches around the crowd, playing his drum with the band.

The only real heartache is the stench, far worse than Springfield in summer. We're near the Potomac River and the Washington Canal, whose waters are rancid, so the hills smell like rotten fish. When breezes come from the north, the odor inside is nearly unbearable. John Hay says it smells like 10,000 dead cats, but that may be a low estimation.

Mar. 29, 1861: Though I had to fight Seward for the right to host it, our first state dinner last evening was a real smasher. All 28 guests stayed late into the night for sherry and cards. I showed Seward once and for all that he is not the President, nor is he in charge of social events in this administration! Abraham will likely be upset when he learns I took the reins from Seward.

He will also be angry if he discovers my recent correspondence with Simon Cameron. I wrote to express my displeasure at being ignored during his visit last week. He answered that he had forgiven me for my past offenses toward him and asked me to pardon his indiscretion. But I'm not forgiving enough to feel lenient toward him, as he passes me so lightly by when he visits, and asked him to be more observant. I will be given respect or know the reason why! I wish Abraham had more time to discuss these issues with me. He wouldn't allow his men to ignore me, but he doesn't see. His life is artificially colored as the land's most important man. Must end now; Tad has tied his goat to a chair and it is braying loudly.

Mar. 31, 1861, Easter: Abraham took a morning from his turmoil to attend church with us, though he went straight to bed afterward with a headache that has been nagging him for several days. Could it be the smell?

Congress has finally authorized $20,000 to refurbish the mansion. The money is meant to last the first four years, but the house is in such terrible shape that I will invoke the doctrine of necessity: Spend what I require now and worry about the remainder when the need arises. I'll leave for NY as soon as possible.

The White House must be the finest home in the country—meriting royalty, honoring America, standing worthy of our nation's leader. Then people won't dare to destroy it or cut edges off the draperies. Abraham and I argue over this constantly. He says I should buy cautiously and not flaunt our success, but I know finery is right. The mansion is a dreary place now, old and worn—not a showplace for the Chief Executive. With the country in turmoil, the citizenry needs to know the Union is secure, that we're not afraid or suffering. They will see all that when the house is refurbished. Embellishing has not even been attempted since Mrs. Fillmore reworked the kitchen and library, so we need new furniture, china, artwork, wallpaper, rugs, crystal, draperies. I am just the woman to tackle the challenge.

Apr. 4, 1861, Tad's 8th birthday: Tad received many birthday gifts from the personnel and visitors, including several pets. The little codger loves animals so much that he proclaims he was a "wabbit" in a previous life! Already we have a zoo of cats, ponies, geese, and goats in the yards. One gift we did not appreciate was the black doll, with stomach ripped apart, posted specifically to Tad. Must the Union-haters attack innocent children? Why won't they just leave us alone?

Apr. 6, 1861: Willie has been ill since Tad's birthday, and I don't like the sound of his coughing. I'm tempted to take him back to see Willie Wallace, but perhaps we'll visit the homoeopathist here first. I wish Abraham would also see a doctor. His appearance worsens each week and sleep is modest. His headaches come nearly as frequently as mine, and he refuses to eat regularly. When he does eat, he does so mechanically, with no notice of the food. I often take a tray to his office and am rudely instructed to leave it outside the door.

Apr. 7, 1861: Abraham met today with John Botts, a Virginia Unionist, to explore ways to save that state. If she secedes, we will be surrounded. He also sent troops to Forts Sumter and Pickens with provisions, though he refuses to evacuate or negotiate. Seward knifed him again by secretly meeting with the Confederate representatives and telling them we would leave Sumter. Abraham is responding with uncommon choler. I sense war in my bones and don't believe we—Abraham and I, the Union, the military, the people—can handle it. Wouldn't a compromise be wise? The *Charleston Mercury* says our reinforcements in SC mean war!

Apr. 11, 1861: Though Abraham rejected my former pleas, I again requested the appointment of William Wood as Commissioner of Public Buildings. I discovered his shrewdness when he arranged our inaugural trip. Since I must work with that commission on all purchases for the mansion, I would prefer him. I don't know why Abraham is rebuffing me on this; someone must be prejudicing him. So I wrote to Hill Lamon, now US Marshall for DC, and asked for his assistance. One can always find ways to get things done without begging.

Apr. 15, 1861: War has begun! The rebels fired on Ft. Sumter, the Union armies surrendered after 34 hours of bombardment, the American flag was torn down, and 2 Union men were killed in an explosion. The relief expedition sat outside in the harbor, unable to help. I fear that what the *New York Times* says is true: "The ball has opened. War is inaugurated." I'm afraid our lives will change for the worst now, and I find myself covering my face with my hands to ward off the spectre of death. Amazingly, Ft. Pickens has been reinforced and remains Union.

John Jay blames Seward for this rebellious act, and I'm not surprised. When Abraham ordered relief to Pickens and supplies to Sumter, Seward apparently interfered. So the naval strength needed to relieve Sumter was diverted to Pickens, and the fleet for SC left without enough arms. I will speak to Abraham about dismissing Seward immediately.

Apr. 16, 1861: After a battle for power with William Seward, a consultation with Stephen Douglas, and an all-night Cabinet meeting, Abraham proclaimed a condition of "insurrection" rather than "war," and called on the remaining states for 75,000 volunteers to fight for 3 months. Much to my amazement, he refused to allow negroes to volunteer! We need all the men we can get, and we are fighting this war for the colored race. Why should they be excluded? I wish he would ask my counsel. I'll have a word with Navy Secretary Welles about this situation. Surely he can see the benefit negroes would provide.

I had to ask John Jay to explain the difference between insurrection and war. The knip is that insurrection is simply a rebellion, an uprising; war is an act of treason. Avoiding the term "war" means southerners can be tried more mildly and held to Constitutional punishment rather than martial. I pray Abraham's estimate of 3 months is too long and these boys, if they answer the call, are home even sooner.

Abraham also asked a fine Virginia man and West Point graduate, Robert E Lee, to head our troops. He is the one who put down the Harper's Ferry raid, and he is married to George Washington's granddaughter! Abraham also asked our darling Ben Helm to take a major's commission, but he refused, possibly to join the rebel army instead! We so wanted Ben and Emilie close to us and on the same side; we love them as our own children. I leave for a shopping trip early tomorrow.

Apr. 24, 1861: Home from Philadelphia, Boston, and New York with carriagefulls of new items for the mansion, and more will arrive via train, including magnificent gold wallpaper from Paris (only $6800, including installation). I won't feel so unneeded when the decorating begins. When Abraham sees what a grand job I plan to do, he'll want to spend more time with me. Imagine, I thought we had too few days together in Springfield!

Mrs. Keckley, Mr. Wood, and I traveled in our private B&O Railroad car, without the boys, and had a wonderful trip. We attended Henry Ward Beecher's church and Laura Keene's theatre. We stayed at the elegant Metropolitan Hotel in NY and were fêted by Alexander Stewart, the city's most renowned merchant. He gave me an extravagant Italian silk-and-lace shawl, and I ordered $2000 of rugs and curtains from him. We were followed everywhere by reporters eager to tell the nation how I plan to make the national house into a grand mansion.

My favorite purchase is the rosewood bed I commissioned for Abraham. I long ago promised him a bed he would not overhang, and this one measures 8' 6" by 6' 2". Abraham will love it! Also purchased a new bed for myself: mahogany with rosewood carvings, large white canopy, spring mattress, fleecy pink coverlet.

Unfortunately, I overspent the allocation for these items, but since Wood approved everything, no one will bicker. He told me Harriett Lane also exceeded her allotment, and Buchanan's administration simply buried the overage in civic appropriation bills, whatever those are. I'll also work with Abraham's secretaries to get the budget increased. The amount isn't enough to manage the intense needs of this house, especially for 4 whole years! Congress did agree to another $6000 annually for repairs, but that will soon be gone as well—spent on new furnaces, gas lights, and other modern conveniences.

While I was gone, my greatest concern was realized: Virginia seceded and we are surrounded by rebels. How I hate to see this stronghold of our past, the motherland of the very area in which we now reside, join against the Union of Washington and Jefferson! In addition, Baltimore was besieged by rioters and Abraham declared their actions an insurrection. Many whom we trusted have left Washington, and the city teems with strangers who hope to stimulate war.

Apr. 26, 1861: Sent Willie and Tad to their room without supper. They are sometimes so disruptive! Perhaps when I finish the playroom, they will spend time there rather than under Abraham's feet. They have turned the entire mansion into a make-believe world, and I frequently receive complaints that they interrupt official meetings. I even heard them referred to as "the Madam's wildcats." I have spoken with them, but they are too adorable to chastise very often!

The vampire press is making light of my purchases, tomahawking me now to slay later, saying Jeff Davis will soon own everything. Surely that can't be, though our protection troops haven't arrived. Abraham paces constantly, muttering, "Why don't they come? Why don't they come?"

He blockaded several Confederate ports and issued another volunteer request for 42,000 men. Where will they all come from? Not Virginia, North Carolina, Missouri, or Tennessee, for they refused the initial requisition. More importantly, where will our ships come from? The navy hasn't been used since 1812. We have only 29 steamships!

Apr. 27, 1861: Oh my God, the troops have arrived! Though they entered triumphantly with music and flags, many have inadequate clothing and some march without shoes. They wear pants too long or too short for their legs, coarse flannel shirts that must itch dreadfully, ugly caps, and tattered, dirty jackets. They sleep in the streets and put up tents on the lawn. I have never seen so many men in one place! Guns and knives lie all about, and many men drink night and day. Soldiers guard our bedrooms and every entrance, so silence is rare.

As these men passed through Baltimore yesterday, they saw the pro-secession flag on Federal Hill. Worse, they were fired on and many are wounded. The plug uglies attacked with bricks, stones, rocks, whatever they could find, and our troops fired in response. On unarmed men! They say 9 civilians and 4 soldiers were killed, with dozens more lying hurt. Now the bridges in Maryland have been burned so additional troops can't traverse, and we hear more serious talk of plans to torch Washington! When I coveted Dolley Madison's experiences, I didn't mean to include war or the burning of the capital. I keep our sons in my sight at all times. They are not allowed outdoors alone and they sleep in my room at night. If Maryland joins the Confederacy, we will have no hope of escape.

Apr. 28, 1861: Robert E Lee not only refused Abraham's offer of command, he has become head of the Confederate Virginia forces! This is frightening, as we know what a fine soldier he is. Can we gain no stronghold in this skirmish? So many of our military's best men are being loyal to their home states and retreating south to fight the Union they once claimed to love. "Must we go to war?" I asked Abraham.

He sighed more deeply than I've ever heard, and answered dully: "I've hoped as sincerely as any man, and I sometimes think <u>more</u> than any other man, that our present difficulties would be settled without bloodshed. I won't say all hope is gone, but if the alternative is whether the Union is to be broken in fragments and our liberties lost, or blood is to be shed, I've got no choice. I don't mean to let them invade us without striking back."

May 2, 1861: Although the arrival of 10,000 soldiers has eased the threat of Washington's overthrow, and Maryland has voted against secession, Gen. Scott has ordered me to take the boys and Lizzie back to Springfield. Assassination and kidnapping threats abound (more than 300, he said). Other people are evacuating daily, especially the women. I asked Abraham to go with us and he emphatically refused. Therefore, I, of course, have also declined, so Scott moved the Frontier Guards and the Fire Zouaves into the East Room for protection, and we will all move into the Soldier's Home next week. It's a charming retreat, once known as the Anderson Cottage, situated a few miles from the city and several hundred feet above our present location. That will make it much cooler, so our time there will be enjoyable. I sense that Abraham is pleased we're still with him, though he feigns annoyance.

May 12, 1861: Lizzie, Mrs. Keckley, and I returned today from a quick trip to NY, complete with military guards. We were fortunate enough to take in a Charles Wilson Peale art exhibit and Washington Irving's new play, *Spectre Bridegroom*. In addition, we saw the impressive St. Patrick's Cathedral, still unfinished but open to the imagination. I'm astounded at the newspaper reports of our purchases there, for we made none this time!

Unfortunately, the Senate did not confirm William Wood as commissioner, so I will have to deal with someone else regarding my expenditures. I was so fond of him and his clever ways of handling money!

May 21, 1861: Arkansas, Tennessee, and North Carolina have joined the Confederacy. England has recognized the rebels as "belligerents," allowing them the rights of a state at war, entitling their flag to recognition on the seas, and granting their war and commerce ships the same privileges as the Union. What is to become of us?

Must go now; my heart is skipping beats and an unknown force is poking hot knives into my brain at regular intervals. I'll write to Willie Wallace tomorrow for more powders.

May 25, 1861: I write through spasms of nausea and tears. Elmer Ellsworth, our great pet, a son in our hearts, was shot yesterday while removing a rebel flag from a hotel roof in Alexandria, Virginia. Only 24 years old! We saw him just two days ago when we went to see the gymnastic drill of his Zouaves. He looked so handsome and virile.

Now his body lies in the Blue Room. His officers presented me with the flag he captured, but I don't want it. I asked the doorman, Edward, to hide it in the attic. Spirits float all through this huge house and not all are friendly. Elmer's presence chills my spine. Abraham is crushed, and we have canceled all receptions and unofficial dinners for the weekend. He sobs at hearing Elmer's name. Our boys are also desolate; they loved him as a brother.

June 1, 1861: How things are changing! Postal ties with the southern states have ended. There will be no more letters between loved ones on opposite sides, even our own families.

And now poor Virginia is not only part of the warmongers, but their capital. Davis has moved his headquarters to Richmond, within a deer's run of Washington. The beautiful south is being ravaged by traitors, and a foreign flag flutters on her shore. I can see that hated banner, and alien campfires as well, from my own windows! How will we survive this? Perhaps it's a sign that we should cross the river and attack. Surely a surprise strike would end this uprising!

June 3, 1861: Once again an icy fist squeezes our hearts. The State Department informed us this morning that Stephen Douglas has died in Chicago from typhoid fever. He was only 6 years older than I. Abraham wept openly at the news, canceled all appointments, and declared a national bereavement of 30 days. I have donned half-mourning purple and sent condolences to Adele. Despite our lifelong competition, Stephen may have been our truest friend. He will be greatly missed, both personally and politically. I always believed he would follow in our footsteps to the White House, or even beside us in 1864, but God had grander plans. May the Lord grant peace for us as well.

June 6, 1861: So much is happening that I don't know if I can continue to write. Our men are now worried that Europe will join with the south against us. If acknowledged as a nation, the Confederate States of America will be sanctioned by Europe to receive money, arms, and men. I am ready to flee to Europe myself. This is not the existence I wanted. I fear for Abraham's life with each breath, and often have to hold my own hands to stop their shaking. Eddy's spirit tells me to hold on, but I am not sure it's possible.

June 8, 1861: A wonderful sermon this morning. It's pleasant going to church without the boys to watch over. They now attend the Presbyterian church with Julia Taft because it's "lots livelier" and because Julia teaches them Sunday School lessons along with her own brothers. Willie has declared his intent to become a minister and no longer romps or rides with us into the country on the "blessed Sabbath." He has always been our dearest boy, and now he looks to a life of godliness! I don't see such a bent in Tad. He attends services only because he goes wherever Willie goes. We continue to tell Tad that he must learn about the Bible because it's Abraham's favorite book and the one we try to live by, but he only grins.

June 14, 1861: The boys and I were almost killed yesterday! We took a carriage with Lizzie and Gen. Walbridge to Virginia to see the camps, but the horses stumbled and threw the driver off the box. The carriage overturned and we all spilled out. No one was hurt, and the boys thought it was great fun, but my nerves are spent and I have just risen from bed to take another dose and jot these notes. I will be selfish about the boys' excursions from now on. God, please let nothing else happen to my family. I could not continue with more loss.

July 4, 1861, Independence Day: We can't celebrate today because we are no longer free. Rebels have torn up the railroad tracks and clipped the telegraph lines into Washington. The streets are deserted, barricades protect public buildings, sentries pace the avenues. Thank Heaven Bob is in school or he would be going into battle. No! I won't allow him to consider it!

I watched Abraham's special session of Congress from the gallery. Even his wife is not allowed on the floor. He appealed to them "to favor, facilitate, and aid our effort to maintain the honor, integrity, and existence of our Union and the perpetuity of popular government." He is now with George Ashmun in his private quarters discussing our strained relations with Canada.

The Confederacy has stopped cotton exportation to England, hoping to bribe Great Britain into backing the south in this rebellion. It may work; if so, the Union is doomed. And yet the daily chores of government go on. I reviewed our troops at Camp Mary Lincoln today in Abraham's absence, and will appear at a reception tonight in the Blue Room.

July 5, 1861: At least 300 people attended our reception last night—all the important people I used to admire from afar. The Marine Band played till all hours and we danced gaily. Abraham has become an acceptable dancer in spite of himself, so perhaps it's true that practice makes perfect. I wore a lustrous white satin gown with a long train, trimmed with one deep flounce of black Chantilly lace. Even the press wrote about the look. Here's an excerpt from *Leslie's Weekly*:

> Our fair Republican Queen was attired in a white satin gown, décolleté of course and with short sleeves, displaying her exquisitely molded shoulders and arms. Her headdress—a coronet wreath of black and white crepe myrtle—was in perfect keeping with her regal style of beauty. Let us add here en passant that Mrs. Lincoln possesses that rare beauty which has rendered the Empress of the French so celebrated as a handsome woman, and which our Trans-Atlantic cousins call la tête bien planté (the well planted head).

July 10, 1861: Nicolay's most recent letter from Alexandria says hundreds of sightseers and souvenir hunters, strumpets and prostitutes, reporters and politicians march and ride alongside the troops. They carry picnic baskets, opera glasses, champagne, and hopes of a grand ball in Richmond under a white flag. Lizzie, Julia, the four boys, and I climbed to the housetop to listen to the battle and wished we too could actually see the festivities as this second War of Independence comes to an end.

July 15, 1861: About 2000 of Gen. George McClellan's troops, under the command of Brigadier General Rosecrans, recently attacked Rich Mountain in western Virginia. Many are dead, but McClellan is considered a hero. The rebels were also defeated at Corrick's Ford and Laurel Hill, and Union pursuit has been discontinued in that area. Now they head into the eastern region and people all around are celebrating. "Forward to Richmond," banners the *New York Tribune*. McClellan says the backbone of the rebellion will soon be broken and the war will be over. The soldiers sing *John Brown's Body* as they march. My soul wavers between elation and terror.

July 21, 1861: The battle is a festivity no longer. It began in earnest today in Manassas, Virginia, and both sides suffered heavy casualties. The silly sightseers ran for their lives when a shell hit a wagon, and some didn't make it out alive. Many soldiers proclaimed their three months up and went home to hide their heads, or simply left their posts and disappeared. By midnight, military and townsfolk alike were straggling into Washington— soaking wet, bleeding, muddy. I visited the hospital and found little hope remaining. I'm afraid we won't see peace in our lifetime, and Abraham himself now says the war will be long. More lives, more heartbreak, more children without fathers. We must find a way to stop this. Would surrender be so horrid?

Abraham meets late tonight with his Cabinet; now, after an apple for supper, he listens to those who arrive with news and watches the telegraph. He has no time to talk with me, and he no longer listens to my advice. I leave him notes but they go unread, or at least unheeded. I advised him to replace Gen. Scott, to meet with Davis and forge out a compromise, to buy ships from Europe, to leave the whole damned thing to Hamlin! I don't know what else to do.

July 24, 1861: President Martin Van Buren has passed away. We also have the toll from Manassas: 460 dead, 1124 wounded, 1312 missing. The rebels' new gamecock, "Stonewall" Jackson (don't know his given name), was very active at Manassas.

Abraham has dismissed the kind Gen. McDowell and appointed McClellan as head of the Armies of the Potomac. I don't like him. He's vain, egotistic, arrogant, and a Democrat. He has no courage and no manners, and he dismisses me as though I did not exist. I'm not the only one who refers to this tyrant as Young Napoleon. Abraham has ordered him to hold present positions, tighten the blockade, and replace the volunteers. I put my personal feelings aside and sent him a bouquet for good luck; it's the least I can do for our country.

July 27, 1861: Abraham hasn't touched his bed in three days. Perhaps we won't be in the White House very long after all. I better find a way to pay my debts so he won't learn about them if we're forced out. Though

Wood approved all the purchases, I'm receiving all the blame, and I sense that Jeff Davis would make much of it.

Aug. 1, 1861, Bob's 18th birthday: Thank God Bob is safely away at Harvard. I wish there were some place to send Willie and Tad for better safety. The heat here is oppressive, the sound of cannon terrorizing, the hospitals filled to capacity, the sight of ambulances never-ending. I have passed through so much anguish without the benefit of companionship that a change is absolutely necessary for me as well — perhaps back to New York.

Aug. 4, 1861: Prince Jerome Napoleon Bonaparte (Eugénie's nephew and cousin of the Emperor) and his suite dined with us and 27 other guests last evening. Prince "Plon Plon," as he is widely known, came across to see the war maneuvers. An excellent opportunity to speak my favorite language and impress him with my French attire: royal purple silk, deeply bordered, with pearl ornaments. He, of course, was in full dress, his breast a flame of decoration. I'm sure he appreciated our hospitality, our French menu, and our manners. Entering the dining room on his arm was a true pleasure, and I was honored that Abraham thought so highly of my language abilities to allow it. What a joy to be able to entertain so lavishly.

Aug. 5, 1861: Finally an opportunity to escape the heat. I just can't endure it any longer. Willie and Tad, Lizzie, Edward the butler, and John Nicolay will accompany me to NY City next week. Dear Hannah Shearer, and perhaps her sons, will join us in Philadelphia, and Bob will meet us in Long Branch for two weeks at the seashore before returning to school. We have invitations from three different hotels, with suites offered at each. Because of our railroad passes and private car, the trip will cost nothing — a good deal for us all in these trying financial times. And, most exciting, we may be able to attend an operatic concert by Carlotta Patti, the only rival of Adelina.

I plan to purchase the necessary china and glassware from Haughwout's while in NY. The ugly red-bordered porcelain Mrs. Pierce acquired is nearly all gone.

Aug. 6, 1861: Abraham has signed a bill freeing the slaves being used by the rebels in the war. It seems many officers took negroes with them into battle to do their cooking, clean their weapons, and keep up their uniforms. I doubt many slaves are fighting for the rebel cause, however.

He also convinced Congress to pass a national tariff, called an "income tax," of 3% on earnings over $800, and even stiffer taxes on purchases. The people won't be pleased with this, but the war effort needs money.

Former VP John Breckinridge has been here several times recently, urging Cousin Lizzie to leave. When she refused again today, he made a play of inviting her to remain as a guest even after the rebels take possession. I spit out, "We'll be only too happy to entertain her till that time!" Until the rebels take possession—how dare he threaten us! I won't allow it! I will get a rifle and fight them every inch of the way to protect what is mine! Damn them all!

Aug. 11, 1861: Another major battle, another defeat, more lives lost— including Brig. Gen. Lyon. The score is two to one for the rebels, and Washington is dressed in mourning. We lost more than 250 men at this battle of Wilson's Creek, Missouri, and it's estimated that over 1000 are wounded or missing. What will become of us? Will Missouri now join the Confederacy? Abraham has proclaimed the last Thursday in September as a national day of humiliation, prayer, and fasting. I doubt our going without food will help the soldiers very much. We leave for NY on Tuesday.

Sept. 3, 1861: We've returned from our excursion to NY much more rested and peaceful, though respite was hard to achieve because of the constant press coverage. We inspected a beach life-saving station, attended a grand hop in our honor, shopped, visited friends, attended many extempore receptions, and tested the waters at Saratoga and Niagara. As always, the falls revitalized my soul.

And how wonderful to see Bob! He has grown much taller than I, and was not so self-indulgent as in the past. Hannah looks and feels well considering her delicate condition. The Carlotta Patti concert was not held.

I'm delighted with the 190-piece Havilland Limoges dining service: solferino purple and double-gilt borders, emblazoned with the US seal. I had the border entwined with two lines to signify the Union soon to return. I purchased an identical set for the Lincoln family with the initials "MTL" instead of the seal.

Much to my dismay, however, Lizzie returned to Springfield. I cried and pleaded for her to stay, but she wanted to get back to her husband and children. I can't fault her for it, but will miss her support. She was frequently the only one I could trust; only she knows how frightened I am under the surface. I feel rather like a swan—tranquil and beautiful on the outside but flippering frantically underneath—and can tell only Lizzie. I have no one else. My husband is unapproachable.

Sept. 6, 1861: Trouble among our own. A NY volunteer troop mutinied near Washington yesterday and refused to obey orders because their petition for furlough was denied. It occurred again today in Maine. Many were arrested and the regiments were put under guard. How can we survive if we fight among ourselves? My husband and I are also fighting among ourselves. We had another loud spat over his inattention to his family. He even threw a small piece of kindling at me! But the stick missed, and the bad humours will pass as always.

Sept. 8, 1861: Abraham was biting angry at supper tonight. He explained that Maj. Gen. John Frémont, once a Presidential candidate but now commander of the Department of the West, declared martial law in Missouri, suppressed several newspapers, then confiscated the property of anyone who had taken up arms and freed their slaves.

We're undermined and ignored from all sides of the military. Our army is worthless. The south will fight this event with new furor, and we'll lose Missouri and Kentucky over the milldam. Abraham called the acts dictatorial, purely political, and not within the range of military law or necessity. He will, of course, override them all, which will make some hate us even more.

Sept. 10, 1861: Abraham sent a much-too-kind request to Frémont, asking him to revoke his orders in Missouri. He says it must be all or nothing, especially now that the rebels have moved into Kentucky. I'm certain he will take my advice and dismiss the usurper as soon as the orders are negated. No man can overrule Abraham Lincoln without grave penalty!

Sept. 11, 1861: Pleasant evening tonight with friends. Chess games and rousing marches on Dolley Madison's wonderful grand piano—such a relaxing time. Hill Lamon has a deep, rich voice and we love to hear him sing! Tad is finally over the lingering cold he picked up at Long Branch, so he joined in the entertainment.

The codgers have raised a soldier company and erected a fort on the roof. Willie is a colonel, Tad a drum leader, and their closest friends, Bud and Holly Taft, are a major and a captain. They have a log cannon and a few wooden rifles. Willie bragged to anyone within earshot, "We're ready for them. We're in a high state of efficiency and discipline." The company is called Mrs. Lincoln's Zouaves, and I've arranged for our boys to get their own red, blue, and gold Zouave uniforms to wear.

Sept. 13, 1861: You won't believe who arrived at our doorstep late last evening: Mrs. Frémont, who traveled from St. Louis to beg for better treatment of her traitorous husband and approval of his illegal orders in Missouri! I wouldn't have seen her, but Abraham is sometimes kinder in heart than I, and he allowed her to present her petition to his deaf ears.

It has rained for several days and the troops stand and sleep in constant mud. We offer them coffee when we can, and I advised the staff to watch out for their health. If one falls, he is to be brought inside. I myself may fall if I don't find more energy. I visit the hospitals several times a week, taking flowers and food. I read to the men, feed them, and write their letters, but it seems so little to do. Reporters don't often visit the hospitals, and it has been suggested that I take the press with me so they can report on the joy my visits bring the soldiers. But I believe charity is a private matter. The visits make the men smile and give me some peace. I don't know whether to dance or die these days, and try mightily to keep up a fearless visage.

Sept. 14, 1861: Abraham has responded favorably to Mrs. Frémont's visit after all. He advised the general that he will order the clauses in relation to property confiscation and slave freedom modified to conform to the acts of Congress, and he hangs fire on dismissal. I don't understand his thinking, but I am not counseled in these matters.

Thanks to Gideon Welles, however, Abraham has finally realized the need to allow negroes to join the army, so we'll soon see more dark faces on this lawn. If only we had been able to employ these extra men yesterday on Cheat Mountain when Lee attacked.

I am forced to dismiss much of the staff. Many are known to be stealing and spreading vicious rumors about us. They have turned John Hay against me, so perhaps he should leave as well. He was appointed illegally at any rate. He serves as Nicolay's aide, but holds the position of Interior Clerk, since we had no money for an assistant. And he has the nerve to accuse me of covert spending! Damn them all!

Sept. 16, 1861: Lee has withdrawn from Cheat Mountain and that part of Virginia has been saved. There is strong fighting in Lexington, Missouri, and Abraham has established Generals Ulysses S Grant and William T Sherman in Kentucky to protect its borders. I fear we will soon see blood on the blue grass, and my heart bleeds. My dear mother and father are buried there. I ache to think their souls will be tarnished with neighbors' blood. My uncles, cousins, and brothers-in-law will soon be forced to fight, if they are not already. I am so torn. My eldest brother and a half-sister swore loyalty to the Union, but another brother and three half-brothers joined the Confederacy. Three half-sisters are married to rebel officers. We're a family in ruins and haven't spoken since the war began.

Sept. 29, 1861: Willie and I have both suffered chills and coughing for several days. I'm sitting up now, but feeling weak again. When so much is demanded from me, I can't afford to be delicate. If a different climate will restore our health, we have to go. If still sick at week's end, we'll head up to Boston and return in November. September and early October are always considered unhealthy months here, and my racked frame certainly bears the evidence.

While we were ill, the Union lost Lexington, Missouri, to the rebels. Approximately 40 dead, 120 wounded. And why? Because Failing Frémont neglected to send help. Surely Abraham will dismiss him now! He is derelict and dangerous. I know Abraham is discussing the issue with his Cabinet and other military men, but nothing is being done!

Oct. 1, 1861: Cousin John Todd has been elected to Congress to represent the Dakota Territory. He took a leave of absence as a brigadier general in Missouri to stand. I enjoy seeing my family in places of honor, though I'm not pleased with the *New York World*'s statement that Abraham has appointed his whole family to government posts. I immediately wrote to the editor about this villainous claim. Abraham has no brother or sister, aunt or uncle, and only a few third cousins. That clears him entirely as to any family connection.

Oct. 6, 1861: Gen. McClellan sent me a box of delicious white grapes from Cincinnati. I wish the sweetness would ease this nausea. Only more powders will accomplish such. Could the cramps be <u>caused</u> by the sweetness?

Hannah Shearer's letter reveals that she has delivered a boy and named him after our precious son: William Lincoln Shearer! I can hear our own Willie outside flying a kite with Tad and the Taft boys. I remember when the world really was as joyful as the children believe it to be.

Abraham and I now occupy the state guest room because of the makeovers in our chambers. The pleasant side of this arrangement is that we're back in the same bed and I know whether or not he sleeps. Sharing a bed has not helped our conjugal life, however. After supper, he changes into his dressing robe and slippers, lights the gas and builds up the fire in his office, and sees visitors till almost sunrise. The diplomatic corps have returned to the city and many strangers come in every day. The Blue Room is quite alive in the evenings with the highest of society.

Oct. 12, 1861: Went to Boston again with Mrs. Keckley, who has become a dear friend and confidante. Only three days, but enough time to spend a day with Bob. He introduced us to many of Harvard's distinguished men, all of whom highly respect him. He's finding life there quite pleasant, and is rooming with Fred Anderson of Cincinnati, a polite young man, son of Maj. Robert Anderson. Bob has joined the Institute of 1770, a social club that promotes public speaking, and is studying Greek, Latin, mathematics, chemistry, religion, elocution, rhetoric, composition, history, and botany. He is still headstrong, but finally using it well.

I'm pleased with the carpets and draperies: Damask curtains, pale green velvet carpet, and gilt mirrors for the East Room; crimson Wilton carpet for the Red Room, green draperies for the Green Room. The mansion improves each week and begins to look like a palace. I also added more books to the library. The collection contained some poor sets of Waverly and Shakespeare, so I replaced each with a fine new edition, plus a set of Cooper. Mr. Watt showed me a way to pay funds out for one purpose and charge them to another so Peter and Paul are both covered.

Oct. 15, 1861: William Wood, the man I once championed as Commissioner of Public Buildings, has turned against me now, as has most of Washington. He brought a charge of dishonesty against Watt, who has been rigidly exact in all his accounts with us. Because of the dishonest way Wood dealt with White House money, he is the last man who should besmirch anyone. He is bitterly disappointed that we displaced him and is capable of saying anything against those who tried to befriend him, myself included. My chosen replacement, Maj. Benjamin French, has taken Wood's place as commissioner, and I look forward to working with him on the remodeling. He served in this position under President Pierce, so he understands how to "handle" money.

Oct. 21, 1861: Abraham came to me in the early evening and my heart raced to see him. It has been a long time since we shared a quiet moment together. But neither romance nor conversation brought him across my stoop. He came to tell me that our dear friend, Edward Baker, after whom we named our precious Eddy, was killed in Leesburg. Ned visited us earlier this week and spent several hours lying on the lawn with Abraham and the boys, talking and tossing leaves. Ned knew he was going into this battle and came to discuss strategy and embrace us all before he left. He wasn't the only casualty—more than 900 killed, wounded, or missing. The defeat was apparently caused by the ineptness of Brig. Gen. Charles Stone, who has been imprisoned for treason.

Abraham is grief-stricken and now admits to a constant pounding in his head that blinds him to other matters. He walks with a shuffle, as though a dagger pierces his back. There are deep furrows around his eyes, mouth, and forehead. I watched him through the window as he later slumped to the stables, both hands to his heart, his face toward Heaven. Even with the distance between us, I could taste his tears.

How long can this continue? How many more sons, friends, and fathers must die before God will stop this travesty? My heart weighs in my chest like a poorly spent cannonball. We feel safe here, but would be so thankful if our purpose could be accomplished without more bloodshed. Abraham says it's now impossible. He whispered as he held me to his chest,

"If being the head of Hell is as hard as what I've got to undergo here, I could find it in my heart to pity Satan himself."

Oct. 25, 1861: Congress has not warmed to us the way I thought it would, and I don't know whom to trust. The city folk seem jealous, divided, angry. They are vicious in their criticism and crude in their remarks. The papers are often violently unfriendly. I have been referred to as a negro-lover, a secessionist, and a southern sympathizer. Abraham is called a backwoodsman, a hick President, a buffoon, an unsophisticated mudsill. They compare him to Andrew Jackson and say he doesn't amount to pig tracks in the War Department or on the battlefield. Many reporters lambaste with great negativity and innuendos because we're both from Kentucky and my brothers fight with the rebels. To my shock, most of the journalists who berate me personally are women.

Where is the respect due the President and his wife? This is the top office, the finest position, in the entire nation! Where is the proper homage? Abraham says it's the price of the Presidency in a time of unrest, but I've stopped reading the rags and am designing a way to fight back. We are not illiterate yokels to be disrespected! My husband is the greatest man in the world! Must close; my head pricks with each word.

Oct. 26, 1861: Western Virginia has voted to become a state, possibly called Kanawha. The Union can use all the strength available right now, so statehood will be granted quickly. Even more wonderful, Abraham has sent orders for Frémont's dismissal and Gen. David Hunter's appointment. The Union will be well served by this decision; it was too long in coming.

Nov. 1, 1861: My trusting husband has never been a particularly good judge of bad characters, and he's just made the biggest mistake of his career. He finally accepted the retirement of feeble Gen. Winfield Scott, but appointed George McClellan to the rank of General-in-Chief. McClellan, called "Mac" by most, is not a fighting man, especially if he suspects a possibility of himself being hurt. He will bring us to our knees and we will live under a slavery flag for the rest of our lives.

Nov. 4, 1861, our 19th anniversary: What of it? We should have stayed in Springfield. I sneaked a glass or two of champagne in the kitchen by myself and have come to bed early.

Nov. 7, 1861: Gen. Grant has lost a camp near Belmont, Illinois. He has a reputation as a self-made failure, a drunkard, a bully, and a vulgarian, and this battle proves the claims. He apparently pushed back the rebels, but then began to celebrate and loot. As he luxuriated in self-indulgence, he was attacked again and had to flee and leave behind his wounded men. What a waste of lives!

A heavy storm tonight, and I'm so on nerve I couldn't stay in the presence of others. I write from my bed, with all lights on and a servant in the corner to mind the fire. I wish Abraham could be with me like he used to be. I fondly remember the days he ran home from his office to hold me until the storm subsided. Will we ever see those moments again?

Nov. 28, 1861, Thanksgiving: A grand lunch with Gov. and Mrs. Newell, Gen. Nathaniel Banks, Col. John Cochrane, and most especially, Joshua and Fanny Speed. Abraham spent the afternoon with us, and I'll never forget him on the big red chair telling Indian stories to the boys after our guests left. Willie sat on one knee, Bud Taft on the other. Holly Taft lay on the chair's arm, holding a gray tabby cat, and Tad straddled the back. The dog slept at Abraham's feet. When I entered the room, he reached out and pulled me into the circle, his child-wife once again. I will always treasure that moment.

Nov. 30, 1861: Dinner alone with the boys and my friend, Chevalier Henry Wikoff. Though an international traveler, he writes for the *New York Herald* and frequently brings me puzzles, fashion columns, or cartoons in advance. He can talk about any subject from love to war, and is abundantly knowledgeable about politics! What fun to be ahead of NY itself! He wrote a book called *My Courtship and Its Consequences*, which deals with his romances and diplomatic adventures in Europe. Very naughty!

McClellan continues to plan, not to do, and this dreary war drags on. Now we hear talk of combat with England and France, especially after the rebel spies James Mason and John Slidell were captured on their way to England earlier this month. This event is being called the *Trent* affair because of the ship on which they sailed. It's rumored that Queen Victoria has sent troop vessels to Canada in readiness. Abraham says he will do all in his power to avert more battles, and meets every day with someone to discuss the affair. "One war at a time," he says.

We can hardly handle this conflict, how would we take on the powers of England and France? We have not received the extra men Abraham wished for, even with the added provision for negroes.

Dec. 1, 1861: Other invoices have arrived for goods I thought were gifts. Can't anyone be trusted to his word? How am I to know what is a present and what must be paid for later? I wrote to AT Stewart about the Italian shawl I believed he gave me last April, thanking him for his patience and soliciting a delay in payment. I know he wanted an audience with Abraham, which I couldn't arrange, but this sudden demand doesn't seem proper. To assure him of my future patronage, I ordered a black India camel's hair cape for $1000. If I continue to purchase large amounts, he probably won't call for my payment as quickly.

Dec. 3, 1861: Oh my God! The *NY Herald* somehow found paragraphs from Abraham's upcoming message to Congress and published them! Abraham's men are searching the mansion for spies. I am terrified the culprit might be Wikoff. Surely not, he's so kind to me! Yes, we discussed the message, but he wouldn't betray me. He is my friend and confidant, yet Abraham suspects us.

Even worse, the evil press is spreading more rumors about me, declaring that proof exists that I shared the speech with Wikoff. In addition, I spy for the south, I'm a secessionist at heart, I had affairs with both Wood and Wikoff, I'm stealing from the White House and the treasury, and I think about nothing but spending money when the military needs it so badly. Can't they see that I care only for the mansion and its splendor? The remodeling is for the soldiers and the war effort, not against it! My loyalty should never be questioned; I have always been, and will forever be, a Unionist. I, who so little desire attention and notoriety, don't understand why they attack me. I wish we had never aspired to this office! It's my fault that Abraham's life is cursed, my fault that he looks so ill and is threatened daily with murder. Assassinate <u>me</u> if I'm so horrid, but leave my beloved husband alone! I'll be glad to relinquish my claims on this position when our term ends. I would go now if it were possible.

Dec. 13, 1861, my 43rd birthday: *The demon in my chest is pounding, pounding to get out, but the doctors with shroud-covered faces have strapped a belt around my ribcage so it can't pierce the skin. The demon knocks, raps, bangs, and yells, "Set me free, you bastards, set me free." Please, God, let it out!*

I search for the paregoric on the table by my bed, but the unholy doctors have hidden it again. Kill me, kill me! For God's sake, kill me!

The oozing black face rises at the end of the bed, its cracked teeth gleaming. It looks like Eddy. I see his little hands reaching out for me, but it can't be. I clench my eyes, scream through stitched lips. I scratch at its pocked cheeks.

Slowly I roll myself to the floor and start dragging across the small room. There are laudanum pills on the dresser. My feet are tied together. I take a stride, fall to the ground, hit my forehead on the floor. No, I can't stop! I crawl to the dresser, reach up, pull the ripped lace covering. The bottles come tumbling down around me, onto me. Over me. Perfume, hairbrushes, creams, toothpowder. The laudanum bottle. I wrestle with the top, and it comes free. I take one, no two or three. I look around. There is no water. I creep back to the bed on chafed hands and knees and see the paregoric on the table. Who replaced it? No matter. One sip to melt the laudanum. Lying on the floor, the demons cackling around me, I sleep.

I woke to Abraham's rough shaking. "Get up, Mother," he commanded. I looked around me slowly, cautiously. I was in my own bed, lightly covered with my own soft pink spread. Abraham continued to shake me. Why was he shouting? I tried to tell him I could hear his voice, but no words came out. The room was hazy, like the canal after an August rain. He lifted me from the bed, wrapped a paisley shawl around my shoulders, and stood me on my feet. I looked at the dresser. It was neat. All the items were in place, but it was wrong somehow. My lower chest hurt, as though a child had been ripped from my ribs. The devil's child. The space inside was heavy, full of foul air.

I could hear Abraham squawking through his invisible cotton mouthpiece. "Wake up, Mother! Molly, wake up! You've slept the whole day. It's time for supper and the boys are worried about you." Then he slapped me. I know only because I heard the wind pass my face and the sound of his palm, not because I felt the blow. I shook my head and looked around. There was a jar of face tint on the floor. It was not a dream.

Dec. 15, 1861: Snowing, dark, cold, and damp outside. Inside, I'm torn between agony and glory as Mrs. President. My heart pulses with black anger and frustration. The party last evening was scant, despite personal invitations and many bouquets sent as reminders. Will these people never accept us? Were Buchanan and his slender niece truly so much more refined? Even if they don't like us as people, shouldn't the office command respect? Even Mrs. Hamlin doesn't attend, though admittedly she and the VP are seldom in Washington.

I sit now at my desk, trying to focus on Willie as he reads *Aesop's Fables*. The book is one of Abraham's favorites, and when they have a moment together, they often discuss the stories. Today, Willie occasionally laughs aloud and looks up to see if I heard. Such a precious child, though somewhat thin now from his recent nausea. So devout, frequently quoting the Bible or writing spiritual stories. He calls himself my boy: "I'm Mama's boy, ain't I, Mama?" Indeed you are, My Darling.

Tonight Abraham and I will attend a much-praised comedy entitled *Family Jars*. We're both greatly anticipating it. Now that we have a private box, the theatre is an even greater diversion.

Dec. 20, 1861: The decorating and remodeling are almost complete, just in time for Christmas. Potomac water now flows through the pipes rather than spring water, all the rooms are painted, furnaces installed, gas light restored. There are custom-made carpets, elegant wall coverings, and draperies on gilt cornices in many rooms—several in Dolley Madison gold and green. Every room except Abraham's offices shines with newness and elegance.

My expenditures are now over by approximately $6700. No matter. Abraham's men will help me resolve the issue and he won't be bothered with this small affair. Perhaps I shouldn't have spent so much with the country at war and money so necessary, but people need to know the government is stable and unconcerned. The mansion belongs to the people. Anyone wishing to see Abraham (he declines no one) simply walks in the front door, climbs the stairs, and waits in Nicolay's office. They wander into our private quarters as well. Our life and family are in public view at all times. Still, I hope they will refrain from snipping off bits of the new draperies. If I catch someone harming our new effects, he will be arrested!

Bob will be home for the holidays; we've sent security passes for his travel and safety. I'm so eager to see him. Unless Abraham releases the spies Mason and Slidell, as England demanded, he will likely not spend much time with his son. I also pray the little ones are well enough to appreciate their brother's presence. I don't know who is the sicker—both suffer from vomiting and fever.

Dec. 21, 1861, Willie's 11th birthday: What a handsome, talented young man Willie is becoming! We gave him a much-wished-for pony, promptly named Jeff, and he hasn't put his feet on the ground since mounting the small steed. Tad begs for a "pwony" now as well. Both are such fine horsemen! They look forward to returning to the Soldiers' Home next summer because it has such wonderful riding trails.

Dec. 23, 1861: Abraham's secretaries and my "special friends" won't help me, so I enlisted Benjamin French to plead my case and make Abraham understand that it's not unusual to overrun appropriations. French must tell him how much it costs to refurnish a house, because he knows very little about such things. I promise I will never overspend again if I'm saved this time. Abraham has too much on his mind to be worried about my behavior. I'm so, so sorry. Why can't I control myself?

Dec. 24, 1861: Abraham is enraged with me, angrier than I've ever seen him in all our years together. After speaking with French, he demanded that I come to his office. He refused to authorize additional money for decorating expenditures, and says we must pay the overage from our own pockets. He screamed at me, his voice going into that falsetto pitch that makes me fear for his heart. His left eye flew up into the socket. His arms brandished on their own.

"Dammit, Mary, it'll stink in the nostrils of the American people to have it said the President spent more than $20,000 for flub-dubs for this damned old house when a hundred thousand soldiers don't have blankets or shoes! This is it—the bottom's out of the tub!

"This place was furnished well enough—better than any diggings we ever lived in before. Why can't you ever leave well enough alone? You've embarrassed us beyond repair. Broken eggs can't be mended. I'll pay the $6700 from my own pocket, but don't ever ask me for anything again as long as we live in this house, including political favors. Just keep quiet. And stop interfering in my affairs! It's better to keep your mouth shut and be thought a fool than to open it and remove all doubt!"

I was actually frightened when he seized me and threw me out of his office. He has never clutched me in rage before. He is not himself.

I didn't realize we are still so poor. Nor did I know that, even though the government pays for our steward, doorkeepers, watchmen, gardener, and laborers, we must pay for cooks, waiters, coachmen, cleaning women, and scullery maids from our paltry $25,000 salary. We must also personally purchase all food and liquor served at official functions; our horses, carriages, and feed; and rooms and food for Abraham's secretaries and their horses. In addition, we have to deduct taxes of approximately $900! I realize now that I truly don't have the means to run this house. If only I had let Seward retain responsibility for entertaining....

What to do? We simply can't afford $6700 from our own purse. No one has the interest of this place more at heart than I. Of course I understand that the country is at war and military funds are critical. How dare he speak to me as though I have never managed a house and family? Did I not plan, oversee, and pay for the entire reconstruction of our Springfield house? Did he complain then? I will not be treated like a common thief! Damn them all!

Dec. 25, 1861, Christmas: Red, white, and blue abound in every room in the mansion. And the most magnificent tree (also decorated in patriotic colors and tiny flags) since Aristocracy Hill. Even more outstanding! Willie and Tad were concerned that "Swanda Closs" wouldn't find them here, but they received what they most wished for: toy guns and rifles, uniforms and mess kits, and a large tent to spread in the East Room and camp out with the Taft boys.

The day is marred only by the fact that my blessed husband and I are still at odds. He speaks to me only when necessary. He enthuses to the country about the "doctrine of necessity" when it comes to war, but can't understand such a philosophy when it comes to image. Material things mean nothing to him. He doesn't notice how the mansion looks, just as he didn't notice our home in Springfield. Beauty is the dominion and world of women only. How long will he keep me locked out of <u>his</u> world?

Dec. 28, 1861: A group of radical anti-slavery senators has formed a committee to review war conduct, and Congress has approved investigation of Abraham and McClellan. They believe, as I do—as all wise men do—that Mac is a coward. He writes that he is sick, but why should his illness stop our army? The committee leader is Andrew Johnson, a Unionist from Tennessee. Charles Sumner and Lyman Trumbull are also involved.

Since I feel so strongly about the need to remove McClellan, I wrote to Sen. Johnson myself. We need a general who is not afraid to fight, who can end this nightmare before more lives are taken. Mac's delays are ruining us! Why can't Abraham see what a straggler he is? You can't bore a hole with an auger too dull to drill. The war would have been over months ago if Mac had been moving, but he doesn't care one whit about the war or the men. All he wants is the Presidency! I've spoken to my silent husband about this matter and sent messages through his secretaries, to no avail.

Meanwhile, DC and most of Maryland and Virginia are insurrectionary. People are burning bridges, destroying telegraph lines, looting, and are kept down only by troops.

Jan. 1, 1862: Our New Year's Day reception began at 1pm and continued most of the afternoon. It was attended by Cabinet members, diplomatic corps, justices, military officers, and residents of DC and Maryland. So many guests, so many requests for favors and positions, so many foul and ignorant people trampling through the mansion and fingering the precious fabrics! I wore my new violet taffeta, but still I heard the "unsophisticated, rural, unattractive" comments and innuendos behind my back.

The new year frightens me terribly. Our foes are in our own household, treason and rebellion threaten our beloved land, our freedoms and rights are invaded, every sacred claim is trampled, typhoid and malaria lurk right outside our doorstep, clouds and darkness surround us. But triumph will surely come. As Abraham says, men who deny freedom to others don't deserve it for themselves, and under a just God, will not long retain it.

To my relief, he released Mason and Slidell. He has also become highly distressed over McClellan's inaction and, in effect, took over the armies himself.

Jan. 13, 1862: Abraham has finally accepted Simon Cameron's resignation as War Secretary. I knew that appointment wouldn't last long. The man has taken too strong an anti-slavery stance without permission and others have demanded his replacement for months. Abraham gave him Cassius Clay's former post as minister to Russia.

Jan. 16, 1862: In another move I battled, Abraham appointed Edwin Stanton, a Democrat and former Attorney General for Buchanan, as War Secretary. Doesn't he hear the horrid things Stanton says about him, calling him an original gorilla, the Illinois ape, an ugly giraffe? My insiders tell me all this, but I myself remember the way Stanton snubbed Abraham in the McCormick reaper case a few years ago. Doesn't Abraham see the malevolence embodied in that short-legged creature with the long black whiskers? Doesn't he ever look through Stanton's thick lenses into his menacing eyes? Why is it that Abraham can see the good in all humanity, but can't see the darkness in individual men? I try desperately to protect him from schemers and traitors, but he no longer listens. I have no more importance than Mr. Hamlin. I feel broken and fragile, just like a tiny child. I just want to reach out my arms to someone and not be pushed away. I want to be hugged, held. I want someone to dry my tears, rub my shoulders, brush my hair.

Jan. 19, 1862: Former President John Tyler has died at 72, and the Confederacy has taken the southern half of the New Mexico Territory, calling it Arizona and allowing it to contain slavery. I'm lonely and scared, but trying to hold up.

Jan. 20, 1862: Abraham agreed I may suspend the usual three state affairs and have one huge private affair. Three dinners would cost at least $3000; we can have a magnificent reception for half that. And public receptions are so much more democratic! The event is planned for February 5th, and I have sent out hundreds of invitations to people who have been kind to us. I ignored those who have not, though Stod said I may need to recant and send more. I didn't ask those with anti-Lincoln sentiments, hoping it will entice them to change their tune! Only the best trappings will be used: Maillard's to cater, Widow Cliquot champagne, Maryland oysters, Potomac shad, Florida tomatoes. No dancing, however; it wouldn't be proper in these times.

Jan. 27, 1862: Abraham is visibly frustrated with the lack of military movement. He sleeps little, eats less, breathes with loud wheezing, curses under his breath, and seldom wears shoes at all. His stockinged feet in the White House offices are an embarrassment, but I have little influence.

He ordered all military units, both land and naval, to move toward the rebels on Washington's Birthday. The military seldom follows his commands, however, so we will see what becomes of this "General War Order."

Feb. 1, 1862: Willie and Tad have again caught chills from this incessant cold, wet, dreary weather. I hope a warm poultice and hot tea will help. They have hardly gotten over the last bout!

Our family continues to drown in the public opinion waters. My sensitive nature is reeling from all the insults and innuendos against me. Pride is a virtue, and I won't allow these pigs to continue to insult me, the Todds, the Lincolns, and the high office of First Lady. I will fight back somehow!

Stod is right when he says Washington is a jury empanelled to convict on every count of every indictment that any slanderous tongue chooses to bring against me. He now opens all my mail and withholds the threats; I can no longer bear to see them. Abraham has always avoided them. "Don't want to be provoked by things I can't properly offer an answer to," he says.

Feb. 2, 1862: A visit from Ralph Waldo Emerson! How we have appreciated his works over the years: *Fate, All to Love, Ode to Beauty.* How inspiring to hear the words from his own lips!

Bob plans to attend our upcoming reception. It will be good to see him, but he will find our lives changed since his last visit. His mother suffers from great pain. My chest is constricted, as though bands of snakes were tightening around it. My bladder is septic again and personal duties are nearly impossible. His two little brothers are weak with fever. His father fights despair, condemnation, and tyranny from all sides, and looks like Methuselah.

Feb. 3, 1862: My heart cried with joy at the one small smile I witnessed tonight on Abraham's lips. He told me of the letter he received from the King of Siam offering to send us a supply of elephants to breed for war steeds. Abraham's response: "Our nation has not reached a latitude so low as to favor the multiplication of the elephant." He chuckled at the thought of Gen. McClellan riding an elephant into Tennessee, and I nearly giggled myself right out of my chair.

Feb. 6, 1862: Though about 400 people attended last night's reception, Abraham and I can hardly remember it. We took turns going upstairs to sit with Willie, who lay listless and skeletal in the Prince of Wales Room. His fever rose seriously in the afternoon, and he was only partially conscious, but Abraham wouldn't allow me to cancel the event at such short notice. Few attendees knew how troubled we were; we tried to put up a gay face. I left when supper was served at midnight, and stayed in Willie's room till 3am when the last diners re-entered the ballroom. I saw the final carriage drive away long after daybreak. I write now by Willie's bedside, but I need to rest for a few moments.

Feb. 7, 1862: Willie has worsened and Dr. Stone has not left since yesterday. He suspects bilious fever of a typhoidal nature and treats Willie with Peruvian bark, calomel, and jalap. Stone says we must constantly watch over the shivering little body. I also treat Willie with beef tea, blackberry cordial, or bland pudding when he will eat. He fades in and out of consciousness, and speaks hardly at all, though he did ask today for Bud Taft. That dear boy has not left Willie's bedside except to stoke the fire for comfort or to relieve his physical needs. Tad is still sickly as well, but the doctor says time will cure his ills.

Abraham looks at me through haunted eyes. With Willie's illness and the troops about to storm Ft. Henry, he has too many things on his mind for one man to handle.

Feb. 8, 1862: What have I done? Apparently a group of men, led by Sen. Johnson, has arrested one of McClellan's generals and imprisoned him in NY. They have now set their sights on additional minor generals, not McClellan himself as I directed in my letter. Why do things never go as planned?

The reception didn't have the effect I hoped for either. Though expenses were covered from my own pocketbook, I'm being assailed in the press for the extravagance. I know soldiers need supplies, but the legislators need joy too. Why can't people see I'm only trying to help? If I have events, I'm criticized for being frivolous and indulging in unpatriotic extravagance. If I forego events, I'm condemned for shirking my patriotic social duties. No matter what I choose to do, I'm maligned. There are no kind words from anyone. Those who urged me to host the bash now ridicule me for it, and not even one has come to console me in the aftermath or publicly taken my defense.

Even worse, I find that I have once again been the victim of evil counselors. Our security officers found that James Watt, whom I trusted, is the one who gave the inaugural speech paragraphs to Wikoff. He has been fired. Wikoff has been arrested and banned from the White House forever, as has another *Herald* reporter named Malcolm Ives. I am so, so sorry to have caused Abraham this grief and embarrassment with my unwise choice of friends, especially with Willie so sick. Still, he erred in thinking I played a larger part in the leak, and I will stand by my demand for an apology.

Feb. 14, 1862: Our armies have attacked Ft. Donelson, Tennessee, and are gaining strongholds in the south. Still people complain: Stop the war, speed the war, slow the war. The conduct committee has reported many improprieties, including waste, favoritism, corruption, and greed, and has severely chastised Abraham. They say our contractors, officials, and generals are greedy, cowardly, and dishonest. They have proof that Simon Cameron purchased poor and often unusable equipment, supplies, blankets, and clothing for the soldiers. They say he was careless, uncaring, and devious on all fronts. As I said from the beginning to closed ears, Cameron is a traitor. Why won't anyone listen to me? Damn them all!

Feb. 17, 1862: Dr. Stone says Willie is now hopelessly ill. His fever has spiked again, and he can't draw breath without rasping. Abraham, Bob, and I take turns sleeping in his room and a nurse stays by his side constantly. Willie is our darling child, Abraham's doppelganger, and we can't lose him.

Dr. Stone called in Dr. Neal Hall, a typhoid specialist. Please, God, Willie must get well, he must! Tad sleeps fitfully in the next room and we're terrified that he may be taken as well.

Feb. 24, 1862: Our precious, perfect little man, our Willie, left this life at 5pm on February 20, 1862. Those whom God loves are always taken from us too quickly. I was holding his comatose hand when he simply ceased to breathe. Dr. Stone says he died from drinking the contaminated Potomac water that runs through the pipes. Abraham says he was just too precious a boy to remain very long on this cruel world. I believe God must have reclaimed him as punishment for my own negligence and interferences. I will never speak again, never set foot beyond my own doorstep. What use am I? Abraham doesn't need me, except perhaps to join in his personal pain for a spell; Bob doesn't need me, he's a man now; Tad doesn't need me, he's dying too. The world doesn't need me.

Feb. 25, 1862: Our boy is gone, he is truly gone! Life will never be the same. I watch through the window as hundreds of soldiers escort his casket to Oak Hill Cemetery through violent rain and lightning. I can't go, can't bear the storm or the event. I have been fogged and paralyzed since seeing my baby lying cold in the Green Room, that room so recently decorated to celebrate life. I will never enter it again. Abraham and Bob will say my prayers over the tomb. Tad is still desperately ill, and I need to be here to protect him—and myself. Thank Heaven Bob could stay on for a while.

I have buried myself in solitude, knowing that many people I would see at the service could not fully understand my feelings. They say weeping is not for public gaze, and I have nothing but tears. I don't care to hear the hollow words of those who claim to share my pain. False, unsympathizing people are repellant enough when we're happy, but when we're otherwise, their presence is intolerable. What good are words on the tongue when truth is not in the heart? What help are comforting arms when the country is killing itself as my darling child has been killed? God wanted me to feel the loss that Union mothers suffer, and that pain will smolder deep in my soul until my own last breath. I will spend whatever time I have left on this earth befriending the men in hospitals and camps. If their mothers can't be with them, I will be a substitute.

Feb. 28, 1862: I have been remembering Willie's exploits. He and Tad would occasionally stop the White House visitors, of any nationality or rank, to ask why they had come to see the President. They charged people to see the small entertainments, circuses, and fairs Willie wrote, and gave the money to the Sanitary Commission. They rigged the roof like a ship's deck so they could watch for the enemy. They delivered minstrel shows in the attic, once employing the flag that bore Elmer Ellsworth's blood. They found a way to summon all the servants in the mansion at one time by pulling all the bell cords simultaneously, causing more uproar than even chasing their goats through the corridors into the kitchen.

Tad is still ailing, but coming around. In this horrid world, sorrow strikes everyone, but it comes with bitter agony to the young because it takes them unexpectedly. He knows Willie was sick, but he doesn't understand death. He realizes only that Willie "wun't ebber talk to me awen." He is sedated and lies peacefully asleep. Oh that I were so blessed.

Mar. 2, 1862: Bob summoned Elizabeth from Springfield to stay with me, and she has brought my diary to me in repose. How can I write? I can hardly read the few words I've just scrawled. Continuous headaches inside, incessant rain outside, my throat as sore as my soul, eyes unable to focus, hands that shake relentlessly. Though Abraham has forgiven my previous indiscretions and looks at me again with love, I can't rally.

Two of my darling boys are gone in their youth! If not for Abraham's sorrow urging me to comfort him, I would never rise again. Why am I being punished so severely? What have I done so horrid that my children must be taken? My heart carries so much guilt and pain that I don't care whether I ever see sunlight again. I have never felt so solitary, so lonely, so desperate. The demons are overthrowing the angels in my mind. Thank Heaven for my medicines. They allow me to sleep and then to rise again.

Mar. 4, 1862: Elizabeth forced me to get up and don one of my new black dresses. I find no joy in the frock or in being awake, but she reminded me that Abraham has been President for exactly a year and I should act like a First Lady. When I mentioned the date to Abraham, he said quietly, "I was frequently told in my youth that I was on the road to Hell, but I had no idea it would be in Washington, DC, staring at an unfinished dome. I have to get the Capitol husked out."

Tad is still feeble, but can leave his bed for an hour or so and has begun to eat. Bob returned to school, but still talks about enrolling in the army. It's impossible to conceive of him in combat. I refuse to give up another son!

Mar. 18, 1862: I learned that Abraham finally dismissed McClellan as General-in-Chief, but in truth it's only a demotion. With his usual blend of patience and blindness, he allowed Mac to retain the Army of the Potomac. I would have exiled him to Cuba. The papers and all White House staff, Abraham included, are overjoyed with the recent battle of the Merrimack and Monitor. Apparently we won.

Apr. 1, 1862: Unwell for some days now. Fevers, chills, back pain, urinary problems, insomnia. I avoid all brightness, including sunlight, because it pierces straight into my brain. Sudden noises cause nausea and hysteria. Dr. Stone told me these are "nervous symptoms," but I heard him say "stroke" to Abraham. The chloral hydrate helps me sleep, but it disposes me to quick anger, and I hate myself when I lash out for no reason. My patient husband stands all he can and then goes back to his advisors. I don't blame him for avoiding me. I only hope he doesn't leave me permanently.

Apr. 4, 1862, Tad's 9th birthday: I have left my bed for my son's sake, but my soul is still an empty shell. The servants made Tad's favorite spice cake and invited the available children in for a small party. All except the Taft boys. I can't bear to see them, or anyone who brings Willie to mind, and Tad understands the ruling.

He received two white rabbits from an ambassador and is tickled with them. Also a nondescript brown puppy, which he immediately named Jip. These, next to Nanko and Nannie, are now his favorite playmates. I don't know who loves those goats more, however—Tad or his father. Abraham says they are the kindest and best goats in the world, though how many he has been intimate with I can't say.

Abraham was at the little party for a while, and I was shocked at his paleness. He said Dr. Stone is treating him for malaria. I have been blind and selfish.

Apr. 5, 1862: The Senate finally voted to abolish slavery in DC, something Abraham has promoted since the House, back when the world was sane. This time he didn't bite his lips and keep quiet, but spoke up for what he wanted. (I used to do so as well, but have learned the folly of it.) The act allows for remuneration of up to $300 per slave. Doesn't it seem that someone should pay the enslaved for all those years, rather than the enslavers?[18]

In the late afternoon, Abraham and I rode awhile in our carriage. We didn't speak much, but eventually he said, "Mother, I think it's time to free the slaves."

I leaned my head toward him and whispered, "All of them?"

He grimaced. "No, I can't do that right now, but I can free the ones still in rebel states. My main objective at present is to avoid secession, and this is a plan to that end. You know that if I could save the Union by freeing all the slaves, I'd do it. If I could save it by freeing none of them, I'd do it. If I could

---

[18] This is the only act of compensated emancipation in the US. By the end of 1862, the government had paid almost $1 million for the freedom of approximately 3100 people.

save it by freeing some and not others, I'd do that too. Much as I hate slavery, I'd consent to the extension of it rather than see the Union dissolved, just as I'd consent to any evil to avoid a greater one. The greatest good for the greatest number.

"But I reckon this is a start. I don't have it all worked out just yet, but I'm going to first offer the Confederate states one more chance to come back. Those that do can exist as before. Those that don't will lose their slaves. Perhaps then those men can join the Union army and fight for their own freedom. Even if they don't, they'll be free and that's a good thing."

We rode the rest of the way in silence, my head on his shoulder, his mind filled with emancipation plans.

Apr. 6, 1862: I attended church today but no one recognized me, because I covered myself in a black body veil. I'm not ready to socialize, so all activities at the White House have also been cancelled.

Rev. Gurley's sermon did not touch my heart. If I could truly believe that Willie and Eddy are happier in Heaven than they were here on earth with us, I could be at peace. Is there a Heaven? Are our boys still here as living spirits, surrounding us like a great cloud, as the Bible says, or are they simply dead and covered with dirt? If they are with me, they hear my cries and know how I chastise myself for my frailties. If they are truly gone and I'll never see them again, how can I live? Why doesn't God, if there is a God, show me the answers? Heaven? I will gladly go if assured of seeing my babies again.

Apr. 7, 1862: We gave Tad the new book *Alice's Adventures in Wonderland* for his birthday on Friday, and I have read it to him in only two sittings. The fantasy gave me a brief respite from my own dreary reality. My favorite scene is when the Queen of Hearts proclaims, "Off with their heads!" How I would love to order such a proclamation for my foes. The Queen of England and the Queen of Hearts can command it, why not the Queen of Washington?

Elizabeth says I have lost my mind, and maybe she's correct! She bore up well under the loss of her child, but then she was always stronger than I.

Apr. 9, 1862: The war continues and other mothers' sons are also dying. A nasty battle Sunday in Tennessee, referred to as Shiloh, spawned 13,000 Union casualties. The rebels apparently caught Gen. Grant unaware when they attacked. Grant counter-attacked and won, but so many lives lost! My grief compounds with each.

My dear husband concurs with Elizabeth that I may be losing my sanity. He pointed out the lunatic asylum across the way and reminded me that people are often incarcerated there when they can't control their heartache.

"You're totally unpredictable," he told me harshly. "One day you're kind and considerate, loving and generous; the next day you're mean-spirited, unreasonable, irritable, and accusing; the next day you're in great pain, despondent, petty, prone to see the dark side, and willing to spend your life in the shadows. Today you love all men, tomorrow you hate them. Today you're full of life, tomorrow you're ready to die. It ain't right!"

He may be correct; I may need to go to the asylum. How many times I feel rebellious and wonder if God has truly forsaken us. I sin with my thoughts, but these musings are for your eyes only. I'm reading the Bible to cure my transgressions, and books such as *Agnes and the Little Key (Bereaved Parents Instructed and Comforted)* to cure my sorrow, but the ache in my heart never lessens. The hole there is large enough for all the country to pass through. All I really need to change my dementia is a little attention and caressing from my husband. Being alone is itself sorrowful.

Apr. 14, 1862: Abraham is furious again, this time thankfully not at me. His friend Commander David Hunter proclaimed freedom for all slaves in and around Ft. Pulaski, Georgia, which he had just captured. But he did so without Abraham's knowledge, and Abraham plans to rescind the order. How I wish he would overlook this indiscretion as he did so many of McClellan's. This edict can't possibly be bad! Instead, he again begs the border states to accept compensated emancipation. And again they refuse.

Apr. 16, 1862: Thank you, God, for sending Elizabeth to stay with us. She has been a source of warmth for me, and has helped Tad recover as well. I can comfort him very little. Sometimes I can't even bear to look at his sad little face. I'm also grateful for the extra time Abraham spends with Tad. He never sends the boy away from his office, even when dignitaries arrive. This permissiveness greatly chafes some people, but both my "boys" relish the experience.

Today I visited the Laurie sisters in Georgetown. They are renowned for being able to communicate with the dead. This session was not successful, but they have great confidence that we will soon reach Willie. Eddy often appeared to me in Springfield, and he sometimes brought my brother Robert. The Lauries believe my "sensitivity" to the process will enable Eddy to also bring Willie forward without much difficulty.

My banished friend Chevalier Wikoff once told of being hypnotized in Romania and reliving his life in another time and place—regression, it's called. A very slight veil separates us from our loved and lost, and I'm comforted knowing that, though unseen, they are very close. The Lauries assure me Willie's death was not my fault and urge me to continue my attempts to reach him. And they have given me a concession on the fee—only $1.00 per visit!

Apr. 19, 1862: Elizabeth has returned to Springfield. Though we all begged her to stay indefinitely, she said she received an urgent summons. I saw no such bidding and believe she simply could no longer remain in this situation. I understand fully; it's hard on everyone. Tad insisted on sending Willie's toy cars to Elizabeth's grandson Lewis, saying emphatically that he could never play with them again.

Now I have no one to help me. All my lady friends except Mary Jane Welles have deserted me or Washington (or both). Abraham is always involved in military matters or reading the Bible. If I must lose him to something, I suppose God is better than the women I once suspected. He goes to church with me every Sunday now, but only because the people expect to see him. Like most true believers, he doesn't need a building in which to say his prayers. God is in his heart, the heart I once had completely.

Tomorrow he goes to Aquia Creek, near Fredericksburg, Virginia, to meet Gen. McDowell, and I'll be alone again. I begged him to remove his hat when he reviews the troops this time. He stands as an obvious target: almost 7' tall, with a high black bull's-eye atop his skinny head!

Apr. 20, 1862, Easter: Rev. Miner, our minister from Springfield, has come to stay a few days, and we took him to services this morning. I hope he can help us through this pain. We both need reassurance on so many things. I feel less agitated with his presence in the house, even though another tragic blow has befallen me. My half-brother Sam was killed at Shiloh earlier this month. They say God never gives us more than we can handle, but I believe I have also received someone else's share. Sam abandoned me when he joined the rebels, but I could never stop loving him. I remember with heartbreak the Thanksgiving in 1847 when he came to Father's. He called me "Mrs. Congressman" and taught Bob to call him "Uncle Sam." A fine, handsome young man! "Uncle Sam" now killed in a battle against the other Uncle Sam.

I am heartbroken, but if I show grief, the papers will crucify me for being a rebel sympathizer. They already call me a spy and blame me for McClellan's inaction and the deaths of all the soldiers. Me personally! How could I, who have suffered so much from this horrid war, be responsible? They say I pass Union secrets to my brothers and cousins, though I've said from the outset that I would see them captured or killed like other rebels. I am the scapegoat for both north and south. Surely no previous First Lady has been accused of treason or subjected to such shame! The charges are even more ludicrous because, for the first time in our marriage, I know almost nothing about what Abraham is doing or planning. Why can't this damned war be over?

May 28, 1862: McClellan continues to drag. Why won't he advance? Abraham is distraught and has written Mac that his move toward the rebels in the Shenandoah is "a question of legs." In other words, go as quickly as you can. For this general, "quickly" never implies much speed. When will Abraham see the truth and replace him with someone of fortitude?

June 1, 1862: I asked Abraham at breakfast if we could proceed with the national emancipation proclamation he has drafted. I believe it's past due and told him so. He thinks about slavery all the time—in legal terms, constitutional terms, Union terms, political terms—but does he truly think about it in human terms?

He replied, "My paramount object in this struggle is not to save or destroy slavery, but to save the Union in the shortest way under the Constitution. I don't agree with those who wouldn't save the Union unless they can save slavery. I also don't agree with those who would destroy the Union if that's what it took to destroy slavery. What I do about slavery and the colored race, I do because it helps save this Union."

"But what about the proclamation?" I asked.

"What good would a proclamation do, especially where we're now situated? I don't want to issue a document the whole world will see as inoperative. Would my word free the slaves when I can't even enforce the Constitution in the rebel states? Would it influence a single court, magistrate, or individual there? And why would it have any greater effect than the Fugitive Slave Law, which offers protection and freedom to the slaves who come within our lines? I can't prove that law to have brought a single person over to us.

"What if the pressure of the war should call our forces away from where they are now to defend some other point, what would prevent the masters from reducing the negroes to slavery again? Whenever the rebels take any black prisoners, free or slave, they immediately auction them off.

"If the people could just keep cool on both sides of the line, the troubles would come to an end and the question would be settled, just as surely as all other difficulties like this have been settled. If the people on both sides would keep cool, this nation could prosper like it used to."

June 3, 1862: Summer is heavily upon us, and Stonewall Jackson continues to evade us. He has beaten us several times in recent weeks, and this week vanquished both McDowell and Shields and slipped away again. Perhaps they should call him "Slippery" Jackson!

The Lauries advised me to clear my debt with Congress, so I've decided to raise money by rounding up all the broken and scratched furniture around here and advertising a sale for Friday. I doubt the pieces will bring much—it's all rubbish—but just being from the mansion should merit a few pennies. I managed to move the tutor's and piano teacher's salaries to the Treasury Department so they will no longer come from our personal budget. And I'll fire some of the servants and run more of the house myself. I wonder if I could arrange to sell manure from the stables? How much would it bring?

Tonight we'll attend a rendition of *King Lear*. Though Abraham doesn't feel his best, it will be good to get out together and perhaps I can persuade him to spend time in my room afterward.

Must close. I hear a dog screaming hellishly outside; Tad must be playing doctor again.

June 8, 1862: The Marine Band has played for the last time. I stopped the concerts, just as Dolley Madison did during the Barbary Wars. The White House should not be gay when men are dying all around us. When we're in sorrow, quiet is necessary.

To help with my money-saving plan, I dismissed the steward today. I can do his job just as well, and I asked Hay to pay his salary to me instead. I also let go other household servants, and brought in a small band of free blacks, including a butler/waiter, a cook who will serve only the simplest meals, and several maids, all of whom are willing to work mostly for the prestige. I'm very proud of my thriftiness!

Also, the Federals have taken Memphis, and Abraham thinks this victory is a good time to bring up emancipation again. We discussed it, and for the first time in more than a year, I felt needed. It's a good proclamation, one I have fervently prayed for. He'll discuss it with Hamlin and his other advisors soon.

June 19, 1862: The crowds showed up on Saturday expecting to hear the band play, and were outraged when it didn't. I don't give a fiddler's damn for their disappointment or disapproval. We all have to make sacrifices in these worrisome times.

Tad has recovered and is up to his tricks again. He aimed a wooden cannon at this morning's Cabinet meeting and demanded full surrender of the members. Much to the Cabinet's dismay and disapproval, Abraham forced them to comply! It's so good to hear Tad's laughter ringing through the house again and his boyish voice singing, "Ode Abe Winkum came out od the widderness...."

July 1, 1862: Abraham has increased the tax levee to 3% on incomes of $600 to $1000, and 5% above $1,000. People won't be happy with this directive. There is little money available to spend, much less contribute. He has also approved construction of rail lines across the west, accepted Frémont's resignation, and signed a law prohibiting slavery in the territories. The rain continues, delaying our departure for the Soldiers' Home. Our 15 wagonloads of clothes, toys, and furniture sit dejectedly under tarps.

Meanwhile, McClellan has done none of the things Abraham ordered him to do—matters that were quite possible from his vantage point—so Richmond remains a stalemate. And now he refuses to communicate! What insolence! I sense he hides in the woods to avoid taking any action whatsoever, but this absence of news is a dreadful anxiety for Abraham. We could win this war today if that boot-licking whiner would come out of his chicken hole. Off with his head!

July 4, 1862, Independence Day: Parades abound, but I feel no joy, even here in our lovely hilltop retreat. After McClellan's failure to take Richmond, Abraham issued a call for another 300,000 volunteers to "bring this unnecessary and injurious civil war to a speedy and satisfactory conclusion." When will our men be allowed to go home? The Lauries say the war won't end in Abraham's lifetime. How many years will that be?

He has begun to sleepwalk again, and he groans so loudly I can hear him through the closed door. He dreams Willie is alive and happily playing, then wakes to the dismal reality. He writes to parents of the murdered soldiers that they need to allow themselves time to recover, but he permits no healing time for himself. He returns to the White House every Thursday and locks himself in the Green Room to weep alone. Teardrops are not for show.

July 17, 1862: I took a quick trip to NY and Boston with Tad to raise money for the contrabands.[19] Shopping in several fine stores revived my spirits somewhat, but I remained frugal. Abraham is still angry with me, and his new tax has taken another $67 from his salary!

While I was traveling, Abraham went to McClellan's camp to see the situation for himself, and is angrier than ever. Mac is now trying to dictate political matters in addition to military ones. I wish Abraham would completely dismiss the laggard from command. He did appoint Henry Halleck as General-in-Chief of all US land forces, a wise choice.

Today Abraham signed the second Confiscation Act, another prediction of emancipation. It provides that slaves of anyone who

---

[19] Runaway slaves.

supported the rebellion will become free when they cross Union borders. It also authorizes him to employ negroes in the war, provide for colonization outside the US, and grant amnesty to anyone he deems fit.

July 22, 1862: Finally! Abraham read the emancipation proclamation draft to his Cabinet this morning. His message included admonitions about the Confiscation Act, renewed his proposal of compensation for gradual emancipation, and advocated freedom for all slaves in rebellious states as of January 1, 1863. Even though he also read them a chapter from Artemas Ward's book of humor, surely they will see the seriousness and wisdom of this proposal. If they would visit the contrabands, as I have, they would know how kind these people are and how much they need help. Brown skin does not mean stupidity or worthlessness. Negroes are human beings and deserve to be treated as more than horses or cows. They must be freed in all states as quickly as possible!

July 27, 1862: We attended church this morning and heard a sermon on forgiveness. I asked Abraham in the carriage home, "Are you willing to forgive?"

He patted my hand. "Forgive who?"

"Everyone, anyone, the rebels, those killing and being killed, me."

He threw out the sarsaparilla from his mouth and answered, "As to you, I'll forgive if you stop spending foolishly and butting into things that don't concern you. As to anyone and everyone else, I reckon I've done a fair job of forgiving since we got here. Those killing and being killed will be judged by a bigger force than me. But the Confederates—I don't rightly know. Still, whether we forgive each other or not, I've got to save this government if possible, and I believe that means we keep on fighting. You need to understand, once for all, that I won't surrender this game leaving any available card unplayed."

Aug. 16, 1862: The Soldiers' Home sorely needs redecorating. Each day brings visitors who deserve more comfort and eloquence. I'll undertake this mission very soon.

Bob has finally arrived. He's very companionable for a change, and helps divert our minds somewhat from the tragedy around us. He's eager to meet Walt Whitman, who lives on the route between here and the mansion, as he recently read some of Whitman's poetry. I'll enjoy that also.

Abraham travels almost daily back to the mansion for meetings and such. I fear for his safety, but he brushes off my concern. I'm not worried for myself; I regularly go to the hospitals with apples, oranges, lemons, other fresh food that might provide vitamins, and the bouquets they all love. Some of the young wounded remind me of my personal loss, and I worry that I dismiss them too quickly. Still I return day after day, facing mortality, gangrene, drug addiction, severed limbs, malaria, insanity. It's the least I can do, and perhaps it will help Willie forgive me.

I'm glad Tad's nurse came up with us. Though still my angel, being together very long makes us both nervous, and I sometimes lash out. I'm trying to stay apart from him until the new medicines take effect. He now sleeps with Abraham when possible. He's too frightened to bunk alone since Willie died, and I thrash too violently in my bed. When Abraham works late into the night at the White House, Tad dozes on the floor, and the two ride back here together on the brown mare, Tad laid over his father's shoulders like a rolled blanket. When Abraham wakes perspiring or trembling in the night, he can reach out and touch the kitten-soft arms of his remaining son. I wish with all my heart that he would reach for me instead, but our time will return. The Lauries say this is true.

Aug. 19, 1862: My God, how much more can one woman endure? We received word that dear, sweet Brother Aleck was killed at Baton Rouge earlier this month. My heart bleeds, but I refuse to cry. He made his choice and it proved a poor one.

Aug. 26, 1862: Abraham was shot at on his route from the White House tonight! He lost his hat to a bullet and it could easily have been his life! We must return to the mansion immediately so there will be no need to venture out. I warned him!

Aug. 30, 1862: The Union was badly defeated at Bull Run and our soldiers have returned to Washington. Sadly, the hospitals have no beds or rooms, and little way to help the men. Ours would be a better army if the men in charge cared more about winning the war than fighting each other. Abraham is on his way to meet with McClellan. God keep him safe.

Stod sent me a paper he thought I would like to see, and he was correct. How badly I need some kind words said about me. The *Chicago Daily Tribune* took up my defense:

Enough! Mrs. Lincoln has become the ridicule of the nation and it's time the false tales stopped. If Mrs. Lincoln were a prizefighter, a foreign danseuse, or a condemned convict on the way to execution, she could not be treated more indecently than she is by a portion of the New York press. No lady of the White House has ever been so maltreated by the public press. The signs and sneers of sensible people all over the land, and the mockery of the comic papers, are the natural consequence. Let us give Mrs. Lincoln her due. She is one of the finest First Ladies ever to occupy the White House.

Sept. 4, 1862: I discovered by listening at the door that Abraham has restored McClellan to full command in Virginia and around Washington. Stanton and Chase are furious, but couldn't change the decision. If they can't move him, I certainly will have no success. Maryland is being evacuated because the rebels are invading, so Washington is at risk, but Abraham chooses to put Gen. Do-Nothing back in power. I just don't understand war.

Sept. 12, 1862: The rebels move more completely and stealthily into Maryland, causing great excitement. Militias are gathering, people are leaving, widows and mothers are weeping. I don't see how we can hold on. Though I feel safer here in the mansion than at the Soldiers' Home, I'm packed and prepared to evacuate at a moment's notice.

Sept. 15, 1862: Hope comes after all! McClellan's men somehow found Gen. Lee's operation plan for Maryland, apparently wrapped around some cigars, and Mac is pushing toward the mountains beyond Frederick. If he can cut Lee off, the war will be ended! But I won't give up our personal guards and cavalry escorts just yet. In fact, they have been doubled. Abraham twitches, grinds his teeth, and does not sleep.

Sept. 17, 1862: The rebels have captured Harper's Ferry and we lost two more strong war leaders. We hear little from McClellan. Contrabands continue to pour into Washington, despite the danger to us all. Thousands are suffering intensely, many without adequate body or bed coverings. Hundreds are dying of want. Mrs. Keckley and I go almost daily to help them, and I sell flowers from the conservatory to raise money for the Contraband Relief Society. Tad sells cookies in the driveway and foyer. We're all doing what we can for the war effort, despite our own terror.

"Why?" I asked Abraham when we finally slipped into the carriage for a quick drive. "Why doesn't God prevail for us? Why are all these young men dying in vain?"

He put a twig of sarsaparilla in his mouth, clucked the horses, and answered grimly. "I believe God always prevails. In great contests like this, each party claims to act in accordance with His will. Both may be wrong, but one must be. God can't be for and against the same thing at the same time. In this case, don't you think it's quite possible His purpose is something different from either party?"

I nodded and stared at the side of that head I worship so much.

He continued. "Yep, me too. And yet humans, working just as we do, are the best way to achieve His purpose. I reckon it's true that God wills this contest, and also wills that it don't end yet. With mere quiet power exerted on the minds of the contestants, He could have either saved or destroyed the Union without a contest. Yet the war began. And He could give the final victory to either side any day, yet it proceeds."

Yes, My Darling, but for what?

Sept. 22, 1862: Soon freedom will be a reality! The Cabinet approved release of the emancipation proclamation to the public: "That on the first day of January, 1863, all persons held as slaves within any state or designated part of a state in which the people are then in rebellion against the United States shall be then, thenceforward, and forever free; and the executive government of the United States, including the military and naval authority thereof, will recognize and maintain the freedom of such persons and do nothing to repress them in any efforts they may make for their actual freedom." [20] Glory to God! Freedom looms!

Oct. 15, 1862: Tad, Mrs. Keckley, and I came to NY last week to purchase fabric for next season's gowns. Though I haven't entertained since Willie's passing, I will soon need to do so again. The materials are beauteous, their warmth and softness comfort me, and shopping in NY makes me feel vibrant and alive again!

Abraham has not written in days, but strangers come up from Washington and tell me he's well, which satisfies me very much. His name is on every lip, and many prayers and good wishes are rendered for his welfare. McClellan and his slowness are vehemently discussed each night in the salons and restaurants here. Allowing this beautiful weather to pass away without a hard strike is disheartening to all. Northerners would almost worship Abraham if he would put a fighting general in Mac's stead. People are also discussing the congressional elections in Iowa, Ohio, Indiana, and Pennsylvania. Apparently the Democrats have won everywhere except Iowa.

Oct. 20, 1862: Tad and I are back from visiting with Bob for a few days. It was good to see the boys together, and Bob "gratefully" accepted the tooth Tad lost while there! Mrs. Keckley stayed here in NY and raised funds to house and feed the additional negroes who will soon be emerging from bondage. I introduced her around before we left, and am in full public support of the Contraband Relief Association. She didn't collect very much, and was the most grateful woman I ever saw when I personally contributed $200. The cause for humanity requires it.

---

[20] The biggest misconception about the Emancipation Proclamation is that it freed all the slaves. In actuality, it freed people only in the states still in rebellion. It meant little unless an amendment outlawing slavery was passed, which didn't happen until December 1865. If the South had won the war, they would have simply ignored the proclamation. But its issuance did free thousands from bondage.

Nov. 4, 1862, our 20th anniversary: It's good to be home again, though we enjoyed the trip. A day or two after my last entry, while still in NY, I had one of my severe attacks. I don't know what I would have done without Mrs. Keckley. That damned monthly curse will someday launch me away!

I ordered a suit for Tad and purchased some fur wrappings for the coachman's carriage. Also ordered two gowns from the new fabrics, but did not specifically mention these to Abraham. No reason to concern him; he has so much to manage, and he no longer asks about my purchases. For now, I'm satisfied with people who can simply make him smile for a moment. Such seldom occurs in this busy time. Tad is correct when he says, "Papa dust dun't hab time to pway wid ud any more." I continue to invite anyone with whom Abraham feels safe and like his former self. If he entertains us with a story, I know my social attempts are successful. If he eats well, I slip a small sum to the cook. Tonight she received a quarter.

Nov. 7, 1862: Abraham finally dismissed McClellan the Snail as commander of the Potomac, and named Ambrose Burnside to replace him. He also dismissed Porter, a corps commander charged with disobedience at Second Manassas, and assigned Joseph Hooker. Perhaps our "gentlemanly war" will now become a fighting war!

Nov. 10, 1862: Julia Ward Howe, author of Battle Hymn of the Republic, visited today and sang the ballad for us. The Marine Band accompanied her, and the rendition brought goose bumps to our ears. She is wonderfully gifted! How I wish I could sing and be admired by so many people for my talent. Mary Jane and Gideon Welles were invited for the recital, but their young son Hubert is not expected to live more than a few more days. He will be the 6th child they have lost. How can a mother withstand so much ripping away of her own flesh?

Nov. 18, 1862: Hoorah! Without the debilitating McClellan to keep them in reserve, the Army of the Potomac is moving toward Fredericksburg. Virginia will soon be ours again! Washington is in full celebration! Must go; I hear a ruckus on the roof that sounds like captive cats.

Nov. 23, 1862: Perhaps I was wrong about Stanton. He released nearly all the political prisoners—a caring and humanitarian act for a War Secretary. He has also taken Tad under his wing, even securing a small lieutenant's uniform and giving him a "commission." Earlier in the week, Tad dismissed the White House guard, put all the servants on sentry duty, and marched around for hours surveying his troops. We watched in glee from the window until Abraham put things back in order by carrying the sleepy soldier to bed.

Nov. 24, 1862: Today Abraham had the worse case of hypo in years: drawn, ill-looking, uncommunicative, and fatigued. His spirit is crushed as more and more die under his thumb. "I'm to blame," he chants to himself. Gen. Burnside requested Fredericksburg's surrender, but was refused. Surely life with slavery could not be so bad as the tension we now live with. Abraham told me, almost in a whisper, "If the war fails, the administration fails, and I'll be blamed whether I deserve it or not." How our life has changed and how I wish we could go back!

Nov. 29, 1862: I felt almost like a close, loving family again today, out for a ride on a bright winter's day, bundled against the snow. Abraham stopped the carriage long enough to have a snowball fight and build a small snow fort with Tad. It was wonderful to see them, so bound to each other in their few pleasures. I haven't felt more mother's love since that grievous day in February. At times like this, I can almost forget the horror around us and pretend we are safe in our own home—a grand home like we've always dreamed about!

Still, I read the papers and know we are not safe. The proclamation hurt the Republican Party, and the recent elections were disastrous. The Democrats took New York, Pennsylvania, Ohio, New Jersey, Wisconsin, and Illinois, giving them 75 members of Congress rather than 44. Cousin John Stuart, who campaigned loudly against our policies, overran Leonard Swett, so the new Illinois governor will undoubtedly be a Democrat, as is New York's. How can our administration continue without support? With this many Democrats in Congress, we will likely be impeached before the year is out! I see no real hope for 1864.

Dec. 1, 1862: We don't have to wait to be impeached! Abraham told the Cabinet informally that he is willing to resign if they can find someone who commands more of the nation's confidence. Many of the Cabinet believe they fit that description.

He also recommended three amendments: compensation for states abolishing slavery before 1900, eternal freedom for slaves who gain amnesty during the war, and negro placement outside the US. He has been pleading for compensation and colonization since he was a young congressman back in Illinois. Will they ever come to pass?

Dec. 12, 1862: How many sad changes time brings. Our home is now quite beautiful, the grounds around us are enchanting, much of the world smiles and pays homage, yet everything is a mockery.

Abraham's moods shift more rapidly than mine—from laughter to hypo, from friendly to silent and withdrawn. He sleeps little, but says he's not ill. Tad has lost the luster of youth, and Bob is far, far away. Willie, our idolized boy, is no longer with us. I killed him by bringing us here to breathe the horrid air, live among the disease, fight the insects and the rats, drink the contaminated water, and endure the constant attention. He died, as did our precious little Eddy, because of my own desire for political advancement. I pray to join them soon to free myself from this guilt.

Dec. 13, 1862, my 44th birthday: *Willie came to me, covered in gauze, speaking in hushed tones. He sat by the fireplace, drinking tea and staring away from me. I tried to touch him, hold him, but he wouldn't respond. Suddenly there was a knock on the door. I opened it to see Mother and Father. I was so glad to see them, but they pushed past me as though in a great hurry. I looked out into the hall and it was as dark as a tunnel at midnight. No one spoke. "What is it?" I cried.*

Willie stood. "I need to see Papa very soon. I don't want to lead him, but he has to come. The train is moving and Papa has to be on it." I heard the train whistle far in the distance.

I jerked my head to see my parents. "What is he talking about?" I asked. My mother replied, "I was always afraid too, Mary Dear. You have so much of me in you that no one ever told you. I may have frightened myself into an early grave, so you must be more careful. Abraham is a good man and the world will long remember him. But prepare yourself."

"Prepare myself for what?" I screamed. The room began to darken until all I could see were Willie's eyes, like the orbs of a cat from high in a densely-foliated tree. "We have to go now, Mama," he said. "I love you."

I woke up crying and unable to catch my breath. Later in the day, I begged Abraham to go to the Lauries with me and try to contact Willie, and he reluctantly agreed. He refused to sit at the table, but leaned on the doorway and watched with his arms folded across his chest. Willie didn't come, as he often does, and Abraham chuckled all the way home. Why am I ridiculed so, even by those who claim to love me? Was the dream prophetic or the result of the wine I sampled after Abraham went back to his office?

Dec. 18, 1862: Horrible defeat at Fredericksburg. We lost almost 13,000 men! Dear God, when will this end? Now Congress itself is calling for a change of Cabinet and the dismissal of Smith and Bates. How long have I cried this sentiment to Abraham's deaf ears? He once heeded my counsel, but no longer. William Seward and his son Frederick resigned from the Cabinet because they are besieged with criticism and constantly in dispute with Salmon Chase, but I sense that Abraham will ask them to stay. Chase is even more evil than Seward; the country can claim no greater scamp. Abraham meets tonight and tomorrow with a committee of Republican senators to discuss these issues.

Dec. 20, 1862: I am livid! Chase resigned as Treasury Secretary but Abraham refused to accept it! My sweet, forgiving husband has been duped again! Doesn't he see what this man is doing to him? That rogue even had his own likeness printed on the new paper currency! If an image appears on the bills, it should be Abraham's, not Slimy Salmon's. Now he has a free campaign handout for the '64 election. "Here, see me, I'm so handsome and important that I'm on the dollar. Who better to vote for?" Off with his head!

Dec. 25, 1862, Christmas: Death and misery surround us on this silent night. I long for the simple Christmases in Springfield when we were all together. Abraham, Tad, and I spent most of the day visiting wounded soldiers in the nearby hospitals. Bob didn't come home; it's too dangerous.

Dec. 29, 1862: I asked Abraham at breakfast this morning if he will indeed enforce the emancipation proclamation on January 1st, and he is adamant. He smiled briefly, then compressed his lips quickly before he responded: "I won't retract the proclamation for any reason. Nor will I ever return to slavery any person freed by that document or any other act of Congress. I only hope the people will understand that I don't act in anger, but in expectation of a greater good." No man or woman can rule my husband after he has made up his mind.

Dec. 31, 1862: Mr. Newton went with me tonight to sit with Nettie Colburn, another spiritualist who can reach across the river of souls. Mary Jane Welles introduced me to her, and she says Mrs. Colburn can see much that others choose not to see. Mrs. Keckley also visited this good lady after her son was killed, and was able to speak directly with him.

She told me about Willie and Eddy's life in Heaven and how they miss me. She advised me confidentially that Abraham's Cabinet contains enemies who care only for themselves and should be dismissed. She sees danger surrounding Abraham on all sides. He's so honest and good that he can't sense the predators who stalk him day and night. He must be warned against those who take advantage and plot against him. I can see through the façades, and I call up the faces in my dreams, but he won't listen. He says I'm being melodramatic and teases by saying, "Mother, if I listened to you, I'd soon be without a Cabinet at all." I am not amused.

Jan. 1, 1863: Our huge reception was gloomy and depressive for me. I'm torn; my heart is still in mourning for my precious son, but the country needs to see vibrancy and life. If I pretend gaiety, the world will smile with me! For that reason, I abandoned black today and wore the half-mourning purple silk trimmed with white velvet and black lace.

Shortly after noon, I accompanied Abraham to meet the Cabinet and sign the emancipation proclamation. He had shaken so many hands that his fingers were limp and highly swollen. Only 12 people attended this historic event, but the decree has gone forth and no unprincipled zealots can eradicate it. It's a rich and precious legacy for our remaining sons, and one for which they will always praise God and their father. If our name goes into history at all, it will be for this act.

Since we last stood in the New Year's Day receiving line, we have passed through a forge of affliction, both personally and in our beloved country. Nationally, we have endured some 2000 battles. Personally, God saw fit to remind us how small and insignificant all worldly honors are. We had become so devoted to political advancement that we thought about little else. Why must we learn so painfully?

Abraham regularly dreams about his own death and about soldiers lying on cold wet ground. He sees again the scalped men of his youthful days in the Black Hawk War. He paces in his slumber—sometimes going outside, often going down the hall to gaze at the portrait of Thomas Jefferson near his office. They have so much in common; does he consult with Jefferson in his sleep? I now insist the door between our rooms be open at all times so I can follow when he rises and keep him from harm. Some monsters would still assassinate him, and his long white nightshirt wandering on the lawn would give them good aim.

Jan. 20, 1863: The rain finally stopped, bringing heavy wet snow in its stead. It occurred to me this week that I don't run so quickly from thunder now. There is much more to fear in this world. As I sit by the fireplace with my tea—safe, dry, warm, and well fed—I weep for the men slogging through the mud who can see this snow only as an impediment and a curse. The weather will likely become our greatest enemy in Virginia. Gen. Burnside is calling his advance a "mud march" and a miserable failure. It must be harder on the rebels, though; they are not accustomed to cold weather.

Jan. 25, 1863: Burnside arrived early this morning to confer with Abraham. Now, close to midnight, my exhausted husband has just stopped by to say goodnight, and I asked the results of his meeting. He told me with remorse that he relieved Burnside and assigned Hooker to command the Army of the Potomac. Burnside was in command for only three months, but caused us to lose more than 13,000 men. He blamed the other leaders, including Hooker, and demanded their removal, but Abraham has become wiser about his men and ignored the petition.

Abraham says that, despite Hooker's reputation, he is a brave, skillful fighter who doesn't mix politics with his profession. He has self-confidence, which is a valuable if not indispensable quality. I heard, however, through White House gossip, that Hooker drinks a great deal and regularly entertains "ladies" in his camp. So many women come that they are called simply "hookers."

Feb. 1, 1863: I hoped to reach Eddy through Mrs. Colburn on this anniversary of his passing, but it did not happen. Abraham decided at the last minute to go with me—for curiosity, I believe, and perhaps some caution for me. He still doesn't trust my spiritualist guides. Eddy sent word that he and Willie are fine, but neither appeared. Abraham says I'm fooling myself, but it's not true. It's not!

Feb. 3, 1863: We entertained the French minister, Monsieur Mercier, after his meeting with Seward. He offered to mediate the war, but Abraham and Seward said no. The world seemed almost normal when speaking the Royal language and entertaining again in the Blue Room. How I long for those days to return!

Feb. 13, 1863: After a particularly unexciting birthday for Abraham last night, tonight we unexpectedly entertained the famous dwarfs from Barnum's exhibit, which the boys and I saw 10 years ago. Gen. Tom Thumb stands 3' 4" tall and weighs only 70 pounds—at 25 years of age! His bride, Lavinia Warren, is almost the same. Even Tad is taller! They married several days ago in NY and were passing through DC on their journey. I worried they might become lost in a snow bank, because the drifts are as tall as they are.

It was so funny to watch Abraham bend down to greet the couple. He's almost twice Thumb's height! When Abraham sat in a chair, Thumb stood in another and they were still not eye to eye. He said shaking Thumb's hand felt like holding an uncooked breast of tiny quail. Thumb's whole hand is not as long as Abraham's fingers!

Miss Lavinia is adorable—like a china doll that can talk! Tad says she resembles a tiny version of me, and the lady agreed she had frequently

heard the sentiment. I'll never forget this evening. Nor will Tad. I doubt he
has ever enjoyed an event so much. Poor Bob, though home on leave,
refused to attend (undignified, he said) and missed all the merriment! Such
a shame; we laugh so seldom these days.

Feb. 14, 1863: The Saturday Valentine's reception was a real crusher,
even in the snow and slush. I have never seen such a crowd trying to attend,
all peering about wildly. I'm sure they came to see the Thumbs, but the
small couple had gone. And soon so did the large people, but not without
snipping a foot or so from my new lace curtains. Also, since last inspected,
someone has cut a piece out of the carpet in the Red Room, leaving huge,
deep scars in the wooden floor beneath. Have people no respect? I should
have left the house as it was. Then I wouldn't have to post guards in all the
corners! Where is the American pride?

Would they treat Kate Chase so shabbily? Oh yes, I know she and her
father long for this residence! They conspire and scheme against us. Chase
whispers his own name throughout Washington as a candidate for
President in 1864. And his daughter, his only hostess and confidante, is a
witch! She had the audacity to receive guests in the White House on the
same day and time I was receiving. It would not surprise me if some of our
recent illnesses were due to poison put in our meals by those who don't
want us here.

Feb. 20, 1863: On this first anniversary of Willie's death, I engaged
Lord Colchester, the celebrated medium I met in New York last year. He
conducted a séance in the Red Room, but Noah Brooks proved him a
charlatan. Colchester himself beat a small drum under the table! I have been
duped—deceived by my own senses again—and can't breathe for the
yellow bile in my throat. If not for Abraham and Tad, I would pray to be
removed from a world so filled with dishonesty and cruelty. I can trust no
one.

Mar. 10, 1863, Eddy's birthday: I can close my eyes and see him. He
would have been tall and muscular, much like Bob, his beautiful face filled
with love as he smiled at me. I went to see Mrs. Colburn this afternoon, a
true visionary and friend, unlike the phony Colchester.

I relish the intimacy of the séance circle: sitting in the dark, holding
hands with others, feeling the souls of loved ones swish over my chair. I
desperately miss the closeness once shared with my loving husband. He
seldom comes to my bed now, but I sometimes find him lounging on my
settee when he should be dealing with affairs of state. He will stretch out
and read his Bible, with Jip or a cat on his chest, shoes and stockings on the
floor, toes wriggling in the cool air. I order him a cup of strong coffee or

sassafras tea, and listen as he reads a passage or two aloud. Unfortunately, it's never long before someone drags him away.

After our session, Mrs. Colburn asked if I might secure a position for her in the Interior Department. A superb idea, though it would take some strong convincing of Abraham. Then she would never be forced to leave Washington, would never be arrested or fined for her craft, and could stay near me as long as we're here! How long will that be? Until we are cold and sightless, most likely.

Apr. 1, 1863: Today Abraham granted amnesty for deserters if they return before the end of the month, and promised court martial for those "leg cases" who don't return. The extent of truancy would astonish most citizens. Scarcely more than half the men being paid are truly serving, but Abraham says he can't condemn a man just because his legs ran away with him.

Because of our low numbers, Abraham has formalized the national conscription. He has requested it many times, but now it's law: All male citizens between 20 and 45, except for some special cases, are required to enter military service. They may, of course, hire a substitute or purchase their service completion for $300. We'll see if this works better than his pleas.

He also agreed to put more negroes in the field. Their entitlement has been recognized and enlistments are being sought. Some black troops are already serving valiantly. I believe they will be honored to help win their freedom. Colonization is not going well, so this race without a home must help create their own homes. These are not popular decisions, and our lives are in danger. My brain throbs from the constant barrage of criticism against the White House, the war, and us personally, and I sleep as often as possible to avoid reality. Abraham seldom rests, and he feels the pressure to his core.

Apr. 3, 1863: After breakfast, we took Tad to Stuntz's toy shop on New York Avenue to pick out a birthday gift. Then we filled the hammercloth coach with flowers and food for the sick soldiers. We were accompanied by Col. Sweney, a nicer man not to be found, who later took Tad for a horseback ride to the navy yard. We were also fortunate to have the company of Dr. Henry, our dear friend from Springfield. He now serves as surveyor general in the Washington Territory. Dr. Henry encourages Abraham to remember his old yarns, which pleases me highly. We also gave Tad permission to accompany Abraham, Noah Brooks, and Dr. Henry to Gen. Hooker's headquarters tomorrow. I hope the "hookers" are not in sight.

Apr. 5, 1863, Easter: An unexpected snow fell as I readied for bed about midnight last night. I hope it didn't impede the men's journey. They were to spend the night on the steamer, go over from Aquia Creek to Hooker's camp this morning, visit the hospitals, review the troops, and remain there till Friday.

This morning, I rode through fresh drifts to attend services with Mrs. Orne, Mrs. Dixon, and Mrs. Hamlin. The sermon about resurrection and life after death was interesting. The minister castigated women like Mrs. Colburn, but I believe she's as saintly as he in her way. She believes in God, and says the spirits are available to anyone enlightened enough to understand the doctrine of the Holy Ghost. I'm inclined to believe her.

Apr. 20, 1863: After much dilly-dally and argument, West Virginia (not Kanawha as previously anticipated) has been approved to enter the Union on June 20th. We should be rejoicing, but so much dissention and irritation about the emancipation proclamation fill the country that tensions are heightening. I no longer comprehend all that's occurring, and don't understand why we're so hated. We've done everything possible to make the country safe and prosperous, but the Democrats have raised such a level of hostility toward us that we'll never be re-elected and may not even live to see the end of this term. The public is weary of battle, so they believe the worst.

Can we really have been at war two years now? People are angry about the suspension of habeas corpus, about the hundreds of people arrested for pro-Confederate sentiments, about newspapers being suspended, about negroes fighting, about the mounting casualties, about the Indians who were hanged, about conscription. My God, they're angry about everything!

I wish we were in our little house in Springfield to enjoy this lovely spring weather. I can't take much more of this madness, and Abraham is so bone weary he can hardly lift his head. He says nothing can truly touch his tired spot. I understand. My spot is also too deep for relief.

Apr. 24, 1863: A fun séance in my suite last night! Abraham attended for a short while, as did Stanton and Welles. Little was accomplished except that a spirit pinched Stanton's short nose and tugged Welles' silly wig. Thank Heaven there is some small diversion to our terror.

May 1, 1863: Good news from the troops and a rare look of pleasure from Abraham. He says the push is on, both east and west. Hooker crossed the Rappahannock in Virginia with 70,000 men. Stoneman's cavalry is close behind. The navy is clearing the way for Grant's army to cross the Mississippi River. Sherman is near Vicksburg. Perhaps there will be peace after all.

I agreed that the Marine Band may resume their concerts in the yard this Saturday. Mr. Welles convinced me of the joy it brings the people, and who am I to deny happiness?

May 12, 1863: The Richmond papers headline that Stonewall Jackson is dead. His own men accidentally wounded him some days ago and his arm had to be removed. Then he was wounded again in skirmish and developed pneumonia. The Confederacy mourns. If he had been a Union general, we would also be disappointed, because he was a fine fighting man. As it is, we are as pleased as one can be. Our own generals seem to be drinking and dragging again. We leave for the Soldiers' Home tomorrow — much cooler there.

June 5, 1863: Tad and I leave on Monday for the Continental Hotel in Philadelphia. Perhaps a change of scenery will cure my aches and help Tad stop sneezing. I instructed Abraham to get more fresh air and eat more than a daily sandwich while we're away.

June 17, 1863: The newspapers report that Gen. Lee is moving northward, but no one seems to know where. Abraham's telegrams don't give much information. This morning's message was cryptic: "I'm tolerably well. Haven't rode out much yet, but have at last got new tires on the carriage wheels and perhaps will go out soon."

He also mentioned that he called for another 100,000 militia to serve for six months, and that Generals Halleck and Hooker, as well as Grant and McClernand, continue to spat between themselves. If the coast is clear, Tad and I may begin toward Washington soon. Philadelphia is in a perfect panic, and they say Harrisburg is packed for evacuation.

June 21, 1863: Back in Washington with the raging heat, humidity, flies, mosquitoes, and that damned smell — like rotting skunks in the gutters. So dusty that breathing is almost impossible. How I despise this city in the summer. The coach is packed and ready; I'm eager to return to the Soldiers' Home.

June 28, 1863: Why does my family insist on embarrassing me so? Ninian was charged with using his position to enhance his personal income and was dismissed as commissary. Why would he do such a thing? Why wouldn't he just ask for money rather than take it like a common hoister? He has never endorsed us or our politics, but why would he steal? Elizabeth will be mortified. I am mortified. Another Democratic bullet aimed at my head!

While I prayed at church for all our souls, Abraham accepted Hooker's resignation because of disagreement over action at Harper's Ferry, although

I sense it had more to do with his failure at Chancellorsville and his ineffectiveness against Lee. George Meade (they call him Old Snapping Turtle) was appointed. He is the 5th general to command the Army of the Potomac within a year! Why can't we keep commanders? If they could only overlook their own egos and fight for the Union instead of their own recognition, we would have been out of this rebellion long ago. Damn them all!

Aug. 1, 1863: I have finally returned to the world of the living after sustaining serious injuries on July 2nd while driving to the Soldiers' Home. I'm told that the screws holding the seat had been removed in an attempt to kill one of us! I flew to the ground and hit my head on a rock. I was treated at the hospital, requiring many stitches, and lay infected, festering, and comatose. Rebecca Pomroy has been nursing me or I likely would be dead. If Abraham had been in the carriage, the Union would now be in grave jeopardy. It can afford to lose an aging First Lady, but it could not survive without Abraham Lincoln!

While I lay ill, Gen. Pemberton surrendered Vicksburg to Gen. Grant, but we lost 23,000 men, and my half-brother David was perilously injured. Abraham thought the war had ended, but Meade let Lee's men escape from Gettysburg.

"These are trying occasions, not only in success, but for the want of success. We had them in the palms of our hands," Abraham said sadly as he paced my room. My poor husband. He has had so very much to worry him. He is sick, both physically and mentally, and I don't know how much longer he can hold on. The circles under his eyes are even deeper and darker than mine. His heart, always slightly off-beat, pounds constantly in a wayward rhythm. His skin is gray and crinkled. We have both aged so much since we moved into this place! I wonder if those before us frayed as visibly?

Bob came home to care for me, though he has not been much comfort to me or Abraham with his surly attitude. I sense a favorite young lady has chosen another suitor, but he won't discuss it. He's also angry that I won't allow him to join the army. How can he even ask such of me? Has he no heart? Can't he understand a mother's grief and concerns? Abraham agrees it is Bob's duty to enlist, and reminds me that we're being criticized for holding out when others are giving so much. But I could not bear another loss.

He told me the first draftee names were drawn and published in New York City on July 12th, and rioting and looting began immediately. Negroes were lynched and beaten. A colored orphanage, among other buildings, was set afire. The mobs, composed mainly of Irish, even attacked federal officials. More than 500 were killed and another 500 wounded in the long rampage. Property losses are estimated at over a million dollars! There were also conscription riots in Massachusetts, New Hampshire, Vermont, and Ohio. I'm glad to have missed that portion of the summer.

Aug. 4, 1863: Tad, Bob, and I leave tomorrow for a two-month sabbatical in the New Hampshire White Mountains. It's so dreadfully hot here that I can't recuperate, and Tad is quite frail again. I've been told that the past three or four days registered 104 degrees in some parts of the city! Not to mention the cholera that creeps through the streets.

Aug. 9, 1863: A low-spirited note from Abraham: Tad's nanny goat has disappeared. The housekeeper saw her in the middle of Tad's bed on the day we left, but now she can't be found! Tad is distraught and I had to promise him another goat. The weather continues dry and pleasantly cool here. Bob is being gentlemanly and solicitous. The hole in my skull and its companion aches are not healing, but the drugs soothe me.

Aug. 29, 1863: We heard from Abraham that Ft. Sumter is battened down and useless to the enemy, that it's likely our forces now occupy both Sumter and Wagner, and that Gen. Gilmore has thrown some shot into Charleston!

My husband seems content and capable without me. I admit it distresses me that I'm no longer needed. I see the way young women gaze at him; does he look back? He seldom comes to my bed, though I know his needs. Could he be finding release with a younger, healthier woman? Should I return to protect my own? Surely he wouldn't indulge in flirtations with silly women as though he were a beardless boy fresh from school!

No, these are the thoughts of a woman whose head has been knocked awry, not one married 21 years! I have no cause to doubt his fidelity, yet I see him so frequently surrounded by young beauties with physical desire and a wish for power in their eyes. Surely no man could resist so much temptation. I must make myself more attractive, stop giving in to my pains and sorrows, wear more face coloring, lose weight, cross the threshold between our chambers more often on my own accord. No, where is the good in it? I'll never be the belle of Springfield again.

Sept. 21, 1863: A wire from Abraham said he's still staying at the Soldiers' Home because Washington continues to suffer intense heat. New Hampshire is ever so much cooler, but he implied he wants us to come home! His message read: "I neither see nor hear of the epidemic here now and would be glad for you to come. Nothing very particular, but I really wish to see you." How nice to hear words of love. So frequently now his messages are sparse and impersonal. It's good to have just one line to say we are remembered and missed!

Sept. 24, 1863: Abraham's wire contains the worst news yet: On the 22nd, the rebels crushed our army at Chickamauga, Tennessee, and our darling Ben Helm appeared on the casualty list! Abraham must be suffering as much as I; he loved Ben like a son. Only 32, a mere boy! If he had stayed with the Union, Abraham would have given him a post and he wouldn't have been in combat. Emilie would have lived with us all this time and Ben would be safe! Why, God, why? When will the dying end?

Despite my bad cold, the boys and I are leaving tomorrow for Philadelphia, then back to Washington. I want to contact Emilie as soon as possible, and I need to be near my bereaved husband.

Sept. 30, 1863: It's so good to be home again and find myself needed! Abraham wants to proclaim a national day of thanksgiving and asked me what day we set aside in Springfield. I reminded him of the date, and he will ask Congress to proclaim the last Thursday of November as a day of national gratitude. Sarah Hale, who has been campaigning for this day for more than 40 years, will be here when the proclamation is signed on October 3rd.

Nov. 4, 1863, our 21st anniversary: I remain unnoticed as wife or advisor. I might as well have stayed in New Hampshire. Abraham's mind is so crowded with fears for the military, shells crashing over Charleston Harbor, preservation of the Union, and upcoming elections that I try to be considerate by not expressing my doubts concerning personal events and the details of my failing health. He is hardly well himself, still furrowed and careworn. His face is tight and pinched, and he's thinner than I've ever seen him, even in those days of hypo while we were apart in Springfield. Where are my medicines?

Nov. 6, 1863: Abraham has been asked to speak at the dedication of a military cemetery in Gettysburg, Pennsylvania, and he solicited my help with the composition! How long I have anticipated that moment, and it fulfilled every expectation! I thought he was lost to me, outside my reach, beyond my touch, but now I see the foolishness of my worry. This dreadful war will be over soon and we will be just Mary, Abraham, Bob, and Tad Lincoln again. I will cherish that day!

Nov. 10, 1863: We drove through a light snowfall to the theatre last night to see John Wilkes Booth in *The Marble Heart*. Abraham is pleased with the recent Union advances in Virginia, West Virginia, and Tennessee, so it was a pleasant evening despite the mediocrity of the performance.

Nov. 12, 1863, State Election Day: Republicans carried every northern state except New Jersey! Springfield voted Federalist by 138 votes, giving us a gain of 440 over last year. *Harper's Weekly* says Abraham is the reason the Union is still alive—because he stood above party to keep the loyalty of Union-loving people. Didn't I say so even back in '42?

And, on this day, probably to mar its importance, haughty Kate Chase married the richest man in America, Rhode Island senator William Sprague. The press reported earlier this week that Sprague gave his bride a tiara of matched pearls and diamonds with a value of more than $50,000! Now if her father becomes President, she will be a true fairy princess!

Nov. 18, 1863: Tad has not been well for several days and Dr. Stone says he has a severe case of scarlatina. But, since he is somewhat better today, we believe it's safe for Abraham to go on to Gettysburg. I'll stay with Tad.

Nov. 20, 1863: Abraham reminisced so warmly about Gettysburg that I cried just to hear of it. I wish I could see the hills where brothers fought brothers, the valleys across which brave men trudged and died, the thousand wooden crosses over the bodies of boys for whom mothers in both north and south are crying.

He said musical groups played in the streets and military bands marched in the square. Beyond the tunes, the echoes of gunfire. Edward Everett, a noted public orator, first addressed the group of 15,000. "Some passages in his talk exceeded even my expectations," Abraham praised. "He made a point against the theory of the general government being only an agency whose principals are the states. That was new to me and I think it's one of the best arguments for national supremacy ever heard. And you'll like this, Mother; he also made a loving tribute to our noble women for their angel-ministering to the suffering soldiers."

When I asked about his own remarks, he said they were "about three minutes and not entirely a failure," though he didn't receive much applause. Unfortunately, he came home bilious, and now I have two boys to care for! It's nice to be needed again.

Nov. 22, 1863: The weather was dreadful today, and Abraham is still not well. He developed a rash and Dr. Stone said he may have contracted scarlatina from Tad. Though sick, he appreciated the note from Mr. Everett: "I should be glad if I could flatter myself that I came as near to the central idea of the occasion in two hours as you did in two minutes." He also enclosed a copy of Abraham's speech from the Philadelphia newspaper:

Four score and seven years ago, our fathers brought forth on this continent a new nation, conceived in liberty, and dedicated to the proposition that all men are created equal.

Now we're engaged in a great civil war, testing whether that nation, or any nation so conceived and so dedicated, can long endure. We're here today on a great battlefield of that war to dedicate a portion of that field as a final resting place for those who here gave their lives that this nation might live. It's altogether fitting and proper that we should do this.

But, in a larger sense, we can't dedicate—we can't consecrate—we can't hallow this ground. The brave men, living and dead, who struggled here have consecrated it far above our poor power to add or detract. The world will little note nor long remember what we say here, but it can never forget what they did here. It's for us the living, rather, to be dedicated here to the unfinished work that they who fought here have thus far so nobly advanced.

It's rather for us to be here dedicated to the great task remaining before us——that from these honored dead we take increased devotion to that cause for which they gave the last full measure of devotion, that we here highly resolve that these dead shall not have died in vain—that this nation, under God, shall have a new birth of freedom—and that government of the people, by the people, for the people, shall not perish from the earth.

But the secesh *Chicago Times* condemned the speech. How ignorant and unfeeling! Surely some of those dead boys were Democrats!

The cheek of every American must tingle with shame as he reads the silly, flat, and dish-watery utterances of the man who has to be pointed out to intelligent foreigners as the President of the United States because he so little looks the part.

Nov. 23, 1863: Dr. Stone has confirmed that Abraham has varioloid, a form of smallpox. My humorous husband said he finally has something he can give to everyone! "Everyone" must believe it; the White House was deserted today. Hamlin has been alerted to assume office if necessary, and I'm dreadfully worried. Everyone here was vaccinated, some were quarantined, and the vampire press is spreading rumors that the President is dead.

Nov. 26, 1863, Thanksgiving: We enjoyed a lovely meal, though we had to contend with a highly upset son. When the turkey arrived last month, Tad immediately made friends with it and named it Jack. He taught Jack to follow him around the grounds like a dog, often with Jip behind Jack. When the cook went early this morning to kill the turkey, Tad was devastated. He burst into a Cabinet meeting in Abraham's bedroom, for he is still confined, screaming, "Zak mushn't be kilt, Zak mushn't be kilt!" Abraham explained the true purpose of a Thanksgiving turkey, since Tad didn't know what happened to "Tom" last year, but Tad would not be swayed. He wailed, "Zak's a good tork and I dun't wan em kilt. Pweez, Papa, dun't kilt Zak!" Abraham smiled reluctantly at his Cabinet members, took Tad on his lap, and wrote a reprieve for the turkey. We had chicken for supper.

Dec. 3, 1863: Congress will convene next week, which will take up much of Abraham's time, so I'm going to NY for several days to help raise money for the Sanitary Commission. It's a good cause—they purchase nursing supplies—and NY is lovely in winter. I'll return by next Tuesday.

Dec. 8, 1863: So glad to be home! The best medicine for my aches is to be back where I can see, hear, and touch my beloved husband. I still see fever in his cheeks, but he is upright and working.

He told me that Grant has secured Chattanooga, the insurgent force is retreating from East Tennessee, and Union troops probably can't be dislodged from their important position. Grant is hotly pursuing Lee, and the road into Georgia is now open. We should have peace before Christmas!

He also related that he issued a proclamation of amnesty and reconstruction, pardoning people who participated in the war if they take an oath to the Union, although "people" doesn't include military and government men. He also offered to help establish a governing body for any seceded state that agrees to rejoin the Union and abolish slavery, and signed an agreement for a colony of freedmen in Haiti. This has been a year of highs and lows. I hope next year will bring peace and be more high than low.

Dec. 13, 1863, my 45th birthday: We are receiving gifts of all sizes and shapes, from all over the world: grapes from Ohio, apple cider from New Jersey, figs from Smyrna, hand-made furniture, jewelry of the loveliest and tawdriest, a linen tablecloth from Constantinople, yards of Swiss lace, silk from China, fabrics embroidered in France, and many books. I love the presents that come with this time of year. How wonderful to feel special for a few weeks.

Tad received a box of tools and immediately began to remodel the mansion. If he continues, we'll be forced to take the implements away. He tested the saw by cutting through the plank leading from the dining room to the conservatory!

Dec. 14, 1863: Emilie has come to Washington, though not of her choosing. My little sister and her daughter Katherine were returning to Lexington from Atlanta when they were stopped at Ft. Monroe, Virginia. The Union officers insisted Emilie take the Oath of Allegiance, but she refused (that old Todd stubbornness). The officers wired Abraham and he told them to send Emilie here immediately. I'm happy to have them safely ensconced with us; no harm can come to them now. I will heal Emilie back to her beautiful self.

Dec. 16, 1863: Emilie and I are strained. We avoid any mention of politics, war, death. These topics form a barrier of silent truth between us. I tried twice to apologize for this horrid war and Ben's involvement in it, but we both know it was not our doing.

Our critics are hard at work again, chastising us for having a "southern spy" in our home. Emilie wants to leave, but Abraham and I are both begging her to stay. My nerves have disintegrated, and she's a calming influence. If anything should happen to Emilie, or Bob, or Tad, or God forbid, my beloved husband, it would kill me in a second's time, which is why I can't allow Bob to enlist. Why don't they understand?

Dec. 20, 1863: I thought I could write an entry before bed, but more words than these are impossible. Emilie has been granted temporary amnesty, so she leaves tomorrow. I am heartbroken.

Dec. 21, 1863, Willie's birthday: Happy birthday, darling Willie. I'll never forget you. Memories and regrets march across my mind with vivid cruelty, but much still needs to be done among the living. Abraham had made no mention, either publicly or privately, of seeking another term, so I finally asked, "Will you seek this office again?"

He hesitated, then stretched his arms out behind him and entwined his fingers. His nose twitched and his eyebrows rose slightly. Then he pressed his lips tightly, firmly, one against the other, before saying, "I can't imagine who else would want it, and we can't hardly leave it unattended. A second term would be a great honor and I wouldn't decline if it's offered. But remember, Mother, no President since Andrew Jackson has been elected twice. Only one's even been nominated. Don't get your hopes up."

No, My Darling, my hopes are not up. In fact, I would prefer to return to Springfield and be a lawyer's wife. But that's not possible yet. Our mission is not finished. We started this journey for eight years and we'll have them! How odd that our individual desires for this place have reversed. I no longer want it and you no longer want to relinquish it.

Dec. 25, 1863, Christmas: Since Abraham has no time for Christmas, I gave myself some lovely gifts this week: diamond ear-knobs, a tiny gilt clock, silver and crystal to go with the china purchased in '61, and a magnificent rosewood piano. The sight of diamonds glittering in the light as I play carols is soothing. It gives me a sense of security little else can provide in these times. It's hard to realize that this is the third Christmas Day we have been at war, though there's little fighting right now. I close my eyes, or engross myself in books or piano, and try to forget the reality.

Jan. 1, 1864: The continuous tide of humans dragging in slush and freezing wind for the reception has finally ended and the re-election campaign has begun. A group of negroes came late in the day and we were proud to greet them. I believe Frederick Douglass, the abolitionist orator who met with Abraham last year, was the first black guest in the White

House, then that large group attended last year to talk about colonization, then the church group who picnicked on the south lawn, and today we welcomed yet another free group. We're pleased with what we've accomplished. This Presidency will never be forgotten!

Jan. 16, 1864: I'm being undermined in planning next week's state dinner, just as I am in everything else. I gave the guest list to Nicolay this morning, but he soon came asking why the Chases were not invited. I replied that I did not want them to attend. Young Nicolay, not knowing his place, went directly to Abraham, and now the Chases must be invited. Why can't men mind their own business? Damn them all!

Feb. 7, 1864: An article by Harriet Beecher Stowe, author of *Uncle Tom's Cabin*, appeared in this month's *Littell's Living Age*. It's the finest description of my blessed husband I have seen in many years:

> Lincoln is a strong man, but his strength is of a peculiar kind—not aggressive so much as passive. And among passive things, it is like the strength not so much of a stone buttress as of a wire cable. It is strength swaying to every influence, yielding on this side and on that to popular needs, yet tenaciously and inflexibly bound to carry it to a great end. And probably by no other kind of strength could our national ship have been drawn safely thus far during the tossings and tempests that beset her way.

Feb. 11, 1864: Our enemies are out to kill us all! Last night they set fire to the stables, destroying all our beautiful thoroughbred horses. Abraham tried to save them, but the guards wouldn't let him enter the barn. We watched from our windows as the poor helpless creatures burned to death, including Tad's pony and Willie's beloved Jeff. The goats also perished. We could hear the desperate whinnies echoing through the pores of our skin, and the sound froze my soul. Abraham stayed with me till after daybreak, holding me close. I couldn't stop shivering. Tad is inconsolable and hasn't left his room since he learned of the tragedy. I must take more doses and rest.

Feb. 16, 1864: Salmon Chase is at it again! A circular has been widely distributed alleging that Abraham's re-nomination is impossible because the honor of the nation and the cause of liberty would suffer for it. The flyer advocates the one-term principle and promotes Chase "in this critical time." It's signed by "C. Pomeroy" of Kansas. I know no such name. I showed the rag to Abraham after receiving it in the early mail. He laughed and said, "I'm determined to shut my eyes to everything of the sort. I'll keep Chase where he is and let him do his electioneering behind my back. If he becomes

President, it'll be all right; we could have a worse man. I'm indifferent so long as he does his duty in the treasury." Bah! Can't he see what's going on? I know his eyes have worsened so that spectacles are always necessary, but has he become blind <u>and</u> deaf? Chase would stab him and watch him bleed to death if he had no chance of being seen! I must put a stop to this!!

Feb. 18, 1864: Now that I have recovered, Abraham is not well. I tried all day to persuade him to take some medicine, food, and rest. He eats such small amounts now: a biscuit for lunch, a single egg and toast for breakfast, an ounce of meat for supper. He's hollow-eyed and gaunt; his skeleton shows whitely through his skin. He's bent over like a graybeard, and his feet swell so badly he seldom forces on shoes, even when meeting with dignitaries. I hear even now the clip-clopping of his open slippers as he scuffles down the hall toward his bedchamber. I'm terribly distressed about his health, but he won't listen and refuses to see a doctor.

Mar. 1, 1864: Abraham made a quick speech today, one that should have been quicker. It was not a noble effort, nor well delivered. For one thing, he announced Grant's appointment to lieutenant general, a rank retired after being merited only by George Washington and Winfield Scott. Washington and Grant compared equally—how horrid! Speeches like this would never have beaten Stephen Douglas in the early days. In fact, it was one of the worst I've ever heard. I wanted the earth to sink and let me through!

Mar. 3, 1864: We had a lovely evening with Tad at Grover's National Theatre watching Edwin Booth in *Hamlet*. Abraham has always loved this play, and tonight's was a fine rendition. We watched Booth's brother John at Ford's last year in *The Marble Heart*, but he doesn't compare with Edwin! The President's box at Grover's is luxurious. I love the crimson velvet seats because they're so sensuous. Sitting in the dark with Abraham made me feel like we were young lovers again. I reached out and placed my hand on his leg, knowing he would smile. I rested my head on his shoulder and could feel his bones pressing into my cheek. We could almost forget the true world around us as we sat in our loge and watched a world that doesn't exist.

Tad loved the theatre so much that he asked for materials to allow Bobby Grover and him to build their own! I agreed to let them use that little room just over the entrance. The White House carpenter, Mr. Haliday, will gave them wood and oversee the construction. Soon we'll have no need of Grover's or Ford's—we will have our own production company right here!

Mar. 6, 1864: To my surprise and delight, Chase's slanderous circular has hurt him and helped us. The papers are beginning to rally behind us, Chase's own home state of Ohio came out for Abraham, and the Union National Committee[21] called for the convention to meet in Baltimore on June 7th, with our name on their lips.

But matters are strained in our personal world. Abraham is receiving more visions. He again saw himself with two faces, one atop the other but paler, the same as he saw just before the first election. The Lauries confirmed what I was told then: He won't survive his second term.

My God, what have I done? I brought him here! He wouldn't be in this place if not for my constant harping and prodding. By forcing this office on him, I have condemned him. How I wish we could go home and leave this nightmare behind us, but he says he must finish the task.

I now believe we are cursed. In my youth, Mammy Sally often told me about a jaybird that watched me at all times and reported my bad doings to the devil. I believed it then, I believe it now. If not, why have we been forced to drink so deeply from the cup of affliction? Disaster has followed all our political luck. Eddy's tuberculosis worsened during our term in Congress, and he died soon after I insisted that Abraham campaign again. Willie and Tad contracted scarlet fever barely a month after our last nomination, and both were struck with measles soon after the inauguration. God took Willie because of my ambition and the foolish ball we hosted. All these scenes appear nightly to me in hideous dreams. My mortal spirit was too proud and made me a blind target. How would I live without my beloved husband? If fate runs true to history, I will take my own life and lie beside him for all eternity.

Mar. 8, 1864: Who should appear at our reception this evening but US Grant himself! We had never met him. What a seedy little man: ugly, gauche, vulgar, smelling of cigars. I was so embarrassed I left the reception and took refuge in my room. I suppose we will meet Mrs. Grant tomorrow when he's named General-in-Chief.

Bob wrote that he met a young lady, Miss Mary Harlan of Iowa but residing in Washington, in whom he has a great interest. Though they met at a dance at the National Hotel in Washington, he hasn't mentioned her until now. I assume they have been corresponding. She is three years younger than he, so they won't consider matrimony for several years. He asked to bring her to our next public event. Of course we'll approve. She attended the same conservatory as Julia Taft: Madame Smith's exclusive French School. To attend there, a girl must know who her great-great-great

---

[21] The Republican Party called itself the Union Party during the war years, allowing War Democrats to vote for Lincoln.

grandfathers were! And all studies are conducted fully in French! I sent the young lady a bouquet of our finest flowers to introduce myself.

Mar. 11, 1864: The Grants joined us for supper last evening before the general left for Nashville to meet Gen. Sherman. Mrs. Grant is much like me. She loves the theatre, dances well, and wears fashionable clothing, though perhaps too low cut. I found myself liking her, despite her crossed eyes. Amazing that she married such a careless fool. Though he eventually manages to claim victory, he loses two men to the enemy's one.

Abraham teased my opinion of Grant by saying, "Well, Mother, suppose we give you command. No doubt you'd do a whole lot better than any general who's been tried." No doubt you're correct, and with fewer lives lost.

Mar. 12, 1864: Tad's little theatre is finished, complete with gas footlights, curtains, the finest background scenery, and handsome china vases on each side of the stage. A bust of George Washington stands in the center of the platform, and a wicket fence surrounds the front. The audience area contains cushioned chairs, covered settees, and small tapestry sofas. Mr. Grover lent them costumes, props, and stage properties.

His first production today was *The Seven Sisters*, with himself in the starring role. He has seen *Sisters* so often that he did quite well! Tad's little friends played the other parts. He charged a nickel for admission. We attended, of course, as did many of the men camped in our yard and most of the staff. Everyone loves Tad!

Apr. 4, 1864, Tad's 11ᵗʰ birthday: Mr. Sumner came to Tad's small party and brought some flags sent over from Stanton's office. He stayed for dinner with me and spent the evening relaxing in the drawing room, entertaining me with stories and poetry. How nice to be shown such interest! I am hugely fond of him. He's brilliant, handsome, aristocratic, gifted, and powerful. Although he's somewhat peculiar, I converse more freely with him than my other friends. And he, unlike others, has time to spend with me. He is always a gentleman, though he does hold my hand a little longer than necessary. Of course, I have no romantic interest in him!

He told me that, since Chase has been publicly humiliated, other names are being mentioned as Presidential candidates: Generals Ben Butler, US Grant, and John C Frémont (though I believe he is a shill for Chase). Bring on your best—we'll whip them all!

Apr. 5, 1864: We passed another enjoyable evening at the theatre, seeing Edwin Forrest in *King Lear*. How we love the bard! Another attack struck me as we drove home—headache, spasms, lights in my eyes—and

I'm off to bed. These attacks leave me without patience, endurance, or the ability to write. It's time for a trip away from the stench and unrelenting talk of death.

Apr. 10, 1864: The Senate approved the 13th Amendment, which abolishes slavery, but the House has not yet voted. Surely it will be passed immediately and that evil will be wiped out!

Probably because of that good news, a vast crowd attended our reception, even with the torrential rain. They came and ate as though they had never, and would never again, be invited out. They stayed until 2am, and we're exhausted! I find no pleasure in these events now, but must go on for sake of the upcoming election. My position requires my presence even though my heart no longer feels allegiance.

Apr. 16, 1864: We hear talk about postponing the Union National Committee conference till summer, so I may have more time to collect money for my accounts. I will meet with certain people during my upcoming NY trip to secure their dedication for the nomination and perhaps also help with my small financial problem. I'm dealing with an unprincipled set of politicians, but such risk is necessary when working for re-election. Abraham is unaware of my actions, because he would never approve such proceedings. He is too honest to take proper care of his own interests, so it's my duty to electioneer for him in any way possible. It's time for me to shake off my illnesses and be with those who can ensure success!

Apr. 18, 1864: A painful rumor reached us this beautiful spring morning of the massacre of some 300 negro soldiers and white officers by 1500 rebel assailants at Ft. Pillow, Tennessee. The public mind now holds some anxiety about whether the government is doing its duty to the colored soldier and to the service. We must give negro soldiers all the protection given to all other soldiers, and Abraham is having the affair thoroughly investigated. If true, the north will surely retaliate and massacre will become routine. When will this savagery stop? I have ordered Tad and his friends to stop playing war games; it's not good education for them.

More states have come to our side. Tennessee supports emancipation, Arkansas installed a pro-Union legislature, Louisiana declared for freedom, part of Virginia declared itself free, and Nebraska was admitted without slavery. The proclamation is working.

Apr. 28, 1864: Tad and I are in NY. I had a battle of my own with him to leave the goats behind. He's afraid for their safety at all times. He has become high-strung, ornery, and undisciplinable. Words often used by his father to describe me.

Many of the people here don't share my interest in re-election. They favor passing the office to someone less undecided and more forceful, someone who will end the war immediately. The *Detroit Free Press* headlines, "Not a single senator can be named as favorable to Lincoln's re-nomination." Damn them all!

This election holds more at stake than anyone knows. Defeat could end our marriage, because I won't have time to pay my debts and will be forced to admit my indiscretions. Abraham would surely pay my dues, but he wouldn't understand them. I'm not sure I myself understand them. I vow not to buy, but the stores are so bright and cheery, everyone is covetous and caring, and the feel and appearance of new items is too enticing to resist. If I had a partner to share my life with, as I was promised, perhaps I wouldn't be so intemperate.

My debts have mounted to approximately $27,000 at the usual stores, particularly here in NY. If Abraham is elected, he will remain oblivious, but if he's defeated, the bills will be sent in and he'll know everything. If the press discovers the extent of the debts before the election, he'll be defeated because of it. Oh what have I done?

I must seek help from those who have grown fat on Presidential patronage. If Abraham loses, they lose as well. These men will help pay my debts in order to remain in office, I know it! I'll call on Isaac Newton, John Hay, Rufus Andres, Marshall Bobs, Oliver Halsted, Simeon Draper, Charles Sumner, others as I think of them. Since I was instrumental in securing the most lucrative post of NY surveyor for Abram Wakeman, he is beholden. And, being so well thought of here, he can surely soothe over issues of payment with the storekeepers. Wakeman also associates with Seward, Weed, and Bennett, and can dun them if he can't manage enough money himself. I'll weep and beg as need be, but I must have help! And then I will never overspend again! These men will help me; they must help me. And the sooner they begin, the smaller will be the amount past mending.

May 2, 1864: Just before our departure from NY today, someone handed me a *Herald* containing another maligning article by Mary Clemmer Ames. Had I committed murder in every city in this blessed Union, I could not be more traduced.

Mrs. Lincoln is again in town. From the early hours until late in the evening, she ransacks the treasures of the Broadway dry goods stores. While her sister women scrape lint, sew bandages, put on nurses' caps and give all to their country, the wife of the President spends her time rolling between Washington and New York, intent on extravagant purchases for herself and the White House. Mrs. Lincoln seems to have nothing to do but shop for lavish goods.

That is a cooked-up lie! I am profoundly affected by the costs and casualties of this war, but I'm only one woman. I have given and given—to hospitals, to the CRA, to negroes, to soldiers, to the nation. Can I have no personal life and enjoyment in my aging years? Besides, when Mrs. Marshall called earlier this year and asked me not to purchase foreign goods, Abraham and Mr. Welles said I shouldn't agree, because the government needs the revenue from the importation of goods. It's patriotic to purchase American goods! The more I spend, the more our treasury has to spend!

Some people also don't understand that I would insult my position if I weren't well dressed at all times. The very fact that we're from the west subjects me to searching observation. Further, if I buy inexpensive goods, they won't bring a high sale price when we leave Washington and I no longer need them. All I have ever done was out of the purest motives, but wicked people intentionally misinterpret.

May 9, 1864: We have learned enough of army operations within the last few days to give special gratitude. All of Grant's armies are progressing in the south, and the war will soon be over! This beautiful weather proves that God watches over us.

We moved today to the Soldiers' Home and Mr. Sumner joined us for supper. How I enjoy discussing Whittier, Longfellow, and Emerson with him. He has met them personally! His time is immersed in his business, yet he insists on hearing all my news. He cares for me, only as a friend of course, and I'm honored that he visits no other lady. Abraham is too distracted to notice me.

May 27, 1864: I was unable to leave my bed yesterday because of a severe headache and debilitating nausea. Though it has almost receded, I'm so weak this morning that I will probably not be able to visit the hospitals. Why does spring bring such suffering attacks? I no longer enjoy being here at the Soldiers' Home, and have told French to request an appropriation for a new summer home. If we're to be here another four years, we need more adequate accommodations.

June 5, 1864: The Union National Committee is pressuring Abraham to tell them where he stands and to help them prepare the platform, but he will not. "I don't want to interfere with the convention," he said. How silly, it's his convention! The only thing he stressed for himself was an amendment to completely abolish slavery. Otherwise, he's staying uninvolved as to policy, position, or platform. He even asked them to choose his VP, likely a War Democrat rather than Hamlin. Names in the air: Leonard Swett, Joseph Holt, Daniel Dickinson, John Dix, Andrew Johnson.

Once again, it's time for my good husband to stand up and be vocal! How can he allow these men to tell him what to do and plan his life for him? Does his reticence denote a lack of enthusiasm for the office? I'll write to the committee myself and inform them that our choice is Leonard Swett.

June 8, 1864: We are nominated! Glory be to God! The only other man to receive recognition at the convention was Grant (22 votes to our 484). The party demanded reorganization of the Cabinet, as expected, so Hamlin was replaced. Abraham will pair with Andrew Johnson, territorial governor of Tennessee. The platform calls for integrity of the Union, suppression of the rebellion with no compromise, and an amendment prohibiting slavery. How I despise the banner of "Abe and Andy!"

Crowds of delegates from the convention swarmed the mansion today in celebration. Abraham still shows little excitement. His comment upon hearing the news, "Well, I suppose they decided it best not to swap horses while crossing the river." How different from the man who came running home from the telegraph office four years ago, his scarf flying in the wind, calling, "Molly, we're elected!" How much we've all changed. If we're elected, God, we'll need more strength to live through the next four years.

June 9, 1864: A bit of humor and entertainment tonight. Stephen Massett, known as "Jeems Pipes of Pipesville," presented a few sketches to amuse us. One of the humors was entitled *Eating Roast Pig with the King of the Cannibal Islands (My Only Essay on Bacon in Foreign Parts)*. Quite silly really, but Abraham enjoyed the evening.

As we were readying for bed, I asked Abraham if he will indeed enact an amendment abolishing slavery. He took my hand, but his mind was not with me. "You're right, I don't like messing with the Constitution. But it's a matter of liberty. The country's never had a good definition of the word and the people need one right now. North and south both declare for liberty, but they don't mean the same thing. With some, the word 'liberty' means for each man to do as he pleases with himself and the product of his labor. With others, it means for some men to do as they please with other men and the product of other men's labor. Here are two not only different but incompatible things called by the same name—liberty. And it follows that the opposite of the thing is called by another incompatible name by the respective parties—tyranny.

"When the people in revolt elected to stand out after being given a hundred days' notice that they could resume their allegiance without the overthrow of their institution, this amendment became necessary. We need a law that will stand for all times." I hugged him so tightly he coughed.

June 11, 1864: I'm honored to read the article about my humble self in the *Daily Union*. God bless them!

> The tales told of Mrs. Lincoln's vanity, pride, vulgarity and meanness ought to put any decent man or woman to the blush, when they remember they do not know one particle of what they repeat, and they would resent as an insult to their wives, sisters, or mothers that which they so glibly recite concerning the first lady in the land. Shame on these gossips and envious retailers of small slanders. Mrs. Lincoln, I am glad to be able to say from personal knowledge, is a true American woman, and when we have said that, we have said enough in praise of the best and truest lady in our beloved land.

June 16, 1864: The House voted yesterday on the 13th Amendment: 95 to 66 <u>against</u> abolishing slavery! I don't understand at all. Perhaps they have been driven insane by the bugs eating up Washington. Bugs on my hair, on my clothes, in my nostrils. I'm being nibbled to death by tiny insects and look forward to spending time in cool New Hampshire with Bob. There are intelligent men there.

June 20, 1864: A wire from Abraham says the rebels (or dissidents) set a fire in the cartridge-making building of the Philadelphia arsenal. 18 were killed, approximately 20 injured. I believed we were safe again, now I don't know, but I'm pleased to be here in New Hampshire. I asked in a letter when he now expects the war to end. His reply: "War, at best, is terrible, and this battle of ours, in its magnitude and duration, is one of the most horrible. We accepted this situation for a worthy object, and it'll end only when that object is attained." Yes, My Darling, but will we ever be able to rebuild and begin anew?

June 24, 1864: Letter from Abraham said all is well and very warm in Washington. He and Tad were at Gen. Grant's camp in Petersburg, Virginia, for several days! Has that man no sense at all? Taking a child to a battlement area? He will be the death of me. And quite possibly of himself and his son as well!

June 30, 1864: Finally Abraham has accepted Chase's resignation as Treasury Secretary! He offered it several times previously, but Abraham held on to him. This time, when he refused to nominate Abraham's choice for assistant treasurer in NY, Abraham fought back and Chase again asked to be dismissed. What a stunner it must have been when Abraham accepted! He told Chase, "You and I have reached a point of mutual embarrassment in our official relation, which it seems can't be overcome." Bravo!

Bob and I leave tomorrow and will arrive just in time to move to the Soldiers' Home. He is eager to see Mary Harlan. I sense he's a serious suitor, though he won't talk about it. I'm astounded how life goes on amidst the horror that surrounds us.

July 4, 1864, Independence Day: Our independence and our very lives are threatened by rebels at our back door. Baltimore and Washington have been targeted for destruction, and the graybacks are less than 30 miles from the capital. We have no protection now, for Grant has all our troops, and Abraham called for 24,000 militia to help the defense. Our belongings are packed and we're ready to leave on command. I will not allow Tad to be put in danger again, although Bob and Abraham say they won't evacuate!

July 9, 1864: Stanton reports that Abraham's carriage was followed from the White House to the Soldiers' Home, where we are now staying, by a horseman not of our troops or security. Some people said he looked familiar, but none could place the "handsome" face. Constant guards have been posted for us, and we were ordered back to the mansion until the threat passes.

Panic-stricken people from Maryland are invading Washington by the thousands, bringing all their belongings with them and seeking protection. We can hear the cannon from Ft. Stevens. The noise destroys my brain; I can't bear the shocks. What if I should lose my only remaining loved ones and yet live on? How would I care for myself?

July 10, 1864: Word today from Gen. Wallace that the rebels defeated him in Maryland and turned toward DC with 10,000 men. Our mail and newspapers have been stopped, telegraph lines are cut, rails are blocked. I am terrified. Mr. Welles says we have absolutely no men fit to go to the field. Gen. Wallace can send no men, and Abraham said those we get from Pennsylvania and New York will scarcely merit counting. We have moved back into the mansion for the safety it offers. This may be my last entry.

July 12, 1864: Maryland is under attack! Abraham and Dr. Henry were standing on the parapet of Ft. Stevens yesterday when it was set upon. Dr. Henry was wounded in the leg. Thank Heaven they missed Abraham. Silly old fools!

Postmaster General Montgomery Blair's home in Silver Spring was torched; there was skirmishing at Frederick; and rebels captured trains near Magnolia. Our untrained Washington militia stands ready, our civilian office personnel is armed, and Gen. Halleck tells us not to be concerned.

The Lauries were right—we won't live to see the end of this rebellion. I will take a large dose of chloral hydrate and paregoric and be totally asleep when the rebels arrive, holding Tad in my arms. I will dose him too, rather than hand him over to the enemy! Abraham seems unconcerned about the city's capture. His only worry is whether the army can destroy the rebel force, not whether we will die. Bob is still here and eager to get into battle. Tad is almost unable to speak or hear because of his terror! No one eats regular meals, no one sleeps proper hours, no one smiles.

July 13, 1864: Troops arrived in Washington today just in time to save us from sure death, but the rebels got away! We have a reprieve, though how long only God knows. Abraham and Bob went back to Ft. Stevens, and Bob said a soldier screamed at Abraham to get down before he got shot! I'm lucky not to be a widow tonight. He has lost his mind! Though Bob and John Hay also went, I worry less about them. They're young; Abraham is too stiff and slow to run.

July 14, 1864: Abraham told us today that he will likely not be able to attend Bob's college graduation; he has no time for anything other than this damned war, the constant quarrelling of his Cabinet, and his campaign.

He has lost all sense of life as it truly is. He is mesmerized by this war and lost to me. But I also see good news in that. The Lauries said the interpretation of his vision of two faces has been revealed: He will not physically die, he will perish only from me and his sons. That is, he will become pale to us. That has already occurred, so I can stop worrying about his death.

July 16, 1864: We returned to the cottage yesterday. The threat of invasion has passed and, in fact, Abraham sent John Hay to NY to consult with Confederate representatives about ending the war! Perhaps, with the threat of immediate attack under control, I can take enough powders to stop this blasted pain in my head.

July 18, 1864: Abraham has called for 500,000 more volunteers to be drafted on September 5th. This is the third call this year, and the public screams that the draft is the act of a despot. Grant has lost too many men, and people are too tired of war to keep sending loved ones to the battlefield. I now believe our chances of re-election are minor. Bob and I leave alone today for Cambridge, and I'm glad to escape the intense heat. Why must Washington be so sticky?

July 20, 1864: Bob's commencement and graduation were lovely, and I'm very proud. He graduated 32nd in a class of 100! I asked what he plans to do now and he said, "Since you object to my joining the army, and you apparently have control of that, I'm returning to Harvard and studying law." Like his father! Perhaps he will also become President someday. I will be his manager and "run" him! He will come to see that my decision about the military is a wise one. We leave tomorrow for NY, where he'll remain awhile as I return to my duties.

Aug. 1, 1864, Bob's 21st birthday: Our dear friends Mercy and James Conkling have arrived in Washington, and we're planning a trip to Gen. Grant's camp at Ft. Monroe to celebrate Bob's birthday. He arrived yesterday. Of course the trip will not be totally pleasure—when is it ever?—because Abraham invited several associates to discuss the command of Gen. Meade.

Aug. 8, 1864: Bob related an excursion he had on his way to Washington. I don't believe he planned to tell us, but the occasion warranted it, and we all found the tale quite humorous since it turned out so luckily. Bob said the crowd purchasing tickets at the train station pushed him aside and suddenly the cars began to move. The motion twisted him off his feet and dropped him partially into the open space between train and platform. Suddenly a man in a dark frock coat pulled him to safety. As Bob turned to thank him, he recognized none other than Edwin Booth, the famous actor! I shall send him a bouquet of our finest roses.

Aug. 12, 1864: My precious Emilie came today for only a short while before throwing her locket in my face—the one from Father that I gave her back in '54 to keep her safe—and fleeing in cold anger. When she left last December, Abraham issued a pass for her return and promised to allow her to ship 600 bales of cotton this year, a privilege every plantation wants, if she signed the Oath of Allegiance. When she came for the license today, she refused to comply. As is proper and legal, Abraham did not grant the license. Further, he won't defend her any longer. "I'm sorry, Mother, I love her too, but I don't intend to protect her against the consequences of disloyal words or acts. I've advised my generals to revoke the pass *pro tanto* and deal with her conduct just as they would with any other." My poor sister, what will become of you? What will become of us? If Abraham is defeated, as is rumorous, we will probably be hanged.

Aug. 15, 1864: I want my husband to go to New York with me to get away from the heat. I asked him when he came to me in the early dawn for a moment of physical release (for that's all it was), "Why can't we get away for a fortnight? It would re-invigorate us both, and perhaps we could have more moments like this one. I would like that very much."

He shook his head slowly from side to side, his thick hair hanging in his face. "Two weeks wouldn't do me any good. I can't fly from my thoughts. My concern for this country follows me wherever I go. I still like being with you, but I don't have time for frivolity right now." Then he rose, put on his dressing gown, and went to his own room.

Aug. 20, 1864: A bitter letter from Emilie condemning Abraham for the deaths of her own mate and our brother Levi, who recently succumbed. She could have her cotton if she would sign the oath. Her words cut through my heart, but she ridiculed and cursed my husband, my country, and my President. She is dead to me from this point. This war kills brothers <u>and</u> sisters.

Aug. 23, 1864: Tonight our re-election looks exceedingly improbable. We seem to have no friends left. Even our closest supporters are deserting like rats from a ship. Henry Raymond, editor of the *New York Times* and chairman of the Union National Committee, wrote: "The tide is setting strongly against us. If an election were held now in Illinois, we would be beaten. Pennsylvania is against us. Only the most strenuous efforts can carry Indiana. Other states feel the same. Only the most resolute action on the part of the government and its friends can save the country from falling into hostile hands."

Abraham replied, "I'm struggling to maintain the government and prevent others from overthrowing it. I've got a strong impression I won't live much longer, but if God permits, I'll remain President till the 4th of next March. Whoever's elected in November will be duly installed on that day. In the interval, I'll do my utmost to cooperate with the President-Elect to save the Union between the election and the inauguration, because he can't possibly save it afterward. I don't think it's personal vanity or ambition, though I reckon I'm not free from those infirmities, but I can't help but feel this nation's weal or woe will be decided in November. No program offered by any wing of the Democratic Party will result in anything but the permanent destruction of the Union."

Abraham authorized Mr. Raymond to arrange a peace conference with Jeff Davis or his representatives if possible. All he asked is that the states be reunited without slavery and the Union be restored. Davis has refused this offer several times. All we can do now is wait.

Aug. 29, 1864: The Democratic convention begins today in the Wigwam in Chicago, where the Republicans once paraded so proudly and shouldered such high hopes for this office and this country. Abraham sent Noah Brooks as our watchman. We know that George McClellan, Horatio Seymour, Thomas Seymour, LW Powell, and former President Franklin Pierce are being considered as candidates. Of course, we also face John Frémont and the radicals.

Sept. 1, 1864: Noah wired that McClellan was named as the Democratic candidate, with George Pendleton of Ohio as VP. The platform includes returning the Union to the way it was in relation to the states before the war began, outlawing emancipation, and disarming and removing rank from all negro soldiers.

Little Mac as President—the horror of it sends me into tremor. He would declare an immediate armistice, repeal the emancipation proclamation, and divide the Union with southern independence. Odd, with all his years of fighting in this war, his platform calls it a failure! Their real strength for election is with the many anti-Lincoln men.

They would have more strength if they learned about my debts, so I must pay them quickly. I have enlisted the help of as many people as I can trust, and some have already responded. I read that the public debt is now almost $4 million. Mine is a speck of that! Somehow I must help Abraham in his campaign and manage my own political strategy as well. I promise to remain free from debt after this, even if I should be numbered with the poverty stricken.

Sept. 2, 1864: The rebels surrendered Atlanta, second in importance only to Richmond, leaving Gen. Sherman free to continue through the south. And Davis rejected the peace offer as expected. War continues.

The anti-Lincoln force is growing rapidly, even in the north, and the newspapers predict McClellan will be elected. An insurgent convention met in Cincinnati this week to nominate someone other than Abraham as the Union candidate. Chase and Butler are behind it, of course, with Wade and Cameron involved. All traitors and killers—friends only in sunshine! Each should be imprisoned and never see the light of day again. What right have they? This is treason! Even Greeley wrote that we are already beaten and the party needs another candidate to save it from being overthrown. He proposes Grant, Butler, or Sherman, with Admiral Farragut for VP. Yes, Mr. Greeley, and who will run the war if all the generals are campaigning for President?

Sept. 3, 1864: God listens after all. A wire from Gen. Sherman reads, "Atlanta is ours and fairly won," and one from Waverly's in Boston says my account has been paid in full. I don't know which of my "friends" came to my rescue but, in truth, it doesn't matter as long as the bills are paid.

Sept. 5, 1864: How fickle men can be! Since our recent military achievements, the rats have returned. Salmon Chase called on Abraham and praised our value through the north. Horace Greeley, once such a peace advocate, declared that we must continue the war and win. The Lincoln withdrawal leaders are now our best friends again. Bah! Off with their heads! They are not to be trusted, but we need them. I write letters and send bouquets to court them. Men like Cameron, Stone, Cook, Maynard, and Campbell must stand behind us, campaigning loud and strong. I wrote each of them several letters reminding them what Abraham has done and will continue to do.

Sept. 19, 1864: We have come to a barrier. The Indiana election occurs on October 11th, and a Democratic win would have a horrid effect on the November election. Since Frémont has thrown his support to Abraham, we have a chance if we can muster enough additional votes. Indiana is the only important October state whose soldiers can't vote from the field. The ones in Washington will cast their votes on the White House lawn!

I asked Abraham at breakfast, "Why not release the Indiana soldiers from duty long enough to go home and vote? They are the ones who know best that we're fighting to save the Union."

He replied, "I've thought about it too, but Sherman says they'll just get drunk, and many might not come back."

"That's not fair to the men," I responded. "Sherman fears what he himself would do. Besides, you're the President! If you tell him to let the men go home to vote, they'll go. If you don't tell him, I will."

Abraham chuckled, a rare and treasured occurrence. "You're right again, Mother. I'll tell the general to release his Indiana men long enough to vote."

Sept. 20, 1864: Shopping today at Galt's. So many lovely things—items to stroke and feel, to make me look young and beautiful, to capture Abraham's eye and keep it from straying, to make myself worthy of the title of First Lady. It's an obligation to always look my best and ensure that the mansion is always at its finest. People steal, I must replace. Clothing goes out of style, I need to follow the latest fashion.

Sept. 23, 1864: Just recovering from a tedious indisposition. Still I felt well enough to rejoice with the others over Gen. Sheridan's triumph at Fisher's Hill, Virginia. This victory practically ends rebel resistance in the Shenandoah Valley, and will be highly beneficial to us in the election. In addition, Abraham asked for Montgomery Blair's resignation, which will increase support from the radicals who have long requested his ouster.

Oct. 10, 1864: Grant has destroyed the Shenandoah Valley to keep Lee from using it. Everything was burned; the beauteous valley is dead. This, with our other recent victories, will help us at the polls, but at what cost? Can't we give up the office and let someone with more fortitude finish this battle? The Democrats have sworn to take the Oval Office immediately upon election, rather than waiting until March. Perhaps that wouldn't be so bad after all.

Oct. 12, 1864: The Union Party congressional results in Ohio, Pennsylvania, and Indiana have restored our future. If the pattern of this early voting is any indication, we're saved! Abraham continues to worry, however. He believes the radicals will show up strongly.

The weather was too cold today for Tad and his friends to romp outside, so the mansion and my temperament are in shambles. Do other mothers suffer too, or are these the only rambunctious children in the nation?

Oct. 23, 1864: I write in great haste to relieve my anger over another spurious article in the *Sunday Mercury*. When will the fabrications and aspersions stop? When we are re-elected? I sorely hope so, for I can't stand much more. I'm taking medications for my head, stomach, and female problem. My nerves are worn thin and may break despite my efforts. I want to scream and cry and yell and punch and scratch. Will Abraham see the new term without a wife or will I see it without a husband? The odds are even.

Oct. 31, 1864: Nevada was admitted into the Union just in time for its electoral votes to be counted! Maryland outlawed slavery at midnight, and we sent a carriage for Frederick Douglass to share tea and celebration with us! The White House has been quite a Mecca lately. Mrs. Sojourner Truth, the former slave who is now a well-known evangelist, also came to visit us this week.

Nov. 4, 1864, our 22nd anniversary: All around us, men are working for my husband's re-election. Patronage and contracts have been awarded to people with few credentials other than their vote. Mr. Stanton appointed himself as campaign manager and speaks on our behalf at every opportunity. Abraham refused, however, to modify the soldier draft, despite many pleas, or to negotiate with the rebels on any basis but a solidified Union. "What is the Presidency to me," he asked, "if I have no country?" I have the same thought: What is the Presidency to me if I have no husband?

Nov. 9, 1864: Election day opened and closed in rain and duskiness, and we haven't tried to sleep, but Abraham believes we won! The final results aren't yet in, but a massive crowd has gathered outside the mansion, carrying lanterns, playing music, and firing a cannon. Tad takes part in each boom with thunderous shouts. Abraham told the people that the result "will be to the lasting advantage, if not the very salvation, of the country. A fair election in the midst of civil war shows how sound and strong we still are." My stomach tosses, my knees tremble, invisible spiders creep up my spine. It's barely 6am.

Nov. 11, 1864: We won by 55% of the popular vote and carried every state except Kentucky, Delaware, and New Jersey! Republicans also increased their majority in House and Senate.

I'm not so joyful as four years ago; this place has taken most of the elation from me. Now that we have secured the position, I almost wish it were otherwise. My poor, poor husband is so completely worn out that I'm worried he won't live through the next four years even if assassins don't take him. Stanton ordered that Abraham never walk the grounds alone and Hill Lamon watches over him day and night, because the most believable threats say he will not survive to be inaugurated. An Ohio company guards the mansion at all times and a cavalry detachment is stationed at the Soldiers' Home. Washington policemen in everyday clothes walk the halls.

Abraham calls these safeguards annoying and unnecessary. "I've not willingly planted a thorn in any man's bosom, so they've got no personal argument agin me. But if somebody's out to get me, he'll get me. Don't you think he'd kill the guards too if he wanted me bad enough? I'm not the emperor, and people who come to see me need to feel safe. These guards give the illusion that we ain't safe in our own home." I sense we aren't safe, My Dear.

Nov. 15, 1864: Abraham told me as we dressed this morning that Gen. McClellan finally resigned yesterday! Good riddance! He is disliked by the country and the men he commands, and I suppose his tail is between his legs since our military backing was so strong in the election. Abraham advanced Sheridan to the rank of major general in the regular army. Meanwhile, Sherman moves through Georgia with a vengeance, destroying everything of use, burning bridges and decimating railroads. He heads for the capital at Milledgeville.

Nov. 19, 1864: A letter from Hannah Shearer today. What vivid memories such correspondence brings, and how poor a correspondent I've been. Since affliction visited us almost three years ago, I have shrunk from communication with those who bring my sorrows to mind. Despite the ties formed in the midst of this fearful strife, friends of long ago are still the most treasured. It has been gratifying to receive so many kind and congratulatory letters such as Hannah's from all quarters—so filled with good feeling, though often concluded with requests for an inaugural pass or a position.

Nov. 22, 1864: Abraham is considering Gen. Banks for a Cabinet post, possibly War Secretary, and I sense it's a bad appointment. Banks is a speculator, a secessionist, and an associate of Gen. Butler. I have spoken adamantly to Abraham, but he no longer listens to me. I'll spend the next four years in brittle silence, addressed only by storekeepers and favor-seekers. If such is my fate, so be it; they are more faithful in their love than some. If my husband won't talk to me, many others in Washington will. I have made friends here. Still, my soul is weary and my bones are chilled in this raw winter.

Nov. 25, 1864: After all the excitement, Banks will return to his command at New Orleans, and the nation will be comforted that he is not in our Cabinet, especially the many men who made pilgrimages here in pious indignation. Abraham hasn't heard from Gen. Sherman in weeks. Though we believe he's heading toward Savannah, he has cut off all communication.

Dec. 6, 1864: In his annual message to Congress, Abraham asked them to reconsider the 13th Amendment abolishing slavery. If these men are too moronic to appreciate the amendment's value, the next House most assuredly will do so. Abraham will see to it!

He is appointing his new Cabinet, and making some wise moves and some unwise ones. The most foolish, in my opinion, is Salmon Chase as Chief Justice to fill the vacancy caused by Judge Taney's recent death. This appointment gives his strongest antagonist—the one who would be first in line to assassinate him—the highest office in the judicial system.

Wiser moves are James Speed, Joshua's brother, as Attorney General, and Mary Harlan's father as Interior Secretary. The latter bodes well for our son's future. Did Abraham consider the connection?

Dec. 12, 1864: Why has my recent life been so cruel? All around me, the world is in chaos. Just now, I fear to do anything, lest I do wrong. Where is the peace? Hide me, oh my savior.

The medication causes depression, I think. But why not be dismayed? My marriage is a façade. Married people talk to each other; they share more than a house and an ambition. I have no one to share my thoughts with. My husband seldom seeks me out, and is frequently silent when he does appear. Yes, he is lost to me. He will live on in this life, but will he live on in mine?

I need someone to tell me I'm still interesting, still intelligent, still fun to be around. I know Abraham loves me, but he never says the words. Is it so hard to say? Does he whisper it to another?

Dec. 13, 1864, my 46th birthday: All I want for my birthday is peace and a return to the way life once was. I'm off to bed now at not yet 8pm to bury myself and my twinging head, hoping for the relief of silence. My youth, like everything else pleasant, has vanished in this horrid war. Each morning as I awaken to dread, I wonder if we will ever be right again. Dr. Stone says I need to go out more in the open air, but it smells too much like death.

Dec. 15, 1864: A message from Hill Lamon has terrified me beyond my threshold. He has substantiated reason to fear for Abraham's safety. "Ensure he doesn't go out alone either day or night," he wrote. And how will we stop my stubborn husband from doing so? Even now, he's standing on the balcony in his nightshirt and wrapper watching the moon ready itself for sleep.

He is more secure since Gen. Sherman reached the Georgia seacoast and made contact with Admiral Dahlgren. Savannah will soon be in Union hands, but what will that matter if Abraham is dead? I must order more powders immediately.

Dec. 21, 1864: We almost had another injury! Abraham and I were riding together when an iron hoop caught under the carriage wheels and pierced through the back seat between us. We could have one or both been killed! These "accidents" increase my uneasiness tenfold. Such threats darken the future even though the war goes well. I am so very afraid of losing Abraham. Thank Heaven my medicines arrived.

Dec. 22, 1864: A wire from Gen. Sherman said, "I beg to present you, as a Christmas gift, the city of Savannah, with 150 heavy guns, plenty of ammunition, and about 25,000 bales of cotton." Surely, though I've said so many times, the war is nearly over! After reading the message, Abraham trotted with a toothy grin to Stuntz's toy shop to buy gifts for Tad. He spoils the boy fiercely. "I want to give him all the toys I didn't have, and all the things we would've given our other little ones. I want him to never need anything." Tad is the center of Abraham's world, as Abraham is the center of mine.

Dec. 25, 1864, Christmas: We had hoped for peace by now, but it's not to be. Tad is happy though, as always when gifts are given. He is most pleased with the navy sword from Mr. Welles. After our meal, Abraham took Tad's new mechanical bank apart to find out how it was made, but couldn't figure how to put it together again. Tad screamed till his father gave him a nickel, proving once again who is really in command here.

Jan. 1, 1865: Peace is in the air; we can all feel it. Sherman remains in Georgia, Grant in Virginia, Thomas in Tennessee. Congress is in session, and Abraham is trying to arrange peace negotiations with Davis. To share my joy with the nation, I wore an exquisite gown of blue velvet and white lace to the New Year's Day reception. I must always express our confidence in my appearance and demeanor.

Jan. 19, 1865: Abraham asked Grant to appoint Bob to a nominal post. At my insistence, he emphasized, "I don't want to put him in the ranks, or give him a commission that those who've already served are better entitled to. And I, not the public, will furnish his necessary means."

Before the letter was posted, I added at the bottom: "If no, say so definitively and without the least hesitation because we're anxious that you not be encumbered. And, as Bob's mother, I don't truly want you to accept."

Jan. 30, 1865: A wire from Grant reported that a group from the Confederate States of America, including VP Alexander Stephens and former Supreme Court Justice Campbell, has asked for safe conduct to meet with Abraham concerning a peace agreement! Oh my God, can it finally be ending? Illinois, Arkansas, Louisiana, Maryland, and Missouri have abolished slavery; Tennessee and Kentucky are nearing the end of it. Little is left for the rebels. Abraham issued the passes and will meet them at Ft. Monroe.

Jan. 31, 1865: The 13th Amendment has finally passed the House! Abraham has been maneuvering, log-rolling, and making promises for weeks to ensure success this time. Illinois wired that she will be the first to ratify, and similar telegrams are coming from many other states. It will only take 2/3 of the states to make this a law and free slaves across the country! We will enjoy a celebration dinner with many friends, then see Edwin Forrest in *Spartacus*.

My beloved husband and I have kissed and reconciled our most recent little spat. I know how much my coolness bothers him, though he doesn't sense it in reverse. He said, "I don't like arguing with you, Mother. It's too hard on my mind, and I can't sleep thinking that one of us might be called away and never have the chance to mend it. Let's try to fight less and promise never to fall asleep without touching when we're in the same bed." Oh yes, My Love, I promise, and let's be in the same bed more often!

Our ability to reconcile is quite fortunate, with our opposite natures. From now on, I'll take special pains not to bring up sensitive subjects, even in jest. Irritating topics don't make for candid communication between husband and wife.

Feb. 1, 1865: Bob was accepted into Gen. Grant's army as a captain, serving as an assistant adjutant general and stationed behind the lines where he will be safest. Now Tad wants to join up too. "I wanda be in da ermy doo," he begged. No, my darling child, never!

Feb. 5, 1865: Abraham and Seward went to Ft. Monroe to meet with the Confederate commissioners, but we won't have peace yet. "Why won't Davis give up?" I asked.

Abraham responded, "He'll accept nothing short of Union severance — precisely what we won't and can't give. His declarations to this effect are explicit and often repeated. He don't attempt to deceive us, and he gives us no excuse to fool ourselves. But he knows the rebels are weakening and peace doesn't appear as distant as it did. I hope it'll come soon, and come to stay, and be worth keeping for all time when it does come."

Feb. 12, 1865, Abraham's 56th birthday: As I watched him sit yesterday with Clark Mills for a new plaster cast of his face, I realized again that Abraham looks much too old. I'm very worried about him. I remember the first cast made by Leonard Volk in 1860 — how much he's changed. Volk's seemed like a life mask; Mills' seems like a death mask.

Feb. 20, 1865: Gen. Sherman has taken Columbia, SC, but it has burned to the ground. Such a beautiful city, gone forever, and no one claims responsibility. Charleston has been evacuated, and Sherman moves toward NC. The war will soon be over.

Mar. 1, 1865: I am so pleased that John Nicolay has been appointed consul to Paris and Noah Brooks has taken his place as Abraham's private secretary. I'll be much happier dealing with Noah; I never liked Nicolay or his thin shadow Hay, who is also leaving, and the feeling was quite mutual. They harmed me in many ways, including trying to stop delivery of my medications for my "own welfare."

Mar. 4, 1865: Abraham's inaugural address was breath-taking and mesmerizing, although one of the shortest speeches he has ever delivered — perhaps only three minutes! He ended by saying:

> With malice toward none, with charity for all, with firmness in the right—as God gives us to see the right—let us strive to finish the work we're in; to bind up the nation's wounds; to care for him who's borne the battle, and for his widow and orphan; to do all that may achieve and cherish a just and lasting peace among ourselves and with all nations.

I will say nothing more about Andrew Johnson than he apparently enhanced his confidence with beverages and embarrassed us with a meandering, garbled acceptance. Mrs. Eliza Johnson has not yet arrived. I'm told she has tuberculosis. If so, she won't find the Washington air beneficial.

Mar. 6, 1865: The inaugural ball was exciting, festive, and loud. I chose Mr. Sumner as my escort, and we had some lovely dances. Crowds overran the Patent Office, where the event was held, and devoured the midnight supper like a swarm of locusts. I stayed only until 2am. Abraham came home not long after — his hands and feet cold to the touch, his head pounding so badly he asked for one of my doses! It's good to have Dr. Henry here with us; I feel more confident knowing our health is in familiar hands.

Mar. 14, 1865: Abraham is so depleted that he held today's Cabinet meeting in his bedroom. I can imagine what the vampire press will make of such! I heard him say to Noah, "I ought not to undergo what I so often do. I may never live to see peace. This war's killing me." I am terrified that he may be correct, as my dreams are filled with his blood.

Mar. 17, 1865: I rode to Baltimore today and purchased almost $1000 of mourning clothes, though I have no idea what they will be used for. I have no desire or reason to don black again. The articles will be returned immediately and no one will ever know about this peculiarity! What in Heaven makes me do such things?

Mar. 20, 1865: Perfectly blissful weather! Early spring is always a pleasant time of year in Washington. Some of the most cordial senators' families remain till June and all ceremony with each other is laid aside. We visit the theatres with three or four agreeable people and dine afterward as though we were truly friends. Mr. Sumner went with us Saturday night to see the opera *Faust*. Tomorrow, a group of us will hear Theodore Habelmann, one of our favorite tenors, in *La Dame Blanche*. We also plan to see the Italian opera *Ernani* and, in April, a comedy called *Our American Cousin*.

Abraham is going to Ft. Monroe again and wants me to go along. I devoutly hope the change of air and rest will benefit him. Although his health has improved in the past few days, he has been ill a great deal lately and now weighs no more than 155 pounds. We'll take Tad so he can see his idol, Captain Bob Lincoln. Our oldest son is now, to my horror, regularly exposed to battle!

Mar. 25, 1865: We arrived safely at Grant's rear headquarters last night after an overnight trip on the *River Queen* that made me quite ill, but events have not gone well. This morning, Abraham left on the military railroad to the Petersburg lines, and then went on horseback to the battlefield at Ft. Stedman. I was forced to ride to the camp in a field ambulance with Mrs. Grant and Mr. Badeau, a member of Grant's staff. Badeau said all wives had been ordered to the rear except Gen. Griffin's young wife, whom the President had permitted to remain at the front. I knew this couldn't be true. If Abraham had allowed anyone to remain at his side, it would have been me. The President's wife ranks higher than a general's wife! For Abraham to have given such permission, the hussy must have been alone with him.

I said to Badeau, "Do you know I never allow the President to see any woman alone?" The horrid man chuckled out loud! How dare he insult me in such manner! I ordered the ambulance to let me out, and sloshed through the muck to correct the injustice. On my way, I met up with Gen. Meade and asked him for the truth. As I suspected, Abraham was innocent. Stanton had allowed the woman to remain near my husband! Although fully justified, I'm ashamed of my public outbursts. I seemed to have no control over my words. What's wrong with me?

Mar. 26, 1865: I am livid! How dare anyone treat me this way! We were scheduled to review the troops today, and Abraham and Maj. Gen. Ord set out on their horses ahead of the ambulance in which Mrs. Grant and I rode. We were going very slowly because the roads were muddy and full of holes—worse than any I ever rode back in Springfield. Suddenly we hit a gap so large that I bounced to the top of the vehicle, hitting the injury from my last fall, which constantly throbs without additional provocation. We were, as feared, late for the review, and I was immediately greeted with the news that Mrs. Ord had ridden out with the men this morning—side to side with Abraham. How scandalous! The soldiers could have mistaken her for me! No woman but the First Lady should be reviewing the troops alongside the President. It is blatant disrespect!

I told Mrs. Ord exactly how I felt and the wimpish woman melted into sobs. She is strumpet enough to steal a wife's rightful place, but not brave enough to face the consequences! She thinks she's so young and lovely, and such a fine equestrienne. Well, she can't have my husband! The army and the whole country must be reminded who is First Lady! Abraham wouldn't be President if not for me, and my position will not be usurped. I also took the opportunity to give Mrs. Grant my opinion of her butcher husband. He shows utter indifference and heartlessness about the lives of our men. Worse, they covet the Presidency, both of them! Damn them all!

Mar. 27, 1865: This morning I feel the grief and shame of my actions. My stomach churns blackly, and I have vomited many times since returning to the ship yesterday afternoon. The lights flashing through my vision frighten me terribly, and I lose track of time and place. I'm sick of being in hell. I sense I am very ill and I need help to….

Mar. 28, 1865: My ink is like myself — failing. I write this morning with a broken heart, bowed with anguish after another night of suffering. Willie's spirit comes no more to soothe me, though I call and plead. Even he has deserted me. My mirror shows a pale, haggard face, and my reason is nearly gone. I weep while writing and pray for relief as Abraham continues to meet with his generals, blissfully unaware of my turmoil.

Mar. 29, 1865: I dreamed last night that the White House burned to the ground and many of our staff were killed! I have remained in my cabin since the distressful review on Monday, tossing and turning with cramps, vomiting, and holding cold compresses to my aching head, but now I must rouse myself and go home immediately. Like Dolley Madison, I have to save the national treasures!

When I asked Abraham to return with me, he stared at his pocket watch and replied, "I ought to, I know, but I hate to leave without seeing nearer to the end of Grant's present movement. Sherman is here now and they've been out since early yesterday. I want to see something happen here, so I reckon I'll stay a while longer. You go on without me."

Apr. 2, 1865: Back in Washington on this warm, beautiful evening, and all is well. No sign of fire. I had planned to stay here until Abraham's return, but he wired that Richmond was captured this morning. Since I'm feeling so much better, I want to go back for the celebration. I asked several friends to accompany me for the festivities and a tour of the captured cities.

We'll have tea in Jefferson Davis' dining room, if it remains. Davis, his family, and his Cabinet escaped by train, but they wreaked havoc before they left. Abraham said most of the city is afire. Perhaps that was the basis of my premonition.

I so regret my behavior at Ft. Monroe. What is happening to my restraint and judgment? Abraham has always made it clear that he has no interest in other women. It was music in my ears, both before and after our marriage, to hear him say I am the only woman he has ever cared for, and the memory solaces me now. He has become so much stronger, yet I seem to be losing strength. When did we change roles? I must see a doctor as soon as possible. Perhaps one at the asylum.

Apr. 4, 1865: I'm expecting many friends tonight to watch as Washington's buildings are illuminated with torches and gas lamps in celebration of Richmond's surrender. Brightness will flow through windows from which rebellious hearts perhaps once gazed.

I leave for City Point again tomorrow on the *Martin* and will tour Richmond with Abraham. Mr. Sumner and some friends from Boston will stay tonight and go with me. The Marquis de Chambrun, Lafayette's visiting grandson, will also accompany us.

Abraham telegraphs every two or three hours, and says my darling sons are quite safe after three days' exposure to rebel shots. I'm eager to see them all!

Apr. 6, 1865: I have arrived, but Abraham is not to be found. Despite my advising that I wanted to view the fallen cities with him, he went on his own. Or perhaps with Mrs. Ord? No, I remember seeing her on the path. Who accompanied him? Tad and Bob, but why did they go without me? Abraham no longer feels responsibility to his wife; he is more absent-minded than ever! Perhaps he even forgot I was arriving? No, he might repress me, but not the Marquis! We have no option but to sit and wait. Where is he?

Apr. 7, 1865: We received word that Seward was seriously injured in a carriage accident, and I must immediately return to Washington. We can't continue our term without a Secretary of State, and perhaps I can nurse or advise him. I insisted that Abraham accompany us to Richmond and Petersburg, as he promised, and then immediately return with us on the *River Queen*. It's much more comfortable than the *Martin*. I'll arrange for Mrs. Grant and her group to return aboard the *Martin*.

Apr. 10, 1865: On the ship last night—on Palm Sunday, April 9th—we received word that Gen. Lee surrendered to Gen. Grant at Appomattox! The rebel army is in our hands and Bob witnessed it! The crowds around the mansion are immense this morning, bands are playing, people are singing. Peace begets such glorious sounds!

Now we can have the life we envisioned. These last years have been horrid—not at all what I envisioned as a child or when molding Abraham so carefully for the position. I wanted the stature, the gaiety, the prominence of being First Lady, not the desolation and death of war. But soon we'll be like other occupants of this mansion and live in the exciting world of Washington as it used to be! The city will no longer be filled with our enemies. Everyone will be our friend now that the end of the war is in sight!

Apr. 11, 1865: What a celebration last evening! The capital was brightly illuminated, thousands sat on the White House lawn and sang loudly, bands played throughout the city (especially *Dixie's Land*, which Abraham favors), fireworks and guns blazed.

Abraham spoke eloquently from our upstairs window. Last week I would have been horrified for him to stand in an open window with a dark crowd below—indeed, Lamon would not have allowed such—but now we're safe. The curse is broken! I no longer have the blinding vision of Abraham's violent death, though he is obviously expended.

His iris is almost invisible, his voice is strained, his ears are the largest part of him left to see. Every step tires him; he has no endurance left. The war has drained him, but he held on to his hopes for the future, and now he has become distinguished above all, as I always knew he would. My noble husband, my light and my life, will live on forever.

Apr. 12, 1865: Mobile, Alabama, the final stronghold of the Confederacy, has fallen. Shortly after hearing the news, Abraham did the most extraordinary thing, flooding me with memories of our secret courting days so many years ago. He sent me a bouquet of red roses, with a tender note in his own hand:

"Molly," (how long since I've heard that name) "let's take a drive today before we leave for the theatre. I want to apologize for all that's gone on between us these past four years. Seems like we've both been pretty contrary. I know I haven't been the husband you signed up for back in '42 and I'm sorry for hurting you. Between the war and the loss of our darling Willie, we've both been very miserable. When the country's restored, we'll have more time for each other, and I promise you a long trip to celebrate. Everything will be all right now."

Apr. 13, 1865: Abraham and I talked this morning about purchasing a home in Michigan this summer, so we can spend time on the lake shore rather than going all the way to New Hampshire for respite.

He also told me about a recent dream in which he heard weeping. He searched for it until he came to the East Room, where he saw a casket atop a catafalque. "Who is dead in the White House?" he asked the soldiers, and the answer came back, "The President." He dreamed just last night about a huge ship racing toward a dark, shadowy shore. I wish he hadn't told me. I'm numb with fear, but advised him not to be concerned with visions of war-related strain. Despite the nightmares, he's sleeping better now, and the sadness he's worn for so many months has been replaced with a certain serenity.

During a long carriage ride into the countryside this afternoon, he seemed so gay that I teased, "Dear husband, you almost startle me with your great cheerfulness."

He replied, "And well I may feel so, Mother. I consider this as the day the war came to a close and the Lincolns started anew!"

Apr. 14, 1865: Today is the "goodest" Good Friday our country has ever experienced. It's so wonderful to be at peace again, and the glorious sunshine forecasts healing. We went to church with smiles and handshakes all around, though Abraham spent the rest of the day meeting with his generals and Cabinet. He is supremely happy and anticipates the future with grand delight. Tad is all love and gentleness, and Bob, who arrived early this morning, has finally manifested himself as a strong man. Dr. Henry gave me a medicine that doesn't cause such deep changes of mood, and I have discarded the laudanum. I am content.

Without such strife and terror, Abraham and I will learn to love again the way we did when young. We'll grow very old together and cherish every single day, knowing from experience that power and high position don't ensure happiness. As it says in my wedding ring, love is eternal, and this war and its horrid occurrences have not truly hurt our bond.

When we have time, very soon, we'll take long walks and carriage rides together again. We'll lie entwined on rainy mornings and listen to the sound of each other's breathing. We'll entertain, see every Shakespearean play, and ride the glory of emancipation. I'll study French again and Abraham will learn to play the piano. Tad will become a famous playwright and Bob will sit on the Supreme Court. How clearly I can see the future today, and it's everything I ever wanted. My blackness has lifted and our deceased boys no longer lurk in the shadows of my mind. I have no need for spiritualists, because the future glows in my own heart.

This afternoon, we rode alone together again as far as the navy yard, holding hands under the blanket. Abraham was almost boyish in his mirth and displayed the nature I remember so lovingly in our Springfield home — free from care, surrounded by those he loves, being idolized in return.

We talked about the misery of the past years and the peaceful times ahead when we'll travel out west to Oregon and California, then to London, Paris, and Rome. Abraham has always wanted to see Jerusalem and Palestine, so we'll put those on our agenda as well. He's eating and sleeping like a boy of 21, and I no longer ride the waves of emotion.

Though weary, we'll attend Ford's Theatre tonight to see Laura Keene in *Our American Cousin*, a British comedy. It will be good for people to see that we're also celebrating, and Mrs. Keene has written many lovely notes inviting us to see her final appearance as Florence Trenchard. Bob declined our invitation, citing fatigue from his trip. We also invited quite a few other people, including the Grants, the Stantons, young Major Rathbone and his fiancée Clara Harris, and nine or ten men whose wives are not available, but I'm not sure whether they will join us. I sense that Mrs. Grant is still angry with me, and I'll try to make amends immediately. I will also write to Julia Trumbull and try to renew our acquaintance. And I'll return the locket to Emilie and invite her to visit in peace.

I asked Abraham, as we moved closer under the carriage blanket, "What would people think if we caressed like this at the theatre? We'll have a coverlet, you know, and I could make you blush in the dark. What will they say about my hanging on to you so?"

He squeezed my arm and replied with a grin, "They won't think anything about it at all."

Must go. More tomorrow.

Factual Epilogue

Abraham Lincoln, 16th President of the United States, was shot in the head at 10:15 PM on April 14, 1865, during the third act of *Our American Cousin.* He died at 7:22 the next morning, the first presidential victim in American history.

The assassin was an actor whom the Lincolns had seen in various productions while in Washington. Even though Mary Lincoln claimed to have visions, she had no idea that John Wilkes Booth had already attempted to kidnap Lincoln at least once, and that the strange rider near the Soldiers' Home was most likely Booth or one of his men. When he stood in the crowd on March 4, 1865, and heard Lincoln say that he favored voting rights for some Negroes, Booth went berserk. Lincoln had told Mary that guards wouldn't help if a man wanted to kill him, but they had no guards at Ford's Theatre on the fateful night to test his theory. Had the Grants joined the Lincolns, the general would have been armed and alert, as would many of the others they invited. Instead, their sentry was a young Washington policeman Mary had recently promoted to White House duty. He deserted his post during the third act, leaving the Lincolns a vulnerable target. The last words in this story are the actual last words the Lincolns spoke to each other before the bullet hit its mark. According to Major Rathbone and Clara Harris, who sat next to the Lincolns in the presidential box, Mary leaned lovingly and playfully into Abraham's shoulder and said, "What will people say about my hanging on to you so?" Abraham replied, "They won't think anything about it at all."

Although urged by the new administration to return to Springfield, Mary and Tad moved to Chicago, where Bob had settled, and Mary campaigned to get a widow's pension from the government. After a few years, she and Tad traveled across the US and abroad in search of health, mental stability, and happiness.

Abraham's estate was valued at approximately $110,000 when it was settled in 1867. Since he had no will, it was divided evenly between Mary and her two sons. She finally received an annual pension of $3000 in 1870, but she continued to be plagued by fears of poverty, insanity, and murder for the rest of her life.

In 1871, Tad died at age 18 from typhoid and again Mary blamed herself. In 1873, at 55, she returned to Chicago. In early 1875, Bob committed his mother to a private asylum in Batavia, Illinois, because he was concerned about her uncontrollable grief, erratic spending, hallucinations, and traveling habits. She remained eleven months, fighting for her freedom every day through the mails. She returned to roaming Europe alone after her release.

In 1879, while hanging a picture over her mantel in Pau, France, Mary fell from a stepladder and injured her spine. Filled with fear and partially paralyzed with pain, she returned to Springfield in 1880. Almost blind and tortured by headaches, loneliness, and guilt, she spent her last few years secluded in the home of Elizabeth and Ninian Edwards on Aristocracy Hill. Mary Todd Lincoln died on July 16, 1882, in the same home where she was married.

Robert Todd Lincoln married Mary Harlan in 1868 and had a daughter, Mary; a son, Abraham Lincoln Jr., who died at 17; and a daughter Jessie. Robert's last grandchild died in 1985, leaving no heirs in the Abraham Lincoln line.

Bibliography

Angle, Paul M. and Miers, Earl Schenck, Eds. *The Living Lincoln.* New York: Barnes & Noble Books, 1992.

Baker, Jean H. *Mary Todd Lincoln: A Biography.* New York: W. W. Norton & Company, Inc., 1987.

Bode: Carl, Editor. *American Life in the 1840s.* New York: Doubleday & Co., Inc., 1967.

Byrd, Cecil K. and Moore, Ward W. *Abraham Lincoln in Print and Photograph.* New York: Dover Publications, Inc., 1997.

Cable, Mary and Buehr, Wendy, Editor. *American Manners & Morals.* New York: American Heritage Publishing Co., Inc., 1969.

Capers, Gerald M. *Stephen A. Douglas, Defender of the Union.* Boston: Little, Brown and Company, 1959.

Carruthers, Olive and McMurtry, R. Gerald, *Lincoln's Other Mary.* New York: Ziff-Davis Publishing Company, 1946.

Davis, Kenneth C. *Don't Know Much About the Civil War.* New York: Avon Books, Inc., 1996.

Helm, Katherine. *Mary, Wife of Lincoln.* New York: Harper & Brothers, 1928.

Keckley, Elizabeth. *Behind the Scenes.* New York: Oxford University Press, 1988.

Long, E. B. *The Civil War Day by Day.* New York: Doubleday, 1971.

Lorant, Stefan. *The Presidency.* New York: The Macmillan Company, 1953.

McCutcheon, Marc. *The Writer's Guide to Everyday Life in the 1800s.* Cincinnati, Writer's Digest Books, 1993.

Mitgang, Herbert, Editor. *Selected Writings of Abraham Lincoln.* New York: Bantam Books, 1992.

Neely, Mark E., Jr. and McMurtry, R. Gerald. *The Insanity File.* Illinois: Southern Illinois University, 1986.

Neely, Mark E., Jr. *The Abraham Lincoln Encyclopedia.* New York: Da Capo Press, 1982.

Randall, Ruth Painter. *Lincoln's Sons.* Boston: Little, Brown and Company, 1955.

Randall, Ruth Painter. *Mary Lincoln: Biography of a Marriage.* Boston: Little, Brown and Company, 1953.

Rothman, Ellen K. Hands and Hearts: A History of Courtship in America. New York: Basic Books, 1984.

Sandburg, Carl. *Abraham Lincoln: The Prairie Years.* New York: Dell Publishing, 1954.

Sandburg, Carl. *Mary Lincoln: Wife and Widow.* New York: Harcourt, Brace and Company, 1932.

Stone, Irving. *Love is Eternal.* New York: Doubleday & Company, Inc., 1954.

Turner, Justin G. and Turner, Linda Levitt. *Mary Todd Lincoln: Her Life and Letters.* New York: Alfred a. Knopf, Inc., 1972.

Zall, Paul M. *Lincoln on Lincoln.* Lexington: The University Press of Kentucky, 1999.

About the Author

M. Kay duPont has been writing since she was six years old. She self-published her first book that year—with a citywide distribution of one copy. When she was about 18, she published a collection of poetry called *Illusions and Dreams* and had a weekly poetry column in a metropolitan newspaper. By the time she was 22, she had won major awards in every category of writing—from children's literature to editorials. She's had articles and stories published in dozens of magazines over the years.

She has also written three successful business books—*Don't Let Your Participles Dangle in Public!*, *Business Etiquette and Professionalism*, and *Diversity in the Workplace: Communication is the Key*. She is a contributing author to *Chocolate for a Woman's Soul*, which hit the *USA Today* Best Seller list.

In addition to her own writing, Kay serves as copywriter, editor, and writing coach to some of the country's top organizations, speakers, and authors. In addition, she is a Certified Speaking Professional and a Certified Professional Development Trainer and

teaches writing and other business communication seminars all over the world.

She also presents fascinating one-woman shows for educational facilities, community theaters, book clubs, libraries, and conference and corporate programs—as Mary Lincoln herself or as Mary's biographer. For more information, visit *www.MaryTLincoln.com*. Additional copies of Loving Mr. Lincoln may be purchased at *www.lovingmrlincoln.com*.